ANN TATLOCK

All the Way Home

A NOVEL

BETHANY HOUSE PUBLISHERS

Minneapolis, Minnesota

Published by Bethany House Publishers
A Ministry of Bethany Fellowship International
11400 Hampshire Avenue South
Bloomington, Minnesota 55438
www.bethanyhouse.com

Printed in the United States of America by
Bethany Press International, Bloomington, Minnesota 55438

Library of Congress Cataloging-in-Publication Data

Tatlock, Ann.
    All the way home / by Ann Tatlock.
       p.   cm.
   ISBN 0-7642-2663-0
    1. Japanese Americans—Evacuation and relocation, 1942–1945—Fiction. 2. Japanese American families—Fiction.
3. Women journalists—Fiction. 4. Race relations—Fiction.
5. Mississippi—Fiction. 6. California—Fiction. 7. Racism—Fiction. I. Title.
   PS3570.A85 A79   2002
   813'.54—dc21   2002002470

To Laura Jane

May yours be a world in which

it's the heart that matters.

All my love,

Mom

ANN TATLOCK is a full-time writer who has also worked as an assistant editor for *Decision* magazine. A graduate of Oral Roberts University with an M.A. in communications from Wheaton Graduate School, she has published numerous articles in Christian magazines. This is her third novel. She makes her home in Roseville, Minnesota, with her husband, Bob, and their daughter, Laura Jane.

ACKNOWLEDGMENTS

This book couldn't have been written without the help of those who were there, living out the events described in this story. For that reason, I would like to thank:

Mary Tanaka and her son, Don Tanaka, who, until 1942, lived in the Boyle Heights neighborhood of Los Angeles, California. After the bombing of Pearl Harbor by the Japanese, when thousands of Japanese Americans were placed in internment camps, the Tanaka family was incarcerated at the Rohwer Relocation Center in Arkansas. Their memories provided a framework for this novel. Thanks, Mary and Don, for sharing your story with me.

Toshiko Ito, another California native, who as a young woman spent the war years at Heart Mountain Relocation Center in Wyoming. Thank you, Toshi, for your careful reading of this manuscript and your invaluable suggestions for improvement. (Thanks too to my cousin Bob Erbeck for introducing me to Toshi!)

William Hodes, one of the student volunteers working in Mississippi during Freedom Summer 1964. For his efforts he was invited to enjoy a brief stay at a jailhouse in Greenwood. Thanks, Bill, for answering my long lists of questions via e-mail. And of course I enjoy having a "former outlaw" for an in-law.

Also, I'd like to thank Anne Koch for permission to use passages from Howard Koch's celebrated 1938 radio play, *War of the Worlds,* of which the first broadcast on October 30, 1938, by Orson Welles' Mercury theater panicked many listeners and amused many others.

PROLOGUE

Down below, beneath a pale gray sky, a ring of colored light floats on a cloud. From my window seat on the plane I can see the whole of it, a shining circular rainbow suspended between heaven and earth, a halo over the world. I have always believed rainbows to be arches with an apparent beginning and end. But now, gazing from above instead of below, I see that this rainbow at least is perfectly round, endless and infinite.

Could it be a sign? I wonder. I'm not one to look for signs, yet I find myself wishing that the rainbow was sent to tell me something, that it's a message from nature, or the universe, or God himself, if he is there.

I want to tap my seatmate on the shoulder and tell her to look at the rainbow, but she's busy crying into her handkerchief, and I'm not sure I should bother her. She's been crying quietly since the plane left the tarmac in Los Angeles.

Obviously she'd said good-bye to someone, and I know—I remember—that good-byes can be hard. Still, I had thought she might pull herself together by the time we reached cruising altitude, but no such luck. Since takeoff, I've kept my face toward the window to allow her some privacy, but I can hardly crane my neck toward the window for the distance of almost an entire continent.

Sighing, I turn to her and touch her arm. "Are you all right?"

"Oh!" she exclaims, as though surprised that I've broken the polite silence between us. Before saying more, she offers me a brief smile even as she dabs at fresh tears. In spite of her swollen eyes and mottled skin, she is beautiful. No more than twenty or twenty-one, she has a narrow face with fine chiseled features and large blue eyes, and her smooth blond hair is neatly coiffed and crowned with a blue pillbox hat.

"I'm so sorry to be blubbering like this," she apologizes, "but I've just seen my fiancé off." Then she blows her nose in the handkerchief, a dainty blow. "He was drafted. He's being sent to Vietnam." She speaks with an accent straight out of *Gone With the Wind*, and with the nose of our plane pointed toward the Deep South, I gather she's taking this flight home.

Before I can respond, she explains, "I wanted to get married before he left, but he said he didn't want to take the chance of my being left a widow. His daddy told him if I was left a widow, I could get benefits, but not even that changed his mind. But, oh, I don't want the benefits. I want him! So I told him he had just better plan on coming back then, because he promised to marry me, and he'd better not break his promise. He said he'd do his best."

She pauses, and I know this is the point at which I'm supposed to jump in with assurances that he'll be back. He'll be one of the lucky ones who somehow survives, who dodges every bullet, avoids every land mine. He'll be one of the ones who comes home from battle with all his limbs attached and his mind and emotions untouched. He'll come home, and they'll marry and have children and live happily ever after.

But I can offer her no such assurance. I silently curse whatever fate has seated us by each other, not for my sake but for hers. Someone else might have been able to say the words, to give this frightened young woman the comfort she needs. Maybe an older woman, a kindly gray-haired grandmother who sent husband or son off to an earlier war and who could pat this young woman's hand and say, "Now, dear, don't you worry for a minute. When my Harry went off to the South Pacific in '43, I thought I'd never see him again. But, thank the good Lord, he came home, and with more medals pinned to his chest than there's jewelry in the cases at Tiffany's."

It isn't something I can do. Instead, I ask, "What's his name?"

"Alan," she tells me proudly. "Alan Hastings the Third. I'm hoping to give him the Fourth."

"Are you both from Jackson?" That's where our plane is headed—Jackson, Mississippi.

She nods. "We've lived there all our lives. Alan is kind of the boy next door, though he actually lives a few streets over. We grew up together." She pauses again, then sniffs and says, "I was just remembering how in school we used to have those air-raid drills where we'd get under the desks and put our hands over our heads. Remember those? I grew up waiting for Russia to blow us all to bits, but now that we're really at war, we're fighting in someplace called Vietnam. I'd never even heard of Vietnam till just a few years ago. Whoever would have thought?"

Her voice trails off, but I notice that the tears have stopped. Maybe it's helpful to her just to talk to someone. She looks thoughtful for a moment. I wait for her to go on.

She turns to me suddenly and holds my gaze. "President Johnson promised in all his campaign speeches not to send our boys to Vietnam. Well, here we are, not even a year into his new term and it seems like half of America is on its way to fight the Commies."

I nod my understanding. It is July 1965, and about one hundred thousand troops have just been sent over. For me, it's eerily reminiscent of Roosevelt's promises not to get involved in the war in Europe back in 1941. I learned long ago not to trust political promises, but evidently my young seatmate has not.

"It isn't fair," she concludes.

"No," I agree, "it isn't fair. Probably lots of people voted for Johnson on the strength of those promises, only to be disappointed."

"Well, personally, I think people should keep their word, don't you?"

"Yes. Yes, I do. But more often than not, it seems, people don't."

Less than fifteen years separate us in age, I suppose, but I have already forgotten what it is to be so young, young enough to still believe life should be fair and promises kept.

The plane hums smoothly over the clouds. A nattily dressed stewardess comes around and offers us a beverage, but we both decline.

When the stewardess moves on to the next row, my seatmate says, "I just *hate* war, don't you?"

The question startles me. Of course I hate war. Does anyone love it? "I've seen three wars so far in my lifetime," I tell her, "and I can't say I've been very glad about any of them."

"Have you really seen that many?" she asks.

"The Second World War, Korea, and now Vietnam," I enumerate.

"They say Korea wasn't really a war."

"It was for those who lost husbands and sons."

The young woman nods. "Funny. Now that you mention it, I guess this is my third war too, since I was born in '44. Mama was only seventeen when I was born, and Daddy was eighteen. Two weeks after I was born, Daddy was drafted and sent to Europe with the infantry." She purses her painted lips, frowns. "We're always busy fighting somebody, aren't we?"

"Did your father come home?"

"Oh yes. He's still alive today."

Thank heavens. "Well, then, that gives a person hope, don't you think?"

At that, her eyes light up. "I suppose it does. Yes, men do come home." She looks past me for a moment, smiles, then comes back to me. "Do you remember anything about the Second World War?"

"Oh sure. Lots. I was a child, of course, but I certainly remember it. A person hardly forgets something like that."

What I remember most vividly, though, isn't the stuff of history books. What I remember aren't the battles and the newspaper headlines, the scrap drives and the victory gardens, Roosevelt's fireside chats and the endless casualty lists. I was scarcely affected by the letters from my brother Stephen, who was fighting in Europe, or by the lack of letters from my brother Lenny, who was in a Japanese prison camp somewhere in the South Pacific. What served to define the war for others meant little to me then, and even less now.

What I remember most vividly from the war years was Jimmy Durante's weekly radio sign-off and how it always left me in tears. "Good night, Mrs. Calabash," he'd say at the end of the show, and then he'd add, "wherever you are," and when he said those words, I felt for all the world that he was looking straight into my heart and he knew exactly how I felt when no one else in my life had even a clue.

The war had separated me from the people I loved most, Chichi and Haha and Sunny. The separation itself was bad enough, but even worse was the not knowing where they were. If I'd had some idea as to their whereabouts and when they were coming back, it would have all been so much more bearable. But I hadn't heard a word from them since the day they left, and it was just as though they'd taken a train to the edge of the world and fallen off.

Every Friday night I listened to Jimmy Durante with my cousin Stella and her landlords, Grady and Cecelia Liddel, in the latter's small but tidy living room. I'd lie on the floor with my arm thrown around my dog, Jimmy, listening to the grown-ups laugh and trying to laugh along with them. But whenever I heard the final words, I was doomed. I don't know how Jimmy Durante sounded to the others, but to me he sounded wistful and lonely, and his voice was filled with the longing of wanting to say something to someone who just wasn't there. And so by the end of the show I was dropping tears onto Mrs. Liddel's carefully vacuumed carpet, feeling dreadfully sad for myself and for Jimmy Durante and for all the people whose lives were shattered beyond repair because the most important pieces were missing.

My seatmate chews her lower lip and asks gingerly, "Have you ever lost anyone? In one of the wars, I mean?"

I hesitate to answer, as this is not a conversation I want to have. Reluctantly, I say, "Yes, I'm afraid so."

"Not your husband?" She glances at my left hand in search of a ring.

"Oh no. I've never married."

"Oh, I'm sorry!"

Her response so amuses me I have to stifle the urge to laugh. The ultimate tragedy for the young—not to marry. She, like so many, believes that life doesn't begin until one has settled comfortably into matrimony.

I want to tell her not to be sorry for me, that my solitude is chosen. Solitude, I long ago decided, is the most effective means of protecting the heart, leaving me assured that mine would never be pained the way hers is now.

"Well," I say by way of explanation, "my career has kept me pretty busy."

"Oh? What do you do?"

"I'm a journalist. I write for a magazine called *One Nation*."

"How exciting!" she exclaims, at once more animated than I've seen her so far. "Are you going to Mississippi to do a story?"

In fact I am. Yet one more civil rights story. I have done so many of them in the past four years I'm growing tired of writing about the sit-ins, the demonstrations, the violence, the injustice. But a woman in Carver, Mississippi, has been begging me for months to come do a story about voter registration in her town.

Why me? I'd asked. "I've been following your stories in the magazine, and I know you can do this story justice," Helen Fulton had responded. I don't think she realized the irony in her statement. "Not one Negro citizen of Carver is registered to vote, and we need your help to change that."

I was trying to carve out a block of time to work on my second novel. My first had been out for a year, and if I didn't produce another one soon, I'd be quickly forgotten in the world of literature. But this Helen Fulton was relentless in her insistence that I come, and finally my editor agreed that I should snoop around Carver and see if there was anything worth writing about.

But I don't want to talk about it. Not right now, not with a stranger. It's all too tiresome. So I tell the young woman I'm taking a little vacation, going to visit a friend who lives in Carver.

"Oh sure, I've been to Carver," she replies. "There's not much there." Then, realizing she's committed a possible *faux pas*, she raises a hand briefly to her lips. "But it's a nice little town, really. I hope you enjoy your trip."

"Thank you." I have little hope of enjoying this trip and can't wait to get back to the unfinished chapter I left on my writing desk at home.

After a moment, tentative again, she says, "I'm sorry about your losing someone in the war. I shouldn't have brought it up."

"That's all right. It was a long time ago." I'm not above resorting to clichés.

"But it must take—I don't know—years and years to get over such a thing."

Does it? Are there ever enough years piled one on top of another to bury the loss for good?

I try to smile. "Why don't you tell me about Alan. Do you have a picture?"

"Of course!" she cries, opening her beaded purse and pulling out her wallet. She points to a photo of a handsome young man and begins to tell me about Alan. But I don't hear much because all the while she is talking, Jimmy Durante is wishing a good-night to Mrs. Calabash, and my dog's rough, warm tongue is pressed up against my moist cheek as he tries to lick away my sadness, and the wound of separation is just as deep as in those days when my heart first cried out for Sunny and Chichi and Haha. They were the joy of my life, more of a family to me than my own family, the gold among the worthless nuggets that made up my childhood. But the war took them away, and week after week I wondered where they were and when they'd be coming home again.

I turn my gaze to the plane window while my seatmate chatters on. The rainbow is long gone. Perhaps it's hanging over Arizona or New Mexico or Texas, or wherever we might have been at the time. Or perhaps the prism of clouds has broken, the sunlight shifted, the rainbow faded. I don't know. But I do know that if that circle of light was painted there in the clouds to tell me something, its meaning is lost to me now. Lost, like Chichi and Haha and Sunny, and never coming back.

Remembering

PART ONE

ONE

The first time I met Sunny, she was sitting alone on a bench in Hollenbeck Park listening to the music of a Salvation Army band. I'd seen her at school, but in the month or so since we'd entered the third grade we hadn't spoken with each other. As a new student at Whittier Avenue School—and having only recently arrived in Los Angeles—I hadn't much talked with anyone. But I'd noticed Sunny, and she intrigued me. She seemed to be almost as alone as I in the midst of the crowds of students.

She sat primly, her pink blouse pressed against the bench's backrest, her blue skirt pulled snugly over her small bumpy knees. The Buster Browns she wore dangled several inches above the ground. Her tiny hands were neatly folded in her lap. I followed her gaze to the group of musicians that dominated the park that afternoon. A dozen staid-looking men and women in dark uniforms blew trumpets and trombones and clarinets, beat drums, and jangled tambourines while a small choir sang what Uncle Finn would call "religious syrupy sap." They were led by a man perched on a wooden box waving a pencil for a baton. Beside him stood a woman holding a cloth banner with the words "God Is Love."

The name of God was heard quite often in our house. Anytime

someone knocked a funny bone, burned dinner, or didn't like what he heard on the news, the name of God rattled the walls, bounced off the ceilings, and if the windows were open, no doubt went so far as to knock on our neighbors' doors as well. The name of God, as it fell from my family's lips, always had a second word tacked on to it, so that for a time I thought the second word was simply God's last name. It took me a while to figure out that the second word was just a regular swear word. At any rate, in our house, *God* and *love* were two words that never occupied the same sentence.

Shyly I ambled over to where my classmate sat and slipped onto the bench beside her. She glanced at me with a quick movement of her eyes, then looked back at the band as though I were only a pesky squirrel come to beg for peanuts. We sat in silence for what must have been a full five minutes while I studied her profile. Her sleek black hair, cut in a short pageboy, caught the afternoon sun in one shiny ribbon of light along the side of her head. The darkness of her hair stood in sharp contrast to the milky white of her smooth skin, though the one cheek I could see was colored lightly with a healthy blush of red. Her dark eye peered out from under a full creaseless lid and was crowned with a black crescent brow. Her nose was barely there. It was just a bridgeless button that stuck out no farther than the curve of her upper lip. She was beautiful, and I longed to be her friend.

It took me a moment to work up the courage to say something. Finally I asked, "Whatcha doing?"

"Listening," she said. She didn't turn her head to look at me.

I listened then too for a moment. The band started a new tune, and the song they played was slow and poignant, the notes somehow rising and settling as sweetly as early morning dew over Hollenbeck Park. But more than the music, it was the girl beside me who captured my attention. She sat motionless, transfixed, her face a study in wonder. It was as though she were aware of something hidden to me. As though, I thought, she could see fairies dancing in the grass or hear angels singing in the branches of the trees. I wished it were apparent to me too, but all I saw was the ruddy, sweaty faces of the musicians playing their instruments under a too hot sun.

At once I felt sad and awkward, set apart as usual from the circles I wanted to step into. I had thought perhaps she would talk to me, had thought she was as in need of a friend as I was, but I decided I was wrong. I was only the pesky squirrel begging for something she didn't want to give. The streets of Boyle Heights that I'd been strolling the past hour seemed suddenly comforting and familiar, and I decided to go back to my wandering.

But before I could slip off the bench, my classmate turned to me finally and, with eyes wide, said breathlessly, "Wasn't that just about the prettiest thing you ever heard?"

I nodded, unable to respond with words. She was looking right at me, talking to me!

"What's your name?" she asked then.

Delighted that she wanted to know, I shot back rather too loudly, "Augie!"

A line formed between her two dark eyes as she frowned. "What kind of name is that?"

"Short for Augusta."

She gazed at me intently while seemingly considering whether I was telling the truth. She eventually formed her small lips into a circle and said, "Oh," willing, I guess, to accept at face value what I had told her.

"What's yours?" I asked. "Your name, I mean."

"Sunny."

I cocked my head. "What kind of name is *that*?"

"American for Hatsune."

"Oh."

"I'm Japanese," she explained. "But my father says I'm not really. He says I'm American. Not even Japanese American, just plain American, that's all."

I nodded eagerly, as though I understood, though I didn't.

She eyed my red hair suspiciously, then met my eyes again. "So what are *you*?"

"Whadaya mean, what am I?"

"I mean, where'd your family come from?"

"San Bernardino."

She shook her head. "Before that. Like my grandparents came from Japan. Where'd yours come from?"

"I don't know." I shrugged. "Maybe New York or someplace like that."

She stared at me blankly. "But what *are* you? Are you Scottish or German or something?"

My brow furrowing in frustration, I said, "Naw, I'm not Scottish or anything like that. I'm American, like you."

"Well, your family must've come from somewhere."

"San Bernardino, like I said. We just moved here this summer."

Sunny sighed, a little sigh of resignation. "Well, it doesn't matter anyway." She swung her feet under the bench and glanced around the park as though looking for the answer I couldn't give her. Then suddenly she turned back toward me and asked, "Why'd your mom and dad give you a name like Augusta?"

"Because I was born in August."

"August what?"

"August ninth."

"August ninth, 1930?"

"How'd ya know?" I cried in surprise.

Her delicate eyebrows arched upward and she broke into a smile. "That's my birthday too!"

"It is?"

"Yup. This year I got a dollhouse and a book and a bracelet from my mom and dad, and a bunch more stuff from my aunts and uncles and my grandma. What'd you get?"

Since my family was busy moving to Los Angeles just at that time, no one had remembered my birthday. I didn't want to admit this to my new friend, though, so I replied evasively, "Oh, lots of stuff."

"I've seen you in school," she said. She seemed not to notice that I hadn't answered her question. "You're new."

"Yeah."

"Where'd you come from?"

"Like I already told you, San Bernardino."

"What for?"

"What for what?"

"Why'd you move here?"

"My dad died." Then, remembering what my mother had instructed me to say, I added, "In an accident. We had to come here and move in with Uncle Finn and Aunt Lucy."

Sunny looked at me again for a long while, but I couldn't read the expression on her face. Finally she asked, "You miss your dad?"

Miss him? I'd never really known him. He'd been a traveling sales-man, and in the eight years that made up my lifetime, he'd rarely been home. I shrugged my shoulders. "Naw," I confessed. "I guess not."

Sunny turned her gaze back toward the band. They had stopped singing, and the man with the baton was preaching to a small crowd. His face was a shiny red beet, his dark hair slick with sweat, and even from a distance I could see the muscles in his neck straining against the stiff collar of the uniform.

When she turned back to me, she said, "I'd miss my dad if he died."

I nodded. Most kids would, I supposed. I'd never been much like other kids, and our family had never seemed like other families.

Sunny stood and brushed imaginary dirt from the seat of her skirt. "You want to come to my house and play awhile?"

From behind her the voice of the preacher reached me. "God loves you," he shouted across Hollenbeck Park. "God loves you, and that's why he sent his Son to die for your sins."

I knew little about God beyond my family's curses, but in that moment it suddenly seemed possible that there was a God of love somewhere. I had just been invited to play at another little girl's house for the first time in my life.

TWO

When I was born, the midwife who helped deliver me made a mistake on the birth certificate. After writing "August," she realized she had written the month of my birth on the line reserved for my name.

"It doesn't matter," my mother muttered from her bed. "Leave it. August is as good a name as any."

"But Mrs. Schuler," the midwife protested, "August is a boy's name. Your baby is a girl."

As the story goes, my mother didn't hesitate. "Then add an *a* to the end," she ordered wearily. And so it was that by someone's carelessness I came to be named Augusta.

My sister Valerie, eleven years older than I, told me this story for the first time when I was about six or seven. She laughed when she told it, as though it were a joke or an amusing family anecdote. But I was stunned. To me, it wasn't funny at all. Young as I was, I was old enough to realize that my parents hadn't bothered to choose a name for me, and that they had largely ignored the fact of my coming until I was suddenly there.

I was the youngest of six, and seven years separated me from my closest sibling, my brother Stephen. I scarcely knew my oldest brother,

Lenny, who was fifteen when I was born and out of the house and into the armed services by the time I was three. In between Lenny and Stephen were Mitchell, Valerie, and Gwen.

My conception roughly coincided with the onset of the Great Depression. As I grew to become aware of such things, I eventually understood the equation: a sixth pregnancy plus a catastrophic economic collapse equals an unwanted child. I wouldn't have fully pieced it together this way at the age of eight, but I did by that time feel the sum of the equation all the same.

My father wasn't particularly successful at his chosen profession. He lacked both the drive and the charm that were necessary for a traveling salesman, so our family limped along on my father's meager earnings. We lived in a small rental house in San Bernardino, California, and while Father talked about one day making good and finally owning our own home and having money in the bank, that day never came.

I was born too late to hear of my father's aspirations from his own mouth, but Valerie told me Father was a big dreamer before the stock market crashed in 1929. After the crash the dreams died, and Father slowly became a defeated man. He continued knocking on doors for another eight years, peddling everything from brushes to encyclopedias, but he finally decided—as the saying goes—that he was worth more dead than alive. After making sure his life insurance policy was paid up, he drank a pint of sour-mash whiskey, then drove our Plymouth coupe onto a railroad crossing just as the Union Pacific was bearing down on the same stretch of track. His death was officially listed as an accident, though Mother told us children he had killed himself. "He spoke more than once of how he would do it," she lamented, "and now he's gone and done it, just like he said."

My father's death had a greater effect on me than his life ever did. It was his suicide that resulted in our moving to Los Angeles. Something came unhinged in Mother's mind the day Father's remains were pulled out of what remained of the coupe, and she never again did anything that made much sense. She might have kept us in San Bernardino where, had we been frugal with the insurance money and whatever she and my older siblings might earn, our lives could have gone on largely uninterrupted.

Instead, she bought bus tickets for herself and the four of us children still under her care and dragged us all to Los Angeles, where we showed up unannounced on her brother's doorstep. When Uncle Finn answered the door, Mother informed him that as her only brother he was responsible for us now. Uncle Finn looked at each of our five faces and, after throwing out a few introductory expletives, said, "Mags Schuler, you've gone completely round the bend this time."

"That may be so, Finn," Mother agreed, "but we still need a roof over our heads and food in our stomachs, and you can't very well turn away your own flesh and blood."

Finn O'Shaughnessy was by then a middle-aged man who, along with his family, lived on Fresno Street in the working-class neighborhood of Boyle Heights. He owned a hardware store on Whittier Avenue, just a few blocks south of his house, and had earned his living by selling nails and pipe for twenty-five years. He was on his second wife, his first having died of consumption—though the running joke among my siblings was that Aunt Arlys had simply become sick of being married to Uncle Finn. After the first wife died, Finn O'Shaughnessy married a woman sixteen years his junior with the startling but genuine name of Lucille Peacock. Between the two wives he had managed to father five children. With Arlys, he'd had Stella, who was nineteen now and newly married, and Maureen, fifteen and still living at home. With Lucy, he had Russell (known as Rusty), Riley, and Rosey. They ranged in age from nine to three.

He had a full house already, and I think he might have turned us away if Mother hadn't reached into her pocketbook and handed Uncle Finn a tattered envelope. "This is what I got from Leonard's life insurance policy," she said. "It ought to compensate for our staying here awhile." My uncle invited us in then and, hollering for Aunt Lucy to join us, told us to all sit down so we could talk this thing through.

And that's how we came to live in Uncle Finn's house, the eleven of us squeezed in there like so many night crawlers in a fisherman's bait can.

It was a small house, typical of Boyle Heights. Three concrete steps, without railings, led up to the front door, which in turn led directly into the living room. The main room of the house, it was, nevertheless, an uninviting room, filled with a slipshod collection of outdated furniture. Under the two front windows sat an old couch decked in a calico slipcover. The slipcover was of the same material as the curtains that framed the windows, all hand sewn by Aunt Lucy. They smelled heavily of cigarette smoke, and considering the way Aunt Lucy burned through cigarettes, they'd no doubt picked up the odor long before they'd been slipped on or hung up, as the case may be. In front of the couch was a chipped coffee table that harbored piles of magazines, half-empty beer bottles, and ashtrays full of cigarette butts. On the other side of the room were a couple of lumpy overstuffed chairs, both of a tired brown material with cream-colored antimacassars draped over the arms. Aunt Lucy would talk for years to come of making slipcovers for those chairs, but she never did. They shared a coffee table between them, on which sat a lamp with a fringed shade and a cathedral-style RCA radio, the latter being the center of entertainment in the O'Shaughnessy household. On the walls hung a number of framed family photographs, a couple of cheap landscapes, and a small ornate crucifix that was the family's one remaining nod to their all-but-dead Catholicism.

The kitchen was an airy room with ancient appliances and a dizzying color scheme. The counter tops were yellow, the cabinets burnt orange, the wallpaper a purple floral pattern with touches of grease, the linoleum floor a pasty white, streaked with a long history of heel marks. A bright red Formica table sat in the center of the kitchen, surrounded by six badly tarnished padded chrome chairs.

Off the kitchen was a small room that might have been a pantry, but Aunt Lucy used it as a sewing room. Once we moved in, this also became Mother's bedroom. It contained a couch, a sewing table and chair, a push-pedal Singer sewing machine, bolts of material in various colors and patterns, and hundreds of spools of thread in glass jars. Aunt Lucy was an excellent seamstress and earned money for the family by making dresses for a small but wealthy clientele, including two or three of the lesser known Hollywood starlets. By day, Mother helped Aunt Lucy with the endless basting and hemming and the cutting out of patterns that needed to be done. By night, she sought comfort in the bottles she hid between the cushions of the couch that was her bed.

The house's second story was reached by a narrow staircase just to the left of the front door and hugging the west wall of the living room. Upstairs were three small bedrooms and the only bath. The hall to the bathroom was at the top of the stairs to the right, and halfway down this hall was the door that opened up to yet another staircase, this one to the attic.

The attic was a spacious empty room that Uncle Finn had long planned to convert into a sort of playroom for his youngest children. Instead, with a couple of secondhand mattresses, a chest of drawers minus its handles, and a couple of beat-up throw rugs, it became a bedroom for Valerie, Gwen, Stephen, and me. We all felt like prisoners in that attic room with its one small dusty window, its single bare light bulb glowing from the spine of the V-shaped ceiling, and its unfinished walls that revealed the yellowed newspaper stuck in there years ago for insulation.

Valerie got a job as a live-in domestic as quickly as she could and moved out of Uncle Finn's house after only a few weeks, but night after night Gwen, Stephen, and I lay awake in that dark attic, listening to the mice nibbling their way through all the old headlines tucked into the walls.

By the time we moved to Boyle Heights, I was already well aware of a hollow place inside of me, like an air bubble caught in a pane of glass. It was always there hanging about, an ache that made life hard to live, a longing for something that I couldn't begin to identify. I had never tasted the joys of a normal childhood, never experienced the wonder of discovering a world in which everything was completely new and mysterious and fascinating. At eight years of age I was already world-weary, though I wouldn't have put it that way at the time.

Reading served as my one escape. I owned a single book of fairy tales that I read time and again, and maybe it was through the pictures, even more than the words, I discovered a world utterly different from my own. It was a world of magic and goodness, beauty and happy endings, and all the sweet things that seemed not to be a part of life in the Schuler-O'Shaughnessy household. I spent hours in that book, devouring it, living in its pages.

But I always came back to my own life, of course. As soon as I reached the final page and put the book aside, I was right back where I'd started. And sometimes when I returned to the real world, it seemed all the more bleak in contrast to the images the book had conjured up in my mind.

It was a kind of childhood nihilism, I suppose, though of course one can only realize that as an adult looking back. But in some sure way even then I sensed that I was just starting out on a life that didn't matter at all, and it seemed a long road to travel simply to reach nothing in the end.

That was my state of mind when I met Sunny in Hollenbeck Park that late September day of 1938. Largely unsupervised by the adults in my family, I was free to leave the house and wander around Boyle Heights without so much as telling anyone where I was going. I don't think anyone much noticed when I was gone. I don't think anyone much noticed when I was home, for that matter. That's why when I went to Sunny's house and met her family, I felt I had found what I'd always wanted, even without knowing that I'd wanted it, and I was never satisfied outside their home again.

THREE

Sunny lived not far from the park on Fickett Street, in a white frame house with blue shutters and trim. The house was well kept up, with a manicured lawn and window boxes filled with all sorts of colorful flowers. It was easy to see that the people who lived there took pride in their home. It wasn't like Uncle Finn's house, where weeds poked up through the cracks in the sidewalk and the awnings over the windows were ripped and faded.

Something on the inside was different too. I began to realize it as soon as Sunny and I walked through the front door and she cried out, "Mama, I'm home!" as though it was a message her mother had waited all afternoon to hear. I would get no response at all if I made such an announcement in Uncle Finn's house, but Sunny's call was answered right away with the greeting, "Hello, dear! I'm glad you're back." The words came from somewhere toward the rear of the house, and in the next moment Sunny's mother appeared, smiling as she wiped her hands on the apron tied around her slim waist. "And who's this?" she asked brightly when she saw me.

"This is Augie, Mama. Short for Augusta because she was born in August." Sunny gave an excited little hop on the wooden floor with her Buster Browns. "We have the very same birthday, Mama! Isn't that something!"

"Why, yes, that *is* something, isn't it?"

Unlike my own mother who was both tall and wide, Sunny's mother was a tiny wisp of a woman who stood scarcely taller than I. Her dark hair fell to just below her ears and had been permed into loose waves. Her skin was porcelain smooth, her features small and precise. Her dark eyes literally sparkled as she smiled, a tiny panorama of stars twinkling in a night sky. She seemed to me a character right out of my fairy-tale book, a fairy incarnate, if she'd only had wings. She was the loveliest woman I'd ever seen.

And yet it was she who complimented *me*. "What pretty red hair you have!" she exclaimed. "It looks just like spun gold."

More bewildered than flattered, I lifted a hand to my head and pulled at the tangled knots with my fingers. As usual when left to my own devices, I had forgotten to brush my hair that morning.

"And what darling freckles!" She laughed lightly while touching the bridge of my nose with the tip of one index finger.

When she dropped her hand, I rubbed at the same spot, as though trying to rub off the freckles. How could she think they were darling? Other kids laughed while calling me "freckle-face," even my own brothers and sisters, who had an only somewhat lighter sprinkling of freckles themselves.

The only message I'd ever received was that I was hard on the eyes. Even my own mother had recently told Aunt Lucy she hoped I'd grow out of the ugly-duckling stage one of these days. Aunt Lucy had waved a hand and told her not to worry because, after all, "Homely in the cradle, pretty at the table." I was right there in the kitchen with them while they chatted, and they must have thought I didn't understand, but I did.

Since I wasn't used to being complimented, I was suspicious when Sunny's mother found something good to say about me. Especially since she and her daughter had smooth dark hair and perfectly clear skin that I knew even at my age were far more desirable than my own knotted red strands and blemished complexion. I didn't say thank you. I didn't know what to say. But she must not have expected me to say anything because she continued, "I'm very happy to meet you, Augie. I'm Suma Yamagata, Sunny's mother."

Her name sounded like a snatch of poetry, or the notes of an unfamiliar song drifting past me on the air. I wanted to hold on to it and repeat it, but as soon as I heard the name, it was gone. How would I ever remember it?

"We found each other in the park, Mama," Sunny explained. "There was a band there playing pretty music, and I was sitting and listening to it, and that's when Augie showed up."

The woman turned her gentle gaze toward me again and asked, "Do you live in the neighborhood, Augie?"

I fidgeted awkwardly and scratched the back of one leg with my opposite foot. "Over on Fresno Street," I murmured. I lifted my arm and pointed, though I had no idea in which direction Uncle Finn's house lay.

"Then you and Sunny must go to the same school."

"We do, Mama," Sunny said, nodding rapidly, "but we just never knew each other before. I asked her if she wanted to come over and play, and she said she did."

Laughing lightly, Sunny's mother said, "Well, don't let me keep you. Your father will be home in an hour, and then we're going to eat. Would you like to join us for supper, Augie?" I was tongue-tied by the invitation and couldn't squeeze any words out of the knot in my mouth, but I nodded. "Why don't you call your mother, then, and tell her where you are. We don't want her worried about you."

The knot unraveled as I shrugged. "That's all right," I said. "She won't worry."

Sunny's mother frowned and shook her head slightly. "Oh, but I'm sure she will. I'll call if you'd like. What's your telephone number?"

I shrugged again. "I don't know."

The woman looked at me with increasing curiosity. "Do you have a telephone in your home?"

"Yeah."

"Well, what's your father's name? I'll have the operator connect me."

When I said nothing, Sunny drew her mother close with the wag of a finger and whispered, "Her father died in an accident, Mama. Last summer. That's why they moved here to Augie's uncle's house."

"Oh! I'm so sorry——"

"Can we go play now, Mama?"

"Yes, of course. . . ."

As we bounded up the stairs I could feel with every step the bewildered gaze of Sunny's mother upon my back. Already I sensed she was someone I could trust. Even though I didn't miss my father, I would have liked to tell her the truth about his death, just so she could offer the condolences I'd never received from anyone. She might even put her arms around me and hold me while saying she was sorry about what had happened. But Mother's warning was all too clear: "Don't you ever tell anyone your father shamed us by killing himself. It's nobody's business but our own. He died in an accident, just like the coroner said. You understand that, Augie?" And I, not understanding at all, promised, "Yes, Mama."

At the top of the stairs Sunny paused and put a finger to her lips, drawing my attention to a closed door with a nod of her head. "My brothers are sleeping," she said. "Mama'll kill me if we wake them up."

I doubted her mother was capable of killing so much as a housefly, but I nodded and put a finger to my own lips to let Sunny know I'd be quiet. "You'll see 'em later," she continued. "One's Sammy—he's four—and the other's George. He's only a baby, and he pretty much sleeps all the time unless he's hungry, and then he cries a lot."

"How come they have American names?" I asked.

"Well, see," she explained, "Sam's name is really Isamu and George's is really Shoji, but we always call them by their American names."

"Then why not just name them Sam and George in the first place?"

"On account of Obaasan, I guess. That's my grandma. She lives with us—that's her room." Sunny pointed toward an open door farther down the hall. "Papa's her only son, so she has to live here, even though she's got two daughters—that's my aunts. They live right here in L.A. too, and I wished she lived with one of them, but Papa says she has to live with us. But what Obaasan really wishes is that we all lived in Japan. She hates it here."

"How come?"

"I don't know. She grew up in Japan and she says she's still Japanese, and she wants to die in Japan too, but Papa won't send her back. But to be nice to her he gave us all Japanese names. She won't call us by our American names. My middle name's Helen, but I don't think Obaasan knows that. She won't even call me Sunny, just Hatsune."

"Why do you call her—what is it, Oboe Sun?"

"Obaasan. That's Japanese for Grandma. Or at least it's one of the Japanese words for Grandma. There's a whole bunch of words you can call your grandma depending on how old you are, but we've always just called her Obaasan because it's easier. I mean, why call her Baachan one year and Obaachan the next year and Obaasan the year after that? The American way is better—just call your Grandma *Grandma,* no matter how old you are. You know what I mean?"

I nodded. I had no idea what she was talking about. "But you can't call her Grandma?" I asked.

Sunny's eyes grew wide as she shook her head. "She'd kill me for sure if I did. She says Grandma is an ugly English word." She paused and once again put a finger to her lips. "She might be sleeping, if we're lucky. Try not to wake her up. She can be a real grouch, especially if you wake her up from a nap."

We tiptoed past the open door to her grandmother's bedroom, but we hadn't yet reached Sunny's room when a frail voice called out, "Hatsune?"

My new friend turned to me and grimaced. "She's awake," she whispered. "I'll have to go say hi to her. Come on."

I followed her into the room. The light was turned off, and the shades were drawn over the windows. But enough sunlight seeped in to reveal a small woman in a large overstuffed chair in one corner of the room. Her feet were propped up on the matching footstool and appeared as only a tiny ripple in the blanket that covered her from the waist down. She wore a silk kimono, the intricate detail of which escaped me in the dim light. As we neared her, I could see that the old woman's round and wrinkled face was almost as small as Sunny's. Her nose was an equally modest bump, with scarcely any bridge for her glasses to sit on. Her eyes were little more than slits behind the lenses, like the narrow buttonholes on the back of my dress. Her graying hair was pulled back from her face in a crisp bun. She reached for a cane that leaned against the chair and pointed it at Sunny, though not in a threatening way. She was more like a theater director singling out the actor she wanted to speak with. She and Sunny began to talk in Japanese. I marveled that they could make sense out of such funny sounds.

After a moment Sunny turned to me and said, "She wanted to know where I've been. I told her I was in the park listening to a band and that I met you there."

The foot of the cane swung around until it pointed toward me. The old woman didn't smile when she looked at me, but she said something to Sunny and nodded. When she finished, Sunny translated. "She says hello and she's happy to meet you."

"Oh," I said dumbly. "Tell her I said hi." Then to Sunny I whispered, "Doesn't she speak English?"

Sunny shook her head. "She never wanted to learn."

"What's that smell?" I asked suspiciously, narrowing my eyes.

"Incense," Sunny explained. "Obaasan's always burning incense and praying at that shrine." She pointed toward the dresser where even in the dim light I could see a thin breath of smoke rising from a jar. Letting my gaze wander around the room, I noticed that the walls were covered with Japanese artwork, and that where there should have been a bed there was only an uncomfortable-looking mat on the floor. The only objects that looked like anything I was used to were the chair Sunny's grandmother sat in and an old phonograph on a small table beside it. I realized suddenly that all the furniture and pictures downstairs had been typically American, no different from Uncle Finn's house except that everything seemed cleaner and better taken care of. But this room where Sunny's grandmother lived was a little sliver of Japan, as close, I supposed, as the old woman was going to get.

Sunny and her grandmother spoke a few more words, and when they finished, the old woman nodded once more and in doing so seemed to dismiss us. As we exited the room Sunny asked, "Want to see my dollhouse?" I did, but even more I wanted to know why her grandmother didn't speak English and why she sat in a darkened room that smelled of spices and burning wood.

Sunny's bedroom was large and bright and uncommonly beautiful to someone who slept in an attic. That it was hers alone—with its large canopied bed, its handsome walnut furniture, and certainly best of all, its bookcase full of books—was almost unbelievable. How could Sunny enter this room and not feel overwhelmed by its beauty? As for me, I stood in the doorway, scarcely able to enter, staring open-mouthed at what my new friend took in stride. No telling how long I might have stood there gazing in wonder if Sunny hadn't interrupted me by saying, "Come on, don't just stand there." She was already kneeling on the floor beside her two-story, fully furnished dollhouse.

"Your dad must be rich," I said in awe.

Sunny laughed. "We're not rich. I only get one new pair of shoes a year." And as though that settled the question of their wealth, she asked, "You wanna play or not?"

I sat down on the floor beside her, but the dollhouse didn't interest me at the moment. The people in this real house were far more fascinating than any dolls in a dollhouse. "I didn't know you could speak Japanese," I remarked, impressed.

"I'm not very good," she said mildly, shrugging off my admiration. "I can only speak enough to talk to my grandma. Other kids have to go to the Japanese school *after* regular school to learn how to talk in Japanese, but Papa says I don't have to go."

"How come?"

Sunny looked at me and laughed. "Because we speak English in America, of course! Why should I learn to speak Japanese?"

"Then how come the other kids have to learn it?"

Sunny lifted her shoulders again, a slightly bored shrug. "I guess their dads think they might go back to Japan someday or something. I don't know. I'm just glad I don't have to go to the Japanese school. I wouldn't speak Japanese at all if I didn't have to speak it with my grandma."

"How come she never learned English?"

Sunny moved one of the dolls from a bedroom to the kitchen as she answered my question. "She was a picture bride. She only left Japan and came over here because she thought my grandpa was a *dekaseginin*."

"A *what*?"

"Dekaseginin. That's someone who came over to America to make a bunch of money but not to stay. Grandma married Grandpa because she thought he'd take her back to Japan after he earned enough money here, but he never did."

"Wasn't she mad?"

"She's *still* mad."

"And she still wants to go back?"

Sunny nodded. "That's why she never learned English. Papa said she thought if she learned English that'd be the same as giving up her dream of going back home."

"Can't your dad just send her back?"

"There'd be no one to take care of her. We have some relatives there, but all her children are here. She wants all of us to go, but Papa says he can't go back because he never was there in the first place."

I chewed my lip in thought. "If she can't speak English, what does she do all day?"

"Mostly just sits in her room. She can't help Mama around the house much because she has arthritis so bad in her hands. She only goes downstairs to eat, but she says even that's getting harder because the arthritis is moving down to her knees. Papa's thinking about building an extra room for her downstairs so she doesn't have to do any climbing anymore. That way the boys could have their own bedrooms too."

"But," I protested, "doesn't she *do* anything? How can she just sit there all day long?"

"Oh, I don't know. She listens to Japanese music on her record player. She reads the Japanese newspapers from Little Tokyo. She's always calling us to come talk to her. And I think she sleeps a lot too."

I suddenly felt sorry for the old woman. It seemed such an empty life. After a moment I asked, "What do you mean she was a picture bride?"

Sunny stopped fiddling with the dolls and resettled herself cross-legged on the floor, evidently resigned to talking instead of playing. "See, my grandpa came to America a long time ago, way back in the eighteen hundreds, when he was about nineteen. When he got old enough to get married, he wrote to some people in Japan, sent them some money, and asked them to send him a wife."

"Really?" I exclaimed.

"Yup."

"You could buy a wife just like ordering something from Sears Roebuck?"

"Yup. He got this picture back of my grandma, and she looked pretty, so they got married while she was still over in Japan and he was here. By the time she got over here and they met each other, they were already married."

I tried to follow, but it was hard for me to comprehend this strange arrangement. My mind was full of questions, but I scarcely knew what to ask. Finally I said, "I don't see why she came over if she doesn't like America."

Sunny sighed, as though weary of explaining. "She came over because she thought my grandpa was going to get rich and then take her back home."

"Did he get rich?"

Sunny shook her head. "No, but Papa says there was some sort of misunderstanding, and Grandpa never wanted to go back to Japan in the first place. Grandpa tried to get Grandma to learn English and make friends with the *hakujin,* but she wouldn't. She says the hakujin don't like us and never will."

"What's that?"

"What? Hakujin?"

"Yeah."

"People like you."

"Like me?"

"White people. You don't have any Japanese in you, do you?"

I shook my head.

"Then you're hakujin."

I frowned. "Well, I like your grandma all right, even if I'm a hog-a-gin," I said, stumbling over the word.

"Papa says most whites do like us, and the ones that don't we can just ignore."

"So if I'm hog-a-gin," I asked, "then what are you?"

"*Sansei,*" Sunny replied flatly.

"Sand-say?"

"Yeah, I'm Sansei, my mom and dad are *Nisei,* and my grandma's *Issei.*"

"Why aren't you all the same thing?"

"How can we all be the same thing when we're different?"

"What do you mean, different?"

"Well, I was born here, not in Japan."

"So?"

"So I'm Sansei."

"Where were your mom and dad born?"

"Here."

"So why aren't they sand-say?"

"Because their parents were born in Japan. That makes them Nisei."

"So it depends on where you were born?"

"Something like that. And how old you are too. So it's where and when you were born, pretty much."

I paused to think it over and decided that no matter how much Sunny and I went around in circles, I'd never understand. I'd have to take her word for it. But what, I wondered, must it be like to be Japanese and to understand such strange and wonderful things?

As though she had read my thoughts, Sunny reminded me she wasn't really Japanese after all. "Papa doesn't talk about stuff like this," she remarked. "He says we're all just plain American like everyone else—even Obaasan, though she's not a citizen. But Papa said she's spent much more of her life here than in Japan, and that makes her more American than Japanese, and he'd make her become a regular citizen if the government would let him, but they won't."

"How come?"

"Because she was born in Japan."

"So?"

"Anyone born in Japan can't be a citizen here."

"Well, what about your grandpa?" I asked. "Is he a citizen?"

"No, he's dead. He died before I was born." Sunny giggled then and raised a hand to her mouth. "But I still hear Obaasan yelling at him sometimes at night, telling him to take her back to Hiroshima. It's really funny. Papa has to go in there and wake her up and tell her she's having another nightmare. Then she tells him the only nightmare she has is waking up and finding herself still in America."

Sunny laughed again, but I didn't join her. "Wow," I said, "if she wants to go back so bad, I think your dad should just send her back. *Somebody* over there would take care of her."

"No. Papa says she should feel lucky to be here where we have freedom."

"Don't they have freedom over there?"

"Not like here, I guess. The people over there have to worship the emperor and act like he's God and all. Papa says he wouldn't bow to the emperor even if someone held a samurai sword to his throat." Sunny placed one index finger against her throat and drew it across her neck. I swallowed hard at the thought of her father losing his head.

"He must really hate that emperor guy," I remarked.

"He doesn't hate him. He just says he's a man like anybody else. He says no one should be worshiped like that because all men are equal and that's why my grandfather came to America in the first place. And, Papa says, America is the land of opportunity. He says there's no better place to live."

I had never heard such talk, and I was more than a little confused. But before I could ask any more questions, we heard a man's voice downstairs. Sunny jumped up quickly and cried, "Papa's home!" And then she disappeared and left me sitting alone in her room to ponder all I had heard that brief and mysterious afternoon.

❧

I soon ventured timidly downstairs, curious to see Sunny's father. From the staircase I spied the two of them waltzing without music around the living room, Sunny standing on her father's shoes. He towered over her and was perhaps even a foot taller than his wife, but still, compared to my own family, he was a small man, thin and compact, with delicate hands and long, narrow fingers. His jet black hair was parted on one side and pulled neatly over to the other. He had a strong jaw and a friendly upturned mouth, and his eyes were slightly magnified behind a pair of frameless glasses.

As I watched father and daughter dance, my breath caught in my throat, and a bitter taste came to my mouth. I would have begun to weep with envy if they hadn't stopped abruptly and turned their attention to me.

"Who's this!" Sunny's father cried in delight, as though I were a neatly wrapped present suddenly placed in his hands.

Sunny hopped off her father's toes. "That's Augie," she said. "We go to the same school and we have the very same birthday and we found each other today in the park."

The man's dark eyebrows sprang up over the rim of his glasses as he gave me a look of obvious merriment. Then, to my surprise, he approached me with his hand outstretched. Only adults shook hands, and yet here he was waiting for me to place my palm against his. I did so shyly, but when he bowed and said, "Delighted to make your acquaintance, Augie," I laughed outright. I laughed in absolute glee, and to my continued surprise the others joined me, so that in that moment a tangible joy fell upon the room like fresh falling snow. Still holding my hand, he said, "My name is Toshio Yamagata"—oh, how *would* I remember their names?—"and if you were born on my daughter's birthday, then you must be as special as she."

"Papa!" Sunny cried, trying to look embarrassed but obviously delighted.

Her father cast a gaze of mock seriousness toward Sunny. "Well, it's true, isn't it? Everyone knows that those born on the ninth of August, 1930, are very special people. In fact, it's duly recorded in the *Government Handbook of Important Facts.*"

He turned then to look again at me, a smile lighting up his round face. I looked up at him, wide-eyed and enthralled. No one had ever told me before that the people born on August 9, 1930, were special. But if this man said it was so, then it must be so. Something bloomed inside of me at that moment, like a leaf unfurling in the spring. *I'm special*, I thought, and the words echoed through my mind and danced their way into my heart. *I'm special.*

"Augie's joining us for supper," Sunny's mother announced, "and it's just about ready, so everyone wash up."

Everyone knows that the Japanese live chiefly on rice and raw fish, so I was surprised when I sat down to a meal of meatloaf, mashed potatoes, and creamed peas. Even Obaasan ate the American food, though out of a bowl with chopsticks instead of a fork. We sat in their modest but bright dining room, and except for the slant of their eyes and the grandmother's kimono, we might have passed for a cover of the *Saturday Evening Post.*

Sunny's mother, before we sat down to eat, must have told her husband about my recent loss, because even though he directed a great deal of the conversation toward me, he didn't ask about my father. He said he was familiar with Uncle Finn's hardware store. He'd even been there a couple of times and was waited on by a smart young lady who knew more about plumbing and carpentry than he did. I told him that was my cousin Stella. She worked for Uncle Finn when she wasn't at the beauty school learning how to curl ladies' hair.

He asked me how I liked Los Angeles, what I thought about school, and whether I enjoyed listening to baseball games on the radio. I responded that I liked Los Angeles all right, I didn't like school at all except for the library, and that I enjoyed listening to baseball games very much. Actually, I'd never listened to a game and had no interest in baseball, but I told him that I did because he seemed such an enthusiastic fan of the sport. I wanted him to believe that I liked what he liked.

Every once in a while he and his wife spoke quietly in Japanese to the grandmother. Saying nothing in return and only occasionally raising her eyes, she'd simply nod while working her chopsticks through the bowl of food. I was fascinated by the deft way in which she pinched at pieces of meatloaf and pulled at wads of potato laced with peas. I watched furtively to see if any food might tumble from the chopsticks before it reached her mouth, but none ever did. It must be like eating with knitting needles, I thought, and I marveled again at how difficult it must be to live as the Japanese did. But my thoughts didn't come with a sense of gratitude that I was American, nor pity for the Japanese. Just the opposite. In my opinion they were extraordinary people. They had to be to make sense out of grunts and unintelligible muttering, to understand who was sand-say and who was knee-say and e-say, to be able to feed themselves with slender sticks without ever dropping a bite. How I envied them!

"Well then, Augie," Sunny's father said, helping himself to another serving of potatoes, "what else do you like to do? What's your very favorite thing to do?"

I had to think a moment. I wasn't used to answering questions about myself. "Mostly I like to read," I responded.

"Aha!" he exclaimed happily. I was startled enough to jump in my seat. "A commendable pastime," he went on. "Did you know that the very first novel was written by a Japanese woman in the year one thousand and four?"

I didn't and shook my head to tell him so.

"It's called *The Tales of Genji*," Sunny offered, "but that's boring. Papa, will you take me and Augie to Little Tokyo next weekend to see a movie?" She looked at her father eagerly, waiting for his reply.

He shook his head and smiled indulgently. "Movies, always movies," he said with a feigned sigh. "You should like to read more, like Augie."

But Sunny ignored his comment and turned to me. "Ojisan (Uncle) Masuo—that's my uncle—he owns a theater in Little Tokyo, and he always lets us in for free!"

I'd never been to the movies, and the prospect of going was terribly exciting. But I was even more thrilled when, after supper, Sunny's father told me to run upstairs and take whatever book from Sunny's bookcase I'd like to borrow. I quickly chose a book of short stories filled with colorful illustrations.

Walking home later that evening, I hugged the book to my chest as if it was a treasure I'd long been searching for. In fact, the whole world looked beautiful as I made the brief journey down Fourth Street from Fickett to Fresno. Sunny had waved me off with the words, "See you in school tomorrow!" and both Sunny's parents told me to come back soon, to stop by anytime at all, and the way they said it, I knew they meant it. I told them I would, and I thanked them for supper and for letting me borrow the book, and all the way home the words "I'm special" went on beating out a rhythm in my heart.

FOUR

Sunny and I had been friends for about two weeks when Uncle Finn found out I was spending time in the home of a Japanese family. I don't remember how he learned about Sunny's being Japanese—I may even have mentioned it myself, being unaware of my uncle's deep contempt for anyone who wasn't white—but I do remember his fit of rage and the family argument that followed.

We were all there, including Stella and her new husband, Jack Callahan. We had just finished Sunday dinner, an informal but filling meal in the O'Shaughnessy household, and we were sitting about languidly listening to the radio.

Uncle Finn was stretched out in his lumpy overstuffed chair, his stockinged feet propped up on the footstool. He was sunk low enough that his head rested against the back of the chair. A wide sliver of his belly—a white and hairy slab of fat—lay exposed in the gap between his sleeveless undershirt and his beltless trousers. His long, burly arms ran the length of the chair's armrests, with one hand dangling off the end like a beached starfish, the other loosely gripping the neck of a bottle of beer. He had two rules for Sunday: He never wore a shirt, and he never shaved. By early afternoon, with more than a day's growth of whiskers, he looked very much like the tramps I'd occasionally see hiking around the neighborhood in search of a handout.

Mother sat at the kitchen table, still cluttered with dirty dishes and the meal's leftovers. She wore her thin cotton housecoat over frilly lace pajamas, a combination quickly becoming her weekend uniform. Aside from their penchant for dressing down, Mother and Uncle Finn also shared many physical similarities. They were both tall and large boned, with a generous helping of meat on those bones. They shared the same wavy red hair streaked with gray and the same hazel eyes set rather close together in their round-as-the-full-moon faces. Their noses were large and hooked and hung like awnings over their thin-lipped mouths. Neither had much of a chin, or if they ever had, it was now lost behind a sagging layer of flesh. They were not attractive people, though an occasional smile might have improved their looks somewhat. As it was, their faces were heavy with frown lines, and I think Mother's lips had scarcely ventured upward since before I was born. My O'Shaughnessy grandparents, though Catholic, had managed to produce only the two of them, which I decided was just as well.

Mother sat at the table that afternoon doing nothing in particular, her arms crossed on top of the red Formica. She might have been listening to the music on the radio, but more likely she was listening only to whatever thoughts were playing out in her mind.

Aunt Lucy was in the other overstuffed chair, beside the doorway to the kitchen. She was darning one of Uncle Finn's socks while puffing on a Lucky Strike. Both she and Uncle Finn smoked Lucky Strikes, the "Mouth Happy" cigarettes. Sometimes Aunt Lucy stuck hers into a long cigarette holder the way the movie stars did, but that was usually when she was passing the time of day with her lady friends. When just family was around, she did without the holder. She had one of those permanent blue bumps on her bottom lip that Stella told me came from holding a cigarette between her lips while she worked. Her cigarette dangled there now while the ashes lengthened and finally threatened to drop onto her blouse. She flicked them into the ashtray just in time to save her clothes, and from across the room I could see the heavy circle of red lipstick on the filter.

Even when she didn't leave the house, which was most of the time, she was always fully made up. In fact, I'd never seen her without her "face" on. Sometimes Uncle Finn would be hollering for breakfast and she'd call from the bedroom, "Hold your horses, Finn, I'm still putting my face on."

Uncle Finn would send up curses, knowing he could starve before the task was done. She had so many bottles, tubes, and compacts on her vanity table that it would take a half dozen women a half dozen lifetimes to use it all. She had an equally large collection of fingernail files, toenail clippers, eyelash curlers, hair curlers, tweezers, razors, scissors, hair brushes, rouge applicators, powder puffs, and cotton balls—as well as a host of unidentifiable gadgets—all of which were meant somehow, in some way, to make her more beautiful.

She had thick, bobbed hair that she weekly subjected to various dyes, bleaches, and perms, with the result that it was dry and brittle and generally a different color than it had been the week before. She also had a little fake mole—a beauty mark, she called it—that some-times appeared at one corner of her mouth and sometimes smack dab in the middle of her cheek. Between her hair, her cosmetics, an ever-changing wardrobe, and that moveable mole, you never knew what Aunt Lucy was going to look like from one day to another.

The sad thing was, for all that work, I never thought she looked very pretty in the end. She just looked like an old woman trying to look young. But I liked Aunt Lucy just the same. She was a nice enough person when she wasn't fighting with Uncle Finn and more pleasant to look at than my own mother.

Her children, Rusty, Riley, and Rosey, were plunked down on the staircase playing with their toys that particular Sunday afternoon. My sister Gwen and our cousin Maureen were upstairs poking around the dumping ground of Aunt Lucy's cosmetics, while Stephen, fifteen and restless, had climbed up to the attic to brood and indulge in his newly acquired habit of smoking pilfered cigarettes.

I sat on the couch where I had wedged myself in between Stella and Jack. Jack's long arm rested around both Stella and me, and I nestled my head in his shoulder. The three of us sat quietly, content to be together and to listen to the radio. When Jack and Stella came to visit, the house seemed a little homier. Though I had only recently become acquainted with them, I liked them and felt closer to them than I did to anyone else in my family.

Jack was a tall, lanky fellow who liked to amuse me with simple magic tricks. He had a quick smile and an easy way about him, and he was seldom ruffled by anything. He worked as a welder, but he was a man with a vision. He hoped someday to earn a degree in civil engineering, and he also wanted to learn how to fly. His dream, he said, was to build roads and bridges and dams that he could admire from the air in the cockpit of his own plane. I asked him if he'd take me up with him once he'd earned his wings, and he said he sure would. I could even be his copilot if I wanted to. Young as I was, I thought Jack a terribly romantic figure, like Charles Lindbergh, and I hoped I'd be as lucky as Stella when I grew up and got married.

My cousin Stella deserved a good man like Jack, I thought. She was pretty and fun loving and always quick with a laugh. A budding beautician, she came around to the house two or three times a week to use Gwen and Maureen and even me as guinea pigs to practice on. When it was my turn, I lapped up the attention as she washed and set my hair, chattering all the while around the bobby pins pressed between her lips. I asked her why she curled my hair when it was already so curly, and she said she had to learn to work with all different kinds of hair, and mine presented for her the greatest challenge. I wasn't sure that was a compliment, but I didn't mind because it was Stella who said it.

She herself didn't have the red hair of the O'Shaughnessys but had inherited the thick and shiny chestnut hair of her mother, Arlys. She was always neatly groomed and manicured and dressed in stylish though affordable clothing, and I was proud to be seen with her whenever we went anywhere together.

I remember sitting on the couch that Sunday afternoon, feeling sated and drowsy from the dinner, curled up in this secure place between Stella and Jack. But then the news came on, and Uncle Finn started swearing and mumbling something about "those low-life imperialist Japs trying to take over China," and that must have been when I turned to Stella for an explanation. Maybe at that point I said something aloud about Sunny being Japanese, because even though the details are vague, I distinctly recall Uncle Finn lifting his head up from the chair and casting me a long and icy stare. Uncle Finn had a wide array of ugly faces to fit every occasion, but I'd never quite seen a look on his face to equal this one for anger and contempt.

Stella must have seen it too because she said, "Forget it, Dad. It doesn't matter."

She may have wanted to appease him, but her words acted like fuel on his fire, and the next thing we knew he was standing over us, shouting, "What do you mean, it doesn't matter?" And to me he hollered, "Are you tellin' me that kid you been hanging around is a Jap?"

I couldn't answer. I stared up at the man and felt myself tremble.

Stella answered for me. "Now, Dad, Augie's friend isn't really Japanese. I mean, she's an American, born here and everything, just like us. She's hardly one of those Japs over there invading China. She's just a kid." Of course I'd told Stella all about Sunny, but it never occurred to me that anyone else would be interested in her one way or the other.

Uncle Finn seemed very interested now, though not in a good sort of way. "I don't care if she was born on the stinkin' steps of the White House," he hollered, "she's still a Jap!" Then he spat out God's name with that second word tacked on and yelled, "What you doin', Augie, hanging around their kind?"

"But, Dad," Stella argued, still trying to keep me out of it, "Japanese people come into the store, and I don't see you throwing them out." I'd told Stella how she'd waited on Mr. Yamagata at Uncle Finn's hardware store, and she said she remembered him. Mr. Yamagata had told Stella she was the first woman he'd ever met who knew the difference between a toggle bolt and a molly bolt, and she replied that as Finn O'Shaughnessy's firstborn she'd become acquainted with every item of hardware available to mankind even before her two-year molars had grown in. He'd laughed at that, and it was a laugh so distinctively gleeful that it made her think of the way a trolley sounds when it's carrying a bunch of kids to an amusement park.

"That's different," Uncle Finn growled. "That's business. Socializing with their kind is something else altogether."

"So," Jack said, "you're willing to accept their money, if nothing else."

"You stay outta this, Jack."

"You're being hypocritical, Finn—"

"The Japs are savages," Uncle Finn broke in. "Don't you kids know nothing? Don't you listen to the news? They're trying to take over the world, and they'll stop at nothing to do it! They're on a killing spree in China! They're slaughtering those Chinks left and right—"

"Yeah, with our help," interrupted Jack, "since America is shipping oil and scrap iron to the Japanese, all of which aids in their war effort—"

"You leave America outta this, Jack." Uncle Finn swung back around toward me then. Pointing at me with the index finger of the hand that still held the beer, he cried, "I bring your family into my home, I give you a place to live and food to eat, and this is the thanks I get. Mags, you get out here!" He turned abruptly toward the kitchen. "Do you know what this kid of yours is doing?"

"Now, Dad, calm down, will you—"

"You stay outta this, Stella—"

"But, Finn, let's talk about this reasonably—"

"You shut up too, Jack. This is a family matter."

"But, Finn! Jack is family. Don't talk to him like—"

"Shut up, Lucy. Mags, I said get out here."

Mother appeared reluctantly in the doorway, standing there on the threshold between the kitchen and the living room. It seemed an effort for her to keep her eyes open, and she tottered a moment before steadying herself against the doorframe. "Wha' is it, Finn?" she muttered dully.

"Look at you!" he cried. "At the bottle again, aren't you?"

Mother shook her head vehemently. "What you yelling about now, Finn?" She raised one hand to her brow and added, "I got a headache."

The thick finger and the beer bottle rose to accuse me again. "This kid of yours is friendly with a bunch of Japs. How you been raising her, Mags? Didn't you teach her any better'n that?"

Mother turned her gaze at me and blinked several times, trying to focus. "What have you been doing, Augie?" she asked quietly.

I couldn't answer. Stella took my hand in hers and held it tightly. Once again she answered for me. "She's made a friend is all. Is there anything wrong with that?"

Uncle Finn shouted, "And I suppose you knew her little friend is a Jap!"

"So what if she is?" Stella challenged, lifting her chin. "What's it matter?"

"Here we go again with the 'what's it matter' business," Uncle Finn hollered, flinging his arms wide. "The kid's associating with that kind of scum, and you're asking me what's it matter?"

"Now look, Finn—"

"Shut up, Jack—"

"Really, Finn!" Aunt Lucy dropped her sewing and jumped up from the chair. On the stairs, Rosey began to cry loudly while the boys looked too frightened to move. Aunt Lucy sighed and climbed up the stairs to comfort Rosey.

"This happens to be a respectable household," my uncle argued. "Those of us in *this* family don't go around spending time with those Oriental types—"

"Dad, we won't discuss this unless you calm down—"

"Who knows you been there?" Uncle Finn snapped, his angry eyes landing on me again. "Who knows you been in that Jap house?"

I felt my stomach turn and thought I might be sick. I opened my mouth, but no words came, so I sat there dumbly with my eyes wide, my jaw slack.

"Leave her alone, Dad."

"What's the matter with her? She can't talk all of a sudden?"

"You got her scared to death, Dad."

"A thousand white kids in Boyle Heights, and you gotta go for the one Jap—"

"There are plenty of Japanese families in Boyle Heights now, Dad—"

"Well, you listen to me, and you listen good, kid." Uncle Finn leaned closer toward me, so close I could smell the beer on his breath. "You won't be going back there, you hear me? I forbid you to go back to that Jap house."

"Ah, let her go, Finn," Mother said. "She's just a kid. She needs some friends." She stepped haltingly into the room as though to referee the fight, but Uncle Finn moved toward her and swung at her with the back of his hand. She gave a surprised cry as the hand met her face, and in the next moment she tumbled to the floor.

"Dad!" Stella jumped up and rushed to Mother.

"Finn, calm down!" Lucy cried from the stairs while Rosey screamed all the louder. The two boys finally found their legs and shot off in the direction of their room.

"Bad enough that they started coming to America at all," Uncle Finn shouted, "but now they have to move into our own neighborhood. If they have to be here, then they all oughta be in Little Tokyo with their own kind and not trying to mix in with the rest of us. They'll never be like the rest of us, those of us who are real Americans."

He stomped around the room spewing out swear words while Stella helped Mother into Aunt Lucy's chair. Blood ran down Mother's chin from a cut in her bottom lip.

"Look what you've done!" Stella accused shrilly. "You've busted her lip wide open!" She fumbled in the pocket of Mother's robe, pulled out a rumpled handkerchief, and pressed it against the wound. Mother's head lolled on the back of the chair as she shut her eyes and moaned. I wanted to go to her, to pat her hand and comfort her because she had stood up for me, but I was afraid to move. As long as I was on the couch with Jack's arm around me, I felt I was in the safest place in the house.

"You oughta be ashamed, Dad," Stella continued. "Your own sister."

"Well, she's got enough alcohol in her that she won't feel nothing."

"Finn, how can you be so cruel?"

"Stay out of this, Lucy."

"I won't!"

I began to wonder, if everyone was supposed to stay out of it, who was supposed to be in it? Maybe only Uncle Finn was entitled to his say.

"This is my house," he went on, "and as long as I'm the head of this house, there won't be no one in it associating with Japs."

"Now, look, Dad, there's plenty of people who don't much like the Irish either, but that doesn't make us bad people."

"Yeah, well, at least we're whites. That's who this country was settled by and who it's meant for. Not a bunch of slant-eyed yellows from the Orient."

Aunt Lucy decided she'd heard enough and pounded up the stairs, throwing expletives over her shoulder to rival any curses Uncle Finn might toss out. Rosey screamed in her arms. In the chair across the room, Mother moaned quietly into the handkerchief covering her mouth.

From the radio came a cheerful male voice, crooning, "You must have been a beautiful baby, / You must have been a wonderful child. . . ."

Uncle Finn, meanwhile, beat his fist against the wall while hollering about the Yellow Peril, which included, in his opinion, not only the "Japs," but also the "Chinks," the "Chicanos," the "Dagos," and anyone else who happened not to have descended from English-speaking Europe. The crucifix on the wall jumped with every jarring thump.

"And when it came to winning blue ribbons, / You must have shown the other kids how, / I can see the judges' eyes / as they handed you the prize, / I bet you made the cutest bow. . . ."

Stella, her own fists clenched at her sides, her face red, stomped one foot on the floor while yelling, "Dad, stop it! Just stop it!" But Uncle Finn went on banging and hollering while spittle flew from his mouth in all directions.

"Oh! You must have been a beautiful baby, / 'Cause, baby, look at you now."

Jack stood abruptly, crossed the room to the radio, and cut the music. Then he took my hand, lifted me up from the couch, and said, "Come on, Stella, let's take Augie home with us for a while. It's not doing anyone any good to stand around here hollering."

Stella looked from her husband to her father and back again. "You're right, Jack," she agreed. "Let's get out of here." She took my other hand, and together the three of us headed out the front door.

But Uncle Finn wasn't finished with us yet. He stood in the doorway as we moved down the walk, waving his arms and threatening, "She's not going back!"

"Oh yes, she is!" Stella yelled over her shoulder.

"Over my dead body!"

"If that's how you want it," whispered Stella.

None of us said a word as we climbed into Jack's car, an old Ford Mercury he'd salvaged from a junkyard and fixed up. Jack gunned it as we pulled away from the curb, just for added effect, I think, while Uncle Finn stood in the doorway waving the beer bottle and shouting something we couldn't hear.

I was silent on the drive to Echo Park, and in fact had yet to say anything since the argument began. I was too stunned, too frightened, too confused. What was it about Sunny's family that could raise such fury in Uncle Finn? And what if Uncle Finn made good on his threat and never allowed me to go to Sunny's house again?

We soon reached my cousin's apartment, a single room over the detached garage of a private home. When we stepped inside I finally found my voice and asked, "Stella, what if Uncle Finn doesn't let me play with Sunny anymore?"

"He will," she said confidently. "He always does what I say in the end."

She dished me up a bowl of ice cream, then she and Jack sat down at what passed for a kitchen table to play a round of gin rummy, just as though the matter had already been settled and Uncle Finn's anger forgotten.

FIVE

I don't know how she did it, but a couple of days after Uncle Finn's blowup, Stella told me it would be all right if I went to visit my "little Japanese friend" again.

"But," she warned, "don't ever invite her home with you. And don't even mention her name in front of Dad. As far as Dad goes, Sunny doesn't exist."

"But why, Stella?" I asked, baffled. "Why does Uncle Finn hate them so much just because they're Japanese?"

My cousin sighed. "Someday, when you're older, you'll understand, Augie."

Would I? Would I really understand why Uncle Finn raged against the Yamagatas when he'd never even met them? The part about hate I understood already, because I hated Uncle Finn. But I knew him and knew he wasn't worth liking. To hate someone I didn't know—now, that was a whole different thing. What did grown-ups know that I didn't know that made something like that make sense?

On the Sunday evening before Halloween that year, I was at the Yamagatas' home drawing pictures of pumpkins and witches with Sunny. We lay on our stomachs on the floor of the living room. Mrs. Yamagata sat stitching Sunny's Halloween costume, and Mr. Yamagata sat reading the paper and listening to the radio "with half an ear," as he would say.

Sunny and I were looking forward to our class's Halloween party at school the next day. We knew we'd come away with a hoard of candy that, if rationed just right, might last us an entire week. But even more exciting for me was the fact that this year I'd have a real costume. The previous Halloween in San Bernardino, when Valerie took me to a party sponsored by the YMCA, I wore only an old pillowcase over my head with holes cut out for the eyes and mouth.

"Can't I have a whole sheet?" I'd complained.

"Can't afford it," Mother had said.

When we arrived at the Y, a snobbish Little Bo Peep approached me and asked, "Just what are *you* supposed to be?"

I was too embarrassed to speak, but Valerie retorted, "Can't you see for yourself? She's half a ghost. Couldn't afford to die all the way."

My sister then left me to fend for myself among the other ghosts and goblins. Being only half dead and shunned and taunted for it, I wished myself entirely dead and had a miserable time.

But this year, thanks to Mrs. Yamagata's needlework and ingenuity, Sunny would be dressed as a circus clown and I would be the World's Darling, Shirley Temple. No little step up from an impoverished ghost. Mrs. Yamagata had even managed to get a Shirley Temple wig from a distant relative of hers who worked wardrobe in Hollywood. I had decided I wanted to be Shirley for Halloween when Sunny's father took us to the theater in Little Tokyo to see her in *Little Miss Broadway*. I suggested to Sunny that we both dress up as Shirley, but she said it wasn't a good idea because everyone would just laugh at a Japanese Shirley Temple. She'd rather be laughed at for being a clown.

Evening was settling in and the house was quiet, save for the background music of the floor-model Zenith and the rubbing of crayons on paper. In spite of my excitement over Halloween, I recognized the peacefulness of the moment and looked up from my coloring to take it in. Mr. Yamagata was half hidden by the newspaper, his slippered feet propped up on the footstool and crossed at the ankles. Every few moments he reached out for the cup of green tea on the table beside his chair. He was California born and bred, but like his relatives in the old country, he did love his green tea. Whenever the cup disappeared behind the paper, a polite but unmistakable sipping sound followed, and then something like a sigh of satisfaction. Finally the hand reappeared and settled the cup in the saucer. He was so unlike Uncle Finn, who sat in his own worn chair alternately drinking beer, hiccoughing, belching, and drinking more beer, until he finally broke the cycle by falling asleep.

It was the sense of satisfaction that spoke to me the loudest that quiet evening. Mr. and Mrs. Yamagata sat there so placidly, occasionally exchanging smiles across the room as though all was well in the world. No one was on edge—waiting for the first angry word, the subsequent volley of shouts, the onslaught of a tirade—as we were at Uncle Finn's house. At Uncle Finn's I felt perpetually ready to duck, to throw my arms up over my head, or pitch myself under a table to avoid the hail of curses and accusations that seemed likely to rain down at any moment. It was a war zone, not a home but a tiny battlefield in a small house on Fresno Street.

How different to be here, in a neutral country completely untouched by the war. Quiet was quiet, not the prelude to a storm. Peace was the backdrop, and I didn't have to be afraid.

I felt comfortable enough to ask the Yamagatas about the questions I'd been pondering. "Mr. Y?" I said.

The newspaper dropped to his lap, and Mr. Yamagata's face appeared, smiling. "Yes, Augie?"

He had invited me to call them Mr. and Mrs. Y after I managed to twist their name like pretzel dough into a variety of odd shapes—Yamamoto, Yagamata, and most often, Yamamama. It had even come out as Mamagota a time or two, but never once did I get it right. "It's a hard name for most hakujin to remember," he'd said, "so we're just as glad to have people call us Mr. and Mrs. Y. You can call us that too, Augie."

"Mr. Y," I said again now, "do you hate Irish people?"

Mr. Yamagata's smile shifted to a frown of puzzlement, Mrs. Yamagata gave a little laugh that sounded more like a sniff, and Sunny said, "That's a stupid question, Augie."

But it wasn't. It was an important question, and I needed an answer.

"Well now, you're part Irish, aren't you, Augie?" Mr. Yamagata asked. When I nodded, he said, "Then I must like Irish people very much."

Sunny giggled and said, "Yeah, but maybe he hates Germans. Then he'd hate the other part of you." I had recently learned from Stella that I was German on my father's side, Irish on my mother's. I'd reported my findings to Sunny in answer to her long-ago question of what I was and where my family had come from.

"I don't hate Germans, Sunny," Mr. Yamagata replied. "Don't be silly."

"Well, who *do* you hate, then?" I asked.

He shook his head. "I know some people I don't like very much, Augie, but I'm not sure I really hate anyone."

"Except the emperor," Sunny laughed teasingly.

"No, not even him," Mr. Yamagata assured us.

Mrs. Yamagata pulled her sewing needle until the thread was taut and said, "What a thing to talk about." She shook her head. "We try to get along with everyone the best we can."

I looked back at Sunny's father. "Then you don't hate Irish people, Mr. Y?"

"Of course not. Why should I?" He smiled again and, the matter seemingly settled, lifted the paper and disappeared once more.

Why, indeed? That's what I was trying to find out. Uncle Finn hated him, but he didn't hate Uncle Finn.

"I thought all grown-ups hated people they don't know," I blurted.

The newspaper dropped again to reveal the quizzical look on Mr. Yamagata's face. He must have been flummoxed by my statement, because it was Mrs. Yamagata who spoke. "Why, Augie, whatever gave you that idea?"

I didn't want to tell them what my uncle had said about them, so I said, "I don't know. It just seems like it, I guess."

"Well," Mr. Yamagata said, finding his voice again, "there's certainly enough hate to go around, but part of being grown-up is being fair to other people, giving them a chance before you decide you don't like them."

Sunny looked up from her coloring. "So, Papa, if you give someone a chance and you decide you hate him, is that all right?"

Mr. Yamagata cleared his throat. Mrs. Yamagata sniffed again. "Well, Sunny," he said, "that's a hard one. . . ."

"Hate only causes problems, Sunny," Mrs. Yamagata jumped in to help. "Of course there's always going to be people you don't like, but it's best just to stay away from them. If you don't bother them, chances are they won't bother you."

Sunny shrugged and went back to her coloring. I was still confused about Uncle Finn. "Mr. Y?" I asked again.

"Yes, Augie?" The newspaper hovered over his lap, waiting to be opened again.

"Why do some people hate other people they don't even know?"

Down went the paper again, and Mr. Yamagata frowned in thought. Finally he said, "I suppose because that's the easiest thing to do. Being fair to others takes a lot of time and effort, and human beings aren't known for their patience."

That said, the newspaper snapped open once again, and Mr. Yamagata disappeared behind it.

Maybe that's what's wrong with Uncle Finn, I thought. He just doesn't want to bother getting to know the Yamagatas. I counted it his loss for being lazy and stupid.

The volume on the radio was low, but I, like Mr. Yamagata, was listening to the music with half an ear while pondering the differences between my own family and Sunny's. I wasn't even aware of what was playing, but the radio momentarily grabbed my attention when an announcer broke in with some sort of special bulletin about some explosions of gas on the planet Mars.

After putting down her crayon and listening for a minute, Sunny asked, "What's he talking about, Papa?"

Mr. Yamagata shrugged as he turned a page. "Nothing important, I'm sure."

After a moment the music resumed. Sunny and I exchanged a curious glance and then went back to our coloring. I thought whatever it was, it must be big news to a bunch of scientists somewhere, like a sighting of Haley's Comet or something, but I couldn't imagine it was worth interrupting the music program with a special bulletin. Not many people would care if Mars had a case of the hiccoughs. I certainly didn't.

Sam came downstairs and climbed into his mother's lap. She put her sewing aside and combed the child's hair with her fingers. "Did Obaasan finish telling you a story?"

Sam shook his head. "She fell asleep before she got to the end."

"Ah, well, you can play down here, then. I'll get you some paper if you want to color with the girls."

But the child seemed content where he was, dropping his head onto his mother's shoulder.

A few moments later the music was cut off again while someone interviewed someone in New Jersey who was supposed to be a famous astronomer, but we didn't really catch it because I think everyone had gone back to listening with half an ear.

But when the third interruption came, some moments later still, we all gave the Zenith our attention. "Turn up the radio, Sunny," Mrs. Yamagata said.

Sunny stood and turned the knob, then lay back down on the floor. It was yet another special bulletin; this time a huge object, something like a meteor, had fallen on a farm in a place called Grovers Mill out in New Jersey. We all looked around the room at each other, save Sam, who had discovered his mother's shiny silver necklace.

"Toshio," Mrs. Yamagata said, "what on earth are they talking about?"

"Some sort of meteorite hit the ground, I guess—" He cut himself off to go on listening to the broadcast.

Mr. Yamagata sounded unconcerned, but it was soon apparent that something really bad was happening out there in that peaceful-sounding place of Grovers Mill. According to the announcer, the meteor didn't really look like a meteor. What it looked like was a huge metal cylinder, and it had landed with such force it was half buried in a deep pit.

Sunny and I sat up and inched ourselves over to the radio, pressing our ears practically right up against the console. The announcer was describing the scene at the farm: a line of cars with headlights glaring, a crowd of curious onlookers gawking and hollering, a flock of police keeping people away from the strange object.

I wished for eyes that could see through the radio all the way to that farm in New Jersey. I wanted to see for myself what was happening in Grovers Mill. If I could just see for myself, I thought it all might make more sense. As it was, the radio offered up only a tangle of pandemonium, panicked and angry voices that were like a fog I couldn't break through to get to the real picture.

The announcer wasn't much help. He seemed just as uncertain as we were as to what had landed in that field out East. He talked to the man who owned the farm, and he interviewed the astronomer who was on the scene, but the farmer could only tell us he'd been knocked out of his seat when the thing crash landed, and the scientist could only give a few educated-sounding guesses as to what the thing might be.

Suddenly the announcer asked for our attention, a useless gesture, since he already had it. There was humming noise, he said, or maybe a scratching sound coming from inside the cylinder. He held his microphone close to the object so we could hear better. Sunny and I looked at each other wide-eyed as we listened. Yes, we could hear it. There had to be something alive in there. And whatever it was, it couldn't be good.

The panicked wave of voices rose again. Men hollered loudly, "Stand back! Keep back, I tell you!" The cylinder was somehow breaking open, the end of it turning like some sort of escape hatch on a submarine. Whatever was in there was coming out!

I was suddenly so frightened I could scarcely breathe. Sunny looked up at her father and cried, "What is it, Papa?"

Mr. Yamagata said calmly, "I don't know, Sunny. Let's listen and see."

"Toshio?" Mrs. Yamagata asked nervously. But her husband put his hand to his lips to indicate she should be quiet and listen.

The announcer said it was a monster! A huge monster was crawling out of the cylinder! It was a creature with tentacles, large dark eyes, saliva dripping from its mouth. . . .

Suddenly the man was cut off, the music resumed. The clock on the wall ticked off the minutes. Already at least half an hour had passed since the first announcement had broken into our quiet evening. Sunny's lips trembled, and she looked as though she were about to cry. She lifted her eyes to her father again and whispered, "Martians!"

Mr. Yamagata tried to laugh. "That's impossible," he said emphatically. "There's no such thing."

"But, Toshio," Mrs. Yamagata countered, clinging more tightly to Sam. "The man said—"

"I know." He waved a hand to dismiss the idea. "But it can't be real. It's some sort of hoax—"

"Listen, Papa!"

Grovers Mill was in complete chaos, with a hundred things happening at once. People screamed, sirens wailed, and then the transmission was cut off abruptly, leaving us slack-jawed and envisioning scenes of death and destruction. And sure enough, by the time the next bulletin came on, forty people were dead. They were lying in a field, and the announcer said their bodies were burned and distorted beyond all possible recognition!

Mrs. Yamagata gasped and raised a hand to her mouth. "Toshio," she tried again, "what do you think's happening out there?"

We were all afraid now, and none of us could hide it, not even Mr. Yamagata. Sam began to cry, and I was very close to tears myself.

"I don't know, Suma," Mr. Yamagata confessed. He took off his glasses and massaged his eyes with an index finger and thumb.

But we got an answer soon enough. The people in Grovers Mill, New Jersey, were being obliterated with something the man on the radio could only describe as a heat-ray gun.

At the thought of such a weapon, Mrs. Yamagata stood, clutching the now howling Sam in her arms. "Toshio!" she cried.

"Don't panic, Suma. It'll be all right."

"But, Papa, the Martians have come! They're going kill us all!"

"Calm down, Sunny. It's all right. This has got to be some sort of joke. It just isn't possible. . . ."

But it was! The man on the radio was saying so even as Mr. Yamagata said it wasn't possible. The Martians had landed in New Jersey, he said! And they were only part of an invading army from Mars! Undoubtedly more Martians were on their way to earth this very minute! And already several thousand men who had attempted to fight them were dead. The alien monster was now in control of the middle section of New Jersey. . . .

"Impossible," Mr. Yamagata whispered to the radio.

"But what if it's true, Papa!"

A loud rapping on the front door interrupted our speculations, and someone shouted, "Mr. Yamagata!" Whoever it was didn't wait for an answer. In the next moment a teenaged boy burst into the house and, stumbling all over himself, announced breathlessly, "Mr. Yamagata! Dad sent me over to tell you the Martians are attacking. They've blown New Jersey to bits already. We've all got to get out of here!"

Without telling us just where it was we should go to seek safety, he disappeared as quickly as he had come.

Sunny and I looked at each other, screamed, and holding hands, ran up the stairs to take shelter in her closet. We crawled into the dark space among the clothes and the shoes and settled ourselves against the wall in the farthermost corner. When Sunny said, "They're gonna burn us up with their heat-ray guns!" we both burst into tears and fell into each other's arms.

"You're my best friend in the whole world, Augie," Sunny said, sniffing loudly.

I pressed my wet cheek against hers. "And you're my best friend too."

"I'll never forget you."

"I'll never forget you either."

We sat there cheek to cheek, crying and wailing and wiping our tears with a couple of dirty socks we found on the closet floor.

"I don't wanna die," Sunny sobbed.

"I don't either."

But we had no choice. The Martians had landed on earth and were bent on annihilating the human race. I didn't know how long it would take them to get from New Jersey to California, but I was sure we had only a very short time before we too were blasted by the heat-ray guns, our bodies burned and distorted beyond all possible recognition. We huddled in that dark closet and waited for death.

I don't know how much time passed; it seemed like an eternity, but it was probably no more than just a few minutes. Finally Sunny said, "Listen! Here they come!"

Sure enough, footsteps approached from down the hall. We squeezed each other even more tightly and braced ourselves against the onslaught of the heat-ray guns. Our screams drowned out the foot-steps, and when someone or something opened the closet door, we screamed all the louder and pressed ourselves deeper into the corner, trying to become as small and unnoticeable as possible. The creature said something, but only after it repeated itself several times did we finally understand the words: "Sunny, Augie, calm down! Calm down and come out of there, for pete's sake. You're likely to leave us all deaf if you keep screaming like that." It was Mr. Yamagata, not a Martian!

It took us a moment to gather our wits and realize that death wasn't imminent. We stopped screaming but went on huffing and puff-ing as we pressed the dirty socks to our faces to stanch the tears. Then, sniffing, Sunny and I crawled out of the closet and into her parents' arms. They knelt on the floor, waiting for us, and while Sunny went to her mother, I flung myself at Mr. Yamagata. Sam was there too, leaning against his mother's back with his chubby arms around her neck.

After a moment Sunny asked, "Is it safe now, Mama? Did we kill all the Martians?"

Both Mr. and Mrs. Yamagata laughed quietly. "There were no Martians, Sunny," Mrs. Yamagata said. "It was all just pretend."

Sunny sounded surprised and skeptical. "It was?"

"Just as I thought," Mr. Yamagata assured us. "It was only a show, a Halloween prank. Orson Welles and his crew acting out *The War of the Worlds*. That's all it was, nothing more."

"How do you know?" I asked suspiciously. My words were muffled because my face was buried in Mr. Yamagata's shoulder.

"They said so on the radio. Mr. Welles announced that it was just a show, just for fun. That's all."

"Then we're not going to die, Papa?" Sunny asked.

I felt Mr. Yamagata shake with laughter. "Of course not!" he assured us. "No one dies from a harmless Halloween prank." Only then did I dare to lift my head and look up at Mr. Yamagata's laughing face.

Just then Obaasan appeared in the doorway of Sunny's room and stared at us, her expression telling us without words that we'd all lost our minds. Finally she said something in Japanese. I could well imagine her complaint, that our screams had once again awakened her from a sound sleep. Mr. Yamagata responded, and as he spoke, I looked at Sunny.

"Papa's telling her we were hiding in the closet because we thought the Martians were going to kill us with their heat-ray guns," she explained.

When Mr. Yamagata fell silent, Obaasan remained in the doorway staring at us. Then, her shoulders began to shake, at first only slightly, and then more heavily, like a rumbling of the earth, and suddenly her tiny wrinkled face broke open and let out a shriek of laughter that rose up out of her chest like a volcanic explosion. She laughed and laughed until tears ran down her face, and she tapped at the floor with her cane as though she were trying to dig her way through to the living room below. Even before the laughter had subsided completely, she turned and went away muttering to herself, and in the next moment a fresh burst of laughter reached us from her room.

The rest of us sat in stunned silence.

At length Mr. Yamagata said, "I can't remember the last time she laughed."

"We should be thankful the Martians came," Mrs. Yamagata replied.

"I'm glad they *didn't* come," Sunny countered, "though it sure was nice to hear Obaasan laugh."

As for me, I was happy about Obaasan too. But there was something else wonderful about that moment, something far more wonderful. I savored it and promised myself never to forget. When I fell into Mr. Yamagata's arms, it was just like falling into the arms of a father. The Martian invasion, however bogus, had given me a glimpse into the unknown territory called Family.

SIX

Not long afterward Sunny told me about a Japanese proverb listing the things one has to fear most: "*Jishin, kaminari, kaji, oyaji.*" Earthquake, thunder, fire, father.

I could understand the first three, but father? When I asked Sunny why Japanese children were afraid of their fathers, she said things were different over in Japan than they were here in America. "Fathers over there are strict, and all they do is sit around and wait for their children to get in trouble so they can punish them. And fathers never hug or kiss their children, or act nice to them," Sunny explained.

"Who told you that!" I cried in disbelief. I thought surely she'd heard wrong or had somehow misunderstood.

"Papa told me," Sunny said, "and Obaasan too. You never see Obaasan hugging or kissing any of us, do you?"

I shook my head. In the weeks I'd known the Yamagatas, I'd never seen Obaasan express affection to anyone. But surely that was because she was where she didn't want to be, and if she could only go back to Japan, she'd be both happy and loving again. Besides, if things were really so bad over there, why would Obaasan want so much to go back? Her undying desire to return to her homeland spoke only of the goodness of the place.

"Well," Sunny continued, contradicting my thoughts, "that's because Obaasan's from Japan. She says over there not even mothers kiss their children."

If that were true, then the families in Japan were more like the Schuler-O'Shaughnessy clan than the Yamagatas, and that I refused to believe. I had already decided that Japan was the happiest place on earth, an inhabited Garden of Eden. It had to be if people like the Yamagatas came from there. Mr. Yamagata was the best father possible—full of love and kisses and kindness—and if he were somehow suddenly transported to Japan, he'd be just as good a father over there, wouldn't he? Why would he be any different just because he lived somewhere else?

I shrugged off Sunny's talk as so much storytelling. Secretly I hoped the Japanese would be successful in taking over the world, as Uncle Finn had said they were trying to do. With people like the Yamagatas in charge, the whole world would be wonderful.

As the school year passed, and 1938 slipped into 1939, I began spending more and more time with the Yamagatas and very little time at Uncle Finn's. I'd go home with Sunny every day after school. We'd play, eat our supper, help her mother with the dishes, do our homework. And then finally, when I could put off the inevitable no longer, I'd say a long, drawn-out good-bye to Sunny and Mr. and Mrs. Yamagata—and sometimes I'd even include Obaasan and the boys just to stall a little longer—and then I'd leave and walk back to Uncle Finn's, where I'd make a beeline for my room in the attic. If I was lucky, I didn't run into my uncle on the way up. Only Stephen and I shared the attic now, with a sheet hung up between our mattresses for privacy. Gwen, like Valerie before her, had moved out after finding work as a live-in domestic.

By spring I was spending every weekend with the Yamagatas. I think the invitation came about because Mr. and Mrs. Yamagata were disturbed by my reluctance to go home every night. No doubt they didn't fully understand the reasons for my reluctance, but they must have come to realize that the house on Fresno Street was not a place I wanted to be.

"Stay here with us on the weekends," they said. "You can share Sunny's room, just like the two of you are sisters." Sunny begged me to say yes, though she needn't have. As soon as the invitation was extended, I eagerly accepted it.

"But," Mrs. Yamagata added, "of course we'll have to get your mother's permission. I'll call tomorrow and speak with her about it."

My first thought was that Uncle Finn might answer the phone, and that would only end in disaster. But then I remembered that even though the next day was Saturday, he'd be at the hardware store.

When the call came I was in the kitchen making myself a peanut butter sandwich. Aunt Lucy wiped the dishwater off her hands, picked up the extension in the kitchen, and sang out her usual, "Hello! O'Shaughnessys' residence." After a pause she said, "Mrs. Schuler? Just a minute. I'll check."

She laid the handset down on the counter, walked across the kitchen, and peeked into the sewing room. Then she stopped briefly at the kitchen table, where I'd sat down to eat my lunch. She was as blond as I'd ever seen her, and the mole was perched way up on one cheekbone, just below her left eye.

"It's your friend's mom," she said quietly. "The Japanese woman."

My eyebrows shot up. "Can Mom talk to her?"

Aunt Lucy sniffed and shook her head. "Not at the moment."

I glanced toward the sewing room and saw the soles of Mother's feet propped up on one arm of the couch. She was asleep again in the middle of the day.

Aunt Lucy frowned at me and asked, "You haven't done anything wrong, have you?"

"No!" I cried. "Honest, Aunt Lucy."

My aunt sighed heavily. "Well, let me find out what she wants." She moved back to the counter and picked up the handset again. "I'm afraid Mrs. Schuler's not here at the moment," she lied. "Can I do something for you?" I listened anxiously to my aunt's side of the conversation. "Oh, I see. . . . Why yes, I suppose it would be all right. . . . Yes, uh-huh. . . . That would be fine. . . . It's a little unusual, but . . . like sisters, you say? I'm sure they do enjoy each other's company but . . . uh-huh. . . . Are you sure it's no bother? I mean, she already spends so much time with you . . . oh, well, okay, then . . . but you be sure to send her home if she starts to get on your nerves. Aha-ha-ha . . . yes, yes . . . what's that. . . ? Oh yes, I'll see that Mrs. Schuler knows about it. . . . No, really, I think she'd say it was fine. . . . Yes, of course. Yes, all right, then. Good-bye."

She hung up the phone and turned to me. "They practically want you to live with them. They wanted to know if you'd be allowed to stay with them on the weekends."

"What'd you say?" I asked eagerly, though I already knew. I just wanted to hear it again.

"That it'd be all right, if that's what they wanted. I'm sure your mother won't mind."

"But Uncle Finn will kill me, won't he, when he finds out?"

"You just let me worry about Finn."

And that was that. To any other kid, it might have seemed strange to be dismissed so easily from one's own family. To me, it felt like being given permission to go home.

I didn't question the Yamagatas' willingness to take me in; I simply accepted it. I was too young, of course, to realize the magnitude of their kindness toward me. I couldn't calculate the work and the responsibility involved in having an extra child in the house. But the Yamagatas were so loving toward me, I had no doubt they wanted me there. And that's when the whole of my life really began to be transformed into something other than what it had ever been, something leaning toward normal.

Sunny's room became my room as well, her large canopied bed, my bed. Most of my scant clothing found its way into Sunny's closet, and she and I might have simply combined our wardrobes if we'd worn the same size. But I was so much taller than she that sharing clothes was out of the question. We shared everything else, though; or I should say, she shared everything she had with me: her toys, her dollhouse, all of her wonderful books.

Best of all, her parents became my parents. Everything a mother and father are supposed to do for a child, the Yamagatas did for me. They fed me, washed my clothes, combed my hair, helped me with homework. They called the doctor when I was sick, took me to the dentist when I had a toothache, and though I didn't think about it at the time, they must have paid the medical bills as well. Most important, when I needed to be hugged, they were there to put their arms around me and kiss my cheek and tell me they loved me.

At the same time my new parents didn't hesitate to discipline me when I needed it. And in those days it wasn't unusual for Sunny and me to get into trouble for being too noisy and bothering Obaasan or for failing to clean up our messes. But the Yamagatas were kind disciplinarians, and once Sunny and I were duly scolded and had served our punishment—usually an hour separated from each other in which we were each to quietly contemplate our bad behavior—all was forgotten and parents and children went merrily on with their lives.

As a member of the Yamagata household, I was required to do certain chores. One of these was scrubbing the bathtub every Wednesday and Saturday, which I hated, but I did it anyway without complaint. I also helped with dishes, swept the front walkway, and together Sunny and I were responsible for keeping our room clean. Sunny had her own set of chores, as did Sam, so doing my assigned tasks only strengthened my sense of being one of the family.

Sunny and I also spent most Saturday mornings helping Mr. Yamagata at the grocery store he owned with his brother-in-law, Hito Miyamoto. He also had a vested interest in the movie theater in Little Tokyo that was owned by his other brother-in-law, Masuo Nakamura, but he spent little actual time there. Most of his six-day workweek found him in the grocery store. Ojisan (Uncle) Hito and his wife Obasan (Aunt) Akemi lived with their two small children in the apartment over the store. Obasan Akemi was Mr. Yamagata's younger sister. His other sister, Obasan Yoshiye, was married to the theater owner.

The grocery store was on First Street, just off Pleasant Avenue in Boyle Heights, not too far from Little Tokyo but still on this side of the Los Angeles River. It was surrounded by hakujin businesses, but the fact that it was Japanese owned didn't keep it from doing well. Mr. Yamagata and Ojisan Hito were always busy, the bell over the front door constantly tinkling. Sunny and I spent Saturday mornings sweeping, dusting, washing the windows, and stocking the shelves, with the promise that when we got big enough we could start to wait on customers.

The store was patronized by Japanese and whites alike, but my favorite customers were the older men and women who had come over from Japan. Whenever one came into the store, I'd always pause in my work to watch the show. These elderly folks still held to the customs of the Orient, so a lot of bowing and polite talk had to be exchanged before they got down to the business of shopping. Sometimes Mr. Yamagata spoke to them in their native language, sometimes in English, depending on whom he was speaking to. When the bell tinkled and an elderly customer stepped in—say, Mr. Tanaka stopping by for his usual supply of green tea and cigarettes—Mr. Yamagata stepped forward to greet him like an honored guest, and the two men bowed, first one, then the other, and said things like, "Ah, Tanaka-san, good afternoon. It's a pleasure to see you again," and "Thank you, Yamagata-san, I trust you and your family are all in good health."

I was enchanted by this ritual and marveled at how polite the Japanese were to one another. When I tried to imagine Uncle Finn bowing to a customer in his hardware store, I found the image so ridiculous I burst out laughing. Uncle Finn would bow to no one, not even for money. He'd sooner kick a customer in the derrière and send him sailing out the door than stoop to such a display of humble etiquette.

After I started spending weekends with the Yamagatas, the one link between my life with them and my life in Uncle Finn's house was the occasional phone call between Aunt Lucy and Mrs. Yamagata. These were always brief exchanges, centered solely on me. I never heard both sides of these conversations, of course, but the women simply talked about my needs, my general welfare, how I was doing in school. To my surprise and delight, Mrs. Yamagata found my aunt to be "a very pleasant woman." I was impressed by the fact that Aunt Lucy was cordial to Mrs. Yamagata, considering Uncle Finn's attitude toward the Japanese. For a time I dreamed of Aunt Lucy and Mrs. Yamagata becoming friends so that Uncle Finn could come to see that he was wrong about these people.

After all, Mr. and Mrs. Yamagata had a lot of hakujin friends. Mr. Yamagata was always saying things like he'd run into Harvey Tucker, or he'd had lunch with Bill McQueen, or old Tom Johnson from Pasadena had called to shoot the breeze about baseball. All conspicuously American names. And Mrs. Yamagata often visited with other ladies in the neighborhood who dropped by the house with fresh baked goods, recipe ideas, and juicy bits of gossip. The woman next door, Vera Eddington, came by all the time.

Mrs. Eddington was younger than Mrs. Yamagata, newly married, without children as yet, and I think she was lonely with her husband at work all day. So Sunny and I would come home from school and find her in the kitchen helping to bake pies or polishing silverware or just chatting with Mrs. Yamagata over a cup of coffee. I thought Mrs. Eddington was kind of flashy—she wore too much lipstick and lots of jewelry that didn't match, and she smoked so many Marlboros that Mrs. Yamagata sometimes aired out the kitchen after she left. She was married to a man named Chester, but everyone called him Eddie.

Sometimes, on Saturday nights, the Eddingtons came over and Mr. Yamagata set up a card table, and the four of them played pinochle or canasta. The Eddingtons seemed very different from the Yamagatas—younger, louder, less refined, and of course hakujin—but the two couples must have found something in common because they laughed a great deal together and sometimes stayed up playing cards and talking late into the night. Mrs. Eddington reminded me somewhat of my aunt, and I thought, *If Vera Eddington can be friends with Mrs. Yamagata, why can't Aunt Lucy?*

The reason, of course, was my uncle. Uncle Finn knew where I was every evening and weekend, but he never mentioned the Yamagatas to me or to anyone. He no doubt still didn't approve of my hanging around with a "bunch of Japs," but, as Stella confided, he most likely appreciated that there was one less person in his too crowded household. One less mouth to feed meant a little more money in his pocket, and he liked having spare pocket change for poker.

Uncle Finn didn't have a wide circle of friends himself, but he did have a loyal clique of poker-playing buddies. They were all white men, of course, and the majority Irish. Once a week or so he'd get together with them to play cards, drink beer, and try to break even. I think his best buddy was Sean McDougall, who happened also to be our mailman. The two of them loved to go down to the pub—a bar called Charlie O'Casey's—to, as they said, "swap stories about the old country." I wondered how they did that, since neither of them had ever actually been to Ireland. They always returned from the bar in an extremely good mood, telling jokes that I didn't understand and laughing uproariously over the punch lines. But it wasn't really a joyous laughter like what we heard when the Eddingtons played cards with the Yamagatas. It was laughter that sent a shiver down my spine. I didn't care much for Sean McDougall, and therefore thought he made a fitting friend for my uncle.

At any rate, the link between my two worlds was a weak one, and eventually I decided it was just as well for the two circles not to overlap. Uncle Finn's house, I endured. The Yamagatas' home, I loved.

When I started spending nights at the Yamagatas', I discovered that what Sunny had told me was true: Obaasan did sometimes cry out angrily in the dark, scolding her husband for not taking her back to Japan. It was always startling to be awakened by her tirades in Japanese, but Sunny just giggled, so I tried to giggle too. But what I really felt was a pinch of sadness. I was sorry for the old woman who wanted so much to go home, because for the first time I knew what it was to have a home. I couldn't imagine being taken away forever from something so wonderful.

So I didn't even try to imagine it. I'd just turn over and fall asleep again. As far as I was concerned, I was home for good. Though I'd been born into the wrong family, I had—for whatever reason, by the working of some unseen benevolence—found the right family at last, and nothing and no one was going to change that.

SEVEN

On Saturday afternoons after finishing our tasks in the grocery store, Sunny and I often sat on the bench out front and ate ice cream or popcorn or licorice sticks while talking about things we thought were important. We'd rehash the plots of movies we'd seen, gossip about which kids at school we did and didn't like, and dream about what we wanted to do when we grew up. Sometimes we talked about whom we might marry and how many children we wanted and what we would name them.

It became apparent during one of our conversations on this bench that even while I was attempting to assimilate myself into the world of the Japanese, Sunny was just as determined to move herself out of it. Though our lives intersected at this particular place and time, our inner journeys were moving us in opposite directions—me toward the ways of the Orient, and Sunny toward the world of whites.

As I remember it, I made a suggestion that if she played her cards right, Luther Huffington might propose to her in another ten years or so. Luther was a boy in the class ahead of us that Sunny thought was a looker. "He's so cute!" she'd whisper breathlessly whenever we saw him. She had never actually spoken to him, but for several weeks she'd more or less been pining after him from a distance.

I was trying to encourage Sunny in her crush on Luther, but she only shook her head sadly, chewed thoughtfully on a handful of popcorn, and said, "Even if he ever noticed me, which I doubt, and even if he ever proposed to me, which I doubt, I still couldn't marry him."

"Why not?"

"Because it's against the law."

"What's against the law?"

"For an American to marry a Japanese."

"It is?"

"Yup. You can only marry your own kind, or you go to jail."

I couldn't believe it! I'd never heard of such a law. "Are you sure?"

"Yup."

"Who said?"

"Papa told me."

"That only Americans can marry Americans?"

"Yup."

"But you're an American," I argued.

"Yeah, but I look Japanese."

I'd been confused by a lot of things since I met Sunny, and this was one more thing that made no sense to me. "Then how are you going to get married?" I asked.

"Have to marry someone that looks like me."

"But what if you want to marry someone like Luther?"

"Can't do it."

"But what if you did it anyway?"

"I'd go to jail."

I was horrified by the thought. Imagine being handcuffed and hauled off to jail just because you married someone like Luther Huffington.

"Are you sure?" I asked. "They'd really put you in jail just for that?"

"Yup. In California they would, anyway. Some states let you get married."

"They do?"

She nodded. "I've heard about couples who run off to Seattle or someplace like that to get married, because they don't have any laws against it there. So they get married there and then come back here. But Mama told me when they come back, no one likes them anymore.

Not the whites and not the Japanese."

Sunny upended her bag of popcorn and let the last kernels fall into her mouth. As usual, being a slower eater, I was only halfway through my own bag.

"What do they do?" I asked.

"Who?"

"The people who get married and then nobody likes them."

"They just spend all their time alone 'cause no one else wants to be with them."

"Even their own families don't like them anymore?"

"Especially their own families."

Things were becoming more and more complicated. "You mean, Japanese people don't like it when a Japanese marries a white person?"

Sunny shook her head emphatically. "Nope. Most of them think the Japanese should stick together."

"They do?"

"Yup."

"But I'm white and everyone in your family lets me be with you!"

"But that's different."

"Why?"

" 'Cause no one has to marry you. You're just there."

"But if I married someone Japanese, then all of a sudden no one would like me?"

"Uh-huh, probably. Except for me, of course."

We fell silent. I picked out a single piece of popcorn and lifted it to my mouth, but I suddenly felt too full to eat it. I was trying to understand what I wouldn't be able to put into words for years, and it was this: that the law of the land and the attitudes of its people didn't leave any room for love. I only knew, at eight years of age, that something wasn't right.

Especially disturbing was the fact that I would no longer be accepted among the Japanese if I married one of them. It almost made the Japanese sound as biased as the whites, and that I refused to believe. Of course they weren't. Mr. Yamagata had already told me he didn't hate anyone. He wasn't like Uncle Finn in his outrageous across-the-board contempt for everyone different from himself. What Sunny told me about the Japanese wanting to stick together was completely opposed to the open and welcoming ways of the Japanese Americans I knew, not just the Yamagatas but others I had met over the past months. Baffled, I filed away the disparities between what Sunny told me and what I'd seen for myself, thinking I could deal with it all later, if I ever had to.

"What are you going to do, Sunny," I finally asked, "if you want to marry a white man when you grow up?"

She shrugged, shook her head.

"Run away to Seattle?" I suggested.

"Yeah, I guess so."

"I wish you could just marry anybody you wanted."

Sunny looked at the butter-streaked bag in her hands. She crumpled it up and tossed it toward the trash can near the bench. She missed but didn't get up to retrieve it. "You wanna know what I wish, Augie?"

"Yeah?"

"I wish I was white."

"No!"

"Yeah, I do."

"But why, Sunny?"

" 'Cause everything would be so much easier."

"But what's the matter with how things are now?"

"What's the matter?" she echoed. "Everything's the matter, that's what."

"What do you mean, everything's the matter?"

She looked at me then, her face expressionless. "You can't know what it's like, Augie. Nobody calls you Flat Face or pulls their eyes back when they see you."

"Yeah? Well, they call me Freckle Face and Carrot Top, and just the other day Jimmy Farnsworth told me I look like Godzilla's cousin. You know. You were there when he said it."

Sunny shrugged stubbornly. "It's not the same."

"Why not?"

"Because you're white. No matter what they say about you, you're still like everybody else. I'm the one that's different."

I didn't know how to respond. In fact I was stunned. Of course Sunny was teased sometimes—weren't most kids? But never before had she told me she wished she were white. Yes, she was different, but I'd always assumed she knew she was lucky to be Japanese.

On that sun-drenched afternoon, as both white and Japanese faces bobbed past us, pedestrians making their way down First Street, I tried to empathize with Sunny. But I failed. For me, the only way to be happy was to be Japanese. Sunny, born that way, had it made. I was the unfortunate one, the one with the task of insinuating myself into the better culture.

"No," I said finally. "You shouldn't want to be white, Sunny."

"Well," she argued, "I do anyway."

"But you're so lucky."

She shook her head. "America's white, Augie."

"What do you mean, America's white?"

She thought a moment, then said, "Well, for one thing, did you ever see a Japanese movie star?"

I let out a breath of air. "I guess not."

"Did you ever see a Japanese president?"

I shook my head.

"Did we ever read a book in school that had a Japanese person in it?"

"Um, I guess not."

"And look." Sunny turned and pointed at an advertisement hanging up in the window of the store—two cherubic fair-haired children smiling over a bowl of Campbell's soup.

"America's white," Sunny concluded.

She was right, and I couldn't argue with her. Incredibly, I was so used to the whiteness of America that I never even noticed it. I needed Sunny to point it out to me.

"But I thought you liked it here!" I cried suddenly, not sure where else to go with the conversation. "Now you sound like Obaasan, like you want to go back to Japan."

"I don't want to go back to Japan. I just wish I fit in around here."

After a long moment of silence I asked, "Is that why you pinch your nose at night?"

Sunny looked surprised. "How'd you know I do that?"

"I've seen you."

"But I always thought you were asleep."

"Not always."

"Your eyes were shut."

"You thought they were. So why do you pinch your nose?"

Sunny sighed heavily and looked away. "Because it's too flat. It's so flat I hardly even have a nose! I want it to be more hakujin, like yours. People say the white girls' noses are prettier, you know."

I frowned and shook my head. "But I think your nose is pretty."

"Thanks," Sunny said, "but I don't."

"Well, how big are you going to try to make it?"

"I don't know. Big as it'll go, I guess."

Our talk of noses made me think of Jimmy Durante. I'd seen him for the first time in *Little Miss Broadway* and couldn't believe the schnozz on the guy. No wonder he was called "The Great Nostril." Picturing Sunny with a nose like that, I laughed.

"What are you laughing at?" Sunny asked, suddenly defensive.

"Just don't pinch your nose so much you end up looking like Jimmy Durante!" I shrieked.

Sunny laughed too, but then remarked that even a nose like Jimmy Durante's was better than hers.

"Are you kidding?" I exclaimed. "If you had a nose like that, you wouldn't be able to hold your head up. You'd have to walk around looking at the ground all the time."

"Maybe," she agreed. "But if I had a nose like that, I could marry anyone I wanted."

"If you had a nose like that," I countered, "no one would *want* to marry you in the first place!"

We laughed together while we waved at a family we knew driving by in their Chevy. Then, instead of returning my hand to my lap, I let my fingers momentarily seek out the shape of my own nose. Sunny had started me thinking. Never before had I paid any attention to what my nose looked like. It'd been a handy contraption for breathing, and that was all. But now I realized it was probably twice as big as Sunny's. Twice as big, I supposed, as any nose in her family.

"How many do you do?" I asked.

"How many what?"

"Pinches."

"Twenty-five."

"Is it working?"

"I think so."

"Think you'll end up looking more white?"

"I hope so."

I felt my nose again, running my index finger over the bridge. "Do you think if I press down on my nose right here, it'll become flatter?"

Sunny frowned and drew back to get a better look at me. "Why would you want to do that?" she asked, her words heavy with disgust.

"So my nose can look more Japanese, of course."

She peered at me through narrowed eyes, and I realized she thought I was making fun of her.

"It's true, Sunny," I assured her. "I'd give anything to be Japanese."

"Ha!" she laughed shrilly while rolling her eyes. "No, you wouldn't!"

"Yeah, I would!"

"Naw. You don't know what you're talking about."

"I do so know what I'm talking about!" I protested loudly. "I think you're crazy to want to look white. Then you'd have to live with people like Uncle Finn."

She sat quietly, her mouth working. Then she said, "It's kinda funny, me wanting to be white and you wanting to be Japanese."

"Yeah."

"I wish we could just trade places."

"Me too." I was certain, of course, that I'd get the better deal in the long run.

"Think you'll really start trying to make your nose flatter?" she asked.

I nodded emphatically. "For sure."

"Well, how about whenever you spend the night, we can do it together."

"Sure!" I was growing excited now. "Do you think it'll work? I mean, do you think my nose will get flatter just like yours is getting bigger?"

We studied each other's noses then, I to see how much bigger hers was, she to decide whether mine could become flatter. I was skeptical that her nose had changed much since I first gazed at her profile in Hollenbeck Park, but if I looked at it from a certain angle and added a degree of wishful thinking, then yes, I could see that the bridge looked a little bit more pronounced. As for my nose, she decided, "I think it'll work. It'll take a lot of pressing, though. You might be old before it's finished."

"How old?" I asked, steeling myself against discouragement.

"I don't know. Maybe twenty, maybe even twenty-five."

The day seemed very far off, but I was determined to reach it. "Then I'd better start now."

Beginning that night, before we fell asleep, we pinched and pushed on our noses, a routine that was to last for the next several years. About once a week we looked at our noses sideways in her dresser mirror, and while we saw no real change in what Jimmy Durante would call the old schnozzola, we continued to hold out hope that one day our noses, at least, would belong to the race we ourselves wanted to be.

❧

The school year ended, summer passed, and Sunny and I turned nine on August 9, 1939. It was the first birthday we celebrated together, and it was on that day, as I remember, that we started claiming to be twins. Mrs. Yamagata laughed and said we'd have to call ourselves fraternal twins because no one in the world would mistake us for identical twins. But it was also on that day that, in spite of my looks, I really began to think of myself as Japanese.

Mrs. Yamagata made us a dinner of our choice—hot dogs smothered with ketchup and steaming bowls of rice with soy sauce. Obaasan said the combination was bad for our stomachs, that our insides would be pulled both east and west, but we ate it anyway. For dessert there was a huge chocolate cake with nine candles that Sunny and I blew out together. We made a silent wish beforehand, and though we didn't tell each other, I think we both wished for the same thing—to become what we were not.

Afterward, Mr. and Mrs. Yamagata showered us with gifts—or so it seemed to someone who'd had few gifts in her life. I remember only two of them, though, a special gift for Sunny and one for me. Sunny's gift came first. Mr. Yamagata momentarily disappeared and came back carrying a crate, the kind the canned goods came in down at the grocery store. Inside, curled up on a nest of old towels, was a puppy about three months old.

"Oh, Papa, I can't believe it!" Sunny cried as she reached into the box and lifted out the tiny dog. "Is he really mine?"

"One hundred percent!"

"Well, you and Augie can take care of him together," Mrs. Yamagata added.

"He's so cute! What kind is he?"

"He's what you call a mutt," Mr. Yamagata explained with a lopsided smile. "He's a mixed breed; a little bit of this and a little bit of that."

"In other words," Mrs. Yamagata added, "no one has any idea what he is."

"Well, judging from the set of ears he's got on him, I'd say there's some hound in him," Mr. Yamagata speculated.

Sunny and I each lifted a floppy ear and inspected it. They did seem to be rather oversized for his little head. But something else caught my attention. "And look at his nose!" I cried, delighted. "He's got a pretty big nose for a puppy!"

Sunny touched the moist black knob and said, "Then I know what I'll name him. Jimmy Durante! Jimmy, for short."

That was how Jimmy came into my life, where he would stay for the next fourteen years.

Sunny held the puppy in her lap and asked, "Well, what's Augie's special present?"

In all the excitement, I'd almost forgotten there was another present for me.

"Ah yes!" Mr. Yamagata said. He folded his hands on top of the dining room table and leaned toward me. "Well, you see, Augie, your last present isn't exactly something you can hold, or even see—"

"But we hope you'll like it, anyway, dear," Mrs. Yamagata interrupted.

I nodded, anxious for Mr. Yamagata to get on with it. He continued, "Well, you know how fond we are of you and how glad we are to have you here with us."

Again I nodded. What was he leading up to? Was he going to tell me they'd decided that, because of Uncle Finn, I shouldn't come to their home anymore? What kind of birthday present would that be? I fidgeted in my seat.

"Well, we know what your situation is in your own home, how you don't have a father anymore and how it's, well, kind of lonely for you there. We've known you for going on a year now and when you're here we just plain forget that this *isn't* your home and that we aren't your real family—"

"Maybe you should get to the point, Toshio," Mrs. Yamagata cut in gently.

"I'm getting there, Suma. Just give me a minute." He cleared his throat, looked at me, smiled. I fidgeted again. I was starting to get nervous.

"We know you can hardly be with us all the time," he continued, "but we thought, while you *are* here, you might as well think of us as family, and you might as well even call Suma and me Mom and Dad. Now we understand that you have your own mother and you have memories of your father, of course, and that they are your real mother and father, but we—Suma and I—thought you could distinguish between them and us by using the Japanese words for mom and dad."

"But, Papa," Sunny said, frowning at her father, "there's so many words for mom and dad in Japanese. It's confusing, like calling Grandma Obaasan." Here, the old woman lifted her eyebrows, no doubt wondering what was being said about her. Sunny went on, "Which one is Augie supposed to use? When she gets older does she have to call you something different?"

Mr. Yamagata shook his head. "No, no, no, Sunny. We have already thought of that. It would be easiest, we think, if Augie used the words Chichi and Haha. They are easiest to remember and to pronounce." Mr. Yamagata turned to me. "What do you think, Augie? Does calling us Chichi and Haha sound good to you?"

Chichi and Haha. The words sounded like laughter. As well they should! Because the thought of calling these two people Dad and Mom was one of pure joy! I could only nod at Mr. Yamagata in response, because the lump in my throat was too big to get any words around it.

Mr. Yamagata—Chichi—smiled at me. "And we thought we might give you a new name too," he went on. "We thought we could call you Musume. When we say that, we are saying 'my daughter.' So that is our gift to you. Happy birthday, Musume."

Chichi, Haha, Musume. With those three magical words, my inner transformation from Irish German Schuler-O'Shaughnessy to Japanese American Yamagata was complete.

EIGHT

I loved being Japanese. I loved everything about the Yamagatas' world, which, even though they were American, had a distinctly Japanese flavor to it.

We celebrated the Fourth of July, Thanksgiving, and Christmas in the usual ways, but in addition to these were the Japanese holidays that the other hakujin kids at school missed out on. Sunny had extended family throughout Los Angeles, and when this group got together to celebrate, say, the emperor's birthday, white America disappeared altogether for me. I was no longer Augie; I was Augie-chan. Aunts, uncles, cousins, in-laws—everyone called me Augie-chan, except Chichi and Haha, who called me Musume, and Sunny, who alone called me Augie. I wasn't considered a guest at these affairs and not even so much a *tomadachi*, a friend, as I was considered *kazoku*, part of the family. With my red hair I was the kidney bean in a pot of black bean soup, but none of Sunny's relatives seemed either to notice or to mind.

Even though Chichi didn't care for the emperor, we attended *Tenchosetsu* every year, the celebration of the reigning emperor's birthday. I think we went to make Obaasan happy, or as happy as she could be while still living in America. It was a formal affair, held in the large American Legion hall that the Japanese Chamber of Commerce rented for the occasion. We sat in folding chairs facing a raised platform on which four gentlemen were seated, two on either side of a square cabinet covered with purple velvet drapes. The men on the left side wore white gloves, and one of these men began the ceremony by walking stiffly to center stage and bowing toward the cabinet, his hands rigid against the sides of his legs, in a deep formal bow called the *sai-kei-rei*. He stayed that way for half a minute. Then, his hands sliding up the sides of his legs again, he stood. He stepped forward and opened the cabinet doors, revealing to all assembled the photograph of Emperor Hirohito. This was considered a sacred moment, because the emperor's picture was shown to the public only once a year. At this point in the ceremony, as if on cue, tears sprang to Obaasan's eyes as she gazed upon the person she thought to be God.

The second man read a scroll called the *Kyoiku Chyokugo*, which were the imperial instructions to all Japanese subjects. Even though I couldn't understand a word of what was said, I listened as though to a concert. To me, the language was music. After the reading the third man stood up and gave a speech, also in Japanese. This was less formal and a little more tedious, as by this time the hall was hot and stuffy and people were beginning to wipe the perspiration from their brows. But that part finally ended and when the fourth man stood, it signaled the best part of the whole ceremony.

He commanded us to stand, and we leapt to our feet. Then raising both arms over his head, he yelled, "Banzai!" Obediently we echoed, "Banzai!" His arms rolled down and upward again as he roared, "Banzai!" and we yelled more loudly, "Banzai!" Once more we repeated our cheer, with no one yelling more loudly than I.

Then, from a piano offstage, came the strains of "Kimi gayo," the Japanese national anthem, and everyone joined in singing. Everyone but me. I could only pretend, since I didn't know the words, but I at least moved my mouth with great gusto. By then the tears were streaming unrestrained down Obaasan's cheeks.

When the music ended and we all filed out into the open air and sunshine, Chichi invariably mumbled to Haha, "Thank God that's over for another year," while I promised myself that before the emperor's next birthday, I'd memorize the words to the national anthem even if it killed me.

Another event we faithfully attended was the Japanese community picnic held at Elysian Park every June. This was a huge gathering that we prepared for weeks ahead of time, especially Haha, who had to do a lot of baking and sewing. She always made new dresses for Sunny and me, even though they were bound to get dirty as we played in the park and ran in the foot races. She also bought all us kids new tennis shoes so we'd be able to compete with the best of them. Sunny and I never once won a prize, but we had plenty of fun just the same.

On the morning of the picnic the park filled up with hundreds of Japanese, all milling about with huge baskets of food while waiting for the events to begin. The morning was devoted to games and relay races open to all the children; the afternoon, to the annual baseball tournament played by the older boys. At some point during the day, a group of young boys gave a demonstration of mass calisthenics while their leader bounced around counting out their time, *"Ichi! Ni! San! Shi!"*

In addition to sports there was an abundance of music at the picnic, provided mostly by the children who attended the Japanese schools. They performed folk dances and sang songs and usually a band or two from the schools performed as well, the children sweating in their uniforms as they tooted and marched about.

At about noon someone would stroll about the park ringing a bell and announcing that it was time to eat. *"Ohiru desu,"* he said. "It's lunch hour." Tired from the exercise and the heat, we'd all gratefully find some shade and settle down to eat. The idea was to exchange food among families, not just eat what you'd brought in your own basket. All sorts of Japanese delights were passed around, like *maki-zushi,* a type of rice ball with ginger, eel meat, spinach, and carrots in the center, and *nishime,* a concoction of small pieces of carrots, bamboo sprouts, mushrooms, taro roots, and pork all fried up together in soy sauce.

The amusing thing was the way in which the women offered samples of food to one another. They were very formal, sometimes bowing to each other and offering something like *otsukemono,* homemade pickles, with the comment, "These are not at all tasty, but please try some." The woman on the receiving end would respond by saying, "Ah, *arigato.* Thank you, thank you. I'm sure they are delicious. I have made some *botamochi;* it is not very good, but please accept some." Even though I was put off by the thought of eel and raw fish, I tasted many other items and eventually developed a liking for some of them.

Also available at the picnic was a large supply of sake, generally indulged in by a small number of men, the same ones every year. I didn't know what it was, but I liked the results when a Mr. Omori and a Mr. Kikumura had finished off a few bottles. A small crowd would gather around them and beg them to sing *naniya bushi*. This, Chichi explained to me, was a type of ballad singing, the songs recounting the classic tales of Japan. Mr. Omori and Mr. Kikumura happily obliged by sitting cross-legged on the grass while alternately singing and nipping at their bottles of sake.

These men had marvelous voices that resonated in the open air, and I listened with rapt attention as first one then the other put his head back and directed his concert to the sky. The hushed crowd grew in size as the two men serenaded us with the old songs of the mother country, and long before they had finished, more then one listener's face was wet with tears. Obaasan, who spent most of the day in a lawn chair, asked to be moved closer to the singers, and she tapped her cane impatiently on her chair if they lingered too long at the bottle between songs.

This might go on for an hour or more until one or the other of the men fell over onto the grass, asleep. I assumed he had swooned from the exhilaration of it all, but Chichi finally explained to me that Mr. Omori or Mr. Kikumura had simply passed out from drinking too much. When that happened, the concert was over and the crowds dispersed to other things.

Each year I looked forward to New Year's Eve celebrated Japanese style. Chichi observed the traditions of paying off as many debts as he could—though I don't suppose he had many—cleaning the grocery store from top to bottom with Sunny and me helping him, and taking a long, hot bath to rid himself symbolically of the past year's grime. Sunny and I both took extra long baths too, scrubbing and scrubbing to make sure we were clean for the new year. Then, at midnight, Chichi woke up Sunny and me so we could join him, Haha, and Obaasan in the traditional meal of buckwheat noodles floating in chicken broth. The first time we joined them for this meal, New Year's Eve of 1939, we felt very grown-up.

The next day members of the extended family met at one home or another, greeting each other with cries of "*Ake-mashite omede toh gozai masu!* Happy New Year!" And "*Konen mo yoroshiku onegai itashi-masu.* I hope that the coming year will find us close friends as ever." We'd gorge ourselves on the food Haha and the other women had prepared. These were all the traditional dishes eaten on the first day of the year: bamboo shoots and taro, spicily flavored burdock root, shrimp and, if we could afford it, lobster, whole red snapper, fillet of raw tuna and sea bass, salted herring roe soaked in soy sauce, fried soybean cake, vinegar-flavored rice wrapped like a jelly roll in sheets of seaweed, and *mochi*—rice pounded into a glutinous mass and shaped into little buns.

I loved this food not so much for its taste as for the fact that it was uniquely Japanese. You'd never see such food on the table at Uncle Finn's house, and that meant these particular dishes were special, as were the people who ate them.

With our stomachs sated, we'd turn our attention from eating to playing games. The older folks and the younger ones who spoke Japanese played the traditional games of *Go* and *Karuta,* while most of us kids spent the remainder of the day playing double solitaire or checkers or Monopoly.

Of course every New Year's Day marked the beginning of another long stretch of everydays, those glorious everydays in my life with the Yamagatas. They appear now like the individual pieces of glass in a stained-glass window, the ordinary colors and shapes coming together to form a lovely picture. All the unremarkable moments of waking up and eating together and going to school and coming home again— especially lovely, the daily coming home again—and all the wonderful mundane happenings that brought us back around to sleep. Our days, those bountiful everydays, ended with Sunny and me lying in bed, Jimmy stretched out between us, licking our faces while the two of us stroked his fur and whispered and giggled in the dark. The stained-glass picture is held together with the memory of Sunny pinching the bridge of her nose to make it look more hakujin, while I pressed down on the bridge of mine to make it look more Japanese.

This was my life for a little more than three years, three wonder-ful, mysterious, and too swift years. I was happy then, as happy as a child can be, and safe as well, like a baby bird still curled up inside the shell, peacefully unaware of the world outside.

NINE

My own family became like strangers to me, almost as though they were people I had known once upon a time. I wandered about Uncle Finn's house like a ghost, unseen, unheard, and largely content to keep it that way.

Aunt Lucy, whenever I was around, expressed some interest in my life, but whenever I responded to her polite inquiries, I sensed her attention drifting away like the smoke rising up from the tip of her cigarette. My suspicions were confirmed when, ten minutes later, she would ask me the same question that I'd just finished answering.

Uncle Finn and I spoke hardly at all, and that was fine by me. I found him an irascible old creature, grumpy and mean, definitely unworthy of my time and attention.

As for my cousins, my conversations with them were largely limited to yelling matches over the use of the bathroom. Otherwise, Maureen was too old to have much to do with me, and Rusty, Riley and Rosey were too young.

My sisters Valerie and Gwen lived somewhere in Los Angeles, but we rarely heard from them. My brother Mitchell was lost to us completely, having jumped the rails during the Depression to try to find work. The occasional letter and postcard eventually dwindled down to nothing, until we no longer knew whether he was dead or alive. My oldest brother, Lenny, wrote to Mother from wherever his outfit happened to be stationed, but again those letters were sporadic and brief. I thought about Lenny sometimes, and wondered what his life in the marines must be like, but he was a brother I'd never known, more of a myth than a real person.

The person I missed was my mother. I'd never been close to her, but always wanted to be. It was she who kept the distance between us. She had a third arm, one that was invisible, locked at the elbow and pressed against my chest so that, try as I might, I could never reach her. Sometimes I'd start casual conversations, maybe ask a question so she'd have to say something, and she'd respond briefly, but that was all. And it only grew worse over time. As she quietly but doggedly went on exchanging her blood for alcohol, she became more and more like Aunt Lucy's cigarette smoke, drifting away, disappearing.

Eventually she started doing strange things, like awakening in the middle of the night and leaving the house at odd hours. She wandered around the neighborhood clothed in whatever she had been wearing when she'd passed out earlier. That might be a housedress or it might be a slip or a pair of pajamas, depending on how far she had got in the ritual of undressing and getting ready for sleep.

Fairly often Sergeant O'Reilly, a poker-playing buddy of Uncle Finn's, called in the middle of the night to say that one of the officers had picked up Mother and taken her down to the station. Since they weren't running a taxi service with their squad cars, could Uncle Finn kindly come down and take her home? Uncle Finn would tell Sergeant O'Reilly to keep her in the drunk tank till morning, at which time he could better decide whether he cared to come rescue her or not. I knew he was tempted just to leave her there for good, but the next morning at breakfast Aunt Lucy would talk him into going down to get her.

Other nights Mother didn't make it out the front door. We'd find her at daybreak on the living room floor, one hand stretched out in front of her as though she'd been reaching for the doorknob when she went down.

She claimed to have no memory of her escapades and was invariably surprised when she woke up either on the floor or in jail. She accused Uncle Finn and Aunt Lucy and even me of dragging her out of bed and leaving her in places she didn't belong. Uncle Finn threatened to start tying her to the couch in the sewing room if she didn't straighten up, but he never did.

Only Stella and Jack and my brother Stephen continued to feel like family to me. On occasion Stella and Jack picked me up and took me to their apartment, where we played games and ate ice cream, or if we had the time we might even take a trip to the beach. Even after she'd earned her beautician's license, Stella continued to work with my hair, brushing and coaxing the stubborn curls into any number of styles. Afterward, she'd let me play with her makeup and jewelry, and when I presented myself for inspection, Stella invariably exclaimed, "Look out, fellas, there's a heartbreaker ready to bloom!" And Jack would say with a wink, "You better be glad she's not ten years older, Stella, or I might just run away with her myself." The two of them had a knack for rubbing a balm over my bruised ego while at the same time making me laugh.

Likewise, my brother Stephen emerged as somebody for me to talk to. In the years he and I shared Uncle Finn's attic, I got to know him better than I ever had before and felt a connection to him that I didn't have with my other siblings. Seven years separated us, and we had really very little in common, but nonetheless Stephen was kind to me. Though I spent the weekends with the Yamagatas, I still slept in the attic on school nights, and Stephen and I sometimes talked for long stretches through the dusty white sheet that separated our mattresses. The smoke of his cigarette wafted over to my side of the room, and if he were turned toward me instead of lying on his back, I could see a small dim circle of light cast upon the sheet when he inhaled.

Most of our conversations have blended into one overwhelming memory of Stephen's unhappiness in those years. In addition to going to school, he held two part-time jobs—stocking groceries and delivering telegrams—because Uncle Finn required him to help with the household expenses. Stephen resented that he had to turn most of his earnings over to our uncle, while he himself had to go on sleeping in an attic and couldn't even afford to buy himself some new clothes. He called our father a coward for killing himself, faulted Mother for bringing us to Uncle Finn's, and was generally bitter at the thought of what our lives had become. He said I was lucky that those "What's-their-names" had practically adopted me, and I agreed that I was. Stephen's one desire was to escape Uncle Finn's and get out on his own.

I do remember distinctly one conversation we had in the autumn of 1940. I was lying on my mattress thinking about Mother when I decided to ask Stephen why she did all the strange things she did.

"She's nuts," Stephen replied simply. "Too much drink."

"Can't we make her not drink anymore?"

"Not a chance. Once a person gets on the bottle, that's it. There's no getting off."

"Are you sure?"

"I'm sure."

"But why, Stevie?"

"Alcohol's got a grip like a vise. Maybe some people could get away from it, but not weak people like Mags Schuler."

I didn't think of Mother as weak, though I remembered a time when she seemed gentler. It was a time when she didn't drink, at least not that anyone knew of. "When I was little," I told Stephen, "sometimes when I cried, Mom would pick me up into her lap and sing to me until I stopped crying. Sometimes I'd just pretend to cry so she'd sing to me. She had a pretty voice. Do you remember, Stevie?"

"I don't remember her ever singing," he said flatly.

"I think she misses Dad. Maybe that's why she drinks."

"Maybe."

"Do you miss Dad, Stevie?"

Such a long pause followed, I didn't think my brother was going to answer. At length he said, "I wish he hadn't done what he did, killing himself like that. Fat lot of good it did the rest of us. Mom just handed over the insurance money to Finn like it belonged to him in the first place. And now you and me are living in an attic, and I still gotta pay Finn to do it. I tell ya, Augs, soon as I graduate high school, I'm on my own. One more year to go. I'm counting the days. The money I earn that I don't give to Finn, I'm saving up for when I can get outta here."

"But what are you going to do, Stevie," I asked, "after you leave?"

"Don't know for sure," he answered. "I just know I wanna travel, have adventures. Maybe I can find Mitch, and me and him can ride the rails together, go all over the country. I wanna see the East Coast— New York, Boston, places like that. I wanna get as far away from here as I can, I know that much."

"Will you write me sometimes?"

"Sure, kid. I'll send you pretty postcards of all the places I go to."

"If you do, Stevie, I'll keep 'em all. And when you're old, try to find me again, all right? I'll write down all your adventures and put them in a book."

"Sure, kid. All right. I'd like it if you did that—put down everything in a book. I'll try not to disappoint you, Augs."

"I know you won't. I know you'll have all sorts of adventures, and it'll make a swell story."

It was that night, I recall, that Stephen mentioned the possibility of going off to Europe as a mercenary to fight in the war. I didn't even know there was a war going on, and I asked Stephen if he was sure there was.

"You bet," he answered excitedly. "Don't they tell you about it in school?"

"Maybe. I don't remember."

"Yeah, they been going at it for about a year now."

"But what are they fighting about?"

"That German guy Hitler invaded Poland, and then everybody just started shooting. I guess Hitler's trying to take over Europe."

"Which side you going to fight on?"

"*Against* Hitler, of course."

"How come?"

"Well, on account of if America ever got in the war, we'd be fighting against Hitler and his Nazi troops."

"Are we ever going to get in the war?"

"Not according to old Roosevelt, and he's the one that says whether we do or not. Wish we would, though. Then instead of being a mercenary, I could just join up with the U.S. Army and get over to Europe that way."

I didn't say as much because I didn't want to disappoint Stephen, but I hoped America wouldn't get involved in any war. That might just cause problems for everyone, and I liked things the way they were. Surely if President Roosevelt said we wouldn't go to war, then the matter was settled.

That night and afterward I tried to dismiss it all—Hitler and the Nazis and Germany and Poland. I knew from Uncle Finn that Japan was scuffling with China, but I had no idea the extent of what was going on, nor did I care to know. Even when Chichi started pacing in front of the radio whenever the news came on, even when rumors of war flittered through the conversations of grown-ups like so much wind-tossed confetti, I didn't worry.

What did news from far-off places have to do with me? My world was safe, the shell intact.

TEN

Sunny and I were dancing the jitterbug together just as the first of the Japanese planes began appearing off the coast of Oahu. Chichi and Haha had given us a record player for our eleventh birthday, and with our allowance we'd been collecting records of the popular music of the time. Everyone was keen on the jitterbug, and Sunny and I didn't want to be left out. Jimmy joined us, doing his own canine version of the dance by leaping and barking and sometimes, if he got really carried away, jumping on and off the bed.

This had become our Sunday routine, dancing for hours in our bedroom, often killing off the entire morning just by jumping around and flapping our arms. So I know that's what we were doing on the morning of December 7, 1941. While I can't be precise as to how our actions lined up chronologically with the Japanese, I figure we must have been looking through our records, deciding what to dance to, when the bombs were being loaded onto the mustard-colored planes with the red sun on the wing tips. There were hundreds of planes—torpedo bombers, dive bombers, high-level bombers, fighters—waiting to take off from the carriers situated some two hundred miles north of the Hawaiian Islands.

Light streamed in through the windows, and we danced in its

slanted brightness while in the still dark Pacific, Commander Mitsuo Fuchida, hero of the China war, was roused from sleep and readied to lead the attack against Pearl Harbor. While the first planes lifted into the sky, Sunny and I twirled about the room, lost our balance, fell, laughed, got up again. We danced so hard the floor shuddered, the record skipped. Jimmy barked and nipped at our heels. Had we known what was coming, we wouldn't have been laughing, but we didn't know, and so we went on belting out the kind of squeals that routinely brought Obaasan to our doorway looking stern, her hands pressed over her ears. Had Chichi ever added a bedroom downstairs for her, we wouldn't have bothered her, and she wouldn't have bothered us. But that room was still in the planning stages, and Obaasan was still living next door, and she was not amused by the amusements of the young.

She came as expected that Sunday morning and told us to be quiet, and while she scolded us in words I couldn't understand, the first bombs were probably falling on the ships of the U.S. Pacific Fleet. Obaasan shuffled back to her own room where she was listening to Japanese music on her ancient phonograph. Ignoring her completely, Sunny and I went on dancing and laughing, Jimmy barking and nipping. Even at that moment a thousand men were drowning while the USS *Arizona* broke apart and sank to the bottom of the harbor.

Haha was in the kitchen preparing our Sunday dinner. Chichi sat in his chair in the living room reading the paper and listening with his customary "half an ear" to the radio. Sam and George played together in their room down the hall. I know this is how it was, because this morning was like a hundred other Sunday mornings in the Yamagata household.

Shortly before noon when Chichi climbed the stairs, the U.S. Pacific Fleet was in ruins, and twenty-four hundred men lay dead or dying. We saw Chichi appear at the top of the stairs, but we thought he was coming to tell us to wash our hands for dinner. We were hungry and ready to eat. We waved playfully as we fell in tired heaps across the bed, but Chichi neither waved at us nor smiled.

He stopped in the doorway to our room and looked at us for a long moment, his face wooden, his eyes without light. We could only stare back at him dumbly from where we lay, wondering what in the world was wrong. Since he didn't tell us to wash our hands, I thought perhaps he was angry with us. And yet, if he were going to scold us for being noisy, he'd have jumped right in with his usual lecture of how we needed to be considerate of others in the house. As it was, his silence was eerie, worse than any scolding. Finally, he said solemnly, "Sunny, turn off the record player. I have something to tell you girls."

Sunny got up from the bed and did as she was told, lifting the needle from the record in midbeat. She turned the knob on the player to Off, and the revolving disk slowed to a stop. We were plunged even further into the silence that surrounded Chichi like a shroud. Sunny slowly turned from the record player and looked at her father, her eyes wide with expectation. I could feel her fear, its iciness leaving goose bumps on my skin.

When he spoke his voice was pained. "Girls," he said, "the Japanese have bombed Pearl Harbor."

No one moved. No one spoke. My mind turned in circles trying to make sense of what he had just said. After several heavy seconds, I asked, "Where's Pearl Harbor, Chichi?"

"It's in Hawaii. The Japanese have attacked us, and many hundreds of Americans have been killed. The U.S. Fleet is destroyed."

Sunny and I still couldn't take it in. "Are you sure, Papa?" Her voice was a hoarse whisper.

Chichi nodded. "I'm sure, Sunny. I just heard it on the radio."

"Maybe it's a joke," Sunny suggested tentatively. "Like that time Orson Welles said the Martians had landed. Remember that? Maybe the Japanese didn't really attack—"

"No, Sunny, this is real. It's not pretend. Go on downstairs to your mother now. I need to tell your grandmother what has happened."

He turned and walked away then, leaving us bewildered and frightened and wondering still what exactly the news had to do with us. We scarcely knew where Hawaii was, let alone Pearl Harbor—though we knew it was far away, somewhere in the middle of the Pacific Ocean. That seemed comfortably far from California, yet the anguish of the situation was visible on Chichi's face, as visible and disturbing as sudden dark storm clouds unrolling themselves across a formerly blue sky.

"What do you think's going to happen?" I asked Sunny.

My friend turned her dark eyes toward me. Her dread was as certain as Chichi's and yet as ill defined as my own. "I don't know, Augie. Maybe they'll come and bomb us next."

"But they can't bomb you, Sunny. *You're* Japanese."

Sunny shook her head. "Let's go ask Mama."

We started down the hall, passing Obaasan's room where Chichi and his mother both spoke at once in quiet, hurried Japanese. We quickened our pace and, holding hands, stumbled down the stairs to find Haha in the living room. She sat on the edge of the overstuffed chair listening to the radio and dabbing at her eyes with one corner of her apron.

Sunny let go of my hand and rushed to her mother, who embraced her for a long moment before making room for her on the wide chair. I sat down on the floor at their feet and rested my head against Haha's knee. She reached down and cupped the side of my face in the palm of her tiny hand. Her skin was warm and comforting. Big band music played on the radio, sounding odd and inappropriate. Like dancing the jitterbug in the middle of a war.

"What's happening, Mama?" Sunny asked. "Why are you crying?"

"Didn't Papa tell you?"

"He said the Japanese bombed Pearl Harbor."

"Yes."

Silence followed, as though no further explanation was needed. The Japanese had bombed Pearl Harbor, and that said it all.

"But," Sunny persisted, "isn't that far away, Mama?"

Haha sniffed, and when she spoke her voice quavered. "The Japanese have attacked an American territory. That means there will be war." She pressed her hand against my face more firmly, as though she were afraid she would lose me. I lifted both my hands and laid them over her fingers so she could not pull away. I wanted nothing to separate us, not at that moment, not ever.

"Will America be fighting Japan, Mama?"

"Yes, Sunny. I'm afraid that's what it will come to."

"Will Papa have to fight?"

"No. I don't think so."

"If Papa doesn't have to go, then we don't need to be afraid, do we?" The question itself was filled with fear.

"It's always hard for everyone when a country is at war, Sunny," Haha answered. "But we will try to be strong."

I turned to look up at Haha's face while not letting go of her hand. "Haha," I asked, "do you mean the Japanese are our *enemies*?" To me, the notion was unthinkable. I'd spent the past three years trying to *become* Japanese. Japan was my paradise, the Japanese my idols.

Haha sighed deeply, as though her heart were broken. And perhaps it was. "Yes, Musume, I'm afraid so."

I was dumbstruck, dizzy with confusion. Only after a long moment could I put the words together to form the question weighing on my mind. "You mean, they *hate* us?"

"Well, war has more to do with greed than hate, I think."

Either way, it didn't make the Japanese sound very good.

"Uncle Finn said they were trying to take over China."

"They still are, Musume. It's terrible, what's been happening there."

"Did you know about it, Haha?"

"Of course. It's been going on for years."

"And now the Japanese are going to try to take us over too?"

"I suppose that's what they want to do." Haha sounded weary and as though she were suddenly very old.

"But, Haha," I ventured, "the Japanese are such good people. Maybe if they do take over the whole world, everything will be wonderful."

I studied Haha's face, trying to read her thoughts. I hoped my words might comfort her, hoped she might realize that, of course, if the Japanese ruled the world, how could we be anything but happy? But Haha only looked at me with what seemed a mixture of sadness and pity, and I couldn't even begin to comprehend what she was thinking.

Before any of us could say more, a car pulled up in front of the house and screeched to a halt. Haha's back stiffened as she said, "I wonder who—"

But her words were interrupted when the front door burst open and Ojisan Hito flew in, followed by Chichi's sister, Obasan Akemi, and their two small children, both of whom wailed loudly.

Ojisan, whom I knew well from the grocery store, was clearly agitated. *"Sensohda!"* he cried wildly, his eyes wide, his arms flailing. He approached us looking for all the world like an otherworldly creature in a creep show at the theater. "Toshio, Suma, sensohda!"

Haha disentangled herself from Sunny and me and, rising, went to embrace her sister-in-law. Then the three adults began to speak rapidly in Japanese. I asked Sunny what Ojisan had said when he arrived. She sighed heavily. "He said it's a war." She got up from the chair and went to comfort her two cousins, Tommy and Beth, whom the adults in their frenzy seemed to have forgotten.

Suddenly Chichi was on the stairs, his face red and pinched, his hands trembling as he clutched the banister. I couldn't stifle the gasp that rose up out of my chest. Never before had I seen Chichi so angry. It frightened me more than anything that had happened so far that morning. "What are you doing?" he cried. "Stop speaking Japanese at once! We are Americans. We are not Japanese. We must speak English!"

Haha, Ojisan, and Obasan stared up at Chichi, their excited conversation abruptly cut off. The only sound now was the quiet sobs of Sunny's young cousins. Chichi kept his eyes upon the small cluster of grown-ups as he descended the stairs. "We must try to remain calm," he instructed, visibly trying to gather his own wits. "We have to be able to think clearly."

But Ojisan pounded one fist against the palm of his other hand and exclaimed, "You expect us to be calm, Toshio? Don't you know what this means?"

"I know, Hito—"

"How could they have done it? How could they be so stupid?"

"I don't know, but we can't change what's happened." Chichi put one hand on Ojisan's shoulder and shook him slightly, as though trying gently to awaken him from a nightmare. "Whatever happens, you must remember that we are American citizens. We are not Japanese. Do you understand?" He gave his listeners a schoolteacher's gaze, as though trying to drill a lesson into their heads.

A news bulletin came over the radio, but we were all too distracted to listen. The telephone rang and Haha rushed to the kitchen to answer it. The street outside, we slowly realized, had become a swarm of activity—people yelling to each other across yards, horns honking, a newsboy hawking Extras on the corner.

"Listen to me, Hito," Chichi continued, "go home and get rid of anything in your apartment and in the store that's from Japan—papers, letters, souvenirs, everything." Ojisan started to protest, but Chichi insisted, "Everything, do you hear? And when you finish with that, put a sign up in the front window of the store that says, 'We are Americans.' Do you understand?"

Obaasan appeared on the staircase then, slowly and painfully making her way down with her cane. Sunny's brothers, Sam and George, rushed past her, nearly knocking her over in their hurry to find out what was happening. Scrambling to their father, they started pulling on Chichi's shirt and shrieking, "What's going on, Papa! What's going on!"

Obaasan called to her daughter, Akemi, who met her at the bottom of the stairs. They began speaking together rapidly in Japanese. Haha came back into the living room, but the phone rang again and called her away. Someone pounded on the front door and a voice called out, "Mr. Yamagata! Mr. Yamagata!" It was the father of one of the other Japanese American families that lived in Boyle Heights. He entered the front hall without invitation and added to the general confusion by saying, "Mr. Yamagata, what can we do? My father is Issei. He says he will be taken away. He says . . ."

The phone rang yet again. The radio newscaster droned on excitedly. Cars outside honked; people shouted. The house was filled with angry, anxious chatter, much of which I couldn't understand. The man whose father was Issei sat down on the couch uninvited and unnoticed. He buried his face in his hands and wept. Sunny, her cousins and brothers, and I huddled together on the living room floor, a tight circle of fear and confusion.

We were all crying by now, George and Beth the loudest. Sam asked in a whisper, "What's happening, Sunny?"

"A war started," she said simply.

"A war? Who with?"

"The Japanese."

Sam stared at his sister, his eyes narrowed, his mouth open as though he wanted to ask something but he couldn't form the words. Finally he pushed the question out. "But aren't we Japanese, Sunny?"

Sunny pursed her lips, wiped at a tear on her cheek with the back of one hand, and said nothing.

Meanwhile, I caught snatches of English among the grown-ups, but I couldn't weave it together into a meaningful whole.

"She says she wants to know exactly what was said on the radio—"

"What do you think Roosevelt—"

". . . should have known, should have seen it coming—"

". . . and I guess we can expect to hear—"

". . . we're citizens with rights like everyone else—"

"But the Issei . . . never allowed to become—"

". . . wouldn't have happened if we'd all just stayed in Japan, she says—"

"Let me help you here, Toshio, and then we can go back to the store together."

"All right. Go out back then and start a fire in the ash can, and I'll—"

". . . wants to know what you're planning to do—"

Ojisan Hito disappeared out the back door. Chichi climbed the stairs. Obaasan and Obasan Akemi both watched him go while directing a barrage of Japanese at his retreating back. The neighbor man on the couch continued to weep, oblivious to the stares of us children who could scarcely take in the behavior of the grown-ups.

A few minutes later Chichi returned with a handful of papers. He exchanged terse, angry words with his mother and sister, speaking in Japanese in spite of his own warning to speak only in English. Obaasan and Obasan Akemi both reached out as though to stop Chichi from doing whatever it was he determined to do, but he pulled away and disappeared down the hall. To my horror, Obaasan let out a scream so piercing I could hardly believe it came from such a tiny person. She followed her son down the hall, weeping and wailing as she hobbled toward the kitchen. Obasan Akemi followed; she too was crying and calling out in Japanese.

I looked to Sunny for an explanation.

She turned to me with tears streaming down both cheeks. She didn't bother to wipe them away. "They're letters Obaasan saved from her family in Japan. Papa is going to burn them. He says he must destroy everything in the house that's from Japan."

"But why?"

"I don't know," she whispered.

The man on the couch finally lifted his face from his hands and drew a handkerchief from his pants pocket. He wiped at his face, patting the crimson blotchy skin as though he were caressing a baby, then blew his nose loudly. He returned the soiled handkerchief to his pocket, sighed heavily, stood, and smoothed out his pants.

Sunny looked up at him and said, "I'm sorry about your father,

Mr. Nishitani." She must have remembered that he came in hollering about his father, though she probably had no better idea than I what there was to fear for the old man.

Mr. Nishitani nodded, said, "So am I, Sunny," then walked to the front door and left.

Screams reached us from the backyard, rolling into the house on waves of loud and frenzied words. I might have thought myself at Uncle Finn's house, had the words not been spoken in Japanese. Beth crawled into my lap and wept; George crawled into Sunny's lap and wailed. Benny Goodman's band played on the radio, the horns and woodwinds sounding like voices from happier days, laughing at our disaster and mocking our tears.

While we children tried to comfort one another, the front door suddenly burst open and banged against the wall, making us all jump. In that moment I, and probably everyone else, pictured the enemy surging into the house with guns and bayonets at the ready, eager to kill and maim as they had done in Pearl Harbor.

But instead of the Japanese forces, it was Uncle Finn. He stomped in, fists clenched, his face screwed up into a ball of anger like a skein of red yarn that had been too tightly wound. He spotted me and, without a word, strode across the living room, grabbed my wrist, and yanked me up from the floor. Beth slid off my lap into a crumpled, howling heap. I screamed and tried to plant my feet on the rug, but it was a futile gesture against Uncle Finn's strength. He dragged me the length of the living room floor while Sunny and the other children looked on in horror.

"Chichi!" I yelled. "Haha! Chichi!"

I caught hold of the doorframe as Uncle Finn tried to drag me through, but he picked me up around the waist and carried me down the sidewalk like a bag of dirty laundry tucked up under his arm. Screaming wildly, I flailed my arms and legs trying to escape, but my uncle only clenched me more tightly until I thought he would squeeze the breath out of me.

When we reached the car, its engine idling, he opened the driver-side door, threw me in, slid in beside me, and put the car in gear. As Uncle Finn sped away from the curb, I turned in time to see Haha and

Sunny standing helplessly on the front steps of the house, seemingly frozen in their effort to rescue me.

The war that started that morning in far-off Pearl Harbor had reached all the way to Boyle Heights in no time at all.

ELEVEN

The nights had always been dark in Uncle Finn's attic, but the night of December 7, 1941, was the darkest ever. I wanted Chichi to come and hold me and even to laugh while telling me it was all just pretend, that, as Sunny had at first hoped, it was only another attack by Martians who hadn't really come. But as he'd said, this was real. The Japanese had bombed the American naval base in Hawaii, and though it hadn't yet been formally declared, everyone knew we were at war.

It wasn't a fear of war that weighed on me that night. I felt immune to war. Fighting was a distant thing, the possibility of death even more remote. But there was something else, something as heavy as a pile of sand dumped on top of me from out of nowhere. What was so crushing was the separation, the being ripped away from my family and being warned by the tyrant Finn O'Shaughnessy never to see them again.

My uncle, who had dragged me from the Yamagatas' house in silent anger, had finally erupted into uncontrollable rage when the two of us reached his house. Clutching my elbow in his tight grip, he pushed me into the living room, where everyone was gathered around the radio listening to news bulletins. Mother sat listlessly in one of the easy chairs. Aunt Lucy was on a chair dragged in from the kitchen, my young cousins on the floor at her feet. Maureen sat on the couch with Stella and Jack. Only Stephen was missing. Still, Uncle Finn seemed not to notice anyone else as he vented his fury on me.

"Do you know what they've done!" he cried, stabbing his thick index finger into a spot beneath my collarbone. "They've attacked us! They've killed Americans! Bad enough they've been slaughtering Chinks, but now they've gone after Americans!" He didn't bother to define who "they" were. I knew, he knew, everyone knew "they" were the Japanese.

"Up to now I've turned a blind eye to your associating with their kind, but not anymore. Do you hear me?" he went on. "Not anymore! From now on you're staying right here in this house where you belong, and if I hear you've so much as talked to one of those Japs, you can consider yourself out on the street. You see or talk to one of them, don't even *try* crawling back to this house."

His face was so crimson, so moist with sweat, I thought he might choke on his own words. He started to pace the room, and I looked to the others for help. But none came. Mother and Aunt Lucy wouldn't look at me, and even Stella dropped her eyes when my gaze met hers. Jack cleared his throat and, pressing his hands together between his knees, said quietly, "They're the enemy now, Augie. This is a serious thing that's happened. Maybe it would be better if you . . ."

The rest of what he said was lost to me as I ran up the stairs to the attic. Facedown on my mattress, I screamed into the pillow until I was exhausted and my voice was hoarse. When I was finally spent, I lay quietly and planned my escape. I'd hop a train and ride the rails from Los Angeles to who-knew-where, just as my brother Mitchell had done and Stephen had talked of doing. I knew I couldn't possibly survive alone out there, but I dreamed of running away anyway, if only to feel I had some small bit of power over Uncle Finn, some measure of control over my own life. "He can't keep me here," I cried, beating my fist against the mattress. "I hate him. I hate him. I hate them all!"

I left the attic only in the early evening when hunger drove me down to the kitchen in search of something to eat. Most everyone was still in the living room, talking and listening to the radio. I ignored them, hardly even bothering to glance their way. Once in the kitchen,

I spotted Mother in the sewing room. She lay motionless on the couch, her right hand dangling over an empty bottle on the floor. Pots and pans on the stove and dirty dishes still on the table told me that supper had been eaten without me. I made myself a jelly-and-cream-cheese sandwich and climbed back up to the attic.

When Stephen came up to bed late that night, I was still awake, crying quietly in the dark. Stephen fumbled about for a moment, then turned on a flashlight that he used when I was in bed. The light bobbed about briefly, casting moving shadows on the sheet. When Stephen laid the flashlight on the dresser, I watched his dark silhouette undress and slip under the rumpled covers that lay across his mattress. Then came the hissing of a match struck into flame and a brief but pungent odor of sulfur. The small circle of flame swelled as Stephen lighted his cigarette. With a flick of his wrist he put out the match. The attic filled with the scent of burning tobacco.

Stephen's arm shadow reached up toward the flashlight and turned it off, plunging the room into darkness again. For a moment all was quiet. I let the tears slide quietly down the sides of my face onto the pillow. Stephen had always been kind to me, a good older brother, willing to talk. Maybe, I thought, he'd be willing to listen now. I wanted to tell him what Uncle Finn had done, dragging me back here like a captured fugitive and forbidding me ever to see the Yamagatas again. I wanted to tell him how much it hurt to be ripped away from the people who were my family. I wanted to ask him if he could help me find my way back to them.

But before I could open my mouth to speak, he spoke first. "Hey, Augs, you awake?"

"Yeah." I turned toward him onto my side.

"This is my lucky day, kid," he said, his voice heavy with satisfaction.

"What do you mean?"

"I got my ticket outta here. I'm gonna enlist—I'm old enough now. Soon as the doors open at the recruiting office tomorrow morning, I'll be there. And I'll be overseas too, sooner than you can say Jack Daniels."

His words fell on me like blows to the gut. He'd talked about becoming a mercenary, but I'd thought it was just that—talk and nothing more. "You mean you really want to fight, Stevie?"

"You bet, kid. I got a real goal now. I'm gonna kill some Japs, and I'm gonna do it with a smile on my face."

What was he saying? Didn't he know that *I* was Japanese, that *I* was among those he wanted to kill?

I rolled over onto my back in a stupor. In another moment Stephen ground the remains of his cigarette into the attic floor, and the last little bit of light went out.

❧

Of course Uncle Finn couldn't keep me from seeing Sunny in school. We were in the same homeroom, and not even the start of a war could change that.

I was already seated the Monday morning after Pearl Harbor when Sunny walked into the classroom. It was almost eight o'clock, and the place was active with children hanging up sweaters and jackets and settling down at their desks. But when Sunny walked in, a strange hush fell over the room, and all eyes turned toward my friend, even the teacher's.

Sunny was suddenly and inescapably Japanese. She looked alarmingly like the people who had killed hundreds of our men in Pearl Harbor. It had never mattered very much before, but it mattered now.

In the eyes of the hakujin, little Hatsune Yamagata was the enemy.

The number of students in our school of Japanese descent barely reached the double digits, leaving Sunny in a frighteningly small minority. Didn't Chichi and Haha know what they were doing, sending her off to school today just like it was any other day? Couldn't they have guessed and kept her home?

From out of the maddening silence, one boy's small voice hissed, "Dirty Jap." And that said it all. She was no longer an American. She might have been on the edge of acceptance before, a *Japanese* American but an American nevertheless. Now she was really on the outside, a foreigner in her own country. Because she was my best friend, I considered myself locked out with her.

Our teacher, Miss Pruitt, rang a small bell to signal the start of the school day. She cleared her throat and said, "Everyone stand at your desks, please. It's time for class to begin. Let's say the pledge of allegiance."

Sunny moved to her desk, which was beside mine. Our eyes locked and glittered with unshed tears.

"Hi, Sunny," I whispered.

"Hi," she said, the word as thin in the air as gossamer.

There were a hundred—a thousand—things to say, but neither of us could have uttered more than that simple greeting, even if we'd been alone. We were only children, after all. Children in a world that was much too big for us.

We both slipped a hand over our hearts and, with the others, pledged allegiance to the flag of the United States of America. But I didn't have the energy to do more than mouth the words. I was working too hard at trying to keep the tears from running down my face.

Around midmorning, classes were interrupted so that the President's speech could be broadcast over the school's public address system. His voice was familiar to all of us through his frequent fireside chats, those pep talks that encouraged our country through the years of the Depression. Chichi, Haha, Sunny, and I had often gathered around the Zenith console to listen to him. I'd always found President Roosevelt comforting, a kindly grandfather figure patting us on the heads through the airwaves to let us know all would be well. But on the day after Pearl Harbor, his voice chilled me, and I felt like he was exposing to the whole country a list of my own wrongdoing.

"Yesterday, December 7, 1941—a date which will live in infamy—the United States of America was suddenly and deliberately attacked by naval and air forces of the empire of Japan." His lilting voice came all the way from Washington to tell us what the Japanese had done, that they had not stopped at Pearl Harbor but had gone on to wreak havoc throughout the Pacific.

"Yesterday the Japanese government also launched an attack against Malaya.

"Last night Japanese forces attacked Hong Kong.

"Last night Japanese forces attacked Guam.

"Last night Japanese forces attacked the Philippine Islands.

"Last night the Japanese attacked Wake Island.

"This morning the Japanese attacked Midway Island. . . ."

As Roosevelt went on hammering home his point, I wondered what in the world had come over the Japanese. How could good and gentle people—people just like Chichi and Ojisan Masuo and Ojisan

Hito—go around dropping their bombs on thousands of innocent people? They must have all gone crazy, like a rabid dog that couldn't help itself. That was the only explanation I could manage. I couldn't believe they'd brought about all this destruction on purpose.

"Hostilities exist," Roosevelt concluded simply, stating the obvious. "There is no blinking at the fact that our people, our territory, and our interests are in grave danger.

"With confidence in our armed forces, with the unbounding determination of our people, we will gain the inevitable triumph. So help us God.

"I ask that the Congress declare that since the unprovoked and dastardly attack by Japan on Sunday, December 7, 1941, a state of war has existed between the United States and the Japanese empire."

With a thump and a scratching sound, the PA system shut off. The room was quiet. Only ten minutes had passed since the President started to speak, but it seemed an eternity. I had to fight the urge to stand up and shout, "It was all a mistake! The Japanese would never hurt anyone on purpose. We're good people. Really, we are!"

I looked over at Sunny. Her face was strangely pale, but a streak of red crept up her neck and fanned out like a rash. She stared, unmoving, at her hands folded on the desk and would not look up, even at me. Gazing at her profile, I could see clearly that all her nose pinching hadn't done any good. Her nose was no closer to being a hakujin nose than it had been on the first day I met her.

I touched my own nose, then let my hand fall slowly to my lap. That's it, then, I thought. We would never pass over into each other's worlds. Not really. The soul was pliable, but the face was set in stone. She would always be a white girl who looked Japanese, and I'd always be a Japanese girl who looked white. And that was what would finally separate us in the end.

❧

As though to underscore the fact that we were at war, an air-raid drill was called that same afternoon. Such drills were nothing new— we'd been jumping under our desks for months—but this time some of the children thought it was real, and there were no few screams and tears. Miss Pruitt, under her own desk, hollered for everyone to stay calm. She assured us that the drill was only practice and the Japanese weren't really dropping bombs over Los Angeles, but the quiver in her voice hinted that she didn't quite believe her own words.

While the drill was on and the teacher was hidden away, I crawled across the aisle to take cover under Sunny's desk. Wrapped up into balls with our hands covering our necks, we spoke for the first time since my uncle had dragged me away the day before.

"Don't worry, Sunny," I whispered. "Everything's going to be all right." Whatever compelled me to say that, I didn't know. I wasn't at all sure myself that everything was going to be all right, but it seemed to be what grown-ups always said to their children, and so I repeated it.

"Everyone's staring at me," Sunny whispered back. "They think it's all my fault."

"They're pretty stupid if they think it's your fault. You didn't have anything to do with it."

"But I'm Japanese."

"You're American. That's what you always told me before."

Sunny didn't respond. What I had come over to tell her would seem the opposite of what I'd just told her, but I had to tell her anyway. "Uncle Finn says I can't ever come back to your house. Never. He says I can't even talk to you, or he'll throw me out on the street."

"Your uncle hates me," she whispered mournfully.

I couldn't deny it. It was true. "I hate *him*," I assured my friend. "He's mean and stupid. And ugly too," I added for spite.

"What are we going to do, Augie?"

"I don't know. I'm thinking about running away."

"Where to?"

"I don't know."

"Why don't you just run away back to our house?"

I thought a moment, then said, "If I did, I'd never be able to talk to my mom or Stephen or Aunt Lucy or anyone again."

"So what?"

Just then one of the boys squealed on us. "Miss Pruitt, Augie's under Sunny's desk, and they're talking."

From beneath the teacher's desk came a sharp warning. "Augie, get back under your own desk and stay there."

I looked at Sunny and started to crawl back to my own desk, but she stopped me. "Hold on, Augie. Gotta tell you something."

"What is it?"

"Mama's going to have a baby."

It didn't occur to me that this seemed a strange moment for Sunny to tell me about the baby. What surprised me was the sharp stab of jealously I felt. "How come?" I asked.

"How come what?"

"How come she's having a baby?"

"I don't know. She just is."

"Augusta Schuler!" It was Miss Pruitt's disembodied voice again.

I crawled back to my own desk feeling like a dog with its tail between its legs. From somewhere came the thought that this baby had been created to replace me, because Haha had somehow foreseen the day that I would no longer be part of the family.

Was that day suddenly here? *Over my dead body,* I told myself. Uncle Finn could refuse to let me see the Yamagatas, and Haha could even make a baby to replace me, but one way or the other, in spite of everything against me, I was going to find my way back home.

TWELVE

Mother's scream sounded like an Irish banshee wailing the warning of impending death.

"My baby!" she cried. "They're going to kill my baby! Oh, Lenny. *Lenny!*"

The Japanese had invaded the Philippines, where my brother was stationed with the marines on Bataan. Mother, on hearing the news over the radio, stood in the center of the living room, pale and shaken, her hands clutched to her heart.

Aunt Lucy jumped up from her chair and put her arms around Mother's shoulders. "Now, Mags, we don't know that. We don't know that he won't come home safely. Come on, now—"

"But they're animals; they're animals. They stop at nothing! Oh, Lenny, my baby. . . ." She burst into sobs while Aunt Lucy looked to Uncle Finn for help.

My uncle was relaxing in his own chair, sections of the evening paper scattered on the floor about his footstool. He looked like a man who didn't want to be disturbed, not even for a war. Frowning, he took a long drag of his cigarette. Smoke rolled out of his mouth as he spoke. "Lenny's a grown man, Mags, not a baby. More than that, he's a marine. He can take care of himself." He cocked his head and deleted the remainder of the smoke from his lungs with a deep sigh. "Besides, he may be a Schuler, but he's got O'Shaughnessy blood in him."

From where I sat on the stairs, I glared at my uncle. His words offered Mother little comfort. Wasn't dying what war was all about, after all—both sides trying to wipe out as many men as possible, the winner being the side that killed the most? Did Uncle Finn think O'Shaughnessy blood would protect Lenny on the battlefield? Just the opposite, I thought, since I considered my own O'Shaughnessy blood the reason for the bad luck I'd known myself.

As I suspected, Mother was not appeased. She clutched at the front of her floral cotton housedress as though she were trying to keep her heart from popping right out of her chest. "But he's my baby," she wailed, "my firstborn. And now Stevie's gone and enlisted too."

Uncle Finn stood and hitched up his pants. "Go make her some hot tea or something, Lucy. See if you can't get her to calm down."

Aunt Lucy obeyed, guiding Mother into the kitchen where the crying and wailing continued, accompanied by the sounds of my aunt putting the teakettle on the stove to heat. Uncle Finn, belching loudly, climbed the stairs in his stockinged feet. He passed right by me as though I wasn't there. I wanted to grab him and yell, "Don't you care about Lenny? Don't you care about *anyone*?" But of course I didn't. I already knew the answer.

Music drifted up from the radio. I looked out over the empty living room and clenched my jaw, stifling one wave of anger and another of sadness. Though I didn't really know Lenny, I was sad for my brother and wondered what would become of him. More than that, I was sad for myself. I had serious doubts that Mother would carry on so if I were the one in danger, and it didn't seem fair. In fact, it made me mad. I was just as much her child as Lenny was. I may have been the last born, but still, I'd *been* born, and surely I deserved my mother's attention as much as he did. Just once I'd like to see her express some concern for me.

The way I figured it, though, I could commit hari-kari right in front of her, my guts spilling out all over her shoes, and she'd hardly stop to wipe up the mess. The child who's born without a name just doesn't stand a chance.

❧

A couple nights later while we were eating supper, Stella stormed in through the front door and slammed it angrily behind her. She stomped into the kitchen, ripped off her hat and sweater, and started pacing the floor in her patent-leather pumps.

Everyone stopped eating and stared at her, openmouthed. After a moment Aunt Lucy found her voice and asked, "Stella?"

My cousin paused abruptly, as though she'd come up against a wall. She turned her gaze of anger on her stepmother and spat out, "Jack's enlisted!"

Forks and knives started to move again, clinking against plates as we went back to our food. We'd been expecting the news. Evidently only Stella had been taken by surprise.

"Well, aren't you going to say anything!" she wailed, throwing up her hands. She started to pace again, banging out her annoyance on the linoleum.

Uncle Finn shifted a mouthful of baked potato into one cheek so he could talk. "What'd you expect, girl? Now we've got Germany and Italy on our backs. If Jack didn't enlist, he'd be drafted anyway."

Stella stared at her father incredulously. "Well, he could have waited until his number was called. He didn't have to jump right in there and volunteer!"

"Now, Stella dear"—Aunt Lucy pushed her chair back from the table and stood—"Jack's doing what he thinks is right—"

"It doesn't have anything to do with right or wrong," Stella cut in. "He says it's his chance to learn how to fly. He wants to join the Army Air Corps. He says it's the war that's going to get him what he's always wanted."

"So the boy's got plans for himself," Uncle Finn said with a nod. "Nothing wrong with that."

Stella brought one heel crashing down on the linoleum and cried, "But what about me! How can he just go and leave me? Doesn't he love me anymore?"

"Of course he loves you, dear," Aunt Lucy crooned. "The war doesn't change that." She put an arm around Stella and guided her out to the living room.

As they walked away we heard Stella moan, "But we just started talking about trying to have a baby. How am I supposed to do that without him?"

Stella churned up little sympathy in the rest of us. Maureen rolled her eyes and yawned. Mother stonily chewed her food, her own blood-shot eyes dark and distant. Riley and Rosey appeared bored and unconcerned. Finished eating, they both sat with chin in hands, elbows on the card table we younger kids shared when we were all in the kitchen eating at once.

Only twelve-year-old Rusty was animated by Stella's announcement. "If I were old enough," he said, "I'd enlist too." He looked to his father for approval.

"You got that right," his father agreed. "No cowards in this family."

Uncle Finn glanced toward the adjacent room from which Stella's muffled cries still reached us. He sighed heavily and shook his head over his plate as if to say, "A war breaks out, and all the women in the world get hysterical. Good thing we men got things under control."

❦

But I don't think the hysterics were left solely to the women. General John DeWitt, chief of the West Coast defenses, was hardly an icon of calm and composure. Maybe he had a tendency toward histrionics, or maybe he actually believed his own words; either way, he made comments that generally stirred up panic in the hearts of his listeners. "This is war!" he'd announce in his frequent statements to the press. "Death and destruction may come from the skies at any moment!"

The trouble was, most people believed him. There were even those who fled California, fearing it was the next target for the Japanese bombs. Those of us who stayed behind took precautions to save ourselves in the event of an attack. After all, the West Coast and Alaska had officially been declared a war zone four days after the bombing of Pearl Harbor, and one can't be too careful when living in a war zone.

The locations of air-raid shelters were posted in strategic places about the city so people knew where to run for cover when the bombs started to fall. We hung up black-out curtains in our homes and shielded the lamps on the streets and started living like moles in the dark whenever the sirens wailed. Air-raid wardens walked through the city in search of the tiniest crack of light that might tip the enemy to the exact location of the city of Los Angeles. Woe to the person who let that crack of light seep out from hearth and home. He was sure to get a dressing down from the warden that he wouldn't soon forget. Not to mention he'd be slapped with a fine.

When we weren't in the black-out mode, enormous searchlights split the night sky, on the lookout for enemy planes. Gun emplacements were set up along the beaches and on rooftops of tall buildings. Once a barrage of bullets was shot off against what was perceived to be warplanes flying over Los Angeles, but there was nothing there. The shell fragments, though, rained back down on the city and injured dozens of people.

I'd lie awake in the attic—alone, once Stephen set out for boot camp—and dream about committing acts of bravery, subterfuge, espionage. Believing it would be best for America in the long run if the Japanese won the war, I was tempted to tear down the black-out curtain Aunt Lucy had tacked over the attic's one dusty window. I imagined how it would be written up in the history books: One small light in the window of Finn O'Shaughnessy's house on Fresno Street in Boyle Heights guided the entire Japanese air fleet to the very heart of Los Angeles, ultimately leading to a Japanese victory in the war! Oh, at first it would appear an act of treason on my part, but after the Japanese took over and our lives became wonderful, everyone, even Uncle Finn, would understand why I did it. The future of the entire world would turn on one small act performed by Augusta Schuler, girl hero.

I never did tear that curtain down, though. I was too afraid of Uncle Finn's wrath when he had to face the air-raid warden.

Still, I wasn't convinced that the Japanese were barbarians. I refused to believe they committed atrocities, that they killed, maimed, and raped like Uncle Finn said they did. I was more inclined to believe Uncle Finn was a liar.

Of course, from time to time I did entertain some doubts about the good intentions of the Japanese. But I'd push those doubts away and go on telling myself that all would be well when Japan finally ruled the world.

It seems I was willing to root for the enemy because they were

Japanese. What I forgot, or didn't consider, was that Chichi and Haha were American. They only looked Japanese. I think there is irony in this: That which caused me to love the enemy—their Japaneseness— caused most other hakujin to hate their own fellow countrymen, those Americans of Japanese descent.

It was a confusing thing to have Americans in your midst who looked just like the enemy.

❧

On the West Coast the war became one of words. I think the very first sign in Boyle Heights that barred entrance to Japanese Americans went up in the front window of Uncle Finn's hardware store. "Absolutely No Japs," it said. Rusty painted it for Uncle Finn the very evening Pearl Harbor was bombed, and it was hung in the window before the store opened the next morning. Not long afterward signs on the doors of restaurants warned, "No Japs Served Here." In clothing stores and movie houses and barbershops: "No Japs." Tacked to the occasional telephone pole or spray painted on sidewalks: "Go Home, Japs!"

Other Asians distinguished themselves from the Japanese by wearing buttons saying "I Am Chinese," or by pasting signs in the windows of their businesses declaring "We Are Filipinos" or "We Are Korean."

And, in understated defiance, in the window of Chichi's grocery store and on the doors of other Nisei-owned businesses, signs began to appear with the words "We Are American."

Except for the *Los Angeles Times,* in which the enemy was still referred to politely as "the Japanese," newspapers stooped not only to using the term "Japs"—which was bad enough—but also "Nips," "mad dogs," and "yellow vermin."

I didn't read the newspapers, but then, I didn't have to. Uncle Finn took to pacing about the house like a mad dog himself, a cigarette or a beer—or both—in one hand, the most recent edition of the newspaper in the other, reading aloud the stories of the Japanese victories in the Pacific. It didn't matter that the news about the Philippines drove Mother into spasms of despair. It didn't matter that Aunt Lucy begged Uncle Finn to be quiet, that his own children ran from him with their hands over their ears, that Stella—when she was there—cursed him and threatened not to set foot in the house again unless he spared us all the ordeal of having to listen to the news. But the pleas didn't reach him. They were rubber-tipped arrows that couldn't pierce his thick skin. Undaunted, he went on pacing and reading wildly, pausing only to add his own ad-libbed commentary in phrases far worse than anything the papers might have printed.

My one revenge was to secretly think up names for Uncle Finn. Red Vermin, for the color of his hair. Crazy Baboon, for the way he acted. Dead Irishman, for the way I would have liked him best.

❧

"Some men from the FBI came and searched our house last night," Sunny told me one afternoon in late December. We stood on the sidewalk in front of the school, where every day we exchanged final words before heading our separate ways. Talking with Sunny made me feel defiant, since I was directly disobeying Uncle Finn's order not to talk with her. I liked the feeling.

"How come the FBI searched your house?" I asked in alarm. All I knew about the FBI was that they were sent to arrest the guys who were so bad even the police were afraid of them.

But Sunny shrugged as though it had happened a thousand times before. "Papa said because Obaasan is Issei."

"So what if she is?"

"He said they think all the Issei are spies or something."

"They think Obaasan is a *spy*?" She was just a little old woman who couldn't see very well and who was by now half crippled with arthritis. She seldom even left her room, let alone the house. How could she possibly be a spy?

"Well, she's not a citizen, you know, so now all the Issei are being called enemy aliens. And if they're enemy aliens, the FBI's pretty sure they're spying for Japan."

"So what'd they do?"

"Just looked around and took some stuff."

"Like what?"

"Papa's camera, and that little radio we had on the kitchen counter. The one Mama and Mrs. Eddington listened to when they baked and stuff. Oh yeah, and a pair of binoculars."

"A pair of binoculars? Why'd they take those?"

"So Obaasan can't use them to spy with, I guess."

Didn't it seem as ridiculous to the FBI as it did to me? I was just a kid, but to me it was perfectly clear that someone like Obaasan would be as likely to spy for the Japanese as she would be to dance with the Rockettes at Radio City Music Hall.

"Lots of Issei men are being arrested, you know," Sunny continued. "They're being taken away, and nobody knows where they're taking them. You remember Mr. Nakamura, Ojisan Masuo's father?"

I nodded. I'd met him on numerous occasions when our families got together for holidays.

"He was arrested over the weekend. I forgot to tell you."

"They thought he was a spy?"

"Yeah."

"And you don't know where he is?"

Sunny shook her head. "Ojisan Masuo is furious. He punched a hole in the wall of the theater when his mother came down and told him his father'd been taken away."

I didn't blame him. I'd have punched two holes in the wall. Mr. Nakamura was a quiet old gentleman who was nicknamed "Smiles" because, even though he didn't say much, he was always smiling. Every Fourth of July he played Uncle Sam in the parade sponsored by the Japanese American community.

Sunny continued. "I overheard Ojisan Masuo telling Papa that the Issei men who are arrested might be sent back to Japan. Either that or shot."

"Shot!"

"That's what Ojisan said. Everybody's saying so."

I was shaken by these rumors of deportation and death. When Sunny and I parted that afternoon, I walked home in something of a daze. The war was in its infancy, only weeks old as yet, but already strange things were happening. The Japanese community was being broken up, little by little, the old folks sent away to who-knew-where and to who-knew-what-fate. What else might come of the government's paranoia? If Smiles Nakamura could be arrested for being a spy, what might become of Chichi and Haha and Sunny?

My fears took on form when Uncle Finn made the announcement that all the Japanese on the West Coast were probably going to be rounded up and sent inland to concentration camps.

"Is it true?" I asked Sunny the next time I saw her.

"Papa says the Issei may have to go, but that they could never do that to the Nisei and Sansei. He says we're citizens and we have rights. They can't just send us off to concentration camps when we haven't done anything wrong."

"Do you think they'll send Obaasan away?"

"Papa says if they try, he'll fight tooth and nail to keep her with us. She's just an old woman. She couldn't survive in a camp without us."

We were silent a moment. Then I asked, "Are you scared, Sunny?"

She narrowed her eyes and shook her head. "I'm not scared, Augie. I'm just sad. Everyone hates me now."

"No, they don't!"

"Yeah, they do." She looked up at the front doors of the school, to the stream of kids tumbling down the steps after the final bell. "All I ever wanted was to be like them," she said wistfully. "Now there's no more use trying."

"It doesn't matter," I said, maybe too quickly. "I'll always be your friend, no matter what anyone else thinks."

"You could have other friends," she replied, gazing sadly at my hakujin face. "They'd probably like you if they thought you weren't a Jap lover."

The word sounded especially harsh coming from Sunny. I winced but said, "Well, I *am* a Jap lover, Sunny, and I don't want any other friends."

Impulsively we threw our arms around each other. When we stepped back a moment later, we both had tears in our eyes.

"I wish you could just come home, Augie," Sunny said quietly. "Everyone misses you."

"I miss everyone."

"Do you think your uncle will ever say you can come back?"

"No, I don't think so."

"Mama said, 'Tell Musume my heart is broken,' and she said if your uncle ever changes his mind, she and Papa want you to please come home."

I nodded. It was all I could do. I turned then and walked back to Uncle Finn's house, which, I told myself, would never, never, *never* be my home.

THIRTEEN

Two things kept me from running away, back to the Yamagatas. One was Uncle Finn's threat to permanently banish me from the Schuler-O'Shaughnessy clan if I did. Not that I didn't often wish for that very thing. But when it comes right down to it, it's not easy to give up completely on the family you were born into.

I've since met some adults who made the break, but I should think it impossible for a child. In spite of everything, I couldn't rid myself entirely of the hope that one day my mother would tell me she loved me. I even occasionally fantasized about Uncle Finn becoming a nice person so that all of us could live together in that house and be happy.

Funny what a child dreams of in the secret corners of her heart. Or maybe it's not so much a matter of dreaming as it is of listening to the preternatural longing for what we were created to have. I was listening to that faint but very real longing to be loved by my own flesh and blood.

The second thing keeping me from running away was trouble at the Yamagatas. The Treasury Department had frozen the bank accounts of all Japanese Americans. That meant they could no longer withdraw money to live on. Shortly after that, the government shut down most Japanese businesses, including Chichi's grocery store. That meant

Sunny's family had no income at all. When Sunny told me what had happened, that Chichi was frantic with worry and that Haha had cried into her apron for hours, I didn't think I could go back and expect them to take care of me along with their other children and Obaasan too.

So I stayed at Uncle Finn's house and tried, however futilely, to find some joy in the coming of Christmas. The city was readying for the holidays in spite of the war. Stores advertised holiday sales, and Santa was scheduled to make his annual appearance at Bloomingdale's. Ribboned wreaths went up on doors, and except for during blackouts, lighted trees shone in living room windows. At school we made greeting cards and cut out paper snowflakes that we taped to the windowpanes, the closest we would get to a white Christmas in Los Angeles. Stella dragged a tree to Uncle Finn's house, saying her apartment was too small for it, and the cousins and I decorated it with homemade paper ornaments and strings of popcorn.

Shortly before the holidays arrived, the Treasury Department relented and began allowing both Issei and Nisei to withdraw one hundred dollars a month from their accounts for living expenses. Chichi filed an application with the Federal Reserve Bank to reopen the grocery store, and he was back in business a couple of days before Christmas. Chichi and Ojisan Hito were greatly relieved. Ojisan Masuo's theater had been shut down as well, but it too was allowed to reopen.

Christmas fell on a Thursday that year, and on Wednesday at noon school was let out for two weeks.

"How are we going to see each other during vacation?" Sunny asked as we walked down the front steps into the school yard.

"We can meet places, like at the park. Or I can even try to get down to the grocery store and see you there."

"I don't know, Augie," Sunny replied, hugging her books to herself. "What if someone sees us together and tells your uncle?"

"I don't care about him."

"He'll kill you."

"Let him try. I'll kill him first." A show of bravado, but it sounded good.

"Papa and Mama bought you some presents for Christmas. They're all wrapped up and under the tree. I want to get them to you somehow."

A sense of shame kept me quiet a moment. "I didn't get any presents for anyone, Sunny. Not even you," I admitted.

Sunny shrugged. "That's all right. It doesn't really seem like Christmas this year anyway."

She was right about that. For the past three years I'd spent the holidays with the Yamagatas. The extended family gathered together and exchanged gifts, ate unbelievable amounts of mochi, and sang Christmas carols while Ojisan Masuo wheezed out the tunes on his ancient accordion. And right on the heels of Christmas was New Year's with all its exotic food and the cries of *"Ake-mashite omede toh gozai masu!"* and the hours of games and laughter that followed. During those celebrations I'd discovered the joy of family that the rest of the world seemed long to have known. But there could be no joy this year, since I was cut off from the ones who'd given me the joy in the first place.

"Last night," Sunny continued, "Mama said to Papa, 'The worst thing about this war is that it's taken Musume from us.' "

We had reached the sidewalk where we always stood before heading in different directions. I leaned against the wire fence that surrounded the school yard, in no hurry to leave. "She said that?" I asked.

"Yeah."

"What'd Chichi say?"

"He said it wasn't the war that took you from us. He said it was your uncle Finn."

I ground my teeth together at the thought of the man. What Chichi said was true. I'd be celebrating the holidays with the people I loved if it weren't for Uncle Finn.

"I wish he was dead," I muttered.

"Who?"

"Uncle Finn."

Sunny nodded. "Yeah, me too."

"I wish the Japanese would bomb us and blow Uncle Finn to kingdom come and back. Just him, though, no one else."

My friend nodded again. "That'd be the best Christmas present we could get." She shifted her weight from one foot to the other and gazed down the street. Then she looked back at me and said, "Well, I guess I'll see ya."

"Will you tell Chichi and Haha and everyone I said merry Christmas?"

"All right."

"I promise I'll see you somehow."

"All right."

"And merry Christmas to you too, Sunny."

"Yeah, merry Christmas."

Our voices were decidedly cheerless, our faces empty of smiles. As we offered our wishes for a happy holiday, we sounded as forlorn as a couple of octogenarians contemplating their future. It's hard to remain a child when there's a war on.

❧

Stella was in the kitchen baking Christmas cookies with Riley and Rosey. "Want to join us?" she asked, sighing heavily. Something was wrong.

"All right," I said hesitantly.

"Wash your hands."

"All right."

"Rosey, quit eating the dough! You too, Riley. For heaven's sake, you're gonna make yourselves sick."

She thrust a baking sheet into the oven and slammed the door shut. Then she attacked a ball of dough on the counter with more force than necessary.

"What's the matter, Stella?" I asked.

She sighed again as she turned to look at me. "Jack's got his orders." In an instant her eyes glazed over with tears, and she turned back to the dough. "He's supposed to head out to boot camp day after tomorrow."

"The day after Christmas?"

"That's right." She picked up a cookie cutter and rammed it into the flattened dough. "Uncle Sam doesn't care one bit about when they take your husband away from you," she muttered. "Not only that, but he has to work late tonight. Can you imagine? What needs welding so bad that he has to work late on Christmas Eve?" Then, more loudly, "Rosey, I said no more dough! Now stop it, will you?" She slapped the child on the wrist, not hard, but hard enough to send Rosey into a fit of tears.

"Mama!" Rosey cried.

"She's not home, so you can scream all you want, but she won't hear you."

Suddenly baking Christmas cookies with Stella was the last thing I wanted to do. She was seldom in a bad mood, but when she was, it was best to steer clear. I just hoped this particular bad mood didn't last for the duration of the war. "Come on, Rosey," I said, holding out my hand to the child. "Let's go upstairs and play."

"Yeah, get her out of the kitchen," Stella agreed. "She's driving me nuts."

"Can I stay, Stella?" Riley asked.

"Only if you don't eat any more dough."

While Stella continued pounding the counter with the cookie cutter, Riley dipped his hand into the bowl on the table and came up with a cap of dough on his forefinger. He held it up a moment, making sure Rosey and I saw it, then popped the stolen goods into his mouth. He then gave us his I-got-away-with-it smile, a smirk that just begged to be slapped off.

I turned and dragged the teary-eyed Rosey from the kitchen, and together we climbed the stairs while she screamed those words that are among the first we learn in life: "Not fair! Not fair! Not fair!"

❦

It was Christmas Eve, and most kids were probably charged with the excitement of that special day, a day even now rolling in on the heels of this special night. Most kids were probably eyeing the gaily wrapped packages under the tree and wondering what was inside. Most, I supposed, were enjoying visits from grandparents, aunts, uncles, cousins. Most, no doubt, were snatching plenty of samples from a cornucopia of candy and baked goods. On this night of all nights, sleep would be long in coming for the children all nestled snug in their beds.

But it wasn't that way in the O'Shaughnessy house, where a heaviness hung in the air, drifting like fog from room to room so that there was nowhere to go to escape it. It was so thick that it seemed to warp everything, as though we were moving about behind a thick piece of distorted glass. Even the Christmas music on the radio seemed weighed down and garbled, played at the wrong speed.

The family's attempts at tradition came across as a mockery of the season. The haphazardly decorated tree, gifts wrapped in last week's funny papers, a row of Uncle Finn's old socks tacked to the wall, a plate of burnt cookies on the kitchen table—all of these only heightened the sense of gloom spilling over into all the places where joy was supposed to be.

Jack arrived, and Stella fought with him, accusing him of abandoning her for the army. Uncle Finn, who never needed an excuse to yell but grabbed at any chance he could find, entered into the argument on Jack's side. Aunt Lucy tried to squelch the bickering but ended up screaming louder than anyone. I sat on the stairs and watched the show like a patron at a play, though every once in a while Uncle Finn dragged me into a scene by cursing the Japs and pointing a finger at me.

At some point my cousin Maureen, now a pretty young woman of eighteen, came clumping down the stairs in high heels and a tight dress, smelling powerfully of toilet water. At the bottom of the stairs she pulled her jacket and hat from the closet and put them on. She then stood watching her family for a short time, long enough to blink once or twice. She appeared to want to say something but knew she wouldn't be able to squeeze a word in edgewise. Finally she sighed, pulled a compact from her purse, powdered her nose, then snapped the compact shut.

"I'm going out," she told me, speaking loudly enough to be heard over the brawl. "I don't know when I'll be back." She glanced toward the others again, then back at me. "Never, if I'm lucky."

She turned and let herself out, slamming the door behind her. No one paid any attention. Upstairs, Rosey began to wail while Rusty and Riley shouted and laughed. The boys seemed to be having fun, probably at Rosey's expense.

I reached for the banister and pulled myself up from the stairs. I didn't know where I was going, but I wanted to move away from where I was. Surely there had to be some comfort somewhere in this madhouse. In the kitchen I discovered Mother facedown at the table, her head resting on her arms. She was dressed, as she so often was, in her worn cotton robe and slippers. At first I thought she might be crying, but she was too still. Perhaps she had already cried herself to sleep.

Tentatively I laid a hand on her shoulder. I wanted to wake her, though I had no idea what it was I wanted to say. I'm not sure we needed to say anything. If she could just wake up and see that I was there, it might clear away some of the fog.

"Mama?"

She moaned. I shook her shoulder more firmly. "Mama?"

She lifted her head slowly then, snorting quietly as she pulled herself up from sleep. For a moment she looked straight ahead, as though trying to focus or trying to decide where she was. Her skin was red and blotchy, her hair pressed flat against her forehead. Everything in her profile sagged, from the bag beneath her eye to the skin beneath her jaw.

"Mama?" I said again.

Hesitantly she turned toward me. She blinked and stared at me openmouthed, her breath sour with alcohol. She narrowed her glassy eyes, and then, as though she had finally met consciousness, she smiled. She was looking at me, and she was smiling.

"Mama!" I felt what I scarcely recognized as a stirring of joy.

But it just as quickly disappeared when she touched my face and said, "Lenny? Oh, Lenny, my baby boy, you've come home."

My last bit of hope that I might win my mother's love was irreparably shattered on the night before Christmas.

❧

"Musume!" Chichi answered my knock on the door, and I lunged at him, throwing my arms around his waist.

"I couldn't stay away anymore, Chichi," I cried, my tears making a moist spot on the belly of his shirt.

"Of course you couldn't. Of course," he said soothingly. "Come in and let's shut the door. It's chilly outside. Where is your jacket? And where are your shoes!" I hadn't even stopped to put them on, I'd left Uncle Finn's house in such a hurry.

Chichi moved with me into the hallway and shut the door. In another moment Haha was with us.

"Musume!" she said joyfully, opening her arms to me. I kept one arm around Chichi's waist—I couldn't bear to let him go—but offered my other one to Haha. The three of us stood there in the hallway for a long moment, clutched in a circular hug.

Then they began to speak in quiet tones over my head. "She can stay here with us," Chichi said, "until things settle down."

"But, Toshio," Haha whispered, "her uncle will only come and take her again."

I looked up at Chichi pleadingly. "Don't let him take me, Chichi! I don't want to go back there—not ever!"

He laid his hand on my head reassuringly. "Don't worry, Musume," he said. "You don't have to go back. You belong here with us."

"But, Toshio—"

"Don't worry, Suma. Everything will be all right."

"Augie!" Sunny's scream reached us from the top of the stairs, and in the next moment she was tripping all over herself running down to meet me. Jimmy followed, barking excitedly and dancing a little jig at our feet as we threw our arms around each other. "Augie, what are you doing here!"

I wiped at my dripping nose with the back of my hand. "I can't stay at Uncle Finn's anymore, Sunny, I just can't! I wanted to come and be with you."

"I'm so glad you came, Augie! It wouldn't be the same without you. Now we can have Christmas just like always."

Even Sam and George appeared then, standing at the top of the stairs in their pajamas and rubbing the sleep from their eyes. "What's happening?" Sam asked eagerly. "Is Santa Claus here?"

"Better than that," Chichi replied with a laugh. "Your sister Musume has come home."

❧

I was home, and everything was all turned around right again, and the sadness I'd felt at Uncle Finn's house was gone like a fever suddenly broken. Haha took Sunny and me upstairs to bed, read *The Night Before Christmas* to us twice, then kissed our noses—even Jimmy's, when we insisted—and told us to have sweet dreams of sugar plums and mochi.

After Haha turned out the lights, Sunny and I whispered and giggled, kissed Jimmy about a hundred times, then curled up to sleep with our arms thrown about each other. I slept untroubled for the first time since Pearl Harbor.

As soon as she left us Haha called Aunt Lucy to tell her where I was. "Well, let her stay," Aunt Lucy said. "She's been moping around the house for weeks like an orphan slave on an auction block. The poor kid'll be happier there with you."

Haha told me about the conversation the next morning, adding, "Your aunt promised she'd handle your uncle Finn. She also gave me Stella's number in case we need anything. So don't worry about a thing, Musume. Just enjoy the day."

We sat in the living room listening to Christmas music on the radio. We were full from a large breakfast and satisfied from the thrill of opening gifts. Scraps of wrapping paper and tangled bits of ribbon lay scattered about the floor. Sam and George played by the tree with their new toys. Obaasan sat in one of the wing chairs, her tiny feet propped up on the matching footstool. Her head bobbed intermittently as she nodded off to sleep. Sunny was curled up with Haha on the couch. I sat on the floor with my head against Chichi's knee.

"Uncle Finn won't come and try to take me away again, will he, Chichi?" I asked. The memory of him carrying me sacklike under his arm made me shiver.

"I don't think so, Musume," Chichi said quietly. "If he does, we won't remain quiet about it this time."

I wrapped my arms around his leg and squeezed. He responded by patting my cheek. "I want to stay with you forever," I said. "I hate Uncle Finn, and I'm never going back."

Haha looked at me sadly from across the room. "You mustn't hate, Musume. Especially your own family."

"Well, *he* hates *me*. They all do. Even my mother."

"Oh no, Musume," Haha countered. "I'm sure they don't. I'm sure they love you. They just don't know how to show it."

"I hate them too, Mama," Sunny said in my defense. "They're not nice people."

I shook my head, rubbing my hair into Chichi's leg. He patted my cheek again. "Everything is in confusion right now because of the war," he said. "But things will settle down when the hakujin begin to realize that we Nisei aren't the enemy. Then we can go back to the way things were before. And you, Musume, can spend the afternoons and weekends with us again."

"But I want to be here all the time," I stated firmly. "I don't want to go back to Uncle Finn's ever again." It was no use listening to my longing for their love anymore. I wasn't going to get it.

"But, Musume," Haha said, "I'm sure they want to be with you. You're their little girl. We wish you could be with us all the time, but it wouldn't be right to take you away completely from your own family."

I frowned and replied defiantly, "But *you're* my family."

Everyone was quiet for a moment, except for Sam and George, who made engine noises as they pushed their toy trucks across the rug. Then Chichi remarked, "Well, like we said, you can stay here with us until things settle down. Don't worry, Musume. Everything will work itself out."

Obaasan stirred and opened her eyes for a moment. She seemed simply to want to know that we were all still there, because once she had looked about the room and accounted for everyone, she shut her eyes and went back to sleep.

"O Holy Night" played softly on the radio, and it sounded like a lullaby that called the rest of us not to sleep, but to peace. Haha laid her hand across her stomach and patted it contentedly. And then I remembered.

"Haha," I asked, "do you want a boy or a girl?" I wasn't yet reconciled to the thought of her having another child, but I thought I should ask anyway.

Haha smiled sweetly. She ran her palm over Sunny's smooth hair while her daughter nestled against her shoulder. "It doesn't matter," she answered. "Either one would be fine." But then, as though she could read my thoughts, she added, "If it's a boy, it'll be our third son, and if it's a girl, it'll be our third daughter. You'll always be our special daughter, Musume."

My heart expanded with joy as she spoke. She hadn't created this child to take my place!

We smiled at each other across the room, and with that all was once again well in my world.

FOURTEEN

I tried to pick up where I'd left off with the Yamagatas, to go on living as part of a family that had hopes and plans for the future. To think that life could be what it was before Pearl Harbor was indulging in a game of make-believe, but I was willing to play, and I think for a time the others were too.

The Japanese didn't make it easy, though. As they continued to rack up victories in the Pacific, the Yamagatas and I went on pushing against the uncertainties brought on by the war, moving in and out of our days amid the rumors of evacuation and the fear of the end of the world as we knew it.

The Japanese, after capturing Guam and Hong Kong in December, took hold of Manila in January, toppled Singapore in February, and were working hard to seize all of the Philippines as quickly as possible. Sometimes I wondered what was happening to my brother Lenny, but thoughts of him made only fleeting passes through my mind, never staying for long. I was too busy taking note of what the Americans were doing to the Japanese in California to have much time to think about what the Japanese might be doing to the Americans in the Pacific.

Hatred for the Nisei and Issei had heated up among the hakujin until it boiled over into physical beatings and death. Thirty-six cases were reported of gangs attacking Japanese Americans all up and down the West Coast, and seven Nisei were killed. We mourned their deaths, the Yamagatas and I, and Chichi called the dead men martyrs.

The lesser tragedies—but tragedies, nevertheless—were the firing of Issei from jobs they'd held all their lives, the pillaging and sometimes near destruction of Japanese businesses, the shunning of a people who were Americans at heart but Japanese of face.

We couldn't listen to the radio without hearing, "You're a Sap, Mr. Jap," and "Good-bye, Mama, I'm Off to Yokohama." War-bond posters and political cartoons portrayed the Japanese as bespectacled, bucktoothed, silly-grinning morons that Uncle Sam was just aching to wipe out. Escape was impossible even at the movies, where Bugs Bunny hurled cries of "Slant eyes!" and "Monkey face!" at the despised soldiers descending from the skies in Japanese warplanes. These Japanese caricatures were outsmarted and single-handedly obliterated by the Bugs himself.

One day Sunny showed me an article in *Life* magazine titled "How to Tell Japs From the Chinese." The first page of the article included two large mug shots, one of a Chinaman, a public servant named Ong Wen-hao, the other of General Hideki Tojo, the Premier of Japan. White lines dissected the faces like lab specimens, pointing out the differences between the features. Mr. Ong's eyes had a "more frequent epicanthic fold," Premier Tojo's eyes a "less frequent epicanthic fold." Ong's cheeks were "never rosy," Tojo's cheeks "sometimes rosy." The humble servant's chin produced only a "scant beard," while the premier's chin sprouted a "heavy beard."

"*Life* here adduces," the text read, "a rule of thumb from the anthropometric conformations that distinguish friendly Chinese from enemy alien Japs."

I studied the two photos, trying to make sense of it all. To me, the one face looked more or less like the other, the differences seemed minimal and insignificant. But I could just imagine someone like Uncle Finn trying to memorize the photos in case he should happen upon an Asian face in the street. Chinese or Japanese? Friend or foe?

The arrow pointing to the center of the Japanese face was feathered with the words "Flatter nose." Sunny sighed heavily when she read the description. "I always knew my nose would make a problem.

And now it's happened. Obaasan was right; the hakujin hate us. They always have."

"That's not true, Sunny," I assured her. "They're just mad right now because of Pearl Harbor." But my excuse sounded lame, and we both knew it.

"Maybe Obaasan was right about Japan too," she went on. "Maybe it would have been better if we'd all lived in Japan."

I couldn't argue with that, but I tried to. "If you lived in Japan," I said, "I never would have met you."

Sunny looked over at me sadly. We lay on our stomachs across her bed, Jimmy curled up between us, the magazine propped up on the pillows. "But what if they send us away like they say they're going to do? I may never see you again anyway."

"Don't say that, Sunny," I cried. "They can't send you away! Chichi said so!"

Sunny shook her head slowly. "I don't know, Augie," she replied. "No one wants us around anymore. They think we'll help the Japanese win the war."

Stories of sabotage on the part of Japanese Americans were circulating furiously about the West Coast, kicking up trouble for the Issei and Nisei that lay in the path of the rumors. One story had it that Nisei fishermen on Terminal Island, just off the coast of Los Angeles, had Japanese naval uniforms hidden in their boats, cleaned and pressed and ready to be donned the moment the invasion began. These fishermen, most of whom had never set foot in Japan and many of whom spoke scarcely a word of Japanese, were allegedly just hankering to cast themselves on the side of the enemy and overthrow the country that had nurtured them from birth.

Rumor also lifted an incriminating finger toward Nisei farmers. Supposedly these farmers were already aiding the enemy by creating guideposts from their crops to direct Japanese bombers to various targets. In one instance, a patch of tomato plants had purportedly been covered with white cloth to form an arrow pointing toward an aircraft plant in Southern California. In fact, the plants had been capped with paper to protect them against frost, and the field itself happened to come to a point. That the point was aimed toward an aircraft plant was only coincidence.

As we pondered the article in *Life* magazine, I had a thought.

"Sunny, let's write a letter to the President and tell him the Nisei want to *help* America, not fight against it. Since President Roosevelt's way out there in Washington, he probably doesn't know what's going on here in California. Maybe he just needs someone to tell him the truth. We could get a whole bunch of Issei and Nisei to sign it—you know, make it a regular petition. . . ."

Before I could finish, Sunny was shaking her head. "He's hakujin, Augie," she said, "and he's just like all the others. None of them trust us anymore. You know what DeNitwitt said."

DeNitwitt was General John DeWitt, the one who, as soon as war broke out, had us all braced for the death and destruction that was to come from the skies at any moment. Sunny and I knew he was a bigwig in the army, but we didn't exactly understand what his job was. Haha told us he was responsible for the safety of the people on the West Coast, but Chichi scoffed at Haha's explanation and said the man was only making matters worse by stirring up all sorts of unwarranted fears. "The man's a fool," Chichi growled. He grumbled about DeWitt so much that Sunny and I eventually came up with the nickname.

Early in January after the Japanese took Manila, DeWitt had said, "I have little confidence that the Japanese enemy aliens are loyal. I have no confidence in the loyalty of the Nisei whatsoever." That statement saw the beginning of a change in Chichi. I think it was the first time he really felt betrayed, though he'd been encountering anti-Japanese sentiment ever since the seventh of December. But this time it was different, as though he finally understood what it all meant for him and for his family. When he read DeWitt's words aloud to us from the *Los Angeles Times*, an odd look came over his face, one almost of surprised pain, as though he'd been seized with the first twinge of a fatal heart attack. His eyes said that something inside of him had been terribly wounded; his face grew unnaturally pale. He laid the paper down on his lap and held one clenched fist to his chest.

"Toshio?" Haha asked, alarmed.

Slowly Chichi looked up at her. "I'm all right, Suma," he said quietly. "I'm just tired. I'm going to go upstairs and lie down for a while."

As he climbed the stairs he appeared suddenly bent over and feeble, like an old man. "Mama," Sunny asked in a whisper, "is Papa all right?"

Haha watched her husband until he had disappeared. Then she turned to us and said, "Yes, I'm sure he'll be all right." But she didn't sound as though he'd be all right at all.

Many statements against the Japanese Americans were to follow DeWitt's, coming from the mouths and pens of those hakujin who feared the Nisei. Each rabid comment was one more blow to Chichi.

"It would be extremely foolish to doubt the continued existence of enemy agents among the large alien Japanese population," wrote Damon Runyon, a Hearst newspaper columnist.

"Ninety percent or more of American-born Japanese are primarily loyal to Japan," warned John Hughes, a Los Angeles radio commentator, though he didn't explain how he arrived at this mathematical conclusion.

"I am for immediate removal of every Japanese on the West Coast. . . . Herd 'em up, pack 'em off, and give 'em the inside room in the Badlands. Let 'em be pinched, hurt, hungry, and dead up against it. . . . Personally, I hate the Japanese. And that goes for all of them," journalist Henry McLemore angrily proclaimed.

And the mayor of Los Angeles, Fletcher Bowron—for whom, ironically, Chichi had voted—made radio broadcasts declaring that all the Japanese "must go."

Sunny was right. And apparently Obaasan had been right all along. Men like these hated Chichi and Haha and Obaasan and Sunny—and me—and they weren't afraid to say so. With hate like that goading them on, anything could happen. And with every word they uttered, Chichi became more and more sad and distant.

Still I persisted in trying to believe what I wanted to believe. "But Chichi said at the start of the war that you're citizens and you have rights, same as anyone else," I argued, closing the *Life* magazine and tossing it aside. "You can't be arrested and taken away if you haven't done anything wrong."

"Sure we can," Sunny countered. "They've already taken all the Issei men, haven't they? And those guys didn't do anything wrong. If they can take them, they can take the rest of us too."

I didn't want to hear it. I didn't want to dwell on the possibility. Because if the Japanese Americans *were* rounded up and sent off to the "inside room in the Badlands," then what would become of me?

❧

Whenever the phone rang at the Yamagatas' house, I felt a small but persistent hope that it might be my mother calling. I was content where I was with Haha and Chichi to care for me, and yet I couldn't rid myself of the wish that just once she would call and tell me she missed me, or even just ask if I was all right. I would have liked to tell her my fears. I wanted to tell her that the people who loved me might be taken away, so that she could in turn tell me not to worry because *she* loved me too and she would always be there for me. But she never called.

Shortly after I returned to the Yamagatas, Aunt Lucy called to tell me that Uncle Finn had cleared the attic of all my things—clothes, books, a doll, and a stuffed bear from Chichi and Haha—and had burned them in the ash can out back. He called me a traitor while squirting oil on the flames to make the fire burn hotter. He told Aunt Lucy that I'd better never try to crawl back to the America-loving O'Shaughnessy household, since I'd defiled myself by taking up sides with the enemy. I cried when I learned that Uncle Finn had burned my things, but I didn't care at all that he never wanted to see me again.

Stella called frequently just to talk with me. She'd given up being a beautician for the duration and was working swing shift at a defense factory building airplanes. "If Jack's gonna fly 'em, I'm gonna build 'em," she said. She wanted to be right there at the factory to make sure the planes were put together right. She kept busy, but she was lonely without Jack. Whenever she called she always started out by asking how I was, but invariably turned the conversation toward her absent husband.

She said she sent him a Saint Christopher medal to keep him safe, but even so she still had nightmares of his dying in a fiery crash. Apparently Jack was having the time of his life, though, soaring through the skies over Texas where he was stationed for basic training. Stella read his letters aloud over the phone, and he always remembered me and said when he got home from the war he'd make good on his promise to take me flying. Stella said he'd just better come home from the war and make good on his promise to have children, or she would kill him with her own bare hands.

"I'll try to see you sometime, Augie," Stella promised often. "It's not as easy to get around as it used to be, ever since I gave the car's tires away to the rubber drive. But don't worry, kiddo, we'll take the streetcar, and I'll take you out for ice cream or something."

I asked Stella once if she thought my mother missed me, and my question was followed by such a long stretch of silence I began to think we'd been cut off. Finally, not unkindly, Stella said the only thing Mags Schuler seemed to be missing was her marbles. "I hate to speak bad of your mother," my cousin apologized, "but you'd be best just to forget about her. You've got a family with those Japanese people. Just be happy where you are."

I told her I was happy but added, "There's talk about them being sent away. If they are, what will I do?"

"I don't know, sweetie," she said, "but don't spend too much time worrying about it. Even Uncle Sam couldn't figure out a way to round up thousands of people and move 'em into camps. It just wouldn't be possible."

I hoped—oh, how I hoped—that Stella was right.

❧

Sunny no longer pinched her nose before falling asleep, and I couldn't blame her. It wasn't hard to understand why she'd given up trying to look white. As for me, I kept on pressing, though I did it quietly without telling Sunny I was doing it. I knew my nose wasn't getting any flatter, but it was one more way that I hoped against hope.

One night, both of us near sleep with Jimmy a warm lump between us, we exchanged a final thought before falling off into our dreams. Sunny's drowsy words reached me right on the edge of consciousness and pulled me back into the waking world for a moment.

"I hate being called a Jap," she said.

I rolled over toward the sound of her voice. "Me too," I agreed. And then we slept.

FIFTEEN

Sunny wanted to try to find God, to talk with him about the war. She thought maybe if she talked with him face-to-face, he'd agree to get everyone to stop fighting. Or at the very least, maybe he could see to it that the Japanese Americans were allowed to stay in their homes and not be moved to internment camps.

Neither of us knew very much about God. There were times, though, when Sunny grew pensive, and I knew otherworldly thoughts were churning around in her mind. Then she'd start speculating aloud about this superior being, about what he must look like and what he must act like and what in the world he did all day in heaven while we went about our business down here on earth.

Most often it was being in Hollenbeck Park that triggered her thoughts about the Almighty, since it was there she'd been so enthralled by the Salvation Army band. I remember one conversation we had about God while sitting on the very bench where we'd met a couple of years earlier.

"You *do* believe in him, don't you, Augie?" she asked wistfully, almost pleadingly, as though my opinion about the existence of God carried great weight with her.

I shrugged. "Sure," I confessed. "Doesn't everyone?" After all, didn't we sometimes sing hymns during school assemblies and listen to prayers broadcast over the public address system? And didn't President Roosevelt refer at times to almighty God or Divine Providence in those fireside chats that Chichi and Haha were always listening to on the radio? And what about that new song that Kate Smith was belting out every time we turned around these days, "God Bless America"? No, if you were alive and conscious in America, you believed in God the same as you believed in our rights of life, liberty and the pursuit of happiness.

"I don't know," Sunny countered hesitantly. "I mean, Mama and Papa never go to church."

"Naw, we don't go either. There's a cross on the wall at Uncle Finn's house, though. One of those kinds that has Jesus still hanging on it. We used to be Catholic, I guess."

"We never used to be anything."

I shrugged again, not sure that it mattered.

"Do you think God watches us and sees everything we do?" Sunny asked.

I pictured God kicked back in a movie theater, entertained by our lives playing out on the big screen. "Yeah, I guess so."

"And that way he decides whether we get to go to heaven or if we go to—you know." She pointed down toward the ground with her thumb.

"Yeah, I guess so," I said again. I didn't much like to think about that part of it all.

"Remember the band that played here in the park that day and sang the songs about God?"

"Sure. I remember them."

"I wish they'd come back. Do you think they'll come back?"

"Sure they will, someday," I said, though we never did see them again.

After Pearl Harbor Sunny didn't mention God for probably a couple of months, though I knew she was still thinking about him when she got that far-off look on her face. I thought she was probably mad at him for what had happened, but when she brought him up again, what she wanted was to find him and talk to him about the war.

"But he's invisible," I argued. "I don't think you can just sit down and talk to him about something."

"Yeah, that's what I thought too," Sunny said, "but looky here." She reached into the pocket of her skirt and pulled out a battered scrap of paper. "I found it on the street a couple days ago. Look what it says."

I took the piece of paper and looked it over. It was small, about the size of an index card, and ragged on one side, as though it had been torn off of something. On the front in big letters were the words, "What will you say to God when you see him face-to-face?" On the back was the address of a gospel mission along with what looked like Bible verses, though I wasn't well acquainted with the Bible. I handed the paper back to Sunny, not knowing what to say.

"See." Sunny tapped at it with the tip of her finger. "It says right here you can see God, even talk to him."

"But . . ." I paused, rubbing my chin with my knuckles. I was skeptical. I'd never heard of anyone talking to God face-to-face, like he was a rich uncle you could go visit when you didn't have two nickels to rub together. But like I said, I didn't know much about God, so if those who did know something about religion claimed you could sit right down and have a chat with the Creator, I figured it was a possibility worth considering. So I asked Sunny, "Well, where do you think he lives?"

Sunny shrugged. "That's what we gotta figure out."

Obaasan, we knew, thought God lived in Japan, because she believed the emperor was God. Sunny and I considered this idea but ended up tossing it out because Chichi said the emperor was a fool. God couldn't be God and a fool at the same time.

When we asked Chichi where God lived, he said we'd have to look for him within ourselves. His answer left us puzzled. Did he mean that God was camped out somewhere between our liver and spleen, or that he was curled up like a baby in our bellies? Haha sometimes mentioned that the baby inside of her had moved or kicked or even hiccoughed. Surely if something like God was inside of Sunny and me, we'd *know* about it.

I sought out Stella then and asked her where she thought God lived. She said she didn't know but that if I ever found out I should be sure to tell her; she had a few things to say to him herself.

Finally we approached Grace Ann Murphy at school during recess. Her father was a Methodist minister, and if anyone knew where God lived, we figured Grace Ann would.

"In heaven," she responded perfunctorily when we cornered her in the school yard. "You know, up there." She pointed one skinny finger up toward the sky. Sunny and I followed with our eyes, took in the clouds, then lowered our gaze to Grace Ann's face.

She continued. "And everywhere." She then opened her hands and stretched out her arms like a ballerina about to dip into a grand plié. "God lives everywhere."

Sunny frowned. "Well, which is it?"

"Which is what?"

"Does he live in heaven or does he live everywhere?"

"Both, of course."

Sunny and I exchanged a glance. We silently told each other that maybe Grace Ann Murphy wouldn't be the fount of wisdom we had hoped for.

"Well," Sunny persisted, "wherever he is, can we talk to him?"

The pastor's daughter lifted her eyebrows in exaggerated surprise. "Of course! *Any*body can talk to him." The implication was that even *we* could.

"But," I pressed, "can we talk to him *face*-to-*face*?"

Grace Ann thought a moment. "I had a great-aunt once who said she saw Jesus standing by her bed the night her appendix burst."

"Did he say anything?" Sunny asked eagerly.

"Yeah. He said he was there to take her to heaven."

"So what happened?"

"She said she hadn't finished her spring cleaning yet and she wasn't about to leave behind a dirty house."

"Yeah? So what'd he say then?"

"He said all right, he'd come back again in a couple of weeks."

"And did he?"

"Yup. First day of summer, she'd just finished hanging up all the clean curtains when she fell over dead."

Sunny and I looked at each other in amazement. Then turning back to Grace Ann, Sunny said, "So God gave your aunt what she wanted."

"Yeah."

"Do you think God would do something for me if I asked him, the way he did for your aunt?"

Grace Ann narrowed her eyes. "My dad says you can't just ask him for any old stupid thing. It has to be something important, you know."

"Oh, this is important," Sunny assured her.

What could be more important than stopping the war? Surely if that old lady could get a few more weeks to clean her house, God would grant our unselfish request for peace in the world.

"Then I guess you can ask him," Grace Ann said warily.

"But where do we go to ask him?"

At the question, Grace Ann wrinkled her nose and scrunched up her face so tightly I thought she might suddenly be in pain. She opened her mouth and seemed just about to say something when the bell rang to signal the end of recess. She looked at the school building, looked back to us, then swiftly made her escape without a word of farewell.

"Well, she wasn't much help, was she?" Sunny sighed.

"At least we know some people get to talk to God face-to-face," I offered. "Least her great-aunt did."

"But there must be a way to do it without having your appendix burst. I mean, there must be a place to go and talk to him the way people go talk to the pope."

For several nights afterward, as we lay in bed talking in the dark, Sunny and I pondered the mystery of God's whereabouts. At length, Sunny came up with a theory.

"I think," she mused, "that God must live in a place like the Emerald City. And I think he must be something like the Wizard of Oz."

"How do you mean?" I asked.

"Well, lots of people say you can't see God, just the same way that funny guy at the Emerald City told Dorothy and the others they couldn't see the Wizard."

I remembered the scene well. We'd seen the movie a dozen times when it was showing at Ojisan Masuo's theater. By the end of the movie's run, Sunny and I practically had the whole thing memorized.

"We wanna see the Wizard," Dorothy requested at the door to the Emerald City.

"The Wizard!" cried the man who answered her knock, his mustachioed face framed by the peephole. "But nobody can see the Great Oz! Nobody's ever seen the Great Oz! Even *I've* never seen him."

"Then how do you know there is one?" Dorothy asked.

The man sputtered a few moments before spitting out his dismissal. "Oh, you're wasting my time!"

I said, "Yeah, I remember. So you mean, you think people say you can't see him, but you really can if you can just get into the Emerald City?"

Sunny nodded. "No one saw the Wizard, but they knew he was there, and he *was* there. And remember how when Dorothy and the other guys saw him—I mean, *really* saw him when Toto pulled back the curtain and there was the Wizard talking into the microphone and pulling all those levers to make the fire work and to make the thunder sounds?"

"Yeah?"

"Well, that's when he gave them all the things they asked for. A heart for the Tin Man, a brain for the Scarecrow—you know, all those things. When they talked to him face-to-face, he was really nice and gave them what they wanted."

I thought a moment. "But still, how do we find the Emerald City?"

"We don't really find the Emerald City, but, I mean, God must live someplace really beautiful like that."

As I thought of the beautiful places I knew in Los Angeles—which weren't many, my experience being limited—I came to realize that God probably lived in a church, and the first church that came to mind was Saint Stephen's Catholic Church right there in Boyle Heights. I'd passed it a few times, and though I hadn't been inside, it looked large and beautiful from the outside.

When I mentioned it to Sunny, she said, "Hey, I bet you're right! And if he doesn't live there, maybe they can tell us where he does live."

"Sure. Why didn't we think of that before? Let's go tomorrow after school. If we're lucky, that'll be where he lives. And if we're really lucky, he'll be home."

❧

Neither of us had been inside a church before and didn't quite know what to expect. When we entered the sanctuary of Saint Stephen's, we were completely awed. The ceiling in the sanctuary went way, way up, so that I had to crane my neck to see how high it reached. I felt as though I was looking right up at the sky, the center chandelier hung so far overhead.

On either side of this cavernous room were enormous stained-glass windows from which the colors flowed and seemed to sparkle all around us. Lining the walls were a variety of statues on pedestals, men and women in flowing robes with bare stone feet. Sunny whispered that they must be the saints, and I wondered which one was Christopher, as he was the saint guarding Jack while he flew.

In one dark corner a whole garden of white candles flickered, casting light and shadows on the wall. I saw someone, a woman, kneel while lighting one of these candles, and I wondered why she would do that and what it meant.

At the front of the church, behind the altar, was a tall wooden crucifix bearing the image of Christ, a much larger version of the one that hung in Uncle Finn's living room. But this one, unlike Uncle Finn's, made me feel a reverence and a certain sorrow for the man who hung there nailed to the wood for centuries on end.

I looked about breathlessly, nodding my head in agreement when Sunny whispered, "He's *gotta* live here, Augie."

"This is the place all right," I whispered back.

"How do we find out for sure?"

"We'll have to ask somebody."

"Who?"

"I don't know."

"Should we ask one of them?" Sunny nodded toward the few scattered people kneeling among the pews.

I thought for a moment, then decided, "They might get mad if we bother them."

"Then what should we do?"

"Let's wait until someone gets up and heads for the door. Then we can stop and ask him."

"Okay."

We slipped into a pew and sat quietly. Only our eyes moved to take in the scene around us. "Do you think we should kneel like everyone else?" Sunny whispered.

Shrugging, I said, "I guess so. Yeah, we might get in trouble if we don't. Look, do you think this thing comes down?" I tugged at the kneeler, which opened with a crash loud enough to give the impression of the church imploding upon itself.

"Leaping lizards, Augie!"

"I couldn't help it!"

"Get down!"

We huddled on the floor between the pew and the kneeler, waiting to be pounced upon by a dozen angry men and women. After several moments passed and nothing untoward happened, we raised our heads far enough to peer over the rim of the pew in front of us. If anyone had turned to look our way, they were back to their prayers now.

Sunny and I looked at each other, shrugged, then climbed up on the kneeler and tried to look reverential, with our hands folded and heads bowed in imitation of the others.

Without lifting her head, Sunny whispered, "I think I'm going to throw up."

I frowned. "Try to wait until after we see God, all right?"

She nodded and pressed her lips together.

We held our reverent posture for a good three or four minutes, until Sunny nudged me in the ribs and nodded toward a wooden box about the size of a small closet along one wall. "Someone just came out of there and then someone else went in. Did you see?" I hadn't and shook my head in answer. "Do you think you have to go in there to talk to God?"

"Could be," I replied. "Let's see what happens when the next person comes out."

"It was the lady sitting up there with the yellow hat. Listen, when she comes out, ask her if she was talking to God."

I suddenly felt shy. "You ask her."

"Come on, Augie. You're better at talking than me."

"No, I'm not."

"Yes, you are. You're not scared of anybody. Shhh, here she comes. Ask her, Augie, pu-leeze!"

"Oh, all right. But come with me."

We walked along the kneeler to the side aisle and intercepted the woman on her way out of the church. She was a pleasant-looking young woman, and when she saw us she smiled.

"Excuse me," I whispered.

"Yes?"

"We'd like to know, did you just talk to God in there?" I pointed with one outstretched finger toward the protruding closet. The woman followed with her eyes and then looked back at me. Her face registered puzzlement, but she continued to smile.

"Well, I guess you could say that, yes."

This was the place! We'd found where God lived on our first try!

Sunny and I smiled at each other with glee. "Thanks, lady!" I cried, then pushed Sunny up the aisle toward the little room so we could be the next inside.

When a man came out, settling a fedora on his head, Sunny and I pushed past him and rushed into the room. Closing the door behind us, we found ourselves in a small dark space. Instinctively we grabbed each other's hand in fear and tried to settle ourselves on the narrow seat. I was just beginning to wonder what was going to happen next when a wooden shutter in the wall slid back abruptly and the silhouette of a head and shoulders appeared on the other side of a grille.

If this was God, I wasn't terribly impressed. I expected light and glory and maybe even music, not something I could scarcely see.

Sunny squeezed my hand to encourage me to speak, but I didn't know what to say. Finally the silhouette spoke. "Is someone there?"

She squeezed again, harder. "Yeah," I croaked. It was little more than a whisper.

"Please begin."

Begin doing what? I was at a complete loss until Sunny cupped my ear with her free hand and whispered, "Ask him if he's God."

I took a deep breath and forced out the words. "Are you—I mean, are you God?"

The silhouette bent closer to the grille. "Excuse me?"

"Are you God?" I repeated, taken aback by the thought that God might be hard of hearing.

The shadow shifted away again. We heard a throat being cleared. "How old are you?"

What difference did that make, I wondered, and why was he answering my question with a question, and anyway, if he was God didn't he already *know* how old I was?

"Eleven," I sniffed suspiciously.

"Then you're old enough to know I'm not God," the voice snapped.

"Oh!" He was the gatekeeper then, just like the funny guy with the big mustache who answered the door at the Emerald City.

"This isn't a place for games," he continued, his voice quiet but tense. "I suggest you run along. Other people want to make their confessions."

I didn't know what a confession was, but I wasn't going to let this guy dismiss us so easily. "I'm not playing a game!" I protested. "I came here because I thought maybe God lives here. Does he?"

"Does God live here?" he repeated.

"Yeah," I said. "I'd like to know."

"Of course he lives here, but——"

"Well, can we see him, please? It's really important. We promise we won't take too long, only a minute or two."

"We? How many of you are in there?"

"Two. Sunny and me."

The silhouette bent closer to the grille and hissed at us. "Listen, girls, you should know better than this. Desecrating a sacred place such as this confessional is a serious sin." The shadow sighed audibly. "Didn't you girls take catechism classes?"

Sunny and I looked at each other through the darkness of the cubicle. "They don't have that at our school," I explained.

"Are you Catholic?"

"No."

"Neither one of you?"

"No."

"Ah." He sounded relieved. "Well, that explains it. I don't know why you came, but I'll have to ask you to please leave. People are waiting, and my time is limited."

For a long moment no one said anything. More than once we had told him why we came, and there was no use repeating it. This man just didn't want to let us see God. The ruby slippers had been Dorothy's ticket into the Emerald City, but Sunny and I had nothing to offer to get us past this surly fellow and into the inner chambers where God lived.

Finally I asked, "Are you sure God lives here?"

Another sigh. "Of course, but——"

"Please let us see him, mister," Sunny blurted out. "I gotta talk to him about something important."

"But you can't just *see* God," the voice snapped impatiently. "No one sees God."

Sunny and I sat in stunned silence. That's what the gatekeeper told Dorothy too, but it was only an excuse to keep her away from the Wizard. Why was this man so determined to keep us from God?

"Then, how do you know he's there?" I asked.

As I suspected, he had no answer. "Girls," he said, his agitation palpable, "I must ask you please to leave. I have numerous confessions to hear yet this afternoon."

We were wasting his time. The shadow shifted, and I thought I heard the soles of a pair of heavy shoes scraping impatiently across the floor on the other side of the closet. "If you're genuinely interested in becoming Catholic, come back another time, and we'll see what we can do."

"Do we have to be Catholic to see him?" Sunny asked sadly.

But we received no answer, and in the next moment the little shutter that separated us from the gatekeeper snapped shut.

Sunny and I sat in that dark box for another moment, unable to move. We'd had such hope that we would see God and never dreamed we'd be so bitterly disappointed. We'd known he might not be home, but we thought in that case we'd be invited back later. Never did we expect to be shooed away like a couple of flies at a picnic.

Poor Sunny took it pretty hard. She cried all the way home and was still sniffling when we found Haha standing at the back door in the kitchen saying good-bye to Vera Eddington. When Haha asked us what was wrong, Mrs. Eddington came back in, and we all sat down at the kitchen table.

After we spilled the story of where we'd been, Haha frowned, but Mrs. Eddington burst out laughing. "Oh, honey," she said, patting Sunny's hand. "You should've come to me first. I could have told you you wouldn't find God in that stuffy old church!"

"Do you know where we can find him, then?" Sunny asked, sniffing loudly.

"Goodness, no!" Mrs. Eddington shrieked, and she laughed again. "Eddie says that as soon as God created the world and saw what he'd done, he turned tail and headed for another universe to start all over again. He botched things up so bad here, he didn't want to hang around to see what happened."

"Well," Haha broke in gently, "no one knows for sure—"

"But Eddie says to look on the bright side," Mrs. Eddington continued. "He says if there's no God, then there's no hell either, and that's probably the best news for all of us. None of us'll have to sit around roasting our toes in a bonfire day in and day out in the next world."

Mrs. Eddington smiled broadly and patted Sunny's hand again, as though all were settled now, all things righted. But I could see from the look on Sunny's face that she was both stunned and bewildered.

"But what about this?" she asked. She reached into her pocket and pulled out the precious piece of paper. She'd been carrying it around for weeks in the pocket of whatever dress she was wearing, as though it were her one link to hope.

Mrs. Eddington looked at it and said, "This! Oh, honey, this is just one of those tracts the holy rollers are always passing around. Eddie calls those people bliss ninnies, says they're crazier than loons. Well, listen, I gotta run. Mom's looking after Larry"—she'd finally had a baby the year before—"and I promised I'd get back in plenty of time for her to make it to the Red Cross meeting. The war, you know." And with that, she left us.

Sunny and I stared silently at Haha. After several long and painful moments, Sunny asked, "Mama, do you think God moved to another universe?"

Haha shook her head. "I don't know, Sunny."

Sunny rose and looked out the window, as though searching for some sign of the universe that God had escaped to. "If I could have just talked to him for one minute," she said, "I could've maybe convinced him to stop the hakujin from sending us away. Now there's nothing I can do about it, and we'll probably all have to go."

Haha rose to stand beside her daughter. "Sunny," she said quietly, so quietly I could scarcely hear, "if he is there, he didn't stop the Japanese from bombing Pearl Harbor, did he? Now, why would he stop the government from sending us away?"

Dorothy and the Tin Man and the Scarecrow and the Lion made it in to see the Wizard and were given what they asked for. Sunny and I were turned away at the door, and the world went on fighting, and the wheels of the government kept on turning, and the little men in Washington worked day and night to make sure we never got back to Kansas.

SIXTEEN

In a good dream you can spread out your arms and fly. You can be with people you haven't seen in years and whom you never thought you'd see again. You can stand in a spotlight and sing an aria, though you've never in your life been able to carry a tune. In a good dream anything is possible and whatever you desire is yours.

In a bad dream everything is out of control. You wander about a house looking for a room you've been to a hundred times, but you can't find it. You read something over and over, and it doesn't make sense. You get backed into a corner of a room by an armed assailant, and you know you can't avoid the bullet. You're heavy with despair, and though you tell yourself there must be a way of making things right—a way to find the room, a way to understand the words, a way to escape death—you know in your heart that there is no way, and even if there were, you'd never find it.

We started living in a bad dream when President Roosevelt signed Edict 9066 on February 19, 1942, designating military areas from which "any or all persons may be excluded." The edict didn't specify the Japanese, but we all knew what was meant.

"Will they send us away for sure now, Papa?" Sunny asked.

We sat at the kitchen table late in the evening of the nineteenth.

The boys were both in bed asleep, and Obaasan was in her room. She had been told about the edict. She had said nothing.

And now Chichi was silent too. It was as though their words had been stolen from them right along with their hope. Chichi sat hunched over the end of the table, his hands clenched together on the tabletop so tightly his knuckles were white.

Haha got up and poured him some more tea, a gesture he didn't acknowledge. When she sat again, she answered Sunny's question. "Nothing is for sure yet, Sunny. The edict means the government can move people, but it doesn't mean they will."

"When will we know for sure?" Sunny's voice was little more than a whisper.

Haha shook her head. "There's no telling, Sunny. We must be patient and wait."

"But I'm tired of waiting. I want to know now."

"It's not that easy, Sunny. We can't know now. Maybe not even the government knows what they're going to do."

Chichi looked up at his wife then and found his voice. "No, Suma." He shook his head slowly. "They know. I believe the government knows very well what they are going to do."

He dropped his eyes again while Haha, Sunny and I exchanged worried glances. Haha said quietly, "But I don't understand how it could even be done, Toshio. There are hundreds—thousands—of us. How can they possibly send us all away? Where can they possibly send us?"

"You worry about numbers and places, Suma?" Chichi asked, his voice tight with restraint. "What I don't understand is how they can send us away when we are American citizens, when we have done nothing wrong. It's a violation of our constitutional rights."

Numbers, places, the Constitution. None of that meant much to me. I wanted to know only one thing. "When you go, you'll take me with you, won't you, Chichi?"

My whole body trembled as I waited for Chichi to look up at me, to answer my question. When our eyes met, he stared at me for a long while, so long I began to think that time had stopped, that we would sit immobile forever, like the unsmiling figures in an old-fashioned tintype. When he spoke, he said only, "Musume. . . ." Then he rose from the table and left the kitchen. We could hear his footsteps heavy on the stairs.

When I looked at Haha, her eyes were lowered, tears ran down her cheeks.

Sometimes a person speaks loudest by saying nothing at all.

❧

I waded through the bad dream day and night. When asleep, I watched as Chichi and Haha and Sunny walked away from me. I tried to cry out to them, to beg them to come back, but the air passed through my hollow throat without a sound.

When awake I watched fearfully while Chichi grew angrier and Haha sadder, until the emotions themselves became a wall between us. My glances went unmet, my questions unanswered.

"But where will you go, Chichi?"

"No one knows, Musume."

"Will you take me with you?"

Silence.

"You have to take me, Chichi, or else what will happen to me?"

"We will make arrangements with your aunt."

"But I don't want to go back there!"

"Musume, I'm busy. Don't ask me such questions right now."

But he wasn't busy. Not really. He was only pacing the floor or staring out the window or kneading his hands into tight fists.

Sunny and I spent hours talking about how we might stay together, whispering at night in the dark, passing notes back and forth in class, searching out every possibility while we walked to school and home again.

"Can't you talk Chichi into taking me with you, Sunny?"

"I don't think so. He said we're being sent away only because we look Japanese, so I guess you can't go if you don't look like us."

"But I'm one of you anyway, even if I don't look like it," I protested, hating more than ever my curly red hair, my round eyes, my high-bridged nose. "Chichi and Haha can tell the government people they call me Musume and that means daughter. If they tell the government people I'm their daughter, maybe I'll be allowed to go."

"I don't know, Augie. I mean, no one's going to believe you're really their daughter."

"I know, Sunny. I don't expect anyone to believe I'm *really* their daughter, but they love me like a daughter. They said so. And that makes me family. You're more my family than my own family is. Besides, I can't go back to Uncle Finn's! I can't!"

We were walking along Whittier Avenue, holding hands, our fingers tightly entwined. We had just spent another day enduring the stares and the jeers of our classmates whose fathers and uncles and older brothers were shipping out to fight the Japanese. Whenever we were bullied by the other kids we tried to remember what Haha had taught us to recite, "Sticks and stones may break my bones. . . ." And yet if words could never hurt us, we wondered at the ache in our chests every time Sunny was called a "Jap" and I a "Jap lover," whenever she was called "yellow vermin" and I a "traitor."

"I have an idea though, Augie," Sunny said.

"What is it?"

"As soon as we get to wherever we're going, I'll write and tell you where we are. Then you can come and find us. Once you're there, I bet Mama and Papa will let you stay. They wouldn't make you come all the way back here again."

"You think so?"

"Yeah, I think so."

"But what if you go really far away? How will I get there?"

"You can take a train."

"But I don't have any money."

"I'll get Papa to leave you some when we go."

"What if it's not enough?"

We were both quiet a moment. Then Sunny said, "Write me back and tell me how much you need, and I'll send it to you."

"All right." I began to feel hopeful.

"Of course," Sunny added, "maybe trains don't go to wherever they're going to send us. One of the kids at school said his father said we're going to be sent into the middle of the desert. I don't even know if they have roads in the middle of a desert."

I hadn't thought of that. "Then how will *you* get there?"

Sunny shrugged. "Maybe they'll make us walk."

I was determined not to be left behind. "Then I'll take the train to the end of the line," I decided, "and after that I'll walk too."

❧

Right up until the first evacuations took place, and even afterward, I nurtured a certain hope that the Yamagatas would not be sent away. The government would change its mind, would realize that looks have nothing to do with loyalty, would allow everyone of Japanese descent to stay where they were. Better yet, maybe the war would end as suddenly as it had started, and there'd be no need for anything to change at all. We'd go right back to living the way we were living before the bombing of Pearl Harbor, with no hard feelings on either side.

But it wasn't to be. The first to be sent to the camps were the residents of Terminal Island. A number of men had already been arrested, mostly fishermen who were supposedly working as spies and agents for the Japanese. On February 25, the remaining residents of Terminal Island were given forty-eight hours to evacuate. Hastily constructed camps were now ready to receive them as guests of the United States government for the duration of the war.

"It's started," Chichi said when the news reached us. "There will be no stopping it now."

Chichi was right. On March 2, General DeWitt announced that all Japanese, regardless of citizenship, would be sent to relocation camps. The West Coast states had been divided into two military zones. Military Area Number One, which included Los Angeles, would be evacuated first, followed by Military Area Number Two.

"They have figured out a way to do it, then," said Haha.

"Of course," responded Chichi bitterly. "DeWitt and the others have been working very hard to figure this out."

"But, Toshio, our home, the business—what will we do?"

"We'll do nothing until they tell us more."

"But—we'll lose everything." She sounded more wistful than angry as she rubbed her swollen belly.

How I wished I were the baby inside Haha so that she would have no choice but to carry me away with her. I envied that child, curled up safe and warm, just as I had once been safe and warm in the life I lived with the Yamagatas. And at the same time I hated that baby because it would be what I could never be, a real Yamagata, a real *musume*.

"If you tell them I'm your daughter, Haha, you won't have to lose *me*," I whispered to her desperately.

She smiled wanly, but it was accompanied by that terrible heart-stopping silence. The silence that said it all.

❧

The American forces in the Philippines were sick, starved, and broken by March 12, and the country started to fall to the Japanese. The forced marches began. The U.S. troops captured on Bataan hiked in long weary columns to distant prison camps. These journeys took days, without food, water, or medical attention. Many men died or were killed along the way.

Knowing Jack would soon be shipped out, Stella kept a close watch on what was happening in the Pacific. She worried about when and where he might be sent.

"You know, Augie," she told me, "your brother Lenny, if he's alive, is probably in the hands of the Japanese by now."

What was that to me? I continued to be more concerned about the Japanese who were in the hands of the Americans.

SEVENTEEN

"It's time, Suma."

Chichi's voice was hoarse, his face pale. Haha only nodded, a taut, almost imperceptible nod.

"Have you been listening to the radio? Did you read the paper?"

"No, Toshio. Not today. I couldn't bear. . . ." She lifted a hand to her cheek as her words trailed off.

"They are posted all over the telephone poles, on the walls of buildings."

"How much time do we have?"

"Six days."

"Six days, Toshio? That's all?"

"Yes, Suma, that's all."

"How will we get rid of everything in so little time?"

Chichi sighed heavily. "I don't know, Suma. But we must."

"Papa?"

"Yes, Sunny?"

"What was on the telephone poles?"

"It's called a Civilian Exclusion Order. It says we must get ready to go."

"But *where* are we going, Papa? *Where?*"

"I don't know, Sunny."

"But why don't they tell us?"

The room fell silent. At length Chichi said, "I think because it doesn't matter. Our lives are here, and if we can't be here, what does it matter where we go?"

"Chichi." My stomach was a sour pit, churning and reeling. "Take me with you. Please, Chichi, don't leave me here."

Chichi slowly lifted his hand to the side of my head, then ran his palm along the length of my hair, my curly red hair. "I must go upstairs and tell Obaasan and the boys."

"Supper will be ready soon, Toshio."

Chichi nodded, then turned and walked away, bent and weary, like a man who has walked too many miles already on a journey that hadn't even begun.

❧

The next morning Chichi went down to the civil control station as instructed on the Civilian Exclusion Order. The address given was a storefront that had been temporarily converted into a clearinghouse for information on getting rid of the Japanese. He came home carrying twenty numbered tags, which he dropped on the kitchen table.

"What are those, Toshio?"

"That's our number. Those tags go on our luggage and on our persons."

"So we are a number now?"

Chichi didn't answer Haha's question. "We can take only what we can carry," he explained. "Bedding, toilet articles, clothing, eating utensils. That's it. We can store some of our possessions in warehouses that have been set aside for us or in one of the Buddhist temples. Start deciding now what you want to keep and what you want to get rid of. Don't try to keep too much."

We had been told to begin, but Haha, Sunny, and I stared at Chichi as though we couldn't understand a word he'd said. It was a school day, but Haha had allowed us to stay home to help her begin packing. We stood with our feet planted on the linoleum as though we had roots descending down through the floor and into the ground, roots that held us firmly in place. "But how . . . how do I even begin, Toshio?" Haha asked.

"Begin here in the kitchen. It's as good a place as any. Sunny, you and Musume make a sign for the front yard that says we have furniture and household items for sale. Write it big on a piece of cardboard so it can be read from the street. I've got to get down to the store now. Hito and I will be trying to lease it out in the next day or two."

"You won't sell it, Toshio?"

Chichi shook his head tentatively. "If we lease it, perhaps we can get it back after the war."

"What will we do with the house?"

"We will try to lease it too, but we may have to sell."

"Papa, if we lease the store and the house, then we'll come back here and live again after the war?"

"Yes, Sunny, that's what we'll try to do."

"Do you think the war will last very long?"

"I can't say, Sunny. I hope not."

Jimmy scratched at the kitchen's screen door, asking to be let in. Sunny opened the door and threw her arms around the dog. "Can we put Jimmy's number on his collar, Papa?"

Chichi looked at Sunny sadly. "No, Sunny, I'm afraid not. Jimmy can't go with us. No pets allowed in the camps."

"Papa!"

"I'm sorry, Sunny."

"We can't just leave him——"

"I have to go now, Suma. Ask Obaasan to help, whether she likes it or not."

"I don't think she has the strength to do any packing."

"Then she can sit and supervise. She can help you make decisions about what to keep and what to get rid of. But she needs to get out of her room."

"All right, Toshio. Can you bring home some boxes from the store?"

"Of course."

"If people come to buy things, I won't know how much to sell them for."

"Sell everything for whatever you can get."

There was a long pause, weighted with fear.

"I don't think I can do this, Toshio."
"You can, Suma. You have no choice."

❧

Haha worked for hours, seemingly oblivious to the tears coursing down her cheeks. George hovered about underfoot and wailed, unable to understand why his mother was crying and what she was doing, but Haha largely ignored him. She pulled items from cupboards and closets, sorted through desk drawers, made piles on the floor of what was salable, what was savable, what was trash. Sunny, Sam, and I carried the piles of trash out to the can in the backyard to be burned. Letters, receipts, paper work—all sorts of accumulated evidence of their lives went up in smoke.

Vera Eddington saw us from her kitchen window and came over with her baby on her hip to ask us what we were doing.

"We're getting ready to go, Mrs. Eddington," Sunny replied.

Mrs. Eddington turned from us and walked into the kitchen without knocking on the door. She spent the rest of the day working alongside Haha, sorting, packing, and crying. Her baby cried too, for want of attention, but he, like George, was ignored until he finally fell asleep. There was no explaining to the little ones what we ourselves couldn't understand.

Haha gave Mrs. Eddington the whole set of her good china. "I won't be needing these dishes where we're going," she explained. "Couldn't get them there anyway."

"Why don't you store them, Suma?" Mrs. Eddington asked.

"They should be used, not stored away."

Mrs. Eddington touched one of the plates, running the tip of her finger along the floral pattern around the rim. "I'll use them, Suma," she said, "but only until you come back. Then you can have them again."

Haha nodded, and we all went back to work.

Obaasan refused to help. She stayed in her room, saying she was sick. When Haha asked her what was wrong, Obaasan said she had pains in her chest. I thought that was no excuse for not helping. We all had pain in our chests where our hearts were broken, but we had to go on packing up the house anyway.

By midafternoon Haha said she was ready for the sign to go up in the yard. Almost at once it drew hakujin to the house like flies to honey. Books, clothing, beds, tables, chairs, the floor-model Zenith radio all went for pennies.

Some men rented trucks and drove around to the homes of Japanese families, buying up their appliances for five, ten, fifteen dollars. When such a truck pulled up in front of our house, Haha sold her washer and dryer for ten dollars, the refrigerator for twelve. The men carted them out to the truck and drove off in a puff of exhaust.

Haha sold Obaasan's record player for twenty-five cents. Her fingers trembled when the quarter was dropped into her palm. She must have felt she was giving away her mother-in-law's life for a pittance. Later that evening, Chichi sold his car for twenty dollars.

A steady stream of bargain hunters flowed in and out of the house for three days, carrying away with them the Yamagatas' home in bits and pieces. We watched the way flood victims might watch pieces of a town washed away by a swollen river. We were numb with disbelief, caught up in the darkest moment of the bad dream, unable to control what was happening all around us.

The house was stripped bare, save for the suitcases and other items, like bedrolls, that would be carried to the camp. The rooms yawned like endless caverns, echoing our footsteps, throwing our voices back at us because there was nothing there to absorb the sound. The emptiness was all-consuming, as frightening as a sudden nighttime power outage that leaves you sitting in the dark.

Haha said she felt as if they were the victims of an enormous robbery. Chichi said it was no wonder; that's exactly what they were.

Not all the hakujin were hateful in those last days. Some were kind, like Vera Eddington, who was at the house every day helping Haha to endure the dismantling of her home. Many others—long-time neighbors, friends, patrons of the store—came by with food, with apologies, with wishes for a quick end to the war.

Chichi and Haha received them with grace, accepting their gifts and their words of consolation. Chichi shook the men's hands; Haha hugged the women. Chichi said, "We'll be back after the war," and the hakujin said, "We'll be watching for you. Best of luck."

It almost restored my faith in Americans. But not quite.

❦

The store was leased, the house sold. "Don't worry, Suma," Chichi promised, "we'll buy another house, a bigger one, when we come back."

The last night came, and Sunny and the boys and I settled down in blankets on the living room floor to sleep. Obaasan slept alone on the mat in her otherwise empty room. The mat would be left behind in the morning, a hermit crab's shell no longer needed.

Chichi and Haha stayed up late, sitting on the kitchen floor with their backs against the empty cabinets, talking in muffled voices. Their words reached us like the droning of bees, a buzz of sound I couldn't understand. Finally the buzzing gave way to weeping, the first thing that made any sense to me. I could understand fully why Haha was crying.

Sunny and I lay each with an arm flung over the other, with Jimmy wedged between us. Behind us were all the years of nights that we'd talked ourselves to sleep, and now, on our final night, we had no words left.

There was only the awful silence, telling me what I didn't want to hear. It's time now, it said.

EIGHTEEN

We stood on the sidewalk in front of the house, shoulders rounded against the early morning chill. The neighborhood was quiet, rows of sleeping houses, an odd backdrop to the drama unfolding on Fickett Street. We were seven players acting out a tragedy that nobody cared to see. While others slept, our whole world was being torn quietly apart, and by the time they awoke, it would all be over, the sidewalk empty, the curtain drawn to signal the end of the show.

We stood on the sidewalk with the piles of luggage scattered at our feet waiting for Mr. Eddington and his brother to come and drive the Yamagatas to the train station. That morning they were going to catch the train that they'd been hoping for months to avoid. They were all dressed up, just as though they were going somewhere grand, though none of us had any idea at all where they were headed. But Haha had insisted that they look their best, because that would mean they still had their dignity intact, if little else. "There are some things the hakujin can't take away," she said.

Dangling from every suitcase handle and attached to every person was a numbered tag. Everything and everyone fell into the category of 18627, except for Jimmy and me.

Sunny pressed the handle of Jimmy's leash into my hand and struggled to speak. "Take care . . . of Jimmy . . . promise."

"I will, I . . ." I was a sleepwalker, straining to pull myself through this nightmare. "Do you have Uncle Finn's address?" I'd asked a hundred times, a thousand times.

Almost impatiently, "Yes, yes."

"Don't lose it."

"I won't. Anyway, I know it by heart now."

"Write to me as soon as you get there."

"I will. The very minute."

Next door an engine started. Mr. Eddington backed his Buick down the driveway. It wouldn't be long before the tires would go to the rubber drive, but now, this morning, they would carry the Yamagatas away to the train.

In another moment a second familiar car, a LaSalle, turned a corner onto our street. It was Mr. Eddington's brother. Both cars pulled up to the curb in front of the Yamagatas' house, and the men hopped out and started loading suitcases into the trunks.

"Sunny!" I cried as we threw our arms around each other. We both sobbed then, while Jimmy, pacing nervously and tugging at his leash, gave off irritated yelps. He knew something was wrong, but he didn't understand what.

Chichi laid a hand on each of our shoulders. "We must go now, Sunny," he said quietly.

Sunny and I drew back to look at each other. "I'll write, Augie. I promise. As soon as we get there."

I nodded. But it wasn't nearly enough. I didn't want letters; I wanted Sunny and Chichi and Haha. I wanted my family.

Haha kneeled on the sidewalk to invite me into her arms. I threw myself at her, and we held each other tightly. I had told myself to be brave, but it was a resolve I couldn't keep. "Don't leave me, Haha," I begged.

Haha placed her hand against my cheek, brushed a strand of curls away from my face. "Musume," she said, her eyes welling with tears, "we love you. We will always love you. But we cannot take you with us. You know we have spoken with your aunt, and she has said for you to come home. Even your uncle says for you to come home."

"But that isn't my home, Haha. It isn't. I hate them."

"Musume, you mustn't talk so. They're your family——"

"They're not my family. *You're* my family. You said so yourself."

Haha only kissed me then, and rose to go.

I looked at Chichi, panic rising in me. Surely they would change their minds and take me with them. I'd hoped that at the last minute they'd say, "Of course you're coming. You're our daughter, the same as Sunny. No one can keep you from us." I believed there was a safety hatch somewhere, that there'd be a way for me to crawl through the government barriers so that at the end of the day, and every day afterward, I'd still be with my family.

But Chichi wasn't saying the words I was willing him to say. He wasn't saying anything at all. He was sullen and silent and something other than the man I'd met three years before. "Chichi," I said, stepping toward him, "Chichi, you'll take me, won't you? You won't leave me here with Uncle Finn." I threw my arms around his waist and clung to him.

"Musume, dear Musume, you can ask us a hundred times more, and still we can tell you nothing different," he said, not unkindly. "The government would never allow it."

"But, Chichi," I wailed, plunging into one last bitter attempt to persuade him. "I'm German. Tell them I'm German. I'm the enemy too. If you tell them that, they'll *want* me to go—"

"Musume . . ." Chichi bent and kissed the top of my head. "Forgive me. Please forgive me, but you cannot come with us."

"We'll write to you as often as we can," Haha assured me then. "And when the war is over, we'll come back. Maybe the war won't last for long. We can hope it will be over quickly."

Chichi unlocked my arms from his waist and gently stepped away. "Go home now, Musume. We will not forget you."

I watched in horror as he placed the last bag into the trunk of Mr. Eddington's car. Then he helped Obaasan into the backseat. I wanted to say something to her, but she would not meet my gaze. She was like stone, like a person already dead.

It was April 9. On the other side of the world, the U.S. troops on Bataan surrendered. The Japanese takeover of the Philippines was complete. Nearly all of the thirty-six thousand American defenders were killed or captured. My brother Lenny, I would later learn, was marching off to a Japanese prison camp even as my Japanese family was marching off to an American prison camp.

The Yamagatas stepped into the waiting vehicles, one by one. Haha and the boys settled into the LaSalle. Obaasan, Chichi, and Sunny rode with Mr. Eddington. Before he slid behind the wheel, Mr. Eddington gave me an apologetic smile, as though to say he was sorry he had to take my family away. Vera Eddington had bid farewell to Haha the night before, saying she couldn't bear to be there in the morning.

At length, the last car door slammed shut. Sunny rolled down the window, reached for my hand. Our fingers locked. Jimmy barked and licked our knuckles.

Mr. Eddington started the engine and put the car in gear. In the LaSalle behind him, his brother did the same. Slowly they pulled away from the curb. Sunny's fingers slipped from mine. Jimmy strained against the leash, leaping and barking frantically. It took all the strength I could summon to hold him back. It took all the strength I could summon not to run after the Yamagatas myself.

Before the cars reached the end of the street, I let go one last strangled cry of "Chichi!" I knew they couldn't hear, and I knew it wouldn't have mattered if they did. In a moment both cars turned the corner and were gone.

How do you say good-bye in Japanese? In all my time with the Yamagatas, I had never once bothered to learn how to say good-bye.

NINETEEN

There was nothing for me to do except return to Uncle Finn's. I put off the inevitable for as long as I could, walking with Jimmy around Boyle Heights until the sun was almost overhead and I knew it was close to noon. Every once in a while Jimmy sat down abruptly on the sidewalk and, panting, looked up at me with doleful eyes, as though to ask me what in the world we were doing. I tugged on his leash, and we kept on walking. Finally I let myself into the house on Fresno Street and stepped reluctantly back into the world of my uncle's angry silences and my mother's crazy shenanigans.

After a week I called Stella and asked if I could live with her, and she said yes, she wanted me to come—and Jimmy too, if her landlords agreed—but that I should stay where I was long enough to finish the school year at Whittier Avenue School. In the fall she'd enroll me in a new school closer to where she lived.

I endured life at Uncle Finn's a few more weeks, and on the day school ended Jimmy and I moved in with Stella, and that's where I spent the remainder of the war years. It was a good arrangement for my cousin as well as for me. She was terribly lonely without Jack, and my being there helped to ease her loneliness. Nevertheless, we cried a lot in those days. She, whenever a letter came from Jack, and I, whenever another week went by without a letter from Sunny. We cried a lot in between as well. I can remember the two of us lying back to back on the pullout sofa bed at night, absorbing each other's stifled sobs and sniffing loudly in the dark. The worst for me were Friday nights. We'd always spend the evening with her landlords, Grady and Cecelia Liddel, listening to Jimmy Durante on the radio. Whenever the comedian signed off with "Good night, Mrs. Calabash, wherever you are," I started to cry. Where, I wondered, were Sunny and Chichi and Haha? Where in the world could they possibly be?

I had hoped to hear from Sunny in only a matter of days after they left, but days stretched into weeks, weeks stretched into months, and not a single letter came. While still at Uncle Finn's, I sat on the front step every day after school, waiting for the arrival of Sean McDougall, our mailman.

"Anything for me today, Mr. McDougall?"

"No, kid. Nothing."

I wanted to call him a liar. I wanted to grab his mail pouch and search through it myself for the precious word from Sunny that I knew had to be there, but I never did. That daily encounter with Sean McDougall left me with a pain so large I could scarcely drag myself back up to my attic room.

Aunt Lucy promised that when I moved to Stella's, she would let me know the minute a letter arrived for me. I wanted to let Sunny know she should send her letters to Stella's and not to Uncle Finn's. At first I called Aunt Lucy every day, then every other day, then every week. Every time I called she said the same thing: "Not today, Augie. Maybe something will come tomorrow."

I couldn't understand it. The Yamagatas seemed simply to have disappeared, swallowed up by some black hole.

"Why don't they write to me, Stella? They promised they'd write as soon as they got to where they were going. They've gotta be there by now!"

"I don't know, sweetie. I'm sure there's a good reason. I'm sure they'll write as soon as they can."

I envied Stella her letters from Jack. At least she still had a connection to him. At least she could read the words "I love you" and be comforted in that. I had nothing but one big impenetrable mystery as to what had happened to Sunny and Chichi and Haha.

About a year into the war, it dawned on me that Haha might have written to the Eddingtons. I tried to call, but their phone line had been disconnected. When I went to their house, I was greeted by a harried-looking woman with one child in her arms and two more clinging to her legs. The previous owners had moved east, she said, something having to do with the war. And no, she didn't know where they had gone or how to get in touch with them. I asked her if any letters came to her house from a woman named Suma Yamagata, and she said no, she hadn't seen any, but she assumed the previous owners had arranged to have all their mail forwarded to their new address.

I felt as though the big black hole that had consumed the Yamagatas was sitting smack-dab in the center of my chest.

"Do you think they're dead, Stella?"

"Goodness, no. Why would they be dead?"

"Why don't they write to me, then?"

"I don't know. Maybe they're not allowed to send any letters out of the camps."

"Do you think they were sent back to Japan?"

"I doubt it. If they sent the Yamagatas back, they'd have to send all of them back and that would be far too expensive."

"Then why don't they write to me?"

"There has to be a reason. Someday you'll know what it is."

"Do you think they've forgotten me?"

"Of course not. How could they?"

I waited, believing that they wanted to get in touch with me as much I wanted to hear from them, but that something—maybe some sort of government policy prohibiting letters between Japanese and hakujin—was keeping us apart.

In the last year of the war, Jack was flying B–17s over Germany when we received word that his plane had been shot down. For a time he was missing in action, and Stella was paralyzed with fear that he might have been killed. How she and I survived those weeks I don't know, except that we had no choice. Finally a telegram arrived with the news that Jack had been captured, and though we didn't know exactly where he was, we knew he was alive. He spent that final year of the war in a German prison camp, and in that time we never received another letter from him.

In a twisted sort of way, this gave me hope. Because Jack was unable to reach us from the camp, I figured perhaps the Yamagatas too were simply unable to reach me from wherever they were. I trusted in their promise to come back for me after the war, and I went on waiting for them. Months before the Allied victory, Japanese Americans started trickling back into Los Angeles from all the places they had been sent, and that was when I really started watching for the Yamagatas. I knew they wouldn't come back to the house, but Chichi had said he'd come back to claim the store. So I'd sit on the bench in front of the store's plate-glass window, waiting and watching with Jimmy for any sign of Chichi or Ojisan Hito.

When at last the war ended, Jack came home, stepping off the train into the open arms of an ecstatic wife. That was when I moved back into Uncle Finn's house, my cousins' garage apartment being far too small for the three of us. At first I lived again in the attic, but only until the telegram arrived with the news that my brother Lenny had somehow, against all odds, survived the war. He was in a veterans' hospital in San Francisco, but upon his release he'd be coming home to Boyle Heights. Boyle Heights had never been his home, but it was the closest thing to a home he was going to get. Uncle Finn decided Lenny would get the attic, and so I moved down a floor to share a room with my cousin Rosey.

It was a different attic that Lenny moved into because, before he arrived, Uncle Finn and Aunt Lucy had spent some time and even a little money fixing it up. They bought a real bed, a wardrobe, and a chest of drawers. Secondhand furniture, but better than a mattress on the floor. Uncle Finn even tacked down a carpet fragment he bought at a going-out-of-business sale, and Aunt Lucy sewed some drapes to replace the black-out curtain that still hung in the window months after the threat of attack was over. The place actually looked cozy and welcoming when all the remodeling was done.

I was a little jealous that my aunt and uncle fussed over the room for Lenny when no one had bothered to fix up the place for me. But when I helped Aunt Lucy hang up the drapes, she said giving a soldier a room to come home to was the least we could do, and I had to agree with that. Lenny deserved something nice because, after all, he'd been in the war, and he'd survived a lot of awful things. Uncle Finn bragged about Lenny to anyone and everyone, saying he was a hero because he had outwitted the Japs. They'd beat him and starved him and forced him to live and work in unthinkable conditions, but in the end they found it wasn't so easy to break somebody with O'Shaughnessy blood in him.

Even though I had no doubt he was one, Lenny didn't look like a hero when he came home. He didn't even look like the picture Mother had kept of him in her room. He was only just past thirty, but he looked like an old man. His hair was almost completely gray, his body was drastically thin, and his shoulders were rounded as though he were an autumn leaf rolling up in the face of winter. One of his cheekbones was sunken so that his face was lopsided, and his eyes constantly watered and seemed unable to focus. He shuffled rather than walked, as if he hadn't the strength to pick up his feet. He chewed aspirin like candy, though he never bothered to tell anyone where he hurt. I think maybe he just kind of hurt all over.

Mother didn't get to welcome Lenny home. She had taken the final turn around the bend sometime in early 1944. In January of that year the newspapers headlined the atrocities of the Japanese prisoner-of-war camps. Some of our men had escaped from those camps, bringing their stories of misery back to a horrified America. I don't suppose anyone was more horrified than Mother, whose firstborn was in the hands of the Japanese. Aunt Lucy told me about the night Mother went around the house clutching a knife and threatening to kill any Jap she ran into. That was the last night she spent at Uncle Finn's.

When Lenny went to visit her at the state hospital, she didn't know who he was. He said he wouldn't have recognized her either if the nurse hadn't insisted that the wild-eyed woman in the chair by the window was indeed Margaret Schuler. Mother and son had become strangers to each other. After that first visit Lenny never went back.

Lenny wouldn't talk about what happened to him during the war. We could only guess what he might have endured as we learned more about the death marches, the beatings, the starvation, the torture, the deliberate murder. We did know that Lenny had ended up in a labor camp in Japan, which meant he had survived the journey on one of the "hell ships" from the Philippines. So many prisoners were crammed into the filthy holds of those ships, the men could barely move. When it got so hot the men thought they'd go crazy—and some of them did—the Japanese tormented them further by cutting off their supply of water. Disease was rampant. Malaria, beriberi, blackwater fever, dysentery, and pellagra were common ailments. Without medicine, body and soul sometimes held together by a tenuous thread known as willpower. Too often, the thread simply gave way or was snipped by despair. Whenever a hell ship docked in Japan, the hold housed a cargo of strange bedfellows, the dying curled up with the dead.

And that was just the getting there. Once the prisoners reached the camps, years of misery followed.

I couldn't compare Lenny to what he had once been because I had never known him. But Stella knew him vaguely. She remembered meeting him several times when the Schulers and O'Shaughnessys visited each other before my father died. She said he was a bright, handsome boy, always laughing, always pulling practical jokes on people. He had a compassionate, sensitive side too. She remembered once when they were roller-skating together—she was about ten, he about fourteen—and she fell and skinned her knees so that the blood ran down her shins and into her socks. "Any other kid would have just laughed at me, I guess," Stella said, "but Lenny—he was real concerned. He wiped away the blood with his T-shirt, then helped me up and let me lean on him while we skated home. I remember thinking I'd marry him if he wasn't my cousin. He was a real nice kid, Augie. You'd have liked him."

I wanted to like him when he came home from the war. I wanted to know him, but it wasn't easy. One evening shortly after he came to live with us, I found him alone on the front steps smoking a cigarette. It would be a good chance for us to talk, I decided. It seemed there was so much to talk about. When I stepped outside to join him, he acknowledged my presence with only a glance and a nod and went on smoking. His fingers trembled as he lifted the cigarette to his lips. His hands always trembled, as though he were still afraid his captors were lurking nearby, waiting to pounce on him with their rifle butts.

"How ya doing, Lenny?" I asked, sitting down beside him and hugging my knees to my chest.

Lenny nodded while blowing smoke out of his mouth. "All right," he said noncommittally.

He looked straight ahead, and I wondered whether it was the street he saw out there or something else. Something I couldn't see. I wanted to know what it was. I wanted to know what he had seen during the war, what he had experienced. Most of all I wanted to know what it was like to be back home after the long years of imprisonment. Wasn't he glad to be here, to be alive, to have survived something that so many hundreds, thousands, hadn't survived? Didn't he feel lucky, even invincible?

"I wrote to you, Lenny, while you were . . . away. Did you get any of my letters?"

He shook his head slowly. "No, kid. I'm sorry. I'm afraid all the Jap mailmen were too busy being soldiers to deliver any letters."

I laughed eagerly, jumping at even this hint of a joke, hoping he would open up to me. But he didn't join in the laughter. He went on smoking slowly, methodically, his eyes forward, his hands twitching.

"Well, I'm glad you're home, anyway," I said.

He squinted against the smoke as he inhaled. He held the smoke in his lungs, then idly let it out, a thin ghostly ribbon blown down toward the concrete steps. He was quiet for so long I didn't think he was going to respond. Finally, his eyes still averted, he muttered, "Yeah." That was all he said.

Why was Lenny so subdued, I wondered, so seemingly ungrateful that he had come back when he could have so easily died over there? I thought that if I had come home alive from a war, I would be dancing in the streets, hugging everyone I met, shouting for joy. But I was only fifteen and still idealistic, and I didn't know what it was to go on living long after you'd had the life beaten out of you.

We all wished Lenny would open up and talk to us, not necessarily about the war but just about anything. Jack thought Lenny might talk to him because he too had been a prisoner of war. If anyone could understand what Lenny'd been through, surely Jack could. Some Friday nights he'd invite Lenny to go out for a couple of beers, but even so, he said, Lenny wouldn't talk much. Mostly Jack talked and Lenny listened. And Jack wasn't even sure he was listening half the time, he seemed so lost, as though his body was in one place and his mind in another and the two just couldn't meet up. Jack thought Lenny might do better if he got married, had someone who loved him, started living a normal family life. But Lenny wasn't interested. Even though some of the women at the roadhouse flirted with him, he wouldn't give them the time of day.

I wondered at the difference between Jack and Lenny. Unlike my brother, Jack had come back from the war battered but not broken. He was working and going to school part-time on the GI Bill to earn his long-desired degree in civil engineering. He also got Stella with child right away and was rather proud of the fact. In some ways he seemed almost better off now than before the war.

I asked Jack how he accounted for the difference, why he was moving ahead with his life while Lenny remained stagnant. Jack said it was because the Germans, ruthless as they were with the Jews, had more or less followed the rules of the Geneva Convention when it came to dealing with Allied prisoners. While the camps weren't exactly home sweet home, they were survivable. The men were given adequate food and Red Cross packages. They worked but they weren't overworked, and officers didn't have to work at all. They even had organized recreation in the camps—games and sports of all kinds.

The Japanese prisoner-of-war camps weren't the waiting rooms the German camps were. Instead, they were the inner circle of hell. The Japanese, Jack explained, had great contempt for anyone who surrendered, even believing a soldier should commit suicide rather than hand himself over to the enemy. Since prisoners like Lenny had surrendered, they were worthy of only one thing, and that was death. But the Japanese figured they might as well squeeze every bit of usefulness out of a prisoner, so they let him work in the labor camp until his body shut down for good. To help the process along, food was almost nonexistent, Red Cross care packages unheard of. Medical attention was unavailable. And as for organized recreation, the closest the prisoners got to that was in the regular beatings they received from their captors.

Lenny gave up his dream of making a career of the military, of course. Still, like anyone else, he had to make a living. The Veteran's Administration would give him only thirty percent disability because they said he had to prove his ailments were service related. Since the Japanese didn't keep any records of the beatings, torture, and starvation, Lenny had no proof.

Uncle Finn gave him a job at the hardware store, stocking and shelving and keeping up with the inventory. "Just until you get back on your feet, son," Uncle Finn said. "Just until you decide what it is you want to do. You might want to take advantage of the GI Bill like Jack's doing and go to college. Or go to vocational school, learn a trade. That might be even better."

Lenny didn't know what he wanted to do, so he accepted Uncle Finn's offer of work without enthusiasm and without complaint. When Uncle Finn left for the store each morning, Lenny went with him. Uncle Finn said he was a good worker until the drinking started to get out of hand.

I think Lenny started drinking to try to get rid of the nightmares. He brought the nightmares back with him from the camp, like a wound that wouldn't heal. My bed in Rosey's room was directly below his in the attic, and night after night I'd lay awake listening first to his footsteps, then to a series of scratching sounds, as though he were clawing at the walls or the floor, trying to escape. After that a brief quiet, and then the screams, the terrifying screams that woke up the whole house. Uncle Finn would order my cousins and me to stay downstairs while he and Aunt Lucy rushed up to try to calm Lenny. After they reached him, the screams would melt into a prolonged weeping, and we could hear Aunt Lucy hushing him like a baby, saying, "You're safe now. You're safe and nothing can hurt you," and Uncle Finn asking, "My God, son, what did they do to you? What in the name of God did they do to you?"

The horror of what had been done to Lenny ate at my heart, but even more unbearable was who "they" were. That I knew. "They" were the Japanese. "They" were the people I had loved. I didn't want to believe that the Japanese—people like the Yamagatas—could cause such unspeakable suffering. But what to do with this huge bit of walking evidence that was my brother? I couldn't deny what had been done to him. Here he was, broken in body and soul, compliments of the Japanese military.

To end the war the atomic bombs were dropped on my Garden of Eden. The vast cities of Hiroshima and Nagasaki were destroyed in an instant. It took longer for my love for the Yamagatas to be replaced by anger and bitterness. It took a while for me to concede that Uncle Finn was probably right about the Japanese. They were not good people, not even the Yamagatas. When Lenny came home an example of Japanese handiwork, that was the end of Mrs. Calabash. Jimmy Durante, on his weekly radio program, could go on wondering where Mrs. Calabash was, but I wasn't going to listen anymore, and I wasn't going to wonder anymore where the Yamagatas were. I told myself that it didn't matter. They had abandoned me. They'd wanted nothing more to do with me, and now I'd have nothing more to do with them. I would not even allow them to live on in my conscious memory.

The only nights Lenny didn't have his nightmares were the nights he was too drunk to dream. Uncle Finn said he needed help and took him to a VA hospital to dry out. But instead of drying out, Lenny Schuler walked out. He walked away from the hospital one rainy afternoon and disappeared. Uncle Finn tried to find him but never succeeded, though I guess he was always just one or two steps behind, because I don't think my brother ever left Los Angeles. A decade later, in the winter of 1957, word reached us that Lenny had been found dead in an alley not ten blocks from Fresno Street. The official coroner's report listed the cause of death as alcohol poisoning. Uncle Finn said that wasn't right. He said the Japs had killed Lenny back in Bataan in '42, but he was so tough it took him a decade and a half to die.

When I learned he was dead, I started having nightmares about Lenny, as though I were picking up for him where he had left off. In my dreams I heard his screams coming from the attic, and night after night I tried to reach him, but I could never make it to the top of the stairs. I would be tortured for years by those dreams of horror and absolute helplessness, those dreams of Lenny being tortured by the Japanese.

Not a soul in my family died on the battlefields of the Second World War, but the war took its toll nonetheless. I lost Lenny, who came back a dead man. I lost my mother, who lost her mind. I lost my brother Stephen who, upon returning from France, made good on his promise to get as far away from Uncle Finn as possible. He settled in New Jersey instead of coming back to California, and I never saw him again. I lost Stella when Jack came back and made her a mother five times over. And I lost the Yamagatas, my real family, the family of my heart, who simply never came back at all.

PART TWO

TWENTY

A chalky dusk shaded the sky as we neared the airport in Jackson. Two hours had dropped out of the day somewhere between California and Mississippi, and I set my watch forward to tally with the sudden coming of evening. My stomach turned as the plane began its descent into a place I didn't want to go. But never mind. I'd resort to my old strategy of survival. Don't feel anything, I told myself. Put the emotions in cold storage, then go in, do the job, and get out.

But it takes a great deal of effort not to feel anything, and I wasn't sure I could manage it. The journey had been a long one already, and I was tired. With the relentless stream of chatter coming from the next seat, the trip so far had become not so much a flight across open skies as a mountainous trek in and out of the story of this stranger's life and, more than that, in and out of the strange but all too familiar story of my own early years. I thought I'd put a safe distance between me and my memories, but my seatmate had me hiking all over those years once again with her questions.

She looked at me now as the plane sighed and eased itself earthward.

"You know," she said as the landscape of Mississippi rose up to meet us, "I couldn't stand it if Alan was killed by one of those gooks."

Of course she meant the North Vietnamese, or a member of the Viet Cong. They were the "gooks," the "dinks," the "slopes." The enemy in this current war.

I looked at my pretty young seatmate and wanted to tell her that using such a derogatory term didn't suit her. It was as jarring as an off-key chord rising up out of a Stradivarius, as unpleasant as a mouthful of saltwater lapped up from a freshwater stream. Not at all what you might expect, and all the harsher for just that reason.

Too, I wanted to ask her whether it would be any easier to accept if her fiancé were killed by one of his own, cut down by an American bullet, blown apart by friendly fire. He'd still be just as dead, wouldn't he?

Instead, I smiled sweetly and said, "I wonder what the women in Vietnam call our American soldiers?"

"G.I. Joes, I think." She had missed my point completely.

But then, she didn't know how much I hated the racial epithets that sliced people up into so many slabs of meat: gooks, dagos, spics, krauts, niggers—loin, flank, rib, chuck, shank. The entire human race all laid out on the butcher's block, stripped of dignity and reduced, like the doomed cow, to ugly piles of flesh and bone.

"But you know," she said, giving up a little laugh, "even Alan said being killed by a gook would be better than being killed by a nigger. Of course, anything'd be better than being killed by a nigger, wouldn't it?"

A wave of annoyance swept over me, but I let it pass and said nothing. Neither justifiable anger nor carefully chosen words could root out the centuries-old ideas of inequality in this young woman, not in the next few minutes anyway.

Our time together was almost up, and suddenly my seatmate seemed nearly panicked at the thought that something remained unsaid between us. She seemed to think I knew something she needed to know, because she asked, "How will I live while Alan's over there?"

Her blue eyes grew glassy again with tears. Those same eyes pleaded with me for help, as though, for whatever reason, she thought I had been placed here in this seat to save her.

"I mean," she went on, "I could be walking down the street or taking a shower or eating a ham sandwich or something stupid like that, and at that very moment over in Vietnam, Alan could be killed.

How can I just go on living a normal life?"

How to tell her that she would, because she had no choice? She would go on walking and showering and eating ham sandwiches simply because there wasn't anything else she could do. Some things are just too big for us, and we can only stand by and watch them happen. That's all. Just watch while the whole world rolls itself up into one big killing machine, crushing everything in its path, including your own small and ultimately insignificant dreams.

Our plane landed, the wheels touching down on the runway with a thud. The engines reversed their thrust, and the plane slowed down.

"While Alan is overseas," I said, "he'll want to think of you doing all those things you've always done. It'll be his link to the life he had before Vietnam, and the life he'll be coming home to. It's the best thing you can do—to go on living as you've always done, except now you'll be doing it for the both of you."

The words tasted sour on my tongue. Where, I wondered, had they come from? Surely not from the journalist in me. From the fiction writer, then. The writer of fiction can create whole worlds that have nothing at all to do with the real world. It's a convenient skill sometimes, a magician's trick, to pull sugarcoated consolations out of one's own bitter heart.

My seatmate brightened perceptibly. "I never thought of it that way," she exclaimed. "That's what I'll do—I'll live a normal life for both of us until Alan comes home." She took my hand in hers and squeezed it. "Thank you," she said. "Thank you for making me feel so much better."

She was smiling as she stood and said good-bye. I, on the other hand, felt as though I had taken on the weight of her sadness. While the young woman eased her way into the slow-moving line of passengers in the aisle, I stayed in my seat and waited for the plane to empty. I was in no hurry.

At length I pulled my bag from the overhead rack and made my way out of the plane and down the metal staircase to the tarmac, stepping reluctantly into the heat of the deepening Mississippi twilight.

TWENTY-ONE

My work had taken me throughout the South on many occasions, but I had been to Mississippi only twice, and then never beyond Jackson. Even though I wasn't well acquainted with the Magnolia State, I had a definite aversion to it that I couldn't quite shake. To me, its past was Negro slaves and white "Massas," its present, Negro subservience and white supremacists. My picture of Mississippi was tainted by stereotypes, I knew, and I normally didn't like giving in to such bias. Before coming, I reread Eudora Welty and William Faulkner, reminding myself that a place that had produced such writers couldn't be all bad. I thought of Faulkner's imagery: the summer of wisteria, a veranda at twilight, fireflies drifting over a deep shaggy lawn. Perhaps this trip would give me the opportunity to approach Mississippi with an open mind, to realize the good of the place while I worked to uncover the not so good.

It was Saturday midmorning. After spending a night at the Belle Motel in Jackson, where my sleep was once again invaded by nightmares about Lenny, I was on the road with my suitcase and my portable typewriter on the backseat of a rental car, driving north from Jackson across the Mississippi landscape toward Carver. It wasn't far, maybe fifty miles straight up Highway 51. Carver was a town of about fourteen hundred that bumped up against the Big Black River and the border between Holmes and Attala counties, the river and the border being one and the same. It was a town that had started out as little more than a jumping-off place for the Illinois Central Railroad but now had an economy grounded in textiles. Its largest employer was a single textile mill, to be exact, and that was owned by Helen Fulton's husband, Tom Fulton.

As I drove I noted that the landscape was greener and more fertile than I had imagined it would be, filled with blooming azaleas and camellias, evergreens, and the magnolia trees the state was famous for. Somehow I always pictured Mississippi as barren and dusty, the desert of the South, a dry patch of land cracking under a relentless sun. It *was* hot, this being July, but I found myself enjoying the scenery as it slipped past me beyond the open windows—the gentle hills, the blooming bushes, the faint scent of pine and honeysuckle in the air. *Okay,* I told myself, *score one for Mississippi.* No one could accuse me of not giving the place a fair chance.

Helen Fulton told me herself that she was trying to learn to appreciate this southern state. "It has the potential to be a beautiful place," she told me over the phone. "It just hasn't reached its full potential yet."

When I said she didn't sound like a native Mississippian, she admitted she wasn't. She'd been living in Cincinnati when she met her husband. He had moved to Ohio several years earlier to escape the South.

"But he just couldn't stay away?" I asked sardonically.

"He wanted to, but his mother begged him to come back when his father became too sick to run the mill. It's a family business, and Tom felt responsible. So two years ago we moved to Carver."

"And you suddenly found yourself in the middle of the civil rights movement?"

"Well, you might say I found myself in a place that has yet to catch on to the civil rights movement. And like I told you—"

I know, I know, not a single Negro was registered to vote in Carver. Only a dozen or so were registered in all of Holmes County. And in the whole of Mississippi, less than five percent of the black population was eligible to go to the polls. That's what Helen Fulton and a handful of other activists were trying to change. They had started a citizenship school in Carver to help Negroes prepare for the task of registering to vote.

But change didn't come easily in a state where Negro men "came up missing" just for forgetting to address a white man as "sir." Change didn't come easily in a state where Negro women were raped by white men while the law turned a blind eye to the act, or worse, took part in it.

Mississippi was where the Reverend George Lee was killed in 1955 for leading a voter registration drive, and where fourteen-year-old Emmett Till was murdered a few months later for speaking to a white woman. This was where in 1959 Mack Charles Parker was taken from jail by a group of white men and hanged without trial; where in 1961 Herbert Lee, a voter registration worker, was killed by a white legislator; where in 1963 Medgar Evers, a civil rights worker, was shot to death in his own driveway in front of his wife and children.

And only the year before, Mississippi had been the site of the Freedom Summer, an event that had less to do with freedom than with a certain kind of war. I hadn't directly reported on it myself, but I'd followed the story with interest. White students had swarmed in from the North, dragging both their youthful idealism and their dogged determination along with them, not to mention no small measure of courage. Those young folks wanted to unravel the wrongs that had kept the South tied up in racial bondage for generations. They and their Negro counterparts set up Freedom Schools to teach the disenfranchised their constitutional rights and to lead them in a massive voter registration drive.

The first volunteers had barely crossed the state's border in June when three of the workers—two white, one Negro—had come up missing. In August the bodies of Andrew Goodman, Michael Schwerner, and James Chaney were found buried under an earthen dam. They had all been shot. Chaney, the Negro, had been so severely beaten that he would have died even without the bullet. Almost every bone in his body was broken. Meanwhile, Freedom Summer had gone on playing itself out against a backdrop of shootings, beatings, arrests, arson, and fire bombings. All because some concerned activists were trying to get the vote for a group of people who, by right and by law, should already have been able to vote anyway.

It was no benign pastime, no Wednesday afternoon ladies auxiliary meeting, no feel-good volunteer work to be campaigning for civil rights. Not in Mississippi.

"I don't think most people here need to know you're a reporter except for those involved in the citizenship school," Helen Fulton had said. "For the sake of your own safety, we'll just pretend you're an old friend of mine who's come to visit."

That was fine by me. I was becoming more cautious with age. I wouldn't have called myself a coward, but neither did I relish the thought of a nighttime encounter with a group of men wearing their bed sheets instead of sleeping on them.

"I don't suppose your newspaper in Carver reports on civil rights?" I asked.

"Not a word," Helen Fulton confirmed. "But that's not too surprising. You could have Martin Luther King Jr. lead a march right through downtown Jackson, and not even the Jackson dailies would cover it. The press around here is dominated by the segregationists, and they want to present a picture that all's well with the status quo. You know, kind of like looking at the emperor and pretending he's got clothes on when he's obviously naked as a jaybird."

Naked as a jaybird. I had to chuckle. Sunny had used that expression at times, and it always sent us into fits of laughter. Weren't all birds naked except for their feathers? We couldn't recall seeing any wearing britches or dresses, fedoras or Buster Browns.

"All right. I'll travel undercover, so to speak. I might even get a better story that way. We're just old friends enjoying a visit."

So there I was, heading to a town not fifty miles from the town where the three civil rights workers had so recently been slain. I shivered in spite of the heat. "You can be proud," my editor had told me. "You've done a good job covering civil rights. If there's a story in Carver, you'll find it." Maybe so, but frankly, I was getting tired of it all. Tired of reporting on the sit-ins and the kneel-ins and the marches. Tired of seeing the abuse, the riots, the arrests. Tired of hearing "We Shall Overcome" being sung by people who were minutes away from getting their brains bashed in. It seemed that hate was all I'd been writing about for years, and every story left me a little more drained and a little more disillusioned. In spite of the good intentions of some, the problem of racism seemed destined to stick around for a good long while. Most likely, it would never end. People would go on clashing till doomsday, and when I and my contemporaries died, the next generation would simply produce another crop of journalists to write the same old story using only slightly different words.

"Maybe after Carver I could cover something besides civil rights for a while, Richard?" I asked my editor.

"Come on, Augie," he countered, "you've done plenty of stories. Elections, assassinations, the space program, the Cuban Missile Crisis." He offered me a brief lopsided smile before adding, "Well, how about Vietnam, then? You want to be a war correspondent?"

Not exactly what I was hoping he'd come back with, but then, there didn't seem to be much good news in the world.

I drove on toward Carver, making an effort to notice the blossoms and all the green growing things that marked the way.

❧

When I saw the sign that said "Welcome to Carver," I glanced again at Helen Fulton's handwritten directions. I had to drive straight through the center of town and on past it to reach the road leading to the Fultons' house. When I drove by the Magnolia Café and caught the odor of burgers frying, I realized it was almost noon and my stomach was growling. I hoped Mrs. Fulton would exercise her southern hospitality and offer me something to eat. Maybe a decent meal would put me in a better frame of mind for doing what I had come here to do.

I followed the directions onto a dirt road. A cloud of dust rose up like a storm and clung to the back bumper of the rental car. I had to roll up the driver-side window so as not to suffocate by drawing too much of the road into my lungs. The car was unbearably hot and stuffy without the benefit of incoming air, and the back of my dress began to stick to the leather seat. "Wretched place," I muttered, shaking my head and momentarily losing my resolve to try to be open-minded.

Suddenly there it was, a lovely two-story clapboard house nestled among tall pines and leafy live oaks. It was fronted by a porch both long and wide, Faulkner's veranda overlooking a carpet of emerald lawn. I could well imagine sitting on one of the cane-bottom rocking chairs or on the porch swing there, watching the constellation of fire-flies at twilight. The house was painted white with green shutters and trim, while dashes of red were provided by the potted geraniums in macramé slings hanging about the porch. The roof of the house peaked into gingerbread trim and was crowned with a weather vane shaped like a rooster. The only thing missing was the wisteria, though there were plenty of azalea bushes planted along the sides of the house, and honeysuckle and wild grapevine flourished at the edges of the yard by the wooded lots on either side.

"Now that's a house," I whispered as I parked in the circular drive. After peeling my sweaty back from the seat, I stood for a moment in the *V* of the open car door, looking up at this grand and well-kept house. It stood in stark contrast to the small and rather homely apartment I shared with a roommate in Los Angeles. Hilda was a nurse who worked the night shift, so we actually saw little of each other. She returned home from the hospital in time to drop into bed just as I was tumbling out of my own to get ready for work. We communicated mostly by hastily scribbled notes left on the kitchen counter. It was a satisfactory arrangement; we shared rent and living expenses and didn't even have to be compatible. If we didn't like each other, we had neither the time nor the opportunity to find out.

"How lucky she is," I thought of Helen Fulton as I continued to gaze at her home. There had once been a time—back in Stella's cramped apartment, back in Uncle Finn's attic—when I dreamed of living in a place like this. "How very, very lucky, and she probably doesn't even know it."

I threw the strap of my pocketbook over my shoulder and climbed up the porch steps. The main door was open to allow a breeze into the hallway, but the screen door was shut. A sound like dishes clanging came from the rear of the house.

"Hello?" I called, then stepped back to look for a doorbell. Before I could lift my finger to the button, I heard footsteps and saw the small but graceful figure of a woman approaching down the hall.

"Hello!" she hollered cheerfully as she stepped across the hardwood floor. When she reached the door she stopped suddenly beyond the screen, her hands pausing on the wooden frame. Her eyes seemed to widen, her face to open, and I heard what I thought was a sharp intake of breath or perhaps a gasp of surprise. But I may have been imagining her response, because in the next moment she was smiling amiably again and saying, "You must be Miss Callahan. I'm Helen Fulton." I had shed the name Schuler and taken on Callahan—Jack and Stella's last name—early in my twenties when I started writing professionally.

Helen Fulton unlatched the screen door and pushed it open. "How wonderful you're here at last. Come in, won't you? I've got lunch all prepared. You must be tired and hungry after your trip."

Without the screen between us, I could better see my hostess. Her voice had been friendly on the phone, and now I saw she had a face to match. Her laughing eyes and honest smile drew me in and filled me at once with an unexpected warmth.

I was surprised by this, completely caught off guard by my reaction to this woman. Normally I worked hard to stay emotionally distant from people, but there was something about Helen Fulton that I liked immediately, and I seemed to have no more choice about it than did the German sailors who were spellbound by the songs of Lorelei.

My reservations about coming to Carver dissipated as I stepped over the threshold into the front hall. "Thank you so much for inviting me to Carver," I said, surprised once more to realize my words were sincere.

We clasped hands in greeting, and as we did her left hand rose as though she were reaching to hug me. But she only patted her wavy brown hair and motioned me toward the kitchen. "Come in and make yourself at home," she invited.

I will, I thought as my gaze took in the pleasant rooms on either side of the hall. And I might even enjoy these next few days, I decided, because in some odd, inexplicable way, I did feel as though I were coming home.

TWENTY-TWO

Helen Fulton had prepared a lunch of chilled turkey salad and warm-from-the-oven crescent rolls served with seedless raspberry jam. She poured us each a tall glass of sweetened tea with a slice of lemon bobbing amid the ice.

Odd, I thought, as I eyed the rolls and jam, a favorite of mine from way back. How did Helen Fulton know what I like?

"It looks delicious," I said as I spread a cloth napkin over my lap.

"I trust you're hungry."

"Starving."

"How was your stay in Jackson?"

"Fine. Just fine."

"And you had no problem finding Carver or the house?"

"None. Your directions made it easy."

She smiled. "That's good to hear. I'm usually not very good with directions."

We started eating then, and both of us, I sensed, were comfortable with the lapse in conversation. We sat at a small gateleg table in a breakfast nook at the back end of the kitchen. The nook's bay window had a cushioned seat with lots of throw pillows on it. I thought it would be a lovely place to sit in the morning with a cup of coffee and a good book.

"You have a beautiful home," I said at length.

"Thank you." Helen Fulton took a long sip of her iced tea. "I like it, but the children say it's too isolated. They miss having kids right next door the way we did in Cincinnati."

I nodded. I could see their point. Children wouldn't appreciate solitude the way I did. "How many children do you have?"

"Two. Ronnie and Joanie. They're seven and six."

"Are they"—I absently looked over my shoulder—"here?"

Helen Fulton shook her head while she chewed on a bit of crescent roll. "They're at their grandmother's. Tom's mother. She lives alone now since her husband died." She sniffed and offered a brief smile. "Or I should say, she lives alone except for the hired help—a live-in maid, a full-time cook, and a gardener who doubles as a chauffeur. Anyway, the kids spend a lot of time there when school's out. It's in town and closer to everything, including their friends."

"Oh. Well, I look forward to meeting them and your husband too."

"Oh yes, Tom's at the mill, as usual. He almost always works on Saturdays. But they'll all be home for supper. They're anxious to meet you too. In fact, we're hoping you'll stay here with us in the guest room. We'd be delighted to have you."

I wiped at my mouth with the napkin. I wanted to accept her offer at once but instead gave what seemed the polite reply. "Oh, but I wouldn't want to put you out."

"Not at all. We just don't want to be in *your* way, while you're working."

"Oh no, I—"

"I do have reservations for you at the Carver Motel, but I can cancel them. It's over by the train station, and I hear it's awfully noisy, trains coming and going at all hours."

"It's very kind of you. I'd love to stay, if you're sure . . ."

"Please do." She looked at me then, her eyes almost pleading with me to stay. I wondered briefly if she was as lonely here in this house as her children were.

"I will, then. Thank you."

She dished some more jam onto her plate. "It must be so exciting," she said, "writing for a magazine like you do."

I laughed. "Well, as they say, it's a living."

"Oh, it's more than that. I can't imagine traveling like you do, writing stories that are read by people all over the country. I subscribe to the magazine, you know. I read all your articles."

She had told me so earlier over the phone. I nodded and smiled.

"I used to work, of course," she went on, sounding apologetic, "before the children were born." She seemed to think, in this age of Betty Friedan and bonfires of brassieres, she had to explain why she was simply a housewife. I wanted to tell her she didn't have to explain, that having a home and a family suddenly made perfect sense to me the moment I walked through her front door. I had chosen my solitude, but when the alternative is laid out in front of you in living color, it's hard not to feel some sense of loss in what you've denied yourself.

"What did you do," I asked, "before the children?"

"I was a nurse, a surgical nurse. Fascinating work, if you go for that kind of thing. I miss it, but I thought it best to stay home for the children. Someday I'll go back, but probably not anytime soon."

We ate again in silence. It was a less comfortable silence this time. After several moments she asked, "More salad?"

"Please, yes. It's very good."

She passed me the bowl, and I scooped a spoonful onto my plate. The moment I handed the bowl back to her, I realized I shouldn't have taken more; my hostess seemed to want to be done with lunch.

"Miss Callahan," she said quietly.

"Please," I interrupted, "you must call me Augie, especially if I'm going to be staying in your home."

After a brief but somber pause she repeated my name. "Augie." Her voice was a whisper, and by the time the word reached me, Helen Fulton's eyes shimmered with tears.

Completely puzzled, I set down my fork and leaned toward her. My mind replayed in high speed the few minutes we'd been together, searching for what might have happened to cause her tears. Finally I asked, "Are you all right? Have I done something to offend you?"

She shook her head quickly and rose from the table. "Forgive me," she said. Plucking a tissue from a box on the counter, she dabbed at her eyes and returned to her place at the table.

"Miss—Augie, I was going to wait a little while, let us get

acquainted, or reacquainted, but I have to tell you the truth. I never was much of one for acting." Her mouth formed the weakest of smiles. "It's impossible to pretend as though I don't know you."

I lifted my eyebrows, my mouth a taut line. Helen Fulton *didn't* know me, so what was this all about?

"I don't understand," I said quietly while thinking to myself, *She's crazy. I've come all this way for a nut case. Wait until Richard hears this one. . . .*

"Of course you don't. How could you?"

She seemed to want me to say something, but I couldn't imagine what. She was the one who needed to start explaining. She said my name again, "Augie," and as she said it she reached out as though to touch my hand but stopped short of where my fingers rested on the table. "Augie, it's me. Sunny."

Suddenly the turkey salad was a cold brick in my stomach. I felt dizzy but didn't dare even to breathe. What was she saying? That she was Sunny? Helen Fulton wanted me to believe that the little Japanese bud known as Sunny Yamagata had blossomed finally into adulthood as a white woman?

That's it, then, I told myself. *Helen Fulton isn't just crazy; she's a full-fledged lunatic.* Great oak trees may grow from little acorns, but anyone in his right mind knows you can't expect roses when you've planted watermelon seeds.

I wondered fleetingly how she knew about Sunny, but what seemed more important was simply how to escape. I told myself to slowly get up from the table, walk purposely down the hall to the front door, and from there run to the safety of the rental car. But I was kept in place by a mixture of mild curiosity and paralyzing fear.

For an interminable amount of time neither of us spoke. We stared at each other, waiting each for the other to say something, anything.

I pushed my chair back an inch or two, lifted the napkin from my lap, and laid it on the table as though preparing to leave. I repeated to myself the order to get up and get away, but my legs wouldn't follow through.

"I know this must seem strange, even unbelievable—"

"Is this some kind of sick joke?"

"No, Augie, no." She shook her head and reached for my hand, but I pulled away. "It's no joke. I'm Sunny. Sunny Yamagata. I never thought I'd find you—"

"Why are you doing this?" Anger was beginning to nudge its way past the fear in my chest.

"Augie, I'm telling you the truth—"

"Who are you really?" I grasped the edge of the table with both hands, to hold on to something solid to keep myself in the real world.

"Augie, please, I'm Sunny—"

"You said you were Helen Fulton."

"Yes, I *am* Helen Fulton. You probably don't remember, but Helen is my middle name. I go by it now. And Fulton, of course, is my married name. But I'm *still* Sunny."

Frantic, I looked around the kitchen, hoping someone might appear who could explain what was going on. Since this woman obviously could not be Sunny Yamagata, why would she want me to believe she was? Someone, for some reason, had orchestrated an enormous practical joke at my expense. Maybe somewhere somebody was laughing aloud, but the kitchen was heavy with a stony silence.

"Augie, let me explain—"

"But you're not even Japanese." I was surprised I could speak, that I could hear myself above the roar of blood in my ears.

She shut her eyes, opened them, demanded my gaze. "Augie, listen to me. A few years ago I had very simple surgery to change my eyes and add some height to my nose. I lighten and perm my hair—"

"I don't believe it." I pushed my chair back another inch.

"It's true, Augie. Please believe me," she said firmly. "After the war, many Asians did the same to make themselves look white."

True, I'd heard vague rumors of such surgery after the war, but I'd thought it was probably an anomaly, a handful of Japanese doing something drastic to elbow their way into mainstream America. It wasn't anything Sunny Yamagata would do.

"What are you trying to do? What is it you want from me?"

For a moment Helen Fulton was speechless, her mouth open in a small circle. She shook her head as though to clear it of fog. "I don't want anything—I mean, I just wanted to find you again."

I didn't know why Helen Fulton was lying to me, but I summoned the strength to try to find out.

"If you're Sunny Yamagata," I demanded, "where in Los Angeles did you live?"

"Boyle Heights," was the quiet answer. "On Fickett Street."

"What kind of business did your father own?"

"A grocery store, with Ojisan Hito."

"What was your dog's name?"

"Jimmy. After Jimmy Durante."

"What was my uncle's name?"

"Finn O'Shaughnessy. And your aunt's name was Lucy."

The answers came back as quickly as I could shoot the questions, but I figured I could trip her up somewhere. These were too easy. Anyone who'd done a little digging into my past could discover these facts. I had to think of something more obscure, something only Sunny would know.

"Where did we meet?"

"Hollenbeck Park. I was sitting on a bench listening to a band when you came along."

I took in a sharp breath. My jaw tightened. "What did we do every night before we fell asleep?"

"I pinched my nose to make it bigger, and you pushed yours to make it smaller."

Would anyone besides Sunny have known this? I searched my mind for another question. "What were we doing when Pearl Harbor was bombed?"

She thought a moment, but only a moment. A smile flickered across her face. "We were dancing in my room. Obaasan came and scolded us for being too loud. And then Papa came. . . ."

Her voice trailed off. I was slowing down myself, wondering where to go from here. I simply couldn't reconcile this white woman with the little Japanese girl I'd known as a child. "What did your father and mother call me?" I asked, one final bid to catch her off guard. "What did they call me when I was a child?"

She didn't hesitate. "Musume. Daughter. And you called them Chichi and Haha, father and mother."

She rose, pulled something from a kitchen drawer, then returned to her seat in the breakfast nook. She slid a photograph to me across the table, a black-and-white shot of Sunny and me sitting on the front steps of the Yamagatas' house, our arms dangling around each other's necks. "Papa took it on our tenth birthday. Do you remember?"

I did.

The brick in my stomach exploded, and I stumbled into the bathroom where I'd freshened up half an hour earlier, this time to lose my carefully prepared lunch down the toilet. I kneeled there by the bowl long after my stomach was empty, feeling sick and dizzy and somehow disconnected from myself and my life. This woman had to be Sunny, but my mind couldn't take it in. It was too much. I would have to accept it little by little, bit by bit, if I was to accept it at all.

In a moment a hand came to rest on my back, and what was meant to comfort me only started me sobbing.

"I'm so sorry, Augie," Helen Fulton—Sunny Yamagata—apologized quietly. "I never intended to upset you so. I didn't think—"

"Dear God," I mumbled, "are you really Sunny?"

"Really, yes. Augie, I—"

"Why didn't you tell me?" I asked, my voice choked with sobs. "When we talked on the phone, why didn't you tell me who you were?"

I couldn't bring myself to look at her, but I heard her sigh heavily. She dropped her hand from my back. "I didn't tell you who I was because, for one thing, I wasn't sure I was talking to *you*. I mean, you're Augusta Callahan now, not Schuler, so I couldn't be certain."

"Why didn't you just ask?"

"It didn't seem good enough to talk to you over the phone after so many years. I wanted to see you, to talk with you face-to-face."

The irony of her statement didn't escape me, and I lifted my gaze to her face. "Why'd you do it, Sunny? Why did you change the way you look?"

Sunny shut her eyes, her hakujin eyes, and opened them again. "It's—well, it's complicated and not really important right now. What's important is that I've found you, and—"

"After all this time you wanted to find me when you couldn't even bother to write to me after you left?" The anger in the words surprised even me. But I went on, "Why did you never write like you promised you would?"

The question had been knocking at my brain for twenty-three years and had gone unanswered. It had in fact gone unasked because there had been no one to ask it of. But now there was. Now Sunny

Yamagata was kneeling right here beside me on the floor of a bathroom somewhere in the middle of Mississippi, and I could finally ask the question. And when it came out into the open, it dragged with it all the days and months and years of pain and anger that I had for so long tried not to feel.

Sunny looked horrified and helpless. "Why didn't I write?" she echoed. "Augie, I wrote dozens of letters, maybe hundreds. Mother and Papa wrote. We never heard back from you, but we kept on writing. Didn't you receive any of the letters?"

I was still on my knees leaning over the toilet, but now I sank to the floor. For a moment I could do nothing more than shake my head in disbelief. "No," I whispered.

"Not one?"

"Not a single one."

"How can that be?"

I didn't know. "You sent them to my uncle's address?"

"Yes, of course."

We sat in silence, wondering what could have happened to all those letters. I remembered waiting for them, sitting on the front steps until Sean McDougall arrived with his mail pouch, then asking, "Anything for me today?" And his unvarying reply, "No, kid. Nothing."

And then I knew. It all came into focus like a slide projected onto the wall. Uncle Finn must have persuaded his best friend and drinking buddy, Sean McDougall—maybe even paid him—to intercept the letters, to keep them from me. I thought of the way McDougall averted his eyes, how he refused ever to look at me when he told me there were no letters. He was a bad man in many ways, but he wasn't a very good liar. And now I could see that; now I knew.

"But tampering with mail is against the law!" Sunny exclaimed when I told her what I suspected.

I couldn't help but laugh. "That doesn't matter to men like Finn O'Shaughnessy and Sean McDougall," I countered. "All that mattered to my uncle was keeping me from you."

"I can't believe it," Sunny said, sinking back on her heels. "I mean, I know he did some crazy things, but I can't believe he'd stoop to something like that."

"Believe it," I retorted. "There's no other explanation."

Sunny shook her head. "I couldn't imagine what had happened to you. I even wrote to Miss Pruitt—our sixth-grade teacher, remember?—and asked her about you. She wrote back and said you must have moved away because you were no longer enrolled in that school district."

I sighed as the situation became even clearer. "I didn't stay long at Uncle Finn's. At the end of that school year I moved in with Stella, and that put me in a different school district. Stella made Uncle Finn promise to give me your letters so I'd know where to write you, and so I could give you Stella's address. But Uncle Finn and Aunt Lucy both swore that no letters ever came for me. Aunt Lucy probably had no idea, and technically Uncle Finn was telling the truth. No doubt the letters never reached the house at all."

"You think the mailman just got rid of them, threw them away or something?"

I nodded, my eyes shut against the thought. "I imagine that's what happened. Oh, Sunny," I moaned, "I should have known not to trust Uncle Finn."

We were quiet a moment, floating somewhere in our disbelief, trying to make sense of it all. Finally I said, "What must you have thought, when you never heard from me?"

Sunny actually smiled, a wan little smile. "I thought you were angry with us for leaving you behind. I thought you decided to hate us because we were Japanese. I thought a million things, but when it came right down to it, I didn't know what to think. I prayed you would write to me, let me know *some*thing. . . ." Her words faded as she shook her head slowly. And I realized for the first time that all the years I spent wondering where she was, she was doing the same, wondering about me.

"Still, why didn't you come back after the war?" I asked. "You'd have found me if you'd have come back."

Sunny shifted her position on the floor, as though to settle herself in for a long explanation. She smoothed her skirt, fingered a button on her blouse as she spoke. "Early in '45," she began, "when many of the Nisei were leaving the camps to return home or settle elsewhere, Papa and Ojisan Hito did go back to L.A. to reclaim the store. But the hakujin who were leasing it wouldn't give it up. The law wasn't on the hakujins' side, but the lawmen were, so there was nothing Papa and Ojisan could do. And you know we'd sold the house. Even the Buddhist temple where we stored some of our things had been broken into and ransacked. Most everything was taken or destroyed. It wasn't hard to see there was nothing left for us in California. Papa decided to start a new life somewhere else, and that's how we ended up in Cincinnati. A Quaker group there was helping Japanese people like us to resettle. They provided temporary housing, and they helped people find jobs. We were welcomed there, not like Los Angeles where we knew we weren't wanted."

I was quiet a moment, weighing her explanation carefully. Then I said, "I used to go down to the store sometimes toward the end of the war. Afterward, too, for a while. Jimmy and I sat on the bench outside waiting for Chichi to show up. I guess I wasn't there the day he came."

Sunny stopped fiddling with the button on her blouse and laid a hand on my arm. "Papa tried to find you when he was in L.A. He went to your uncle's house hoping you'd be there. But your uncle told him you'd moved north early in the war to live with relatives. Papa asked where you were and if he could have your address, but your uncle wouldn't answer any of his questions. He only shut the door in Papa's face."

"Moved north?" I lifted my eyes to the ceiling, trying to swallow the taste of bitterness that had risen to my mouth. "Well, I did move north but only by a few miles."

Sunny shook her head, a faint smile of amusement on her lips. "And I always pictured you living in Seattle or Portland, someplace like that. I thought it would be impossible ever to find you again."

I shrugged as I held up my hands, palms upward. "Well," I said, "you found me."

It was then that we fell into each other's arms.

❧

"So, how *did* you find me, Sunny?"

We were back at the table in the breakfast nook where Sunny replenished our glasses of iced tea. I still felt slightly sick, but sipping the tea helped. I was struggling mentally to accept the oddity of the moment: here I sat with a woman who was my oldest friend and at the same time a complete stranger. Only an hour earlier Sunny Yamagata was to me an oft-buried memory, never to be resurrected in the flesh. Yet here she was, not only resurrected but transformed into something completely different. A two-pronged surprise that knocked me for a loop, a situation so surreal that even while I was living it, I had to convince myself it was happening.

Sunny smiled at my question. "Last year I read your book. When I picked it up at the library, I had no idea Augusta Callahan was my old friend Augie Schuler. I checked the book out just because the author's name was Augusta. I guess that sounds silly. But I took the book home not even knowing what it was about. As I read it I began to wonder whether it could possibly have been written by you. I didn't know you'd become a writer, of course, but I remembered how much you loved books, how much you loved to read. Also, I remembered you had a brother in the Philippines at the start of the war, and I wondered whether the soldier in the book was based on your brother. I noticed the book was dedicated to someone named Lenny, but I couldn't remember if that was your brother's name."

I nodded. My book, *Soldier, Come Home,* wasn't actually about Lenny, but he had been the inspiration behind it.

Sunny went on, "The dust jacket said you were a reporter for *One Nation,* so I figured I could contact the magazine and find out whether Augusta Callahan was Augie Schuler. Of course, if there'd been a photo on the dust jacket I'd have known for sure it was you." She paused and smiled once again. "I'd have recognized you anywhere, Augie. The moment I got to the front door, I knew I'd found you."

I offered her a half smile in return, one corner of my mouth pulled back. "You mean, I've changed so little in twenty-three years?"

"Well, of course you've changed, but I could still see in you the Augie Schuler I knew in Boyle Heights."

I couldn't say the same for her, so I said nothing. She went on, "I could have fainted dead away when I realized who was standing at my door. I'd been hoping Callahan was your married name, and I guess I was right."

"Well, not exactly," I corrected. "I've never married. Callahan is Stella's last name, which I legally took on when I was in my early twenties."

"Oh?" She looked surprised. "But why?"

Why did I never marry, or why did I take on a new name? I assumed she was wondering about both, but chose for the moment to answer only the one.

"I was young and rebellious and idealistic, I guess. After the war when I learned what the Germans had done in the death camps, I didn't want to carry around a German name. Schuler never meant anything to me anyway. I can scarcely remember my father, and I was never close to my mother. But Stella was good to me during the war. We helped each other through those years when Jack was gone and you were gone."

"Wasn't Stella the one who worked in the hardware store but wanted to be a beautician?" Sunny asked.

I nodded and laughed as I thought of Stella in her Rosie-the-Riveter getup. "Yes, but in the end she became a welder! During the war she worked in a factory building airplanes, and then as soon as Jack came home she became a mother. Anyway, I considered her my only family, so when I was old enough to make the decision, I took her name."

"I guess that makes sense," Sunny agreed. "But didn't you figure you'd just get married and change your name that way?"

Ah, the question of marriage. There was no avoiding it. "No," I said, looking at my hands. "I wanted to devote myself to my work. It's hard to write when you're taking care of a family, so I made a choice. . . ." I lifted my shoulders to signify indifference, but I think instead the gesture hinted at defeat.

"Well," Sunny said, trying to sound cheerful, "as long as you're happy."

Was I? It had been a long time since I'd allowed myself to think in terms of feelings, happiness or sadness, satisfaction or dissatisfaction.

I changed the subject. "Do Chichi and Haha still live in Cincinnati?"

Sunny nodded as she swallowed a sip of tea. "Yes, though Papa's retired and they travel a lot these days. They bought themselves a motor home a couple years ago, and they've driven that thing all over the country."

"Do they know I'm here?" I asked excitedly. "Can I call them?"

Sunny let out a long breath. "Unfortunately, just last week they decided to up and take a trip through New England. So no, they don't know you're here, and no, you can't call them. They never have a set itinerary when they travel—they go when they feel like it and stop when they feel like it. So I have no idea where exactly they are."

"You didn't tell them I was coming?" I tried not to sound hurt, but I must have failed because Sunny looked apologetic.

"I'm sorry, Augie, but I didn't. Like I said, I wasn't sure it'd be you showing up on my doorstep, and I didn't want to get their hopes up if it wasn't. They'd have been heartbroken if I told them I'd found you and then Augusta Callahan turned out to be a total stranger. My plan was to call them as soon as I knew for sure. I didn't know about their trip until the day before they left, and to tell you the truth, they probably didn't either. Papa gets the itch to go, and off they go."

"Do you know how long they'll be traveling?"

"No idea."

"Will they call here?"

"They might. I don't know. We'll probably be receiving some postcards soon from Boston or Kennebunkport, but that's about the best I can guarantee."

My disappointment must have shown on my face because Sunny quickly added, "But I'll give you their number, and you can call them when you get back to L.A. They'll want to hear from you, Augie. I wouldn't be surprised if they jumped in their motor home and sped out to L.A. to see you."

I was still wading through the moment in a haze of disbelief, trying to feel my way to the other side where I could accept it as real. "I long ago gave up all hope of ever seeing them again," I said. "Only now I realize how much I went on missing them anyway—all of you."

"You have no idea how much we missed you when we were in the camp," Sunny said. "We talked about you all the time. When my little sister was born, Mother and Papa decided to name her after you."

Little sister? Oh yes, the baby that Haha was still carrying when they left. I had almost forgotten.

"They named her Augusta?" I asked. Then I laughed quietly. "Poor thing, to be burdened with such a name."

"We called her Gus when she was little, so we wouldn't confuse her with you. But she goes by Augusta now."

"And where is she?"

"Cincinnati. She's married, has a little boy. Sam and George are both in Ohio too. Sam's a dentist, and George is a chemical engineer."

I shook my head, remembering the two little boys I'd once known. "It's hard to believe. And they both have families?"

"Oh yes. Papa and Mother have nine grandchildren."

"They must have hated to see you leave Ohio."

"They did. Tom and I didn't want to move south either, but like I told you on the phone, Tom's father became ill, and there was the mill to consider."

"He has no brothers or sisters?"

"One of each, both younger, both living outside Mississippi. Tom, being the oldest, felt it was his responsibility to come back and take over the mill. We don't intend to stay here forever, though. Eventually we'll sell the business and move north again, when the time is right."

"How do you explain it when Chichi and Haha come to visit? I mean, they still look Japanese, don't they?"

Sunny laughed. "Oh yes. They weren't terribly pleased when I had the surgery, and they've certainly never had any intention of making hakujins out of themselves. Anyway, they won't come to Mississippi. They say the state's uncivilized, with all the lynching that goes on and the vigilante justice and whatnot. No, we have to visit them in Cincinnati when we want to see them."

"So they've never been here?"

Shaking her head, Sunny replied, "Only a miracle would set their feet on Mississippi soil."

I was quiet then, looking at my old friend, searching for the Sunny I once knew. I thought I caught a glimpse of her in the placid smile, the way she lifted an eyebrow as though to ask what I was thinking. "I still don't know where you were during the war," I said.

"We were sent to Manzanar. There were ten camps across the country, as far east as Arkansas, but my family never left California— not until after the war, anyway."

"Manzanar," I repeated. I'd heard of the place but knew little about it. I reached across the table and took Sunny's hand. "I have so much to ask you, so much I want to know. But I'm just so . . . shocked, I guess, that I don't even know where to begin."

She squeezed my hand. "There's so much I want to ask you too. But we have lots of time. Let me show you to your room, help you get settled in, and then we can take a drive around Carver. You still want to do the story, don't you?"

"You mean, there really is a citizenship school? That wasn't just a ploy to get me out here?"

"Yes, there really is a school. And there really is a story here that I hope will make your trip worthwhile."

"Are you kidding!" I exclaimed. "Make my trip worthwhile? You think it's not more than enough to find you? Imagine if I'd decided not to come, or if my editor had said no."

Sunny thought a moment. "Well," she said, "I guess in that case I'd have told you who I was over the phone."

"What—and miss the chance to watch me lose my lunch?"

We laughed then, and my gaze dropped to the photo on the table. Sunny and me on the front steps of the house on Fickett Street, our arms around each other. Time folded up like an accordion so that the present moment touched that long-ago day, and I was Musume again.

Sometimes the unbelievable happens.

TWENTY-THREE

After fetching my suitcase and typewriter from the rental car, I followed Sunny up the stairs to a spacious bedroom decorated in shades of blue and rose and furnished with antiques. I felt very much as I had the first time I walked into Sunny's bedroom in Boyle Heights. Once again I was the attic child looking in wonder at a room that seemed an artist's canvas come to life: a wide four-poster bed covered with a hand-stitched quilt of morning-glory vines; a mahogany chest of drawers covered with a white linen scarf and laden with knickknacks; a full-length standing mirror framed in white wicker; a bookcase, shelves brimming with books, its top covered with doilies and family photographs; a bay window filled with cushions and pillows overlooking the side yard; and by the lace-curtained window overlooking the front yard sat a large desk with plenty of drawers and a chair with a needlepoint seat. It was a picturesque yet homey room and very nearly as large as the apartment I shared back in Los Angeles with Hilda.

"It's beautiful," I commented, then added, "much nicer than anything the Carver Motel has to offer, I'm sure."

"At least it's quiet, and it faces east so you get the morning sun."

I settled my typewriter on the desk. A slight breeze drifted in through the open window. "It'll be the perfect place to work." I turned to look at Sunny. "Shall we get started?"

"Why not?" she responded, smiling.

I wasn't nearly as interested in Carver and the citizenship school as I was in Sunny, but she was right—there was plenty of time for us to get reacquainted. First I simply needed some time to get used to seeing Sunny as a white woman. I needed time to accept that I was with her at all. A drive around Carver would be a good diversion, something to occupy my mind while the rest of me—spirit, soul, heart, whatever it is that cradles one's emotions—adjusted to the unexpected turn my life had taken.

We set out in Sunny's '65 Buick Roadmaster with the windows up and the air conditioner on. "I spent four years in the desert during the war," she told me as we turned out of the drive and onto the road, "but I've never gotten used to the heat of Mississippi." Almost as an afterthought, she added, "But, then again, I've never gotten used to a lot of things in Mississippi."

"Maybe you have to be a native Mississippian to appreciate the place," I suggested.

"That could be," she agreed, "but Tom was born and raised here, and one of his primary goals at this point is to head north again. And preferably sooner rather than later."

Sunny turned to look at me. With her eyes hidden behind dark sunglasses, I caught a glimpse of Sunny Yamagata as a grown woman. There was the round face, the creamy white and flawless skin, the small rosy mouth—a more mature face now and yet reminiscent still of that little girl on the bench in Hollenbeck Park. For a moment I wished that behind the glasses were the same eyes with the creaseless lids, the Japanese eyes I'd thought so beautiful. It seemed to me that something had been lost—something more than just the shape of her eyes—when she submitted herself to the surgeon's knife.

But I wouldn't talk about that now, not just yet. Instead, I said, "It's a shame you and Tom have to live where you aren't happy."

Sunny took a deep breath. We turned off the dirt road onto the paved streets of the town. "Well, we keep in mind that it's only temporary. We don't know when we'll leave, but someday we will. In the meantime we do what little we can about the situation around here. All the injustice, I mean. Tom deals with it constantly at the mill, and I do my bit with the citizenship school."

Sunny knew about injustice—more than the people of Carver could possibly imagine.

I turned my gaze to the window as we entered Carver proper. When we reached one of the main streets, Sunny pulled the car into a diagonal parking space but kept the engine idling and the air on. "Well, here we are in downtown Carver," she announced, and I looked about me at what appeared to be a pleasant enough place, clean and tidy and even quaint. The sidewalks were swept clean, trees grew on the strip of grass between sidewalk and street, and here and there patches of flowers bloomed. The buildings, mostly brick facade, had obviously been standing since the turn of the century or before, but they were well kept up. Behind us was the town square, a large swath of startling green grass crisscrossed by a sidewalk and embellished with strategically placed beds of impatiens and pansies. On one side of the square was a small gazebo, painted white, and on the other, a statue of a man wearing eighteenth-century garb and holding one hand to his heart. On the far side of the square was City Hall, a handsome, two-story building with a prominently displayed American flag. The steps leading down from the double front doors grew wider as they descended, giving the impression of open arms inviting one and all to come inside.

I took it all in, noting too the way men and women moved unhurriedly along the sidewalks, through the square, in and out of stores, as though they had nothing more pressing to do this Saturday afternoon. And who knew but that perhaps they didn't? What, after all, did one have to be anxious about in a little town like Carver on a warm and sunny summer afternoon?

"It looks like an illustration for the *Saturday Evening Post*," I commented.

"Never let appearances fool you," Sunny responded. "The evil queen's apple may look enticing in the hand, but eat it and you're dead." Snow White and her wicked stepmother. Chichi used to read the story to us at bedtime. I nodded at the recollection.

"If you look back over there," she went on, "that's a statue of Lucius Carver, the town's founder. The townsfolk around here are proud of his story, how he started out with nothing and ended up a wealthy man. A typical rags-to-riches tale of a man who made his fortune off the land. But Old Lucius was a slave owner way back when, and as the Negroes tell it, when his slaves spoke of him among themselves, they called him Lucifer. Dear old Lucifer Carver, the man who would be Satan. Gives you an idea as to how well he treated his Negroes."

"All part of what makes him a hero to the whites, I suppose."

"Exactly. Now, that's City Hall there, of course, and this building we're parked in front of is the library." Ahead of us was a white brick building with a pillared porch and double front doors propped open by heavy doorstops. Like City Hall, it looked inviting.

"Negroes allowed?" I asked.

"Only through a back door. But that's improvement. Three years ago they couldn't get in at all."

"Do many use it?"

"Some. Those who think reading a book today is worth the risk of entertaining the Klan tomorrow. There are some whites who still believe ignorance is the best way to keep the Negro in his place."

"And they're probably right."

Again Sunny nodded. "That's what the citizenship school is all about. Most of the places around here are about as integrated as the library. See the Big Black River Bijou back there?" We both twisted around in our seats to look at the theater. "The Negroes buy their tickets at the box office along with the whites, but then they go around to the alley and climb the stairs up to the balcony. No Negroes allowed on the main floor. And over there, the café"—we turned to the Magnolia Café, which was directly across the square from the theater—"they'll serve Negroes there, but they have to enter through the back door and sit in a designated section."

I hadn't expected to hear anything different, but for emphasis I said, "It doesn't matter that there are laws now against such segregation?"

"Not one bit," Sunny confirmed. Then suddenly she tapped at the window with one index finger. "Look, there's the chief of police just about to walk into the café." I followed her gaze and spotted a uniformed man pushing open the door to the eatery. "Bill Sturges, Chief of Police of Carver and Exalted Cyclops of the Carver Klavern of the White Knights of the Ku Klux Klan."

I sniffed. "Now, that's a mouthful. He must be a busy man."

"It takes a certain skill to simultaneously protect and break the law," Sunny said. After a moment, she added, "But maybe it's easier to do when you're convinced both sides of the coin add up to the same nickel anyway. Lynch a few Negroes, keep the whites happy, and all's well in Carver, U.S.A."

Though I'd reported extensively on civil rights, I'd written little about the Klan. Most likely I'd met a few Kluxers in my day, but who exactly they were, I didn't know. The Klan was a group surrounded by secrecy, squirreling themselves away in hole-in-the-wall meeting places, identifying each other by ever changing passwords and handshakes, emerging only under the cover of darkness and robes, so as not to be identified by either white or Negro. I wasn't surprised at the police chief's dual role, but I was surprised that Sunny knew about it.

"How do you happen to know this guy is Exalted Cyclops of the local Klan?" I asked.

Sunny smiled. She took off her sunglasses as she looked at me, and once again I was startled to find myself gazing at a white woman. "First of all," she explained, "it's pretty safe to assume that most police officers in Mississippi are Klan, as are many of the white shopkeepers and businessmen around here. That's just the norm. But on top of that, Tom has an informer of sorts, a woman down at the mill. See, Tom has an open-door policy. He wants all his workers to bring their complaints directly to him. Many of the workers feel free to talk with him now and again about any problems they might be having there at the mill, but one woman—a file clerk—seems to have an exceptional number of complaints." Sunny smiled at me again before going on. "Actually, she's obviously infatuated with Tom and looks for excuses to visit him. Tom makes sure the door literally stays open whenever this lady's there, of course, so his secretary can see inside his office, even if she can't hear everything. But anyway, this woman's husband is in the Klan, and he has a big mouth—tells his wife everything without knowing she's in turn passing it all on to Tom. Of course, Tom has no interest in her whatsoever, but when she comes to talk, he listens. That's how he knows who's in the Klan and often what position they hold."

"And what does this woman expect Tom to do with the information?"

"Nothing, really. But I think she thinks it'll impress him."

"Interesting."

"Yes, well, Tom is seldom surprised by anything she has to say. Like I said, it isn't hard to guess who might be Klan around here. Only on a rare occasion are we surprised, like when this woman told Tom our church organist is a member."

I shook my head. "Do you think it's true?"

Sunny shrugged. "Probably. She has no reason to lie about it. It's strange, though, because this guy, Howard Draper, he just doesn't fit the mold. Not just because he's a church organist. I mean, down here you're lucky if the pastor himself isn't out terrorizing Negroes after dark. But Howard—he's really a very nice guy. People love him, can't say enough good things about him. During the school year he teaches music at the high school, and the two years he's been in Carver he's been voted most popular teacher. He's polite, friendly—but it isn't that, really. Lots of men in the Klan can appear polite and friendly. I guess what's really strange is I've seen Howard having apparently friendly conversations with Negroes. Once I saw him outside the café there talking to a colored man, and I don't know what they were saying, but there was a lot of smiling and laughing going on. And then before they parted Howard offered his hand to the Negro, just like he was used to shaking their hands. I mean, that's pretty much unheard of down here, especially in a public place. In fact the Negro backed away, stuck his hands in his pockets. You could tell he was afraid, and Howard dropped his hand and started shaking his head like he was saying he understood. So I don't know"—Sunny shrugged again—"go figure. I guess Howard puts on a good show. The only way I can make sense of it is to figure he's one of those people who believe they're doing something good—I mean, actually carrying out God's will— when they go around lynching Negroes. Howard Draper thinks it's just one more good deed, I guess."

"Unbelievable," I sighed.

"Well," Sunny went on, "it's a mentality that's handed down from generations. When you've been raised in it, and it's all you've known, hate seems normal. It's what keeps this town locked into Jim Crow laws."

I nodded. I was well aware of the Jim Crow laws throughout the South, the rules both written and unwritten that kept the Negroes separate from the whites. No racial intermarriage allowed. No Negroes permitted in country clubs, tennis courts, golf courses. No riding on elevators in public buildings. Separate waiting rooms in doctors' offices. Separate educational facilities. Separate sections on trains, boats, buses. Separate barbershops, hair salons, churches, hospital rooms. And separate cemeteries to keep the tradition going even after death.

"But the funny thing about Howard," Sunny continued, "is that not only is he not from Carver, he's not even from the South. He was born and raised in Chicago. He just showed up in Carver one day and decided to make the place his home."

"What?" I couldn't hide my surprise. "You've got to be kidding! From Chicago to Carver? Why here, of all places?"

"No one knows for sure. Rumor has it he fled the North to escape a relationship gone sour. But Howard doesn't talk about himself much, so no one knows for sure."

"It doesn't seem likely that he'd come all the way down to this backwater just because of a bad relationship."

"That's what I think. Most likely the story's only hearsay, a bit of gossip to pass along on the grapevine. But then again, people do strange things. I don't know. There's obviously something in his background he doesn't care to discuss, so he remains our local mystery man."

"Well, I always like a mystery."

"I'd like Howard Draper if I didn't know he was Klan." Sunny turned back to the steering wheel and put the car in gear. "Well, let's drive around a little more, see some more of the town."

We turned up the street where the Magnolia Café was wedged in between a beauty parlor and a Piggly Wiggly on one side, a bank and a large department store on the other. Sunny pointed to the department store. "See that store there?" she asked.

"Frohmann's?"

Sunny nodded. "It's owned by Cedric Frohmann, who's also the mayor of Carver. His family has long been one of the wealthiest and most influential around here, along with the Fultons," she added.

"Don't tell me," I said. "Our Mayor Frohmann is Imperial Wizard of the Carver Klavern."

Sunny laughed. "Actually, no. The mayor isn't Klan. Not even a member of the White Citizen's Council, though I hear he's often called upon to speak at their meetings. He's another funny one, Mayor

Frohmann. I haven't quite got him figured out. Tom says he's a fair man at heart, and if he'd been born and raised in the North, he'd be against segregation. He did go to school in the North. He was all ready to enter Ole Miss when apparently at the last minute he changed his mind and went to school in New York——I forget where exactly. Or maybe it was Boston. Anyway, he spent nearly a decade up north before coming back here to get involved in the family business and local politics, so he had a good taste of life outside of Carver. Tom says if he'd only stayed there, he'd be campaigning for civil rights today. But you can't be for integration around here and be elected mayor."

"So Frohmann's Department Store still has one drinking fountain for whites and another for coloreds."

"You got it."

"And he hasn't taken steps to integrate the store in spite of the Civil Rights Act?"

Sunny shook her head. "The only way for him to stay in office is to keep the status quo."

We drove out of the business district, past a park and an elementary school, into the sprawling white residential district. The neighborhood through which we drove was quiet and tranquil, streaked with sun and the shade of large old live oaks, magnolia trees, and a variety of evergreens. Most of the homes were modest, sleepy little cottages with neat green lawns and boxes of petunias or impatiens in the windows. Like downtown, it was a pleasant place, kept up by people who weren't wealthy but who had a sense of pride in their hometown.

We passed only one house that bordered on the pretentious, and I wasn't surprised when Sunny pointed it out as the mayor's residence. It was a white brick two-story gated affair with a large front porch lined with tall white columns. It sat way back off the road in the middle of an immaculate lawn. Though we weren't in Georgia, I could almost imagine Scarlett O'Hara strutting across the grass huffing, "Fiddle-dee-dee!"

"It's big," I commented.

"Has a staff of twelve to keep it up."

"All Negroes?"

"Every one. But I have to add that Mayor Frohmann is very kind to his Negroes. He actually treats them like human beings. You'll see tomorrow. We're having Sunday dinner there with the mayor and his family."

"We are?" I asked.

"Don't look so surprised." She laughed. "It's nothing special, just our turn. It's a Frohmann tradition to entertain his constituents every Sunday after church. Two or three couples at a time. Tom and I and Tom's mother were invited for tomorrow, and when I mentioned you'd be in town, they said you were certainly welcome to come along. Oh, and Howard Draper is a weekly guest. I think the mayor and his wife are trying to snag him as a son-in-law. They have an unmarried daughter still at home. Betsey's got to be fifteen years younger than Howard, but most of the men her own age are over in Nam. It's not a good time to be a twenty-year-old woman looking for a husband."

"It's probably a worse time to be a twenty-year-old man looking to stay alive."

"Yes. No doubt."

After a moment I asked, "Does the mayor know Howard's with the Klan?"

Sunny shrugged. "I don't know. He probably supposes as much."

"He doesn't mind having a night rider for a son-in-law?"

"Better than no son-in-law at all. Heaven forbid Betsey Frohmann should end up an old maid."

We drove beyond the residential district to the outskirts of town, where Sunny pointed out a large box of a factory surrounded by a chain link fence. "That's the mill," she explained. "It employs thirty percent of Carver's population, both whites and Negroes. Tom wants to integrate—get rid of the separate lunchrooms and all that kind of thing—but the whites won't have it, and the blacks are too afraid to make waves. When Tom promoted one Negro into a position of foreman, he took the job for three weeks and then asked to be returned to his old position. He didn't say as much to Tom, but it was obvious he'd had too many late-night visits from the Klan to think the promotion was worth it. Tom says he can't even set the policies at his own mill, because tradition has done it for him. A tradition of prejudice that's so hard set he can't get around it."

"What about Tom's family, Sunny?" I asked. "Any of your in-laws in the Klan?"

"Some have been, and yes, some are now. Tom has a couple of cousins on the board of directors of the mill that are Klansmen, which of course doesn't help matters."

"What about Tom's father?"

Sunny shook her head. "He wasn't a Negro-loving man, but he wasn't Klan either. He went along with the status quo without trying to make things any better or any worse. He never rocked the boat either way. Tom says that's the shining characteristic of a coward." Sunny looked at me, then back at the road. "Tom never felt much affection for his father."

"But—how is it that Tom's the way he is, considering where he came from?"

Sunny smiled knowingly. "It has to do with a man named Hollis Hardy. When Tom was a boy, six or seven years old, his father hired Hollis to do some part-time gardening work around their house. He wasn't there on a regular basis, just as the need arose. Hollis was about fifty, Tom guessed. He had a whole bushel and a peck of kids and grandkids—that's how Hollis used to put it. Tom wasn't really sup-posed to associate with the Negro help, but he used to hang around Hollis, because in spite of everything, Hollis was always smiling, and he always had a story to tell. Too, he had the time for Tom that Tom's own father never seemed to have. Fulton Sr. was kind of a distant, overworked man—not really very paternal. So Tom actually started seeing Hollis as kind of a father figure. Once he even asked Hollis if he could come live with him, saying if Hollis already had a bushel and a peck of mouths to feed, one more wouldn't matter.

"Hollis knew Tom was a rich white kid who had everything in the world but his parents' attention. He told Tom he'd sure like to take him home, but he just couldn't do that." Sunny paused and chewed on her lip thoughtfully. I wondered if she were remembering the little white girl in Boyle Heights who was taken into a Japanese home when she needed to be loved. "Anyway," she went on, "after that, every time Hollis came to work at the Fulton house, he brought Tom a little wooden animal he'd carved himself. He'd give it to Tom and say, 'You know what that animal says?' Tom would make an animal sound, and Hollis would laugh and say, 'That's just a noise, is all. What that animal *says* is Daddy Hollis cares about you. Every time you look at that animal, you can know Daddy Hollis is thinking about you.' "

I waited for Sunny to go on. When she didn't, I said reluctantly, "Don't tell me—Hollis met up with the Klan."

Sunny nodded and took a deep breath. "One night Tom's uncle—

his mother's brother, not his father's—woke him up and said he was old enough to see how niggers ought to be dealt with. Tom didn't know what his uncle was talking about, but he got dressed and went with him anyway—"

"Did his parents know?"

"They had no idea. They were asleep. Apparently this uncle—a guy named Billy Wayne—was staying with the Fultons for a while. He was Corinne's younger brother, kind of a good-for-nothing who was constantly between jobs. He always boasted that his main business was the Klan and he didn't have time for anything else. Anyway, Tom went with him, and when he asked what was going on, Billy Wayne said a nigger'd made a pass at a white woman and now he had to pay the price. Tom asked what they were going to do, and Billy Wayne told him to wait and see.

"Tom has a hard time talking about it even now and won't go into details. All I know is that he had to watch while about a dozen of the Klan, including his uncle, beat Hollis to death. He wanted to defend Hollis, he tried to run to him, but one of the men held him back. Hollis saw him, though, and Tom says he'll never forget the look in his eyes. First there was this terrible fear, but when Hollis saw him, Tom says the fear changed to sadness. Tom was screaming and crying and struggling to get away from the man holding him, and Hollis just kept looking at him with this terrible sadness until he finally closed his eyes and never opened them again."

"Dear God," I whispered, hardly willing to believe what had happened.

"Tom thinks now Hollis was sad not because he was dying, but because Tom had to watch him die. Tom's had nightmares about it ever since. He's still trying to save Hollis from the Klan."

Sounds familiar, I thought. Hollis and the Klan. Lenny and the Japs. Same dream, different colors. I suddenly had an affinity for Tom, though I had yet to meet him. "Didn't this uncle realize Tom was fond of Hollis?"

"That's probably why he did it," Sunny sighed. "To show Tom the worth of a Negro and to keep him from befriending them in the future. Tom says Billy Wayne was a sick man, all crippled up with hate. He probably thought he was doing the right thing."

"Surely Hollis didn't do what he was accused of doing."

Sunny shook her head slowly. "He may have said something that angered a white woman. Maybe he looked her in the eye when he spoke to her or didn't step off the sidewalk into the gutter fast enough when she passed by. Who knows? But Tom doubts he ever made any sort of pass."

"What a horrible thing for Tom to witness."

"He promised that night he'd never have anything to do with the Klan, and that if he was going to hate anyone, it'd be people like Billy Wayne."

"Did Tom's parents ever find out what happened?"

"Tom tried to tell them. He thought they'd want to do something about it, bring about some sort of justice for Hollis's murder even if it meant sending Billy Wayne to jail. But every time he tried to tell them about that night, they told him to be quiet, to never talk about such things. Tom finally gave up. Eventually he assumed his parents' silence meant they approved of the killing and of Billy Wayne's involvement. Well, maybe they did approve and maybe they didn't. What Tom didn't know back then was that white men never go to jail for killing a Negro. Another dead nigger is just another dead dog. All Fulton Sr. did was hire on another gardener to take Hollis's place, and Hollis was never spoken of again."

"That probably didn't do much for Tom's relationship with his parents."

"What it did was drive a permanent wedge between them. When Hollis died, Tom realized he loved that Negro gardener more than he loved his own father, or his mother for that matter. He still has the collection of wood carvings Hollis gave him. He says what those carvings told him after Hollis died was to go north, and that's what he did, against his parents' wishes."

"And yet he came back."

"Out of a sense of responsibility, yes. Oldest son to the rescue of the family business and all that. Now we both hear Hollis's animals telling us to go north again—and we will, someday. As soon as we can."

Just as Sunny finished speaking, the paved road ended and the car began to bump over what was little more than a rutted dirt path. Sunny looked around and waved a hand. "Now we're entering what is commonly known as Coloredtown. Still Carver but a whole 'nother world."

Our entrance into this other world was abrupt, as though in a flash one picture had been replaced with another. We'd left the neat homes and manicured lawns behind and began to pass instead a scattering of shotgun houses; shacks made of wood and tar paper; hovels without glass in the windows, without grass in the yards, without sidewalks rolled out in front. No flowers grew in window boxes. No flowers grew anywhere at all. Instead, here was an old car without wheels, there, a pile of appliance parts rusted by rain and dew. A few chickens strutted about between the shacks. Faded laundry hung unsecured by clothespins over lines of frayed rope. Scantily clothed children played barefoot in the dirt, their curious brown eyes following our car as we passed by.

"The Negro section is a strip of land between Carver proper and the Big Black River," Sunny pointed out. She waved a hand toward the passenger-side window. "Down that way, beyond the trees, is the river. There's a joke about it being conveniently located for waste disposal." She glanced at me to see if I understood. I did. "Some say it's called the Big Black River because of the bodies it occasionally gives up."

"Lovely," I commented.

Sunny nodded absently. "We're coming into the business district now."

It looked like something out of the Old West, what she called the business district of Coloredtown. Or maybe just a second-rate movie set where a western was being shot. A number of connected false-front buildings lined one side of the street, facing a sparsely wooded area across the way. An elevated wooden sidewalk fronted the shops in case rain turned the road to mud, though when the buildings ended the sidewalk ended too, and the people would have to walk home in the mud anyway. All the shops were wooden structures with wood-shingle roofs, though a couple were covered with corrugated tin.

"The lucky Negroes own these businesses," Sunny explained. "They don't have to work for any white folks; they're their own bosses." She drove slowly as she pointed out Harold's Barbershop, Bernette's Clothing Boutique, Reese's General Store, a café called the Chat and Chew, the Robinson Bros. Funeral Parlor, and finally, an office with the name Daniel Dawson, M.D., on the shingle out front.

"They have a saying around Coloredtown that Dawson's losses are the Robinsons' gain," Sunny quipped.

"Handy that they're right next door to each other," I noted.

"Dr. Dawson is the first Negro doctor in Carver. Before he came, people skipped over the medical care and went straight to the Robinsons."

"You're kidding, I hope."

"Not completely. Anyone who was sick or hurt had to go over to Goodman or even up to Lexington to get help. Or else they did without."

"No white doctor in Carver would see them?"

"There was one that would, if he had time. But he rarely had time."

She pulled up in front of the general store for a moment. Its spacious front porch held a number of rocking chairs and a soda pop dispenser. Three men wearing overalls lounged about the porch, drinking RC Colas. Two more men sat facing each other over a small table, playing a game of checkers. Sunny offered the men a wave of her hand; each nodded, a couple of them waved, the two or three wearing weathered fedoras tipped them toward the car. Apparently it didn't seem strange to them that a couple of white women had suddenly appeared in the business district of Coloredtown. We didn't stay, didn't even turn off the car. After the brief acknowledgment Sunny backed the car out and headed down the road the way we'd come.

"They obviously know you," I said.

"Yes, through the school. You'll meet them all later. Right now"—she glanced at her watch—"I want to get home and start dinner. Tom'll be home around six, and he'll be bringing the kids with him."

"Tell me more about the school," I prodded.

But Sunny waved away my request. "That can wait till Monday when I bring you over to meet T.W. and Mahlon. They're the ones who really run the school, and they can tell you all about it." She looked over at me and smiled. "Anyway, that's enough of Carver for one day, don't you think?"

"Well, would you mind answering just one more question?" I asked.

"Sure. What is it?"

"I know the Klan doesn't like Negroes, Orientals, Jews, Catholics, communists, or immigrants, right?"

"Right."

"Well, what about redheaded, third-generation Irish Germans who make their living writing about civil rights?"

Sunny gave me a deadpan look. "Why? You thinking about joining the ladies' auxiliary?"

"I'm just wondering whether I'm automatically on their bad side or whether I can sleep relatively soundly at night."

"You'd better keep a pistol under your pillow, just in case."

"I was afraid you'd say that."

"Tom keeps a rifle in our bedroom closet."

"What in the world don't they like about Tom?"

"Augie, the Klan doesn't like anything about anyone, period."

I nodded. We drove back through Coloredtown toward home.

TWENTY-FOUR

Sunny and I were in the kitchen preparing a meal of fried chicken and corn on the cob when suddenly two small whirlwinds blew in the back door, laughing and chattering unintelligibly between themselves. Then the whole space of the doorway was filled with the huge frame of Tom Fulton. Sunny's husband was a tall, lumbering bear of a man, husky but not overweight, with wavy blond hair and eyes the color of a summer sky. He pounded into the kitchen like a man to be reckoned with, and I thought for a moment that he might be angry—until I saw the smile on his face. Then I realized he walked heavily because there was no other way for a large man to walk.

Sunny greeted the children with hugs, then turned to her husband and, standing on tiptoe, accepted the kiss he bent down to give her.

"Tom, kids," she said, waving a hand at me, "I want you to meet Augie Callahan. Augie, this is Tom, Joanie, and Ronnie."

The whirlwinds turned into two silent children who stood staring up at me. I tried to find Sunny in their faces, but she wasn't there. This little boy and girl were hakujin, with round eyes, slender noses, wavy hair several shades removed from black. Sunny had borne them, but Tom had more greatly influenced their appearance. Little from the Orient had survived the conception.

A small sadness pinched at me, but only for a moment. The children smiled and said hello, and Tom reached for my hand and pumped it enthusiastically. At once I knew I belonged in this home just as I had belonged in the Yamagatas'. That knowing was sealed when Tom, smiling broadly, exclaimed, "So you're Musume!"

"Yes," I said with a laugh of surprise. "Well, that is, I was, once upon a time."

"But you still are," he said warmly. "What a pleasure to finally meet you. I couldn't believe it when Sunny said she thought she'd tracked you down. I've been hearing about you for years but never imagined I'd get to meet you. I have you to thank for this pretty little lady marrying me, you know." Only then did he let go of my hand as he gave Sunny a one-armed squeeze around the waist.

"You do?" I asked, bewildered. I looked from Tom to Sunny, searching for an explanation.

"We can talk about that later," Sunny said. "Supper's ready now. Wash up, everyone, and be quick about it."

In a few moments we were all seated around the large oak table in the dining room, platters of warm food spread out in front of us. No one moved to take anything, and I noticed Sunny nod toward Tom as though indicating that he should help himself first. But instead he lifted his hands to take Joanie's on one side and mine on the other. "Let's return thanks," he said quietly. I wasn't accustomed to saying grace, but after a quick glance around the table, I bowed my head and closed my eyes. "Father," Tom prayed, "for these gifts we are about to receive, we give you thanks. And, Father, we thank you too for bringing Musume to us safely"——he gave my hand a squeeze——"and allowing such a wonderful reunion to take place. Amen."

"Amen!" the children echoed as they eagerly reached out for the food.

Sunny passed me the platter of chicken while Tom turned his shining grin on me. "Musume, Musume," he repeated, shaking his head and clicking his tongue. "Where in the world have you been all this time?"

I couldn't help laughing once again. "Oh, here and there," I quipped. I liked this man, just as I knew I would. Mild-mannered and affable, he was easy to like. He seemed the lifelong friend he was making himself out to be instead of the new acquaintance that he was.

For a moment I envied Sunny, even while I was glad for her.

Tom took a large bite of chicken, chewed, and swallowed. "Sunny tells me you were like two peas in a pod when you were kids." The words rolled out in a friendly southern drawl.

I looked at Sunny and smiled. "Yes, I practically lived with Sunny's family for a few years." Then for some reason, I added, "Before the war."

Tom nodded. "And I'm glad you did," he said, "or I might not be the happily married man that I am today."

I frowned, unable to make the connection. "How so?"

"What he means," Sunny answered for him, "is that he had this crazy idea that Mother and Papa wouldn't accept him into the family because he's hakujin. I told him it wasn't so, but he wouldn't believe me at first."

Tom nodded, took another bite of chicken, and chewed contentedly, as though my question had been answered. "So?" I asked, prodding him on.

"Well, you know," Tom said. He picked up the napkin from beside his plate and wiped at his greasy fingers. "We met, what—five, six years after the war? Sunny's father, Toshio, well, the war had been hard on him, what with the relocation camps and all that. He lost his business and his home, lost his whole way of life, really. He came out of the camp something of a broken man, wouldn't you say, Sunny?"

Sunny nodded, saying nothing.

"I figured he resented us whites for what had been done to him and his family. I wouldn't blame him if he did. Treated like criminals, all of them, when they hadn't done anything wrong. None of them was any more Japanese than President Roosevelt himself. They just happened to look Japanese at a bad time.

"Well, here I am a white man in love with pretty little Miss Yamagata, wanting to marry her the first time I laid eyes on her." He glanced at Sunny across the length of the table and smiled. She smiled in return, and my heart tightened at the intimacy of this simple exchange. "I knew Sunny's family had been in the camps," Tom went on, "and I thought I had the chance of a snowball in July of making her my wife, but she assured me her family would accept me. It took me a while to work up the courage to meet Toshio, but I finally did."

I smiled, amused at the thought of this Goliath of a man afraid of being knocked dead by Toshio Yamagata's little rock of resentment.

"And you know what, Augie?" Tom gestured with the knife he was using to butter an ear of corn. "Sunny was right. Toshio was as gracious as a man could be. He accepted me right off. Later, after we got to know each other better, I asked him point-blank. I said, 'Toshio, did it bother you at first that I'm a white man?' And he said, no, it didn't bother him. I asked him why, and he said that when his family lived back in Boyle Heights, Sunny had a white friend who became just like a daughter to him and Suma. He said they even called you Musume, which means daughter in Japanese, because they loved you just like you were their own. And I remember he had tears in his eyes when he said they lost you because of the war."

A wave of emotion gripped me, and I felt the tears welling up in my own eyes. But I took a deep breath and forced myself to smile at Tom. "Well, then, I'm very happy to know I paved the way for you to enter into wedded bliss."

Tom smiled as he winked at Sunny. "That's a good way to put it." He started in on the ear of corn then as though he were playing a harmonica.

I couldn't help but wonder whether Sunny had been so graciously accepted into Tom's family, having looked Japanese at the time. I wondered how Tom had felt when his Japanese wife became hakujin. I wondered how the children felt when their Japanese mother went away one day and came back looking like a white woman. I wondered about so many things, but now was not the time for my questions. Bit by bit I would learn what I wanted to know.

"Mom," Ronnie asked, his voice a squeal, his eyebrows raised, "were you really friends with this lady when you were little?"

"Miss Callahan, not 'this lady,' " Sunny corrected. "And yes, we were the best of friends."

"Well, how come we never saw her before?"

"Remember what I told you?" Sunny said patiently. "We got separated during the war."

"When you and Gramps and Grandma got put in the camp?"

"Yes. When we moved to the camp, Miss Callahan couldn't go with us."

Two pairs of young eyes stared at me briefly until Joanie piped up, "But now you're friends again, even though you're old."

Sunny's lips trembled as she suppressed a smile. She glanced at me knowingly. "Yes," she said, "Miss Callahan and I are friends again, even though we're old."

"Your mother will never be old, Joanie," Tom commented mildly, "even when she's a hundred."

"That's older than Gramps," Ronnie noted, "and Gramps is pretty old."

"Never mind, Ronnie," Sunny said with a laugh. "Why don't you tell us what you did today?"

We spent the rest of the meal talking about the children's day at their Grandmother Fulton's—she was pretty old too, they said, though she tried to look like she wasn't—and how the maid Flora, who was the one who actually took care of them, had taught them how to make Jacob's ladder and cat's cradle with a piece of string. I felt warm sitting there among them, listening to their chatter, watching their exchanges and their every little gesture, marveling at the miracle that I was there at all.

When we finished eating, Tom stood and started clearing the table. "The kids and I will do the dishes," he offered, "while you two ladies rest yourselves out on the porch or something. You've got twenty-some years to catch up on, and I suppose you've barely got started."

"You've got a gem of a husband," I remarked to Sunny while Tom was still within hearing. "I don't suppose he has an unmarried brother?"

Tom answered himself. "Got a brother, but he's married already, going on ten years."

"Missed my chance, then," I responded with a laugh, though the laughter rang hollow in my ears.

"Come on, Augie," Sunny said, pushing back her chair and rising from the table. "Let's take advantage of Tom's chivalry and have some iced tea out on the porch. It isn't often I get out of doing the dishes."

I rose from the table and followed her.

❧

"What happened to you, Sunny, after you left Boyle Heights?"

That would be a good place to begin, I decided. Go back to the beginning, to the day they left, when Mr. Eddington and his brother drove them to the train station.

Sunny sighed heavily, as though I had placed a weight in her lap. We sat side by side in the rocking chairs on the porch, each with a cold glass of iced tea in hand. "Do you know anything about the camps?" she asked.

"Very little," I confessed. Until now I hadn't wanted to know. Until today I had wanted only to forget the Yamagatas.

"How much do you want to know?" Sunny asked.

"Everything. Everything and anything you want to tell me."

She rocked quietly for a moment, gathering her thoughts. Then she began. "Well, first we were taken to an assembly center, where we stayed for about six months before being sent to Manzanar. The center we were assigned to was the racetrack at Santa Anita. The first thing we noticed when we arrived was the barbed wire, the search-lights, the guards with guns. We felt we were being sent to prison, and like Tom said over supper, we hadn't even committed a crime.

"Families were crammed into the horse stalls and expected to make themselves at home. The stables had been whitewashed, but they still smelled like horse manure. We were given cots and blankets, but we had to stuff our own mattresses with straw. There were separate toilets for men and women, but other than that there were no com-partments. There was no privacy at all. We even had to wash together in what had been the horse showers. It was humiliating. Some of the Issei had grown up in Japan and were used to communal bathing, but those of us born in America had never experienced such lack of pri-vacy. I for one hated those showers, and Mother did too. Poor Mother was pregnant—imagine how she felt. Not that she was the only woman expecting to deliver at the racetrack.

"Then there were the three daily trips to the fly factory, as Sam and George called the mess hall. There were three of them in the camp, but none was any better than the others. Bad enough that the food was terrible, but even worse were the flies. All the posts and rafters of the mess halls were decorated with fly paper, that yellow spiral stuff. Not that it stayed yellow for long. After a while those strips turned black from all the flies stuck to them. The food was hard enough to eat as it was, without all those dead flies dangling over your head. Not to mention the live ones that kept buzzing around and land-ing on your food.

"Everyone was so angry in the camp. People fought with each other all the time, even at night when you were trying to sleep. You could hear everything in the stable; it was just like being in a big open barn. People cursing, arguing, weeping. It was endless. Night after night, day after day. We were all so lost.

"Mother wept for weeks. Papa was quietly angry and only grew more sullen over time. Obaasan was in absolute despair. For her, being forced to live at the racetrack was the final humiliation, her lowest point in a lifetime of unhappiness in America. As with everything else, she blamed my grandfather for our ending up in a horse stall because he didn't take her back to Japan like he'd promised. She cursed him day and night, even in her dreams, just as she'd always done. Only I didn't laugh at her anymore. For the first time I understood and was sad for her.

"One night she cried out my grandfather's name for the last time. Papa shook her and tried to wake her, but she didn't wake up. She never woke up again. My grandfather's name was the last word she ever spoke." Sunny paused a moment and smiled wistfully. "I could just imagine her being gathered into the bosom of her ancestors, all the while complaining that she'd had to die in America in a place fit only for animals."

"Poor Obaasan," I whispered.

"When we arrived at the assembly center, she kept saying to Papa, 'I told you the hakujin hate us. I told you we should have all returned to Japan.' Like me, Papa no longer laughed at her. He never said as much, but I think he wondered whether Obaasan had been right from the beginning. After all, look where we were.

"The only good thing to happen to us in the assembly center was that the baby was born. There was a makeshift hospital at the race-track, so at least we didn't have to say she was born in a barn. As I told you, she was named Augusta, after you. Though we welcomed her, of course, it was hard at first because she seemed such an unhappy baby. She cried at all hours, day and night, and sometimes nothing would console her. Mrs. Sensaki in the next stall said it was colic, but Mother said no, little Gus was trying to rid herself of all the tears Mother had shed when she was carrying her."

I shook my head as I listened and looked out over the yard. A trace of daylight lingered, but a coolness had settled in with the evening, and the day began winding down to a certain stillness. "What about you, Sunny?" I asked. "What was it like for you, being there?"

"It was hard," she said without emotion. "I was lucky I was young, I think, because the living conditions didn't bother me as much as they did the adults. You know kids are more resilient when it comes to roughing it. We can sleep just as well on the ground as on a bed. And of course we didn't have as much to lose. It was our parents who lost what they'd worked a lifetime for—they were the ones who lost everything. We kids still had our whole lives ahead of us, and the thought never entered our minds that we wouldn't lead normal lives again. We knew we would. The war was just an interruption, not the end of everything, as it appeared to be for the grown-ups.

"The hardest thing was seeing what it did to Papa and Mother and Obaasan. They were so devastated, and that's what really hurt. I thought if the hakujin could do this to us, they really *must* hate us." She looked over at me for a moment before going on. "I started to become bitter, and for the first time I started to hate white people. I knew there were good hakujin, like you—but then, I didn't really think of you as a white person. You were just Augie. Not white, not Japanese, just Augie."

She took a long swallow of tea, ice cubes clinking in the glass as she lifted it to her lips and set it down again. "It wasn't like me to have bad feelings toward other people, but when you think people hate you, I guess you naturally begin to hate them back."

I rocked quietly for a moment, thinking. "And yet," I said, "here you are married to a white man."

Sunny lifted her shoulders. "Yes," she said simply.

"So you must have gotten over your resentment."

"Oh yes, of course." She sounded a bit surprised, as though I shouldn't have expected otherwise.

After another brief silence, I said, "After the assembly center, you were sent to live at Manzanar?" When Sunny nodded, I continued, "And what was it like?"

She smiled faintly. "It was dusty," she recalled. "We arrived during a dust storm, and from then until the end of the war, we were plagued by dust. Manzanar is in a desert valley at the foot of the Sierras, and it seemed like the wind never stopped blowing. When it got bad enough to create a dust storm, like it did on the day we arrived, it was thick as fog, and you could hardly see your hand stretched out in front of your face. So it wasn't until the next morning that we could actually see where we were."

"And I don't suppose it was a pretty sight," I interjected.

"Not exactly," Sunny agreed. "I guess you could say it was a step up from the horse stalls, but where we were made Boyle Heights look like Beverly Hills. The place was laid out like an army base, with so many barracks to a block and with a mess hall, bathrooms, and laundry facilities for each block. It was one square mile, and all around the perimeter was barbed wire and eight guard towers where the soldiers kept watch over us with their machine guns. The government called it a relocation center, but that was just a polite way to put it. It was a prison, with more than ten thousand prisoners of war crammed into that small space.

"Well, because there were four children in our family we were given one of the larger apartments. That meant it was a room twenty feet by twenty-four instead of sixteen by twenty. One room, that's all.

"The barracks had been so hastily thrown together there were spaces between the boards that let wind, sand, and dust in. We tried to seal up the holes the best we could with leftover tar paper and plywood, but no matter what, the dust always seemed to find its way in. We'd wake up with it in our beds, and we had to shake out the sheets every morning. No matter how many showers we took, we never felt clean. There was dust in our clothes, in our hair, in our mouths. There was dust in the food, and we tasted dust all day long."

"Sounds awful," I commented quietly.

Sunny nodded placidly. "You'd think you'd get used to it, but we never did." She pointed out over the driveway. "I've asked Tom to pave this driveway a hundred times because I can't stand the dust devils that rise up when the wind blows. And the porch is always dusty." She ran one hand along the armrest of her chair, then felt the tips of her fingers with her thumb. "See? Tom says we'll pave the drive someday, but it's one of those things you never get around to."

I nodded appreciatively. I had been there only one day and already had witnessed those little whorls of dust that rose up from the drive. You could even smell the dust that hung invisible in the air. "And you lived like that for almost four years," I said.

"Yes. But as I think back on the experience now, I'm amazed at the way Manzanar became like a little town, and how we tried to go on living normal lives in spite of where we were. I mean, there were schools, and people had jobs they went to every day. There was a general store, a bank, Christian churches and Buddhist temples, beauty parlors and barbershops, a newspaper called the *Manzanar Free Press*, a hospital staffed by the Nisei doctors and nurses. Many of the people in the camp had been farmers, and they were able to develop a system of irrigation from a nearby creek, and eventually crops were planted and animals were brought in—cattle, pigs, chickens and whatnot—so that the camp became self-sufficient when it came to food.

"Then, of course, there were those people like Papa who'd been merchants. A number of them, including Papa, formed the Manzanar Consumer Cooperative to set up and operate all kinds of businesses, like the general store and the canteen. That kept Papa busy, and Mother had a job making camouflage nets. More than five hundred nets were made every day in Manzanar. It was quite a little industry.

"My brothers and I went to school, of course, and got involved in all sorts of things. I joined the girls' glee club and took lessons in baton and calligraphy, things like that. The boys joined the Boy Scouts and Little League. And there were dances and movies and picnics—all sorts of things. We even celebrated the Fourth of July every year, because, in spite of everything, some of us were still proud to be Americans. I don't know, Augie, I think you'd be surprised at how normal life became, right down to the flower gardens that sprang up everywhere. It wasn't at all like the camps in Europe where Hitler slaughtered the Jews."

Nor, I thought, like the camps in the Pacific where the Japanese slaughtered the Americans. I tried at once to dismiss the thought, but it seemed like dismissing Lenny, and I couldn't do that. I found myself in a strange place, foundering between two opposing worlds. On the one hand I was still angry at the Japanese for what they'd done to Lenny, while on the other, I was angry with white America for what we'd done to our Japanese residents after the bombing of Pearl Harbor. I couldn't fall entirely into one camp or the other, couldn't align myself with one side or the other. But I was sorry for the suffering of both. And I came to realize, perhaps in that moment, that in the end what it all boiled down to was that everyone had suffered.

Finally I said, "You don't seem bitter at all, Sunny."

"I'm not bitter," she said simply. "Like I said, it was harder on Papa and Mother than on me. Oh, it was hard. Sometimes it was very hard. But something good came out of it all, and I can't regret that."

"Honey?" Suddenly Tom was standing in the doorway. "Sorry to interrupt, but Joanie says she has a stomachache and she wants you to go rub her tummy. She says I don't do it right."

"Tell her I'll be right up." When Tom disappeared, Sunny turned to me with an apologetic smile. "She probably just wants attention. She gets that way whenever she thinks I'm spending too much time with anybody else. No doubt I'll have to stay with her till she falls asleep." She stood and laid a hand on the back of the chair to still its rocking.

"You go ahead," I said. "I suspect I'll be turning in pretty early myself tonight."

"Yes, I'm sure you're tired. It's been a long day."

It *had* been a long day. So long, I could scarcely recall the start of it, the waking up at the Belle Motel, the showering and dressing and eating breakfast, the drive from Jackson to Carver with all the windows in the rental car open. The morning was years away from where I stood now, the far end of a very long tunnel.

"I think I'll stay put awhile first and enjoy the evening," I said. "It's so pleasant here."

"Can I get you anything? More tea?"

"No thanks." I shook my head. "I'm fine."

"Well, good night, then."

"Good night." I stood, and we hugged. She felt so small in my arms, a mere child. For a moment I was back on Fickett Street on an April morning in 1942, hugging Sunny, saying good-bye.

She stepped back, smiled. "Good night," she said again. This time, 1965, it was only good night. "See you in the morning."

When she went inside I sat again and listened to the muffled hum of insects singing their lullabies. Twilight began to fall, a sweet coolness rose, the sun would soon be setting on this longest day of my life. One can be blindsided, I thought, not just by tragedy but by goodness. I remembered the news of Lenny's death—the stunning blow, the disbelief, the initial numbness. Finding Sunny was the same, only this time I was stunned by the sudden joy.

I would have to be quiet and let the numbness pass, let the realness of what had happened sink in. I wasn't there yet, not quite. I still needed to tell myself, "Helen Fulton is Sunny Yamagata. Helen Fulton is Sunny!"

A twenty-three-year-old mystery solved in a day, in a few moments, really. From California to Mississippi, from not knowing to knowing, a strange and unexpected journey. How funny life can be with all of its twists and turns, all of its surprises—some of them losses, some of them gifts.

Today was a gift, and I was thankful. "Let's return thanks," Tom had said. And so I offered my thanks to the fate that had brought me here, to Sunny who had found me, to the stars, to the wind, to God—whoever or whatever he was—who had given me the gift of returning home.

TWENTY-FIVE

All I could see of Howard Draper was the back of his head. The organ was front and center of the choir stall, built into a pit from which the organist could play and direct the singers at the same time. All well and good for the choir members who could see his face, but it seemed a rather unfriendly posture as far as the congregation was concerned.

Nevertheless, that's how it was arranged at the First Methodist Church of Carver, where I sat alarmingly close to the pulpit, settled into a pew with Sunny, Tom, and Corinne Fulton, Tom's mother. We had picked Mrs. Fulton up on the way and brought her to church with us. She was, not surprisingly, the vision of southern charm—impeccably groomed, soft-spoken but confident, polite, reserved. She was also terribly prejudiced.

"At first our relationship was what you'd call a bit strained, but that's changed," Sunny had confided over coffee early that morning. "Corinne's liked me fairly well since the surgery." She gave a little laugh as she said it, but it was a laugh at once sad and sarcastic.

Why hadn't Tom's mother accepted Sunny before the surgery, and what had she done to make her disapproval known? The answer to the first part was obvious; the answer to the second I didn't want to know.

It made me angry just to imagine how Corinne Fulton had regarded Sunny Yamagata before she became the round-eyed Helen Fulton.

The elder Mrs. Fulton was sixty if she was a day, but she was trying desperately to hold on to her youth. Her unnaturally blond hair, twisted into a sleek French knot, heightened the bronze-colored sheen of her evenly tanned skin. Her face was a palette of rosy blush, fiery red lipstick, and pale blue eye shadow. Spidery false lashes crested her eyelids, and her eyebrows were plucked into pencil-lead arches. She wore a blue-and-white suit, white gloves, a pillbox hat with a bit of a veil that dipped down over her forehead, and narrow high-heeled shoes that had been carefully polished white. She had pearls in her ears, around her neck, and around one wrist. Once we sat down she removed her gloves, folded them primly and tucked them into her white patent-leather purse, snapped shut with a tortoise-shell clasp. Her hands were bony and freckled with age spots, but the nails shone with flawless red polish, and the ring fingers of both hands carried stones of grandiose proportions, one a diamond and the other an impossibly oversized ruby. She must have bought her gloves at least a size too large in order to have room inside for the rings.

I had never liked flashy dressers, especially when they were aging women who refused to age gracefully, but it wasn't the outer appearance that bothered me so much about Corinne Fulton. What bothered me far more was the story of Hollis Hardy. What kind of woman, I wondered, would refuse to listen to her little boy's tale of murder? What must have gone through Corinne Fulton's mind when little Tom Fulton had told her he'd seen Hollis beaten to death by the Klan? Hadn't she been horrified to think of her own brother dragging her child out of bed to witness a bunch of good old boys beating the life out of a Negro? Not just any Negro, but Hollis Hardy, their own gardener, a man her son had befriended and loved.

There she sat, looking devout and dignified, fanning herself daintily with the church bulletin as the choir sang a song of wondrous love, O my soul. I wanted to jump up and call her a hypocrite, but I supposed most everyone in the church was a hypocrite of one sort or another—including the organist-cum-Klansman whose day job was leading hymn singing and whose night job was terrorizing Negroes—so there was no use in singling out Corinne Fulton.

I myself might have easily fallen into the category that morning.

There I was bowing my head at the prayers, singing along with the hymnbook cradled in the palms of my hands, feigning attention to the platitudes tumbling from the preacher's lips. Didn't I look just like everyone else? And yet I'd never attended a church service in my life, and the last time I was even inside a church was when Sunny and I went to St. Stephen's on our ill-fated search for God. My mother's funeral was held in a church, but I wasn't there. I thought my absence a fitting farewell to the one who'd never been there for me. Lenny's service was held in a funeral parlor with only Uncle Finn, Aunt Lucy, Stella, Jack, and I in attendance. You hardly need a whole sanctuary for a handful of mourners.

Sunny said she and Tom went to church regularly now, which seemed to be what most people did when they got married and had children. Stella and Jack did. They started attending St. Stephen's while they were still expecting their first baby and eventually had all five of their children baptized there. I told them they shouldn't bother going because God wasn't there, but they turned a deaf ear to my arguments and went anyway. I teased Stella, saying she'd got religion when Jack came back alive from the war—something like a foxhole conversion by proxy. She said she wouldn't quite put it that way, that I just didn't understand how thankful she was.

The windows of the First Methodist Church were open, and a series of ceiling fans whirled overhead, but still the air was hot and close. I was anxious for the service to be over. I was looking forward to lunch at the mayor's house, where I would meet Howard Draper face-to-face. I had a journalist's interest in the man, and so far I was less than satisfied. All I'd learned about him this morning was that he was a splendid organist and he had a full head of hair, but I was certain there was much more to him than that.

It was a relief when the pastor sent us off with the words, "Go in peace," and we all filed out of the pews smiling and shaking hands and acting very peaceful indeed as Howard Draper played one final song to accompany us on our way.

❧

We collected the children at Sunday school and took them back to Corinne Fulton's house to be watched over by the faithful Flora. When we reached the mayor's residence, Cedric and Suellen Frohmann welcomed us like long-lost relatives, and I realized I was receiving a taste of genuine southern hospitality. As the mayor shook my hand and said he was glad to meet me, I could only believe that he really was. I liked him at once, and though his wife seemed a bit reserved, she too exuded an inviting warmth.

Cedric Frohmann was a round man, plump with a full-moon face. His hair was graying, his cheeks ruddy, his nose an ill-defined mound that looked like a lump of clay. He was not a handsome man, but his laughing blue eyes were magnetic, and he radiated a friendliness that was his drawing feature. Suellen Frohmann was small and slender, tastefully made up, and she wore a stylish pale green suit that matched her eyes. Not only were those eyes a striking color, but they were kind eyes and gentle—the kind of eyes you'd like to have watching over you if you were sick.

After their enthusiastic welcome, the first couple of Carver waved us into the dining room, a large airy room of white linens and polished silver. They introduced me to the two people who were already there, a man and a woman standing beside a buffet, each with a drink in hand.

"Howard," the mayor called, "Howard, come shake the hand of this lovely young lady, Augusta Callahan."

This, then, was the enigmatic Howard Draper. As he moved toward me, hand extended, the woman he'd been speaking with frowned visibly.

"I'm very glad to meet you, Miss Callahan," he said, his midwestern accent a startling contrast to the southern drawls I'd been hearing all morning. As we shook hands, I wondered briefly why he wasn't married. He was far more attractive than I had imagined, or than the back of his head had implied. He was a tall man, slender, with thick, wavy hair as dark as coal and deep brown eyes reminiscent of Swiss chocolate. He had a dimpled chin, a well-proportioned nose, and teeth that conjured up the image of a row of white piano keys. His honey-colored skin and overall appearance suggested a Mediterranean ancestry, perhaps Italian or Greek. Sunny's comment that he was fifteen years older than the Frohmanns' daughter put him around my age, thirty-five or so, but he was the type of man who appeared ageless and would probably never be old.

"And this is our daughter, Betsey," Mrs. Frohmann added quickly as she placed a hand maternally on her daughter's shoulder. Betsey Frohmann, it was clear, had been groomed for womanhood since the day she was born. Her poise, her very demeanor, spoke of years of charm school; even the way she held her head smacked of something regal. Maybe she'd been one of those adolescent girls who walked around the house balancing books on their heads in an exercise of posture and stride. That afternoon she wore a sleeveless yellow dress that on anyone else might have appeared simple and even frumpish, but on her it managed to accentuate her shapeliness. Her blond hair, teased into a small swell at the top of her head, fell to just above her shoulders and ended in a flip. Her features were fine, her skin unblemished. The only negative thing about her face was that her eyes were somewhat too close together, but in the overall picture that seemed a trivial flaw.

She offered me a weak, tight-lipped smile. "Happy to make your acquaintance, um—I'm sorry, but is it Miss or Missus?"

When I said that it was Miss, the forced smile disappeared altogether. I was amused to think she saw me as a possible rival for Howard Draper's attention. She must be desperately in love with him, I decided, as well as desperately unsure of their relationship.

She touched my hand briefly in a sort of pseudo handshake as she hissed, "*Miss* Callahan." I almost felt the need to disarm her by assuring her she had nothing to fear from me. If I had any interest at all in Howard Draper, it was strictly professional.

The rest of the group, all known to each other, said their hellos. When Betsey turned her gaze toward Sunny, her countenance changed entirely, and she smiled brightly. "How are the children, Mrs. Fulton?" she asked. Without waiting for an answer, she went on, "Oh, I do wish you had brought them along. They're the most adorable children in Carver. Don't you think so, Howard? Couldn't you just gaze on those two adorable faces all day long?"

She lifted her eyes to Howard Draper's face and stood awaiting his response. Howard, looking slightly bemused, nevertheless smiled at Sunny and said, "Yes, they are beautiful children."

"Thank you," Sunny said with a laugh, "but you may not find them so adorable if you had to sit through a meal with them."

"Oh no, I just *love* children," Betsey gushed, her eyes still glued to Howard Draper's face. If she was trying to hint at her hopes for the future, Howard seemed not to notice. He was instead looking at me as though he wanted to say something, and he turned away only when Mrs. Frohmann invited everyone to sit down for the meal.

The elegantly arranged table, laid with genuine silver and china, looked like a piece of art that begged not to be disturbed. I felt almost guilty when I lifted the cloth napkin from beside the numerous forks and spread it across my lap. It seemed almost criminal to sully the plate with food, to use the carefully polished knife and fork for something as urbane as eating. The Frohmanns' dining room was a far cry from my own small kitchen where Hilda and I ate our solitary meals using plastic plates and mismatched flatware.

Sunny, Tom, and I sat on one side of the table, Howard and Betsey and Corinne Fulton on the other. The mayor was at the head of the table, just to my right, and his wife sat at the other end across from him. With Howard Draper, who sat across from me, and Cedric Frohmann both in my line of vision, I could study them simultaneously. The mayor was a round man, while Howard was tall and thin, and yet I thought I perceived the ghost of a resemblance between them, something about the eyes, maybe, or perhaps it was that both of their chins had a rather pronounced dimple.

I was pondering those dimples when a young Negro girl, neatly uniformed in a black cotton dress and white ruffled apron, entered through a swinging door beyond the mayor's seat. She balanced a silver tray on an arm that appeared too thin to carry much of anything. But she must have been stronger than she looked, because she began effortlessly ladling soup into our soup bowls from the tureen on the tray.

"Speaking of children," the mayor boomed, as though we were in fact still speaking of children, "little Celeste here just presented the world with a bouncing baby boy a couple of weeks ago. Cutest little Negro child you'd ever want to lay eyes on. Isn't that right, Celeste?"

Celeste pressed her lips together but couldn't keep the ends from curling up into an embarrassed smile. She didn't lift her eyes when she spoke. "Yes sir," she said shyly. "That's right, sir." She went on ladling the soup while she tried hard to still her quivering lips. I had the feeling it was her perceived protocol surrounding white bosses and Negro servants that kept her from breaking out into a wide and toothy grin.

"Don't be shy, Celeste," Mrs. Frohmann said, patting the young girl's arm. "We're all proud of baby Jeremiah. I know his daddy's popped a few buttons off his shirts."

The young girl gave a close-lipped giggle as she moved on to Tom. "That's right, ma'am," she said. "I been staying up late nights sewing them buttons back on."

Laughter flowed freely around the table, and for a moment there was a sense of ease in the room that hadn't been there before. Celeste looked delighted and very pleased with herself, though still she didn't allow herself to join in the laughter. She moved catlike around the table, ladling the soup.

Corinne Fulton patted her pearl necklace self-consciously and said, "Yes, our darkies do manage somehow to produce such adorable babies." She smiled at Celeste, a little supercilious smile, though the servant didn't lift her eyes to receive it.

"Is he your first?" Howard asked breezily.

The girl nodded. "Yes sir, he is."

"I'd like to see the little fellow sometime."

Celeste pursed her lips again and gave what appeared to be a small curtsy. "Yes, sir," she said. "Thank you, sir." And without ever once looking at any of us, she disappeared with her tray beyond the swinging door.

Across the table Betsey was saying to no one in particular, "Oh, I just love little babies. . . ." but no one was listening.

I had just dipped my spoon into the murky folds of pea soup when the mayor leaned forward, lifted one eyebrow, and said, "Shall we return thanks?"

Ah, the opening act to the southern meal! I dropped my hands into my lap like I'd just been caught shoplifting, and when the mayor decided everyone was adequately poised for prayer, he bellowed, "For what we are about receive, O Lord, we give you thanks. Amen."

There was an echo of "Amen" around the table, followed by the clanging of spoons against bowls. I was amused to see the mayor tuck his napkin into his collar, but in the next moment when a spattering of small green spots appeared on the impromptu bib, I could see the need for it. Mrs. Mayor was probably tired of trying to remove three meals a day from her husband's ties. But in an odd way the napkin at his neck rather endeared me to the man. He was so genuinely human.

"So," he said, shining his smile in my direction, "you've come all the way from Los Angeles to visit our humble town of Carver. I hope you're enjoying your stay with us."

"Oh yes," I assured him. "Very much. Carver is a lovely town." I could just feel the amusement rolling off of Sunny beside me like waves of heat. "Sunny's been showing me around, telling me about some of the town's history."

"Sunny?" the mayor asked.

"Oh," Sunny said, looking up abruptly from her soup. "That's me. Sunny was my nickname when I was a child."

"How charming!" Mrs. Frohmann exclaimed from the far end of the table. "It sounds like such a happy name."

"So your friendship goes all the way back to childhood," noted the mayor.

"Oh yes," Sunny said. "We knew each other when we both lived in Boyle Heights, in Los Angeles. We went to grade school together in the late thirties, early forties."

"My, you *are* old friends, aren't you?" This was from Betsey, who obviously wanted to emphasize the length of our lives over the depth of our friendship.

Howard gave me a knowing look across the table, and a small crooked smile of amusement. I smiled in return and sensed in that moment that Howard's relationship with Betsey Frohmann was a one-sided affair, but he was unsure of how to politely disentangle himself from the web of romance that Betsey and her parents had spun around him.

"And what do you do back in Los Angeles, Miss Callahan?" the mayor asked me.

"Oh, I do a bit of writing——" I began, deliberately cutting myself off with a spoonful of soup. I hoped the conversation would move in a different direction.

But Betsey Frohmann, apparently discovering something worthwhile about me, was suddenly animated. "You're not one of those movie writers, are you?"

"No, I'm afraid not——"

"She's a novelist," Sunny interjected quickly.

"Well, now," Suellen Frohmann said, leaning forward over her soup bowl, "that *is* interesting." The last word came out sounding like "intarestin' " and I almost wanted to laugh.

Betsey, obviously disappointed, said, "But I thought all the writers in Los Angeles wrote for the movies—"

"You must write romance stories," the mayor stated confidently. "Suellen, she loves those romance stories. Reads 'em by the dozen. You like 'em too, don't you, Corinne?"

"Why, no, I haven't time for—"

"Maybe I've read some of your stories," Mrs. Frohmann said excitedly, interrupting Corinne Fulton. It seemed this would be a conversation of interruptions. "Do you write under your own name, or do you have a pen name like most of those writers of love stories?"

"I write under my own name but, you see, I've only had one book published, and it certainly isn't—"

"I love those stories by—oh dear, what *is* her name? Do you remember who I mean, Corinne, that one who always sets her stories in big cities like New York and Paris?"

"Like I said, dear, I don't read—"

"Oh, but I'm sure she's not half as good as you are, Miss Callahan. Tell me, where *do* you get your ideas for your stories?"

"Well, I don't write romance novels, I'm afraid. I can't imagine that I'd ever write a story like that."

A hush fell over the table, and I wondered briefly whether I had insulted my hostess. I hadn't intended to sound snobbish, but it irked me that people assumed I wrote romance—which most people did upon learning that I was a writer—just because I happened also to be a woman. Such stereotyping I found depressing and tedious, as I was always having to contradict it.

But now, in what I hoped was a lighthearted manner, I offered, "I'm afraid I have neither the experience nor the imagination necessary to write about romance."

This elicited a few nervous chuckles from my critics, though I noticed Howard Draper didn't laugh. Instead, he went on gazing at me intently. "What do you write about then, Miss Callahan?" he asked.

Celeste came at that moment to clear away the soup bowls, and I was thankful for her sudden appearance. I disliked talking about my work, was uncomfortable trying to discuss plots and characters with others, especially strangers, and yet I had so far been unsuccessful in coming up with any standard replies to questions posed by the curious.

But Howard looked at me with such sincere interest, waiting for my reply, that I didn't want to disappoint him. "Well, Mr. Draper," I said, "I guess you could just say I write stories about people, everyday people and their struggles."

It was the best I could do, but Howard seemed satisfied. He smiled. "You must know a great deal about human nature."

I looked at the mild-mannered Mr. Draper—the Dr. Jekyll and Mr. Hyde of Carver, Mississippi—who sat beaming a smile at me from across the table. "I'd like to think I do. But then, sometimes I think I understand nothing at all about the human psyche."

Silence returned to the table as Howard and I momentarily locked eyes, two people studying each other the way a curator studies a rare museum piece.

"I don't know," said Betsey finally, breaking into the hush, "but if I lived right there in Hollywood, I'd want to write for the movies."

Her irrelevancy fell to the wayside as Celeste, who had disappeared, entered through the swinging door again, followed by a man who may have been her husband or her father—or then again perhaps no relation at all. Together the two dark servants moved around the table dishing out the main course of thinly sliced roast beef, boiled new potatoes, and French green beans with almonds.

Tom spoke up for the first time to say, "Well, it looks like we've got the arts just about covered here, don't we? Augie's a writer, Howard there's a musician, and Betsey's a local celebrity for her watercolors."

"Oh my, yes," Suellen Frohmann chimed in enthusiastically. "Betsey won second place in an art contest down in Jackson not six months ago. Of course I thought her piece was far better than the first-place winner, but then I wasn't asked to be one of the judges."

We ate our dinner then to the background music of benign conversation while periodically I sensed that Howard Draper's eyes were upon me. It took me some time to work up the nerve to meet his gaze once more, but when I did, I was rewarded with another furtive smile. This went on throughout the meal; our eyes met briefly, we'd smile, look away. We'd offer a comment to the group, trying periodically to join in the conversation, but always it came back around to Howard's gaze, my glance, a passing of something unsaid between us.

He wasn't flirting with me, that much I knew. It was something else. A curiosity, maybe. Or perhaps a recognition of something there—I don't know what. I was curious myself, wanting to become acquainted with the mystery man of Carver, wanting to penetrate the cloud of unknowing that surrounded him. Just who was he, and why did he do the things he did? I hoped I would have the chance to find out during my brief stay in Carver.

At length Celeste came to collect the dessert dishes, and the mayor instructed her to bring our coffee to the drawing room.

"You did bring your violin," the mayor said to Howard as he rose from the table, tugging the napkin from his collar. It wasn't a question so much as a statement.

"Yes, of course," Howard replied, rising and settling his napkin on the empty tablecloth in front of him. He pulled out Betsey's chair and offered her a hand as she rose. She smiled up gratefully, admiringly, at him.

"You must play for us, then," instructed Mrs. Frohmann.

"Certainly. I'd be delighted."

In the next moment, we were seated in the drawing room, sipping coffee from dainty floral tea cups—all except for Howard, who stood in front of the empty fireplace tuning his violin. "He's the finest musician our town has ever seen," the mayor said proudly. "We sure got lucky when he suddenly showed up in Carver, right out of the blue. Just wait till you see what he can do with a violin, Miss Callahan."

I settled my cup of coffee into its saucer before answering. "Well, after the service this morning I certainly know he can play the organ."

Howard didn't look up from the violin strings, but his eyebrows peaked in amusement at my comment. Maybe he didn't like being spoken of in the third person, as though he weren't right there in the room with us.

"Howard can play any instrument you can think of," Betsey added, apparently addressing me.

"Well, not quite," Howard countered, "but thanks for the vote of confidence."

Suellen Frohmann replied, "We have him play for our guests every Sunday afternoon." Then she added hurriedly, "Not that you're not a guest here too, Howard—it's just that, well, you've become like part of the family."

Howard fidgeted slightly as he went on fiddling with the violin's tuning pegs. He lifted his eyes and offered Mrs. Frohmann a brief smile, obviously reluctant to make too much of her comment. When he was satisfied that the violin was properly tuned, he asked, "Any requests?"

"Play the one you played last week," Betsey cried, "that Brahms thing!"

Howard gave an amiable little bow. "Brahms thing," he said, "coming up."

With the bow poised over the strings and his fingers in place along the neck of the violin, Howard paused a moment in statuelike concentration. And then he began to play. He gave us Brahms, gave him up beautifully, the bow rising and dipping, fingers caressing the strings. It took only a moment to realize that this wasn't just music, it was magic. We were all of us transfixed by the shining notes that fell from the strings like a healing rain. The music filled what we would otherwise not have recognized as our parched souls, helping us realize the beauty that we longed for only when we heard it. As Howard played I thought of wind, I thought of stars. I thought of sunlight spinning needles in the leaves of trees, snow falling silently on the branches of evergreens, larks ascending, waves breaking, moonlight on water. I breathed it in, drank it in, drew it in as though all my life I'd been blind to beauty, and then, suddenly, all senses open, I could see it, hear it, feel it. I had heard this piece before, but not like this. Never had I been so moved by this or any other piece of music. It was as though Howard brought something transcendent into the room, as though his music called down something from beyond the world, something from a place of order and goodness. I wanted to be surrounded by it forever. If somehow time and the world stopped and I was caught in this room with Howard and his violin for all eternity, I knew I would be perfectly content.

I looked up at Howard and felt like Betsey, staring at the man with an admiration I didn't want to acknowledge. *He terrorizes Negroes*, I reminded myself. *He's a member of the Klan.* But how could it be? How could the soul that made such music be tainted by such madness? Here was a man who ought to make his place on the side of angels, but who chose instead to dance the devil's dance under the cover of darkness.

When the melody was finished, Howard slipped seamlessly into another and then another. It might have been only moments, and it might have been hours, I don't know; time was lost. No one moved. No one seemed even to breathe. We were all under a spell, and I thought, *My God, who is this man?* I was more baffled now than I had been when we came.

At length, when we said our good-byes, Howard Draper held my hand in his clasp a little longer than seemed necessary. He looked into my eyes, seemed about to say something, didn't. I thought things I didn't want to think, felt something I didn't want to feel. *There's poison in the apple*, I reminded myself.

"I hope we will meet again, Miss Callahan, while you're here in Carver."

"Yes. Yes, I hope so too." I reluctantly pulled my hand from his and turned to go.

TWENTY-SIX

We sat again in the rocking chairs on Sunny's porch, cold glasses of iced tea in hand as we watched the gathering shadows of dusk settle around us. We had left the Frohmanns' in the late afternoon, about five o'clock, and dropped off Corinne Fulton at her home, where we picked up the children. After a light snack for supper, the five of us played a board game at the dining room table until Tom volunteered to give Ronnie and Joanie their baths and get them ready for bed. He sent Sunny and me out to the porch to relax and spend some time together, and as we marched off with our tea I said again to Sunny, "Gem of a guy. How'd you ever find him?" Her only response was a smile; how, after all, does one explain the unexpected gifts that life kindly offers us now and again?

"Tomorrow morning," Sunny said when we'd settled ourselves on the porch, "I'll take you to meet Mahlon Jackson and T. W. Foss, the leaders of the citizenship school. They're a couple of bright, competent young men. They can tell you everything you want to know about the school and the voter registration drive."

"You mentioned, I think, that they're not originally from Carver?" I wasn't terribly interested in Mahlon Jackson and T. W. Foss at the moment. My mind was stuck on the image of Howard Draper and had been ever since we left the mayor's house. Sunny's comment came back to me with startling clarity: "I'd like Howard Draper if I didn't know he was Klan." Of course she would. Who wouldn't? He was so likeable, and his music so lovely. I knew I should dismiss all thought of the man, but try as I might, I was unable to pull my mind's eye away from him.

"Yes, they're from Jackson," Sunny confirmed, "but they both have relatives here. They were involved in the Freedom Summer last year and afterward wanted to go on working for civil rights. They saw Carver as something akin to virgin territory, untouched by the idea of equality for the Negro."

"How old are these two guys?"

Sunny shrugged. "Twenty," she replied, "maybe twenty-one. I'm not sure."

"Just a couple of kids," I muttered, "out to slay a really big dragon."

"That's about the gist of it," Sunny agreed. "But I'd say Mahlon and T.W. are equal to the challenge."

"I have to admire them."

"You'll admire them even more after you meet them."

"Does the mayor know about them and the school?"

"Oh yes. Tell you the truth, I think he's secretly in favor of it all. It's just a feeling I have. I may be wrong. But I think he'd like to see the Negroes registered to vote."

"One thing I noticed—you're right about his being genuinely kind to the Negroes who work for him. He was obviously fond of Celeste and proud of that baby boy of hers. It's too bad he's all caught up in the status quo and won't speak out for change. A man in his position might make a real difference around here."

"I guess he figures he has too much to lose. If he starts talking in favor of civil rights, he can kiss his job as mayor good-bye as soon as the next election rolls around. It's the whites who vote, you know."

"Yes, I know. But still, doesn't he consider how much the Negroes have to *gain*?"

Sunny thought a moment, then said, "It takes a certain greatness to see beyond your own ambitions, let alone sacrifice those ambitions for the sake of other people. Cedric Frohmann is a good man, but I'm not sure he's a great man."

I nodded my understanding. From where I sat beside her I studied Sunny's profile as she looked out over the front lawn sipping her tea. Now was the time, I decided, to give vent to my curiosity. "If I didn't know better," I quipped, "I would say all that nose pinching you did as a child worked after all."

Sunny turned to me and laughed. "That and the surgeon's knife," she said. "Weren't we a pair, thinking we could change the way we looked with all that pinching and pressing? I can't believe we did it."

"Children do funny things."

"Yes, how well I know. Especially now that I have two of my own."

"You always said you wanted to look more hakujin, but to tell you the truth, I didn't really believe it."

"Oh, it's true, Augie. As a child I always wanted to look white."

"But why, Sunny? You were perfectly beautiful the way you were."

Sunny sniffed as the corner of her lips curled into a smile. "It had nothing to do with wanting to be beautiful," she confessed. "I guess I thought things would be better for me if I was white. I mean, I was always so different from everybody else. There were so few of us Japanese. . . ." She paused, shook her head. "I just wanted to be like the other kids. Of course if I'd lived in Japan, I wouldn't have wanted to be white. I'd have fit in there, been normal, you know?"

I frowned at the thought. "So it wasn't that you wanted to be white, but that you just wanted to look like the majority, whatever the majority happened to be?"

"Yes, I guess you could put it that way."

I drank some tea, an excuse to spend a few moments in thought. At length I said, "Once on our birthday, when we were blowing out the candles on our cake, I wished I could wake up the next morning looking Japanese."

"Oh, I know you wanted to look Japanese, but—I probably said it when we were kids, but I'll say it again now—you didn't know what you were asking for."

"I think I did," I said slowly. "I wanted to look like the people I considered family."

"Even if it made you an oddball everywhere else?"

"I never thought about that part, I suppose. Everywhere else didn't matter; only home did."

"In your perfect world, maybe. In the real world you step out your front door, and you find out real fast that it does matter what shape your eyes are, what color your hair and skin are. You can hardly spend your whole life safe in the bosom of your family, you know."

I sighed. "I guess you're right, Sunny."

"I know I am," she said gently.

A heavy silence hung between us. I wanted to understand Sunny, why she had done what she did in changing her appearance. "Forgive me for saying this, Sunny, but I'm not convinced you should have had the surgery. I mean, here you are working for civil rights for Negroes, and yet when it came to the Japanese—your own people—what you did was give up and join the enemy, so to speak. You should have demanded respect for yourself as you were."

Sunny nodded, and I saw the muscles in her jaw work. "I thought a long time about that very thing, Augie. What was I saying to myself, to my children, to the world even, by becoming white? Was I taking the easy path instead of taking a stand for my own people? To tell you the truth, Augie, I still wonder about all that."

"Then why'd you do it, Sunny?"

There was another long silence, interrupted by a series of heavy sighs from Sunny. The ice cubes in her glass clinked each time she raised the tea to her lips. As she lowered the glass to the arm of the chair, she looked back out over the lawn. "You know, by the time I had the surgery, I really didn't care anymore about looking white. If we'd stayed in Ohio, I suppose I'd still look Japanese. I had the surgery because I knew I was coming here."

I wanted to slap my forehead with an "of-course-how-stupid-of-me" slap. "Oh! Of course. Better to live in Mississippi with a white face than a Japanese face."

"Yes," she agreed, "but it was more than that, really. My children are so-called half-breeds, remember? They look white, but one glance at me, and everyone would know they're mixed. So, bottom line, I did it for them. Are we living a lie?" Sunny lifted her shoulders in a resigned shrug. "In a sense, I suppose we are. We're passing ourselves off as white to be on the safe side. But I knew from my own childhood what it was to be different, and I didn't want that for my own children. And it wasn't just to spare them the ridicule, but to keep all of us from the attention of the Klan."

I frowned, cocked my head. "You really think there'd be any danger?"

"I don't know," she said. "Probably. At least this way we won't find out."

"So Tom agreed to the surgery?"

Sunny nodded. "Reluctantly. Angrily. But he agreed. He's a powerful man around Carver because of his position at the mill, but that alone doesn't make him immune to the Klan's shenanigans. The Klan doesn't generally take kindly to mixed families."

The iced tea in my glass dipped and fell with the rocking of the chair. "And what did Chichi and Haha think?" I asked. "Weren't they opposed to the surgery?"

"Yes and no. They understood why I had it done. In fact, Mother told me she was relieved I wasn't coming to Mississippi as an Oriental. But they were sad too, in a way. You know Papa: 'We're not Japanese, and we're not Japanese American, we're just American.' He thought I should be free to live anywhere in the country, and that the surgery was something I shouldn't have to do to protect myself and my family."

"So how'd you respond to that?"

"I told him to head south and preach it to the Negroes, see what they had to say about being free to live in safety anywhere they pleased in the good old U.S. of A."

I took a deep breath, let it out slowly. "You've got a point there. And I can understand your fears and concerns for the children. Still, in a way, it seems like a permanent solution to a temporary problem, since you'll be heading north again someday."

A shrug, and then, "There's no temporary way to look white—not that I know of, anyway."

"No. No, I guess not. Still . . ." I was wrestling with a thought, and it took me several minutes to put it into words. "I guess, Sunny, it saddens me to think you had to give up who you were to satisfy the prejudices of other people."

Sunny frowned and started her chair rocking, as though the motion might help her think. Finally she said, "That's a hard one to answer, Augie. I guess I can only say that I didn't give up who I was. I changed my features, but I didn't change my *self*. I mean, they're two different things, you know. Of course it was strange at first. After the surgery, when the swelling had gone down and there I was looking like a white woman, I'd stand in front of the mirror and wonder 'Where in the world did Hatsune go?' It was something of a shock every time

I saw myself. And I guess you could say I was a little sad too. It seemed at first as though I *had* lost something.

"But eventually I came to realize that when I was away from the mirror and couldn't see what I looked like—which of course is most of the time—I was just going along the same as I always had before. I had the same interests, I was thinking the same thoughts, I experienced the same feelings I'd always known. The surgery had given me a different face, but it didn't make me a different person. I mean, nothing had changed on the inside. And finally I could look at myself in the mirror and say, 'Hatsune hasn't gone anywhere. She's still right here.' "

Her words tumbled about in my mind, and I had to give them time to settle. The challenge was in understanding what Sunny had experienced, but that I could only imagine. At length I asked, "But doesn't a person's race contribute to who they are? You know, your Japanese heritage and all the traditions that made up your life."

"Of course. My race and the fact that I grew up in a Japanese American home, certainly all that influenced the person I became. Those things undoubtedly help shape you, and you can't get away from them. Maybe your question is, am I the same person now that I would have been had I been born white and raised in a white family?"

I nodded. "That's a good way to phrase it, I guess."

Sunny laughed again. "Well, now that we have the question, I'm not sure I have the answer!"

"Give it a try, anyhow," I urged.

More sighs. Another deep breath. Then she said, "Well, again, a person's race and life experiences contribute to what a person is, but I think there's something beyond what we are, and that is *who* we are. I've come to believe that the essence of a person, who that person is, would be the same no matter what kind of body that person happened to be born into. Because we're more than the physical, you know. We're spiritual too. We have a spirit, or a soul, or whatever you want to call it. And what does the spirit of a person look like? What does the essence of a person look like?" Sunny shook her head slightly. "It's beyond looks. My spirit isn't Japanese, and it isn't white. It's"—she paused a moment, waved a hand into an open palm—"like air, I guess. You can't see it, but it's where the life is. And it's what's eternal about us, if you can believe in eternity."

Could I? I wasn't sure that I did. "Do you mean what's generally thought of as the part of us that lives on after death?"

Sunny nodded. "When we were children, I wanted to believe in heaven, but I didn't. Now I do."

I shifted positions in the chair as my mind traveled back to our childhood. "If I remember correctly," I said lightly, "the gospel according to Vera Eddington tells us that God turned tail and ran shortly after creation, leaving us to our own devices. The good news being, of course, that none of us will ever end up in hell, since there is neither heaven nor hell to end up in."

Sunny laughed at the memory. "Yes, well, Mrs. Eddington's version of the gospel wasn't canonized, thankfully. It wasn't very hopeful, was it?"

"So you don't agree with her." It was a statement, not a question.

"No. For a time I thought she might be right, but I don't think so now."

I sniffed, took a deep breath. Rarely did I talk about spiritual things, but I was curious. "What made you change your mind about it all?" I asked.

More tea. More rocking. More thinking. "Well," she answered finally, "there wasn't any one thing, but a lot of things, I guess, over time. It began in the camp with a woman named Shidzuyo."

When she didn't go on, I prodded, "Okay. So tell me about this woman."

"Shidzuyo?" Sunny smiled briefly. "She was a nurse, and I met her because I became very sick. Shortly after we got to Manzanar, I came down with dysentery. It was common because of the food. Lots of people got what they called the 'trots.' For most people it was no big deal, other than being an embarrassing inconvenience, but I was so sick I ended up in the camp hospital. I couldn't eat, and I lost a lot of weight that I couldn't afford to lose. I became weak to the point that I couldn't lift my head up off the pillow. Sometimes my fever was so high I was delirious. Hours, maybe days, went by when I didn't know what was going on. At times I was aware enough to realize I was wearing a sort of diaper, and I was so humiliated, but then again much of the time I just didn't care.

"Mother and Papa were frantic, though they tried not to show it. But I could see it on their faces—at least when I was lucid enough to see their faces. It scared me the way they looked when they came and sat by my bed in the hospital. I was afraid they thought I was going to die. Years later Mother admitted that was exactly what she thought. Every time she came to see me, she was certain it was for the last time. But no one talked about my dying, not to me and not to each other. No one said anything.

"Shidzuyo spent a lot of time with me, even when she wasn't on duty at the hospital. Her name means peaceful or calm, and it was a good name for her because that's what she was. When Mother and Papa weren't with me, she'd come and sit beside the bed and sing little songs, or hold my hand, or help me drink water through a straw. Sometimes she looked like she was praying. In fact she was very devout, but in a quiet sort of way. I almost preferred having her there instead of my own parents, because she didn't look afraid."

"You weren't her daughter," I said, breaking in to defend Chichi and Haha. "Of course she didn't worry the way your parents did."

"No, I understand that, of course," Sunny conceded. "Though she did grow to love me, and I her. In the years we were together in the camp, she became like a second mother to me, when my own mother was so unhappy and distracted. When I was sick with the dysentery, I needed the peaceful presence that Shidzuyo brought to my bedside. It was like there was a strength in her that poured out over onto me. When she was with me, I knew I'd get better. And I wasn't afraid."

"How long were you sick?"

"I guess I was in the hospital for about three weeks. By the time I reached the worst of it, I was nothing but skin and bones. I had no strength at all. But I knew I was getting better when I could smell the dust again, when I could feel it on the pillow and in the sheets. One of the first things I said to Shidzuyo when I had strength enough to talk was, 'I hate the dust. There's so much dust.' And I thought she'd agree and say the dust was nasty and terrible, the way everyone else did. But instead she brought her face close to mine and whispered, as if she was telling me a secret, 'Here in dust and dirt, O here, the lilies of his love appear.' "

Sunny was quiet a moment, as though listening again to Shidzuyo's whispered words. Then she went on, "I had no idea what she meant, and at first I wondered whether she was crazy. There weren't any lilies around, and on top of that, just whom was she talking about anyway? But she said it like it was the most wonderful thing in the world to be living in the middle of all that dust and dirt. And the way she smiled at me and put her hand on my forehead gave me a sense of comfort, even if her words didn't.

"Well, after a while, flowers did begin to grow in the camp. In spite of our being in the desert, the soil there was really quite rich, and people were determined to have gardens. Flowers sprang up everywhere—in front of the school, outside the stores and the post office, in the firebreaks, in the alleys between the barracks. Some of the professional gardeners even built a little park with ponds and waterfalls and curved wooden bridges. One day, months after I had recovered from the dysentery, Shidzuyo took me by the hand and pointed them out to me. 'You see,' she said, 'they bloom, even in the dust.'

"But I was so literal. I said, 'There's lots of flowers around, Auntie, but I don't see any lilies.' She just smiled at me in that quiet way she had and said, 'There are many different kinds of lilies, Hatsune. Some of them aren't even flowers.'

"She quoted those lines about the dust and the lilies about a thousand times over the years. Eventually, when I asked her, she told me they were from a three-hundred-year-old poem by Henry Vaughan, and eventually too, I began to understand what they meant."

She fell silent again. I sat quietly as well, picturing God on his hands and knees planting lilies in the dusty byways of the camp.

"I started going to church with Shidzuyo there in the camp," she said. "It wasn't much of a church, really. Just a simple room with hard benches and a cross hanging up on the front wall. It wasn't at all like that Saint Stephen's church we went to in Boyle Heights. No vaulted ceiling, no stained glass. Remember how we thought God lived there because the place was so big and fancy?"

I nodded. "Yes, and I can hardly believe we actually went into that confessional thinking we'd somehow get to talk personally to God. That poor priest. No wonder he was mad enough to spit. Couple of crazy kids like us asking for an audience with God while a dozen people are sitting around waiting to confess their sins."

Sunny laughed. "Yes, we were pretty confused, all right. But what could we do? Nobody told us."

"Where to find God?"

"No. *How* to find him. That's what I learned from Shidzuyo."

"Okay." *I'm game,* I thought, shrugging. "So how do you find him?"

Sunny gazed off somewhere beyond my shoulder before looking back to me. "Would you laugh if I said it's a matter of faith?"

"I'm not laughing."

She nodded slightly, then went on. "Well, you see, Shidzuyo was the first person I ever met who had faith. I remember I asked her early on why God allowed the war to happen and why he let the hakujin send us away to the camps. What she said was, 'I don't know, but I do know he has a reason, and that's good enough for me.' You see, she just kept on believing in a loving God in spite of everything. And things weren't easy for her. I don't think her life was ever what you'd call easy, but things got far worse after the war started.

"Her husband had been a fisherman, though not a very good one, because he tended to go off on drinking binges. After Pearl Harbor, they lost what little livelihood they had, and they lost their home, like everyone else in the camps. It was then that things became even worse with Shidzuyo's husband, Mr. Miyosha. Some of the men set up stills in the alleys between the barracks where they made a crude form of sake. Drink became Mr. Miyosha's escape from the bitterness of life in the camp.

"I don't think I ever saw him when he wasn't either drunk or passed out. Sometimes he became violently angry and took out his anger on Shidzuyo and their grown children. Sometimes his sons would have to restrain him when he threatened to kill somebody, any-body—whichever unfortunate soul happened to be in his line of vision at the moment. Finally, late one night when Mr. Miyosha was walking home from another binge, he stumbled and cracked open his head on the steps of the barracks. No one heard or saw him, and he bled to death before morning. Shidzuyo found him when she was leaving for her shift at the hospital.

"Well, by that time, all of her children had left the camp. Early in 1943, the young men were allowed to volunteer for service in the army, as the government was putting together a Nisei fighting group. And women were allowed to volunteer for the WACs or the Red Cross. A questionnaire was sent to everyone in camp, and a couple of questions had to do with whether or not you were willing to help defend the country by serving in the armed forces. Those who said no to both questions were considered disloyal to America. They earned the name of the No-No Boys, and were separated from the rest of us and sent to another camp as punishment.

"Shidzuyo's twin sons, Wesley and Harry, turned twenty that year. Harry became one of the No-No Boys. He was angry about what the government had done to us. He thought America was crazy to ask our young men to go off and fight for the very country that had put us in the camps. His bitterness got him sent to Tule Lake. But Wesley volunteered and became a part of the 442nd Combat Team that fought in Italy and France. By the end of the war, almost ten thousand Purple Hearts were awarded to the men of the 442nd. Wesley earned one of them for wounds that required three surgeries and a year of rehab.

"Shidzuyo's daughter, Mary, was a nurse, and she joined the Red Cross at the same time Wesley joined the army. While she was working with a mobile unit in Italy, she contracted typhus. We didn't even know she was sick until we got the telegram telling us she had died. I was with Shidzuyo when the telegram came. I thought it would be the end of her world, and for a little while it very nearly was. But something pulled her through, and that was when I knew there was something more to faith than just believing in a God. It was knowing him in such a way that you could go through hell on earth and still say he is love."

When Sunny finished, I didn't respond. I didn't quite know what to make of it all. Finally, lamely, I asked, "So what happened to her after the war?"

"She moved to Cincinnati too, where she worked for years as a public health nurse. She's retired now, enjoying her grandchildren. Both her sons live nearby. And we're still in touch, of course. All of us came to love her. Mother and Papa are close to her now too—especially Mother. She and Shidzuyo often get together for coffee and just to chat. Mother says their friendship is one of the few good things to come out of the camp."

"She sounds like a very special person."

Howard Draper, who had stepped momentarily into the background, slipped out again. He and his music—so likeable, so lovely—both appeared tainted beside a person like Shidzuyo Miyosha. Best to see him for what he was. Even Satan, I'd once heard somebody say, could appear as an angel of light.

Sunny nodded. "Yes, she is. I owe her so much—my life, really."

She was talking, I knew, about more than just Shidzuyo's sitting beside her in the hospital and nursing her through her illness.

I looked out over the drive where the night breezes kicked up little clouds of dust. Here in dust and dirt, oh here . . .

A Mississippi moon rose up over the trees, full and luminous, and down below light and shadow danced together on the grass.

TWENTY-SEVEN

Coloredtown. Colortown. Colorfultown. I toyed with the word as Sunny and I bumped over the rutted roads in the Negro section of Carver. We should be entering a place of colors, I thought. Where are the colors? Green, of course—in the trees, the longleaf pine, the wild grapevine, the patches of kudzu. And the blue of an early morning sky. But otherwise, mostly brown. The dirt road. The unpainted wood of the shacks. The rusty automobile up on blocks. The skin of those who lived here, all shades of black and brown. Ah, but of course, not colored. *Culud.* Culudtown. Niggerville. Dark because the darkies lived here.

Telltale eyes followed us. The eggshell white, dark-pupil eyes of the young, the yellowing, watery eyes of the old. Eyes heavy not just with the cares of the day, but heavy also with history, with the long span of years that stretched far back into the past. They peered at us from windows, from porch steps, from the sides of the road, speaking even yet of the long, long trip from Africa.

Sunny pulled up in front of the general store, which wouldn't open for business for another hour. Curtis Reese, the owner, stood on the porch and looked out over the road. He was a large man, tall and solidly built. He wore a faded red T-shirt and denim overalls. A red handkerchief was tied around his neck. When we arrived, he stepped forward quickly and bounded down the steps, meeting the car in time to open the door for Sunny even before she had turned off the engine.

"Mornin', Miz Fulton," he said. Sunny slipped out from behind the steering wheel, and Curtis Reese shut the door.

"Good morning, Curtis," Sunny greeted him. I got out of the car and came around to the other side to join them. Sunny waved a hand at me. "I want you to meet Augusta Callahan, reporter for *One Nation*. Not to mention a dear friend of mine. Augie, this is Curtis Reese."

I smiled broadly, held out my hand. "Pleased to meet you, Mr. Reese."

He returned my smile briefly, though his gaze was intense. He seemed to need to size me up. A reflexive action, I decided. Years of sizing up whitey as friend or foe. He took my hand, which got lost in his large, fleshy palm. "Thank you for coming, Miz Callahan," he said. His features relaxed as I smiled at him again. "We been anticipatin' your visit," he added.

He took a step backward toward the porch. As he moved, his eyes darted down the length of the road. He was alert, but not afraid. A nod of his head told us to follow him. He seemed to want to usher us inside as quickly as possible. Two white women in the heart of Culud-town early on a summer morning—surely the White Boys sniffed something in the air? "Mahlon and T.W."—T-dub-ya, he pronounced it—"are upstairs waiting for you. Gloria's making coffee. We sent the young'uns to family so we could talk without their disturbance."

"That's fine, Curtis," Sunny said. "We're right behind you."

A bell tinkled over the front door as we entered the store. Curtis paused to turn the lock behind us; then we walked through the aisles of merchandise to a storage room in the back. There a narrow wooden staircase led to a small four-room apartment where Curtis and Gloria Reese lived with their five children. Sunny, who had been there many times, warned me on the way over that there was no bathroom, only a two-holer in the woods out back.

"They do have running water in the kitchen," Sunny had explained, "but they're embarrassed that they don't have an indoor bathroom."

"In other words," I assumed, "it'd be best if I didn't ask to powder my nose?"

"Try not to if at all possible."

The stairs opened up into a narrow kitchen, where a very dark-skinned woman, plump and perspiring, stood beside an outdated Westinghouse stove waiting for a teakettle to boil. She wore a white wrap-around apron over a sleeveless cotton dress of faded lavender. Her feet weighed heavily on a pair of beach thongs so that the creamy soles were squeezed out over the sides. She stood with one hand on her hip, poised, it appeared, to scold the water for taking too long to boil.

When she realized we were there, she turned and offered us a smile that would have warmed the kitchen had it not already been so hot her face glistened with tiny diamonds of sweat. She had a pleasant, friendly face, surrounded by a halo of hair that she had coaxed into large curls. "Mornin', Helen!" she sang out. "Come on in, hon. This must be your writer friend. Come in, come in. Water's almost boiling."

"This is Augusta Callahan, Gloria—" Sunny started, and before she could say more, the woman approached me with hand extended.

"Lawdamercy, let me shake your hand, Miz Callahan," she said. "Helen tells me you wrote a book. Well, I never shook a real writer's hand before. It's an honor, Miz Callahan. Won't my students be thrilled when I tell them! By the way, I'm Gloria Reese. Call me Gloria. No need to be formal around here. Sure is an honor to have you here, Miz Callahan."

She pumped my hand vigorously, and I couldn't help but laugh inwardly at her enthusiasm. "Well, I'm not exactly a best-seller, Mrs. Reese—Gloria, I mean."

"Doesn't matter, doesn't matter," she assured me. "You got a book in print, and that makes you a real writer."

"Gloria's one of the teachers at the elementary school for the Negro children," Sunny explained.

"Been teaching for more than twenty years, trying to get our young folks interested in books. Sometimes I succeed, sometimes I don't. But I love them myself, books and stories. What a thrill to meet a real writer, and here you come all the way from California to write about us."

The teakettle whistled, and only then did Gloria Reese let go of my hand. "Well, water's hot. Go on and sit yourselves down in the living room. Curtis, you lead the way. I'll be right behind with the coffee."

Sunny and I followed Curtis through the kitchen and into the adjoining room, a spacious, neatly kept room that smelled of Pine-Sol. The bare wood floor looked as though it had been polished only that morning. The front wall facing the street was the only one with windows, but they were large and immaculately clean and adorned with curtains that had obviously been carefully ironed and hung. The windows were thrown wide open against the heat, and a small fan in front of them was working wholeheartedly to draw some air into the room.

Just beyond the door to the left was a long table with benches running the length of the sides and two cane-bottom chairs on either end. To the right was a short hallway that led, I supposed, to the bedrooms. In the living room itself was a couch and a coffee table along one wall, and across the room, two upholstered chairs with a table between them. On the table was a pull-chain lamp with a red-fringed shade. Framed prints and family photographs hung in various arrangements on the walls about the room.

When we entered, two young men stood—or rather, jumped up from the chairs like marionettes whose strings had been pulled too sharply. They shifted nervous eyes in my direction, and I realized that they, like Curtis, were sizing me up while at the same time desiring to make a good impression on me. It was a double-edged sword: Could they trust me, and would I respect them? The answer to both would have to be yes, or else we'd stumble before we even got started.

"Augie," Sunny said, interrupting the unspoken conversation already under way. "I'd like you to meet T. W. Foss"—one of the men nodded—"and Mahlon Jackson"—the other nodded. To them, she said, "This is Augusta Callahan, the reporter I told you about."

Both men mumbled, "How'd do?" politely, but neither offered a hand nor smiled. That'll come later, I decided, when the issue of trust and respect was settled.

"Miz Fulton, you and Miz Callahan have yourselves a seat on the couch," Curtis Reese offered. "It's more comfortable, I think, than these old chairs. Mahlon, you take one of these"—he passed a cane-bottom chair to the young man—"I'll take the other, and we can let T.W. and Gloria have the easy chairs."

Mahlon carried the chair across the room and sat down next to

T.W. Sunny and I settled ourselves on the couch. I had carried my briefcase in with me, from which I pulled a yellow pad of paper and a couple of pens. I had thought about bringing a tape recorder but decided against it. Though handy for reporters, those little machines often backfired by putting a clamp on jaws that should have been wagging. I'd have to trust myself to listen well and write quickly.

Gloria came into the room then, carrying a tray filled with cups and saucers. She'd removed her apron, but it had left a band of sweat around her middle where it had been tied. "Coffee for everyone!" She seemed to sing rather than talk, and the mood of the room lifted as soon as her smile entered it. She moved slowly around the room, allowing each of us to select a cup, beginning with Sunny and me. Cream and sugar weren't offered. "There's more coffee on the stove, and if you get a hankering for a soft drink, I can go downstairs and get some bottles from the cooler. You all just let me know."

As the coffee was being handed around I took the opportunity to study T. W. Foss and Mahlon Jackson, both of whom sat forward in their chairs as though ready to spring again at any moment. T.W. was a lanky young man, more legs than anything else. He looked like a long-distance runner, light and lithe, fleet as a young deer. He was dressed in gray trousers and a button-down, short-sleeved shirt with a pocket over the left breast. On his long, narrow feet he wore loafers without socks; a recent polishing couldn't hide the fact that the shoes had traveled a good many miles. His face too was long and narrow, his cheekbones prominent, his jaw severe. The almost skeletal appearance of his face was accentuated by his skullcap of closely cropped hair. He wore a pair of horn-rimmed glasses reminiscent of Bob Moses or Malcolm X.

Mahlon was a more casual dresser: faded jeans, plain white T-shirt, black high-top sneakers with laces that had broken and been knotted together in numerous places. He wore his hair in an Afro that framed his round face like a scrubby bush. He was of above average height, muscular, compact, the quarterback to T.W.'s sprinter. He had hands as large as melons and feet that made me think of Chaplin in his oversized shoes, except that Mahlon filled his sneakers. He was a big man. While T.W. appeared bookish, Mahlon looked like a man of action. I thought they must make a good team.

The most notable difference between the two men was the stark contrast in the color of their skin. Seen separately, they would both have been simply Negroes. Seen together, the varying degree of their blackness was stunningly evident. Had they been two cups of coffee, Mahlon would have been double brewed, T.W. with extra cream. High yellow, as his fellow Negroes might describe him. Meaning that somewhere in T.W.'s familial past there'd been a mingling of black and white blood. Undoubtedly more than once. A little more mingling—a little more cream in the coffee—and T.W. almost could have passed for white. Plenty of Negroes did. Those who were fair enough often headed north and called themselves white, while in the South their darker-hued relatives continued to live under the burden of their skin.

Gloria returned the tray to the kitchen, then came back and settled with a sigh into the remaining upholstered chair. "Whew!" she complained. "It's a hot one today. Well, boys, let's not waste Miz Callahan's time. Go on, get to gabbin'."

The two young men fidgeted and looked at each other, as though wondering how to begin. I wanted to make this as comfortable for them as possible.

"Why don't you start," I suggested, "by telling me a little about yourselves. Your background and how you happened to come to Carver—"

"Mahlon there," Curtis interrupted, "he's my nephew, my sister's boy. She and her husband moved to Jackson soon as they married, so that's where Mahlon grew up. Right now he's living here with me and Gloria and helping out in the store, when he's not busy with the citizenship school."

Mahlon nodded his agreement.

"And what about you, Mr. Foss?" I looked at him directly, hoping that at some point one of the boys might begin to speak for himself.

T.W. cleared his throat and said, "I grew up in Jackson, too, Miz Callahan, but I've got relatives in Carver, like Mahlon does. I'm staying with a cousin, and I pick up odd jobs here and there to help pay expenses. Mostly I help out in the clinic, working for Doc Dawson. I'm interested in medicine, and he lets me look at his books, even lets me help out with the patients some."

I was impressed. T. W. Foss was obviously well educated—largely, perhaps, by his own efforts. "Would you like to become a doctor, Mr. Foss?" I asked.

"You can call me T.W., Miz Callahan."

"All right, T.W."

The young man looked at me intently while his jaw worked. "I'd like to, Miz Callahan," he said. Then he added, "Someday, maybe." I couldn't help but hear the wistfulness in his voice, as though he feared he were admitting to a pipe dream.

"They was both involved in that big voter registration drive last summer, that thing called Freedom Summer, when all those white students come down from the North to try to help out," said Curtis.

"Yes, I followed the event closely," I replied, "though I didn't write about it myself." I'd found other things to do with the summer of 1964—a book tour, for one, as my novel had just come out. But even after the tour I avoided Mississippi, having, I thought, already seen enough of it in the couple of times I'd been there. On top of that, while I was still touring, the three civil rights workers came up missing, with the unspoken assumption that they were dead. Although it often fell to the reporter to solve such mysteries, I didn't want to be the one to do it. My fear was that I'd find them by joining them, and I wasn't in the mood to make news headlines myself, at least not under those circumstances. Fortunately there were enough reporters hankering to get a byline out of Freedom Summer that I was able to spend those months following other pursuits.

Curtis continued, as though reading my thoughts. "They knew them three boys that was murdered. Ain't that right, Mahlon?"

Mahlon shrugged, lowered his eyes. T.W. answered. "We met 'em once. Didn't have a chance to get to know 'em. The Klan got to 'em first."

Silence hung over us as heavy as the heat in the room. Curtis untied the handkerchief from around his neck and wiped methodically at the sweat on his face. "Well, tell her about the school," he urged. "That's what she's here for." He pulled a pocket watch out of the bib pocket of his overalls, popped it open, then snapped it shut again. "Got an hour before the store opens." He nodded at the young men to go on.

Mahlon spoke up for the first time. "Where should we start, Miz Callahan?"

"Well, I have a pretty good idea what you do at the school, but why don't you tell me in your own words?"

When Mahlon hesitated, T.W. stepped in again. "The Negro's got the right to vote, Miz Callahan. You know that," he said. "Every one of us knows about the Civil Rights Act that was passed last year—"

"Hold on a minute, T.W.," Mahlon interrupted, his voice animated. "Who's talking about the Civil Rights Act like that's the magic word? The Negro's had the right to vote since 1890 and the Fifteenth Amendment. It's just we can't get registered. The crackers've got a thousand ways to keep us from gettin' registered." As abruptly as he began, he stopped. He looked at me apologetically, as though he suddenly remembered that I too was a cracker, a white.

"Mind your mouth, son," Gloria chided.

"Sorry, Miz Callahan. I meant no offense."

"It's all right, Mahlon," I said. "Please go on."

T.W. picked up where Mahlon had interrupted him. "You're right, Mahlon. Can't argue with you. We got the right to vote, Miz Callahan, but only about five percent of the Negro folk here in Mississippi is even registered. There's too many roadblocks in our way. I guess that's what we're trying to do in the school, get rid of the roadblocks."

"That's a good way to put it, T.W.," Curtis interjected.

T.W. nodded toward Curtis to acknowledge the compliment. "What we do in the citizenship school is teach the folks how to fill out the form they need to fill out in order to register."

"Lots of the folks can't read or write, especially the older folks," explained Gloria. "That's where I come in, and some of the other volunteers. Hester Mumford—she's another teacher like me—she and I go in there and just get down to the basics, starting with the alphabet. People got to know how to read and write before they can vote."

"Fortunately, there are those who *can* read," added Curtis, "so leastways they're a little ahead of the game. With them, we work on the form, and help 'em get ready for the test."

"You see," T.W. continued, "whites don't got to take the test, but the Negro—we're expected to interpret a portion of the state constitution. Now, the constitution of Mississippi, it's got two hundred eighty-five sections. And the registrar, he might pick any one of those sections and ask the Negro to explain it. We got to go over the constitution again and again and again so when a Negro goes in there trying to register, he'll have some idea what he's talking about."

"Don't really matter none, though," Mahlon interrupted gloomily.

"No matter what the Negro say, even if he give a perfect answer, the registrar might fail him on account of he just wants to fail him."

Curtis nodded in agreement. "Not only that," he added, "but the registrars, they ask those crazy questions ain't no one can answer. Like how many seeds in a watermelon? Or how many bubbles in a bar of soap?"

"Those questions aren't meant to have an answer, Curtis," T.W. explained. "That's the whole point."

"Anyway," piped up Mahlon again, "don't matter what he asks. If'n the registrar decides you fail, then you fails."

"And so you're defeated from the outset," I said, "even if you know the constitution backward and forward."

"Seems kinda hopeless just trying, don't it, Miz Callahan," Curtis said slowly, quietly, as though he were only now beginning to see the situation clearly.

"We do it to test the law," T.W. said firmly. "The law says we can vote, and the law says we can register. And so we gotta keep on trying. Just showing up at the registrar's office tells the white folks, 'We know the law; we know our rights. And one day the law's gonna stand, even here in Mississippi.' "

Mahlon nodded, but even as he agreed with T.W., he said, "There's more to it, though, than just the crazy questions and being told you failed the test. Worse things happen than that. Lots worse, and people's scared."

"Got every reason to be," added Gloria.

"People lose their jobs for trying to register to vote," Curtis said.

"They're beaten up bad," said Gloria.

"They come up missing," added Mahlon. "Sometimes the body's found, sometimes not. Either way"—Mahlon shrugged—"he's dead."

"A person can be killed just for trying to register to vote," I said, summing it up. Across the room from me, four dark, solemn faces nodded.

For a moment no one said anything. The fan by the windows blew hot air about the room. No one touched their coffee, which grew cold in the cups in spite of the heat in the air.

Finally Curtis spoke up. "These two boys know. They both been doin' civil rights work long enough to meet up with the white man's sticks and stones. Show her, Mahlon. Show her what happen that time last summer you got arrested." Curtis turned to me then and explained, "He got hisself arrested in Jackson when he took some peoples from the Freedom School to register."

Mahlon looked at his uncle and then at his aunt. They both nodded, telling him to go on. The young man stood, turned his back to Sunny and me, and lifted his T-shirt. I gasped when I saw the dark skin crisscrossed with a web of gray scars. It made me think of a Jackson Pollock painting, only this was of splattered wounds instead of color, pain instead of paint. After a moment Mahlon lowered his shirt, sat back down, and said simply, "One of the deputies had hisself a whip."

"Praise the Lawd he stopped using it before he killed the boy," said Gloria.

"Mahlon almost did die there in the jail," explained Curtis. "Probably woulda, if they hadn't finally let him out to see a doctor."

"Dear God," I whispered, gazing at the young man. He stared back at me dispassionately, though I could sense and understand the anger that burned behind those oddly placid eyes.

Mahlon tilted his head toward T.W. "He been beaten too. I ain't the only one."

"My scars aren't so bad," T.W. muttered, shrugging off his own experience.

"It's the culud man's lot," Curtis mumbled.

"It shouldn't be," I said lamely, unsure of what else to say. I'd been writing about civil rights for years, had seen all kinds of injustice, had heard any number of horrifying stories, but there was something about these two determined young men that made it all more real to me than ever before.

"We've had a hard time trying to convince people to register," explained T.W.

"Yes, I can understand why," I said.

"Fact is," added Mahlon, "ain't no one from Carver been to see the registrar yet."

"But that's about to change," said Sunny, speaking up for the first time since we'd sat down. "We've finally persuaded four from the school to try to register. Two men and two women, all in their twenties. They all work at the mill, so they're in no danger of losing their jobs. In fact, Tom's giving them this Friday off specifically so they can go register."

"Mr. Fulton, he's agreed to pay the poll tax of any Negro from the mill who wants to register. Two dollars a head," T.W. said.

Sunny nodded and started to say something, but Gloria interrupted. "Mr. Fulton's paid for most of the supplies at the school—paper, books, pencils, and whatnot."

"It's Tom's way of helping out," Sunny explained casually.

"Helen here, she comes down and helps with the tutoring," Gloria added. "She's been with us from the git-go."

"Who else is involved with the school?" I asked, looking around the room, not sure where to direct my question.

T.W. answered. "Well, let's see, there's Mr. and Miz Reese, Miz Fulton, Hester Mumford—the teacher that Miz Reese mentioned. They all help with the tutoring. Also Doc Dawson. He comes around when he can to help out with interpreting the constitution. He's a smart man." He thought a moment before finishing. "I guess that's about it."

"And how often and where do you meet?"

"We try to meet once or twice a week. But we've got no set night, and we gotta change the location every time."

"So's the Klan don't know when or where we're meeting," explained Mahlon.

"We've got several places, and about an hour or two before we meet, we get the word out. Could be the Baptist church, might be here at the store, or over at the funeral parlor. Sometimes we just meet out by the river."

I nodded as I jotted notes. When I finished, I looked across the room at the two young men. "So the Klan here in Carver does know about the school?"

"Sure they do," confirmed T.W. mildly. "Can't keep much from the triple-K."

"We've had plenty a threats, T.W. and me both," added Mahlon.

"The Klan just hasn't acted on those threats so far. Someday they will, though. You can be sure of that." Gloria spoke so nonchalantly, so lightly, it was as though she were anticipating the day that an old friend might return home for a visit, or the day she might enter her homemade jam at the county fair.

Both young men nodded. "The Klan won't be satisfied with threats forever," T.W. muttered.

"They's just waitin' for us to take someone up to Lexington to register," Mahlon added. "They ain't gonna like it when we finally get out of the school and try to do something. Come Friday, something's gonna happen. Maybe Friday, maybe later, but it'll come sure 'nough."

I wondered what exactly it was that would come. A firebomb? A lynch mob? "Aren't you afraid?" I asked, feeling silly as soon as the words left my mouth. Of course they were afraid, but would these two young men want to admit it?

T.W. leaned forward in his chair and clasped his hands together. "Miz Callahan," he said quietly, "we've been afraid all our lives on account of the whites. Fear ain't nothing new."

Mahlon shrugged. "That's how we live. We gonna be afraid if we do something, and we gonna be afraid if we don't. The way I see it, we might just as well be doin' something."

"Besides how to read and how to register, we teach our students one more thing," said T.W. "We teach them the best way to protect their head and their gut when they're beaten up by the whites. It's just part of the course."

Once again I was met with dispassionate stares. I dropped my eyes, feeling all too keenly my whiteness, my free ticket to privilege and security in an unfair and dangerous world.

I cleared my throat, pretended to read my notes, tried to gather my thoughts. Finally I said, "On Friday, if these four young people are prevented from registering, what's the next step?"

"What we're thinking, Miz Callahan," Curtis spoke up, "is boycotting Frohmann's store till that time we're allowed to register. Mayor Frohmann depends on his Negro customers to keep that store open and running. I'm the only general store in Coloredtown, and I ain't got all the supplies people need. Nearly everyone in Coloredtown shops at Frohmann's one time or another."

"Seeing as it's the mayor that owns the store," Gloria said, "you'd think he'd be able to do something about getting us registered if he doesn't want to lose his earnings from the colored folks."

"And he won't," asserted T.W. "He depends on us—more than he'd like to admit. Another thing, the mayor is old buddies with Evan Hoopes, the registrar. We're thinking maybe Mr. Frohmann can influence his old friend to let the Negroes start registering, if it's the good of his store he's worried about."

Cedric Frohmann, it appeared, was in a more difficult spot than he might have imagined. If he turned one way, he'd be facing the wrath of the whites and the loss of the mayoralty. If he turned the other, he'd be facing the defiance of the Negro and the loss of their patronage at Frohmann's Department Store. He was a good man, certainly. But I had a feeling the days ahead would be a test as to whether he might also be a great man.

"Where will you get supplies during the boycott?" I asked.

"Plenty o' surrounding towns where we can shop," said Mahlon. "We'd have to travel some, but we won't go without. It's the mayor that'll be hurting if we boycott."

"I hope it won't come to that," I commented.

"Another option is to try to bring in a federal registrar," Sunny said. "He can set up a temporary office and start to get people registered."

"But temporary's the word there, Miz Fulton," Curtis said. "What we want is for the Negro to be able to go to the registrar in the county seat and get registered, period."

Several heads around the room nodded in agreement.

After a quiet moment T.W. said, "Tomorrow night we're having the last meeting of the school before we try to get the folks registered on Friday. We don't know yet where it'll be held, but we'll let Miz Fulton know when we decide. We'd like you to come if you would."

I nodded solemnly. "I'll be there," I promised.

❧

As we bumped our way back over the dirt roads of Coloredtown, I asked Sunny, "Do they know you were once Japanese, that you spent time in the camps?"

She shook her head. "No. Only Corinne knows that."

"Shouldn't they know?"

"Would it make any difference?"

"Well, they'd know you understand."

"Can't a white person understand?"

After considering this a moment, I said, "Not in the same way.

Something called privilege gets in the way. Whites can be angry—indignant even—but still the injustice is done to others, not to us."

Sunny shrugged. "Really? Would you care to argue that point with Lenny"—she glanced at me, then back at the road—"that is, if he were alive to talk about it?"

When I said nothing, she went on, "What I'm trying to say is, civil rights isn't just about Negroes. It's about everyone. See, injustice is a funny thing. It doesn't limit itself to the Negro or the Oriental or the Jew. I mean, it likes to spread itself around, you know? Even if you're the one throwing it out, it's going to find a way to come back on you. Even if you don't throw it out, it's going to come back on you. Live long enough, and you're going to get rained on. It's as simple as that."

TWENTY-EIGHT

Thoughts of Howard Draper rose up time and again, wrapping themselves around my mind the way a cat rubs figure eights around your legs while you're working at a desk. I don't like cats, and neither did I like the fact that I was entertaining thoughts of Howard Draper. I kicked his image aside the way I might scoot the cat out from under the desk with my foot, but back it came, slinking silently in, pausing to lick a paw before brushing up against my brain once more. On the one level I had a journalist's curiosity about him, but I knew it was more than that. His gaze when he shook my hand good-bye still haunted me and left me unnerved. What was it he wanted of me? What was it he wanted to ask, or to say? And just what did I want from him?

I sat alone at a table in the Magnolia Café nursing a cup of coffee. It was three o'clock, the middle of the afternoon lull, and I was the only customer in the place. Two pink-uniformed waitresses were taking a break in a corner booth, eating hamburgers and smoking cigarettes. Even while they ate and smoked, they chatted furiously, as though they were up against a stopwatch that threatened to cut off their gossip in a matter of seconds.

As for me, I was trying yet again to kick the pestering cat when

Howard Draper himself walked in. Startled by his sudden appearance, I felt my face grow warm. At the same time the chattering from the corner booth stopped abruptly. I was reminded of birds falling eerily silent right before a tornado strikes.

Howard nodded toward the ladies in the booth, then turned his eyes on me. He smiled. As he walked toward my table, I felt the glare of the waitresses burning on my skin like a heat lamp. My breath caught in my chest. Suddenly I wished I hadn't lingered so long over my coffee, yet I couldn't deny a sense of pleasure and excitement at this unexpected meeting with Howard Draper. The thought crossed my mind that I was acting like a schoolgirl, but I didn't have time to dwell on it.

"Enjoying a late lunch, Miss Callahan?" Howard asked when he reached me. He wore dark trousers and a pale blue button-down shirt. His dark wavy hair was somewhat disheveled, as though he'd been driving with the window down. He looked tanned and young and healthy. For some reason I thought of the war and was suddenly glad for whatever was keeping this man out of Vietnam.

I dropped my eyes as I answered, "Just coffee."

"Are you waiting for someone, or may I join you?"

I'd been reading the local paper, which was spread out by sections over the table. I hastily gathered the pages and folded them awkwardly. "No. I mean, I'm not waiting for anyone. Please sit down."

As Howard pulled out the chair to sit, a large man burst through the swinging door of the kitchen and leaned both hairy arms on the counter. The bib of his apron was streaked with grease and flour. A chef's hat sprouted from his head like a huge white mushroom. "Afternoon, Howard," he bellowed. "What'll you have? The blue-plate special's meatloaf and mashed potatoes."

"Thanks, Jerry, but I'll have the usual," Howard called back.

Jerry tapped the top of the counter with one thick finger. "One o' these days I'm gonna get you to try one of the specials," he said. "Who knows—you might even like it."

"I'm a creature of habit, Jerry," Howard confessed with a sheepish smile.

"I've never known a man to survive solely on egg salad, Howard. Once in a while you got to eat a nice hunk of meat."

"I do, Jerry. I had a hamburger with all the fixings just the other day. By the way, it was delicious."

Jerry clamped shut his heavy jowls and shook his head. "Must've been when Al was working the grill. I don't recall frying you a burger. I think I would've remembered a red-letter event like that. Well, one egg salad coming up. Suppose you want a Coke with that."

"You got it, Jer."

"How's about giving your buds a jolt, douse 'em with a 7-Up for once."

"I'll stick with Coke."

"A little vanilla in it?"

"I'll take it straight."

"You're boring as all get-out, Howard."

"Just easy to please."

Jerry shook his head while feigning great disgust. He looked at me. "Sure I can't get you something to eat, miss? Piece a pie to go with the coffee?"

"Oh, uh, no. No, thank you," I replied. "Just more coffee, please."

Jerry retreated into the kitchen, and Howard turned his attention back to me. I was glad for the brief interruption on Jerry's part that had allowed me to tap down the adolescent giddiness in my gut stirred up by Howard's appearance.

"Well," Howard said, resting his arms on the table and leaning toward me, "it's a nice surprise to run into you here. Helen is . . ." His eyebrows went up, and his voice trailed off to indicate a question.

"Oh, she's at home," I explained. "I've just been doing a little shopping on my own." Actually, after Sunny and I left Coloredtown, she'd dropped me off at the library so I could do some background research on Carver. But I didn't want to tell Howard what I was up to.

Howard nodded as he unrolled the napkin at his place. A fork and knife tumbled out of the paper cocoon, landing on the table with a clatter. "Any luck? Shopping, I mean?"

I shrugged nonchalantly. "I've just been browsing." How deep would my lie take me before I could veer out of it? I'd have to take the wheel, get us moving in a different direction. "Sunny tells me you're from Chicago."

"Sunny?" He looked dubious a moment before his face brightened in recognition. "Oh yes, Helen. Those childhood nicknames tend to stick with us, don't they?"

I nodded noncommittally, then repeated, "So you're from Chicago?"

"Chicago, yes. Lived there all my life before coming south a couple of years ago."

"That's a big change." I lowered my eyes again to the coffee cup. It was almost empty. A cloud of dregs swam lethargically in the shallow brown pool.

"Yes," Howard agreed. "Well, I was ready for a change."

I remembered the rumor of a relationship gone sour and wondered whether there was any truth to it. But if I were to enter the territory of Howard Draper's life, I would have to tread carefully. "Did you teach?" I asked.

"In Chicago, you mean?"

I nodded. Howard frowned, clasped his hands together on the table. He didn't quite seem to know what to do with them. "No, actually, I didn't. I was with the symphony."

My eyes widened reflexively. "The Chicago Symphony?"

"Yes, for a number of years."

His confession left me speechless. It was an awkward moment in which Howard smiled at me apologetically, almost as if to say, "I know you want an explanation, but I'm not certain I want to give one."

I slowly formed the question anyway. "You left the Chicago Symphony to come *here?*"

Howard shifted his position, glanced over at the waitresses. It was a nervous glance, as though they were women not to be trusted. Leaning forward and speaking softly, Howard said, "Just between you, me, and the lamppost, yes, I left the symphony to come here. Not many people know I was with the symphony because . . . well, I'm sure it must seem"—he shrugged slightly—"odd. Suspect, even. But you not being from Carver, well, you can just carry that bit of my history back to Los Angeles with you. I'm sure you understand."

I didn't understand. Not by a long shot. But just then Jerry came back to the table carrying a fresh pot of coffee in one hand and Howard's lunch on a tray in the other. He poured my coffee, then set the pot on the table while he placed Howard's sandwich and Coke in front of him. A toothpick had been poked into each half of the sandwich, and the plate was crowded with potato chips and a long slice of dill pickle.

"Eat hearty," Jerry said, tucking the empty tray beneath an armpit. He picked up the coffeepot, looked at me, nodded toward Howard, and said with a snort, "The guy's in here every day, all hours of the day and night. Must be nice not to have to work for a living."

"Ha!" Howard shot back. "I happen to work hard for a pittance, Jerry, old man. You know it's not easy giving music lessons to rebellious adolescents."

Jerry continued directing his comments toward me. "Can't argue with him there. I'd rather flip burgers than try to teach a bunch of rascals how to make music."

"Rosemary being the exception, of course."

Jerry nodded. "He's teaching my Rosemary how to play the clarinet—"

"A model student," Howard broke in, winking at me.

"Yeah, she's a good kid, but she's as tone deaf as all the rest—"

"Not all my students are tone deaf. Some are quite—"

"Sometimes when she plays that thing it squeaks so bad the dog howls like he's been whipped. Gets bad enough and that crazy hound dives for cover under the couch. Sometimes I'd like to join him, and I would too, if I weren't too big to fit underneath the thing. I tell you, either she's got to quit soon or our whole house is gonna go nuts. But she won't quit, and you know why?" Jerry waited for me to shake my head. "Because she's got a mad crush on Howard here. Twelve years old, and all she can talk about is a middle-aged music teacher—"

"Thanks, Jerry—"

"—who should've been married long ago, and would've been, if he'd played his cards right."

Howard laughed heartily. "How do you know how I played my cards, old man?"

"Ah, come on, Howard. Half the ladies in this town are in love with you, including, everybody knows, the mayor's daughter. Pretty good catch, that one."

"Now, Jerry—" Howard began, shifting in his seat.

"And what does old Howard here do about it? Nothing! Seems our Carver girls ain't good enough for him! Eh? Eh?"

"Jer—"

"Take them two, for instance." He lowered his voice and nodded toward the two waitresses. "Either one'd give both her eyeteeth for just one date with Howard here. Yeah, but them two dames don't have a chance in—"

Howard coughed and gave Jerry a look that said he didn't like the way the conversation was going. I felt my face begin to burn, but I caught Howard's gaze long enough to give him a brief but sympathetic smile.

"By the way," Jerry said, "I take it you two know each other?" He flipped a thumb first toward me, then toward Howard.

"Of course. Well, that is, we met just yesterday," Howard stumbled. "Miss Callahan is a friend of Helen Fulton's."

"That right?" Jerry asked. "Nice lady, Mrs. Fulton. How long you here for, Miss . . . uh . . ."

"Callahan," I repeated for him. "About a week. Just a bit of a vacation."

Jerry snorted again. "Never heard of no one taking vacation in Carver before! But, each to his own, I guess. Where you from?"

"Los Angeles." He was getting tiresome, and I wished he'd go away.

"That right?" he bellowed. He couldn't seem to find any middle ground as far as volume was concerned. "Howard, here, he's another city slicker. Chicago." He snorted once more, or rather gave a brief series of staccato snorts that quivered the nostrils of his large, doughy nose. I decided that was his way of laughing. Though what he was laughing at, I couldn't imagine. "Well," he said at length, "you two city slickers probably got a lot of gabbing to do. Me, I got to get back to work." He turned to the waitresses and hollered, "Hey, Barb, Irene, you ladies are ten minutes over break. You wanna get back to work, or should I take it out of your paychecks?"

"Aw, Jerry," one called back, "ain't no one even here to wait on."

"So?" Jerry responded indignantly. "You think the counter's gonna wipe itself down? You think the coffee's gonna make itself? I didn't hire you two so's you could be playing at Hedda Hopper grinding out the gossip. I wanna see less sitting and more doing around here."

The two women rolled their eyes, stacked their dishes, and got up from the table. Jerry turned back to Howard and me and said *sotto voce*, "Those two"—he shook his head—"sometimes I think they ain't worth the dirt on a nigger's shoe."

Howard's eyes narrowed, and I thought I saw a flash of anger cross his face, but all he said was, "Don't be too hard on them, Jerry."

"Got to stay on top of 'em," Jerry countered, "or nothing gets done around here. Well, listen"——he turned to me——"you enjoy your time in Carver, hear? But let me just give you one word of advice. If you're planning on spending much time with Howard, watch your back. Plenty o' ladies gonna be jealous, know what I mean?"

Howard started to protest, but Jerry simply snorted one last time before walking back to the kitchen.

Howard sighed heavily as his face took on a hangdog expression. "I'm sorry about that, Miss Callahan."

"Don't be——"

"Jerry's a nice guy, but sometimes he goes a little too far."

"Listen, I understand. You don't have to explain. I've known plenty of people like him."

"That's one of the hazards of a small town," he continued, seemingly not assured by my assurances. "Too much talk. People know everything about you, or *think* they do. Or *want* to. No one's immune from the gossip." Howard ventured a smile before adding, "Other than that, Carver's a great little town."

I hesitated a moment, weighing his statement. "Really?" I asked. "Do you really like it here?"

"Yes." Howard took a bite of his sandwich and chewed thoughtfully. "I really do, believe it or not. It's a quiet, unhurried place to live. The people are . . . well, let's say there are lots of colorful characters around here, people who would make for some interesting reading if you put them in a book. They keep me entertained. On top of all that, I'm happy in my work. I count myself fortunate."

"But don't you miss Chicago and the symphony?"

"Sometimes," he answered truthfully. "But not enough to make me go back."

I sipped at my coffee while half his sandwich disappeared. Contrary to Jerry's opinion, I myself wouldn't have described Howard Draper as boring. In spite of his penchant for egg salad, this northern transplant to Carver was anything but dull. Finally I said, "May I ask how you happened to choose Carver?"

He lifted his head, and his eyes drifted to somewhere beyond my shoulder, settling on the far wall of the café. He was lost in thought, and I let him think. At length he answered, "I know it would probably be hard for most people to understand, but you're an artist, Miss Callahan, so perhaps you would appreciate my reasons for coming here."

He looked at me then and paused, as though waiting for some word or sign of assent. I wasn't sure I'd understand his reasons any better than anyone else, as I didn't quite understand anything about Howard Draper so far. But I said, "Why don't you try me?"

He smiled briefly, wistfully, before he spoke. "It's very simple, really. I wasn't satisfied—I mean, I felt I could do something more than what I was doing with my life. You'd think for a musician, being part of a symphony would be enough . . . *more* than enough. And I can't deny it was a fulfillment of a dream for me. But, you see, I guess that's the problem. It *was* for me. I guess that's all right, to go as far as your talent will take you, to satisfy your own ambitions. But I wanted to do something else as well. I wanted—and please don't laugh, Miss Callahan—but what I wanted was to bring beauty to a place that needs it. I thought I could do that for Carver."

How noble! How very sublime! To bring beauty to the needy little town of Carver while simultaneously adding something putrid to the lives of its Negroes. I almost did laugh, and might have if I weren't stopped by the fact that it would appear rude, the same as spitting on his egg salad sandwich and calling him a hypocrite. Which he was, but I didn't want to get on Howard Draper's bad side, not until I had a better idea as to what was *in*side. "Can you," I asked, successfully stifling my mirth, "can you possibly explain what you mean by that in a little more detail?"

Howard nodded slightly while he swallowed a bite of sandwich. "In Chicago, I was just another musician. I was dispensable, replaceable. Dozens of violinists could have taken over my spot with the symphony and been every bit as good as I was. In fact, my replacement was found even before I was gone.

"You see, I wanted to do something that was uniquely my own. Something not for me but for other people. I wanted to give the gift of music to a group of people who needed it, not just to the so-called cultured elite who thought they wanted it." He paused and gave a little laugh. "Often when I was playing with the symphony, I wondered how many people in the audience were there only because their wives had tickets and had dragged them to the concert, or because they thought it might make them look sophisticated to be there. I wondered how many people weren't hearing the music at all but only daydreaming, or tamping down their impatience as the clock ticked off the minutes, or even sleeping while we offered up our little sacrifice of Schumann or Beethoven or Chopin."

He shook his head. "I became dissatisfied. I decided I wanted to live in a small place where my life could make a difference. I think I'm doing that here, through my music and by being a mentor of sorts for some of the young people. A lot of the kids kind of look up to me. I want to help them develop their talents, whatever their talents may be. I want to help them learn to appreciate the life they've been given. Do you know what I mean?"

I nodded. For a moment I wanted to believe him. Wanted to, but couldn't. Undoubtedly he was doing something worthwhile for the young people here, but it seemed overshadowed, even canceled out, by what he helped to do for the Negroes.

I tapped my cup and watched the coffee ripple as I sorted through my thoughts. "What did your parents think when you left Chicago to come here?"

"My parents are no longer living," he replied simply. "They both died some time ago, within a year of each other, I'm afraid. I was their only child."

"Oh, I'm sorry."

Howard shook his head. "Don't be. They left me with many good memories. They were fine people."

"I'm sure they must have been."

"Anyway"—he looked directly at me and held my gaze—"I think they'd approve of what I'm doing. By the time they died I'd already spent a couple of years with the symphony, and they were proud of that. But they always told me to follow my heart, and that's what I did. It brought me here."

And again, why *Carver*? Of all the little towns in the South, why Carver, Mississippi?

In the momentary lapse of conversation, I glanced around the café. One of the waitresses eyed us openly as she wiped circles on the counter with a dishrag. I had the feeling she was storing up gossip for the bridge table later that night. From the kitchen came the sound of dishes clanging and Jerry swearing. "Irene!" he called, and with that the hawk-eyed young woman disappeared through the swinging door. I let out a sigh of relief.

"And what about you, Miss Callahan?" Howard asked then. "You've published a book. Your parents must have been very proud of your accomplishment."

I shook my head. "I lost both my parents before I was twenty."

Howard gave me a look of genuine sadness, but one without pity. "It must have been hard for you," he offered quietly.

"I wasn't close to either one, really. When they died, I barely noticed." I pursed my lips, thinking how callous that must sound. But it was true. I couldn't take it back.

"Do you have brothers and sisters?"

"Yes, but I never see them. I have a cousin I'm very fond of. We get together when we can. But other than that, I'm on my own."

Howard laid his napkin over the potato chips and pickle on the plate. "Well," he said, "we're just two birds of a feather, then, aren't we?"

We were both solitary artists, yes. But surely the similarities ended there.

"Do you think," I asked, "you'll ever go back to Chicago?"

"I suppose I might," he answered, "but I don't know when. I have no plans to go back at this point. I intend to stay in Carver for as long as I'm needed."

Needed? How long would the students of Carver need him? How long would the Klan need him? When would he feel his usefulness was spent? "But it must be"—I took a deep breath—"it must be rather lonely for you here. . . ."

"I'm far too busy to be lonely." He smiled wanly, and I knew that what he'd said was not entirely true. I wondered just how much of his story was fact and how much was fiction.

"But what of culture?" I prodded. "Where are the museums, the theaters, the literary readings, the coffee houses where the artists gather?"

He gave me a knowing smile. "I make my own culture," he said quietly. "It isn't difficult. I have my music. I brought all my favorite books from home. In my apartment I have a little framed print of Monet's water lilies, a landscape by Pissarro, and a third piece by Mark Rothko. That last is untitled, of course." He smiled again.

In the kitchen a dish shattered; Jerry swore loudly once more. "Oh," Howard added, "and Jerry, he's a man of culture. He has a poster of Andy Warhol's Campbell's soup cans back there on the kitchen wall. He says it lends dignity to his work as a cook."

I laughed in amusement. I liked Howard Draper's subtle sense of humor. At least that part of him was genuine and neither a lie nor a front.

Two teenaged boys entered the café just then and, seeing Howard, hollered, "Hey, Mr. Draper!" and "How are ya, Mr. Draper?" while one slid into a booth and the other went to the jukebox. Howard called out a greeting, then said to me, "Two of my students at Carver High."

In another moment the café was filled with the music of a new group called the Grateful Dead. The notes were a loud and jarring interruption to the otherwise quiet afternoon, but Howard only laughed and said, "I haven't managed to interest them in Dvořák and Pachelbel yet. But I'm working on it."

He glanced at his watch. I found myself hoping he would stay—I had so many unanswered questions—but he said he had to give a piano lesson in twenty minutes. He dug around in his pants pocket until he had pulled out enough change for a tip. He started to rise, hesitated a moment, then sat back down. "I don't suppose," he said, speaking loudly over the music, "you'd care to have lunch with me tomorrow?"

I didn't even have to think it over. "I'd like to, yes."

"Good." He smiled. "Same place but . . . ah, say noon?"

"Sounds fine. I'll be here."

He stood and offered me his hand. "It's been a pleasure seeing you again, Miss Callahan. I'll look forward to tomorrow."

I smiled but found I could say nothing in return. I was suddenly thankful for the blaring jukebox that served as an excuse for my silence. Howard turned and left, and after he was gone I stared at the front door of the café for a long time. I told myself he was a man who naturally attracted women—Jerry had made that much clear—and I'd be smart to steer clear of the trap. I reminded myself yet once more that he was a member of the Klan and that the pleasant façade hid a dark interior. I warned myself that even if in some ways Howard Draper was genuinely good, in others he was surely unthinkably evil.

If only, I thought, *you could be all that you appear to be.*

But even so, even though I knew he was Klan, I also knew it was already too late for my heart to get away untouched by Howard Draper.

TWENTY-NINE

I was trying desperately to make it up the attic stairs to save Lenny when the sound of gunfire sliced into my dream. I didn't know whether it was the Japanese who were shooting or someone else; I'd never heard actual gunshots in my nightmares before—only Lenny's screams. One shot came, and then another, and then a third, and a man's voice commanded, "Stay down!" I was still on the stairs trying to reach the attic door and at the same time trying frantically to make sense of what was happening when a familiar voice, a woman this time, demanded, "Augie, wake up!"

Finally I pulled myself up out of my dream to find Sunny calling to me from the doorway of my bedroom. She was crouched down, beckoning me with one hand. She appeared as little more than a silhouette against the dim night-light in the hall. "Augie, get down! Get off the bed!"

Instead, drowsy and disoriented, I sat straight up. "Sunny, what's going on!"

"Get off the bed!" she ordered shrilly.

Yet another shot rang out, followed by a shattering of glass somewhere in the house below. At once I rolled off the bed and crawled across the floor to Sunny, who grabbed my hand and led me to her own room next door. The children were already there, huddled behind the bed. "We're safer here away from the front of the house," she said. She pulled Joanie into her lap, and I put an arm around Ronnie's shoulders. Both children were wide-eyed and trembling.

"For goodness' sake!" I yelped at Sunny. "Tell me what's going on!"

"Someone's shooting at the house."

That much I had discerned on my own. "But why? What happened? Who would want to shoot at your house?"

Sunny shook her head at my barrage of questions. "Probably the Klan, trying to scare us."

"Well, it's working," I retorted, aware that my heart was knocking up against my rib cage with amazing strength. "I thought you said you were safe from the Klan, thanks to the plastic surgeon."

"Well, safer than we might have been, anyway. But I guess the Klan always looks for that window of opportunity. Any small excuse will do."

"So what's their excuse tonight?"

"The school, maybe? I don't know for sure."

Just then Joanie started to cry. "I want Daddy," she wailed. "Where's Daddy?"

A good question. Where *was* Tom? It must have been his voice that first broke into my dream, barking out the command to stay down.

"He's downstairs, honey," Sunny said soothingly. She ran her hand over the little girl's hair, just as Haha used to do to comfort her, and me. "He went to see what's happening."

"Do you think he's been shot?" Ronnie asked.

"Of course not," Sunny replied quickly, breathlessly.

"What if he's downstairs bleeding to death, Mom?" I felt the boy's muscles stiffen against me, as though he were about to spring up and go to his father's rescue.

"Ronnie! Don't say such a thing—"

"I want Daddy!" Joanie wailed.

Sunny shushed the child, saying, "He'll be back in just a minute, honey."

"I want Daddy!"

"I'm here, Joanie." Tom's voice reached us from the doorway, where he stood clutching a rifle in his hand. He wore a pair of jeans with the belt unbuckled, and he hadn't bothered to put on a shirt.

Joanie broke free of her mother's grasp and ran to her father, throwing her arms around his waist. He hurried her back to the side of the bed and crouched down. He laid the rifle on the floor, within reach. "We have to stay here for a little bit, sweetheart," he said gently. "Whoever it was is gone now, but I can't be sure they won't take a second swing by the house."

The five of us huddled there on the floor in the dark like schoolchildren waiting out an air-raid drill. For a moment no one spoke. We all seemed to be listening for the sound of a returning car.

Finally Sunny asked quietly, "Was it the Klan, Tom?"

"Could have been," Tom speculated. "It's a common enough scare tactic for them, going around shooting at people's houses in the middle of the night. Then again, I had to let go a couple of men down at the mill this past week. Maybe they were just coming by to let me know they didn't appreciate it."

"Well, whoever it was," I pointed out nervously, "they could have killed someone."

To my surprise, Tom shook his head. "Only by accident. They were aiming downstairs, assuming we'd be asleep upstairs. They did manage to shoot out the porch light and the living room windows, but still they only meant to send a message."

"Consider it received," I snorted.

Sunny frowned. "Did you call the police?"

"Not yet."

"Don't you think you'd better?"

Tom gave a little humorless laugh. "If it *was* the Klan doing the shooting, Chief Sturges was probably one of the men who just rearranged our living room."

"But, *why*?" I begged.

"Well, like I said," Sunny repeated, "if it was the Klan—and we don't know for sure that it was—they probably got wind of what's planned for Friday, that we're taking the group down to register."

"And the Klan knows you're involved in the school, right?"

Sunny nodded. "Hard to keep secrets from the Klan around here."

We were quiet again, thinking our own thoughts, waiting for I don't know what. The all clear? Something to tell us it was all right now? Barring such a sign, how would we ever lie down again and, feeling safe, fall back to sleep?

I was beginning to think we might venture out from behind the bed when the night's stillness was fractured by a crunching of tires over dirt and gravel. Tom's back stiffened as he cocked his head. "Car," he whispered. The car's engine ran rough, like it needed a tune-up. "It almost sounds like . . ." His voice trailed off.

"Who, Tom?" Sunny asked.

"I can't be sure." Tom reached for the rifle, his fingers curling around the butt. He rose up slowly and moved bent over toward the bedroom door. By now the car had stopped in front of the house, its engine cut.

"Be careful, Tom," Sunny called out.

"I'm just going to look out the hall window," he whispered, adding the unnecessary order, "Stay where you are."

Ronnie fidgeted beneath my arm. "Mom," he whispered, "I'm scared. Don't let them shoot us."

My eyes locked with Sunny's as we held the children more tightly against us. "Nobody's going to shoot anybody," she said. Ronnie wasn't convinced. Neither was I. Sunny probably wasn't either.

"I don't wanna die," the boy moaned.

"Hush, Ronnie," Sunny said, almost angrily. "No one's going to die." She lifted her head slightly as she looked out toward the hall. "Tom?" she called. His name quivered like a faulty arrow sailing through the air.

For a moment there was no response. I thought I heard Tom release the safety on his rifle.

Finally, after another breathless moment, Tom called to us, "Just as I thought. Looks like Lee Henry's station wagon. Hard to see anything much without the porch light." Another pause. Then, "Yeah, it's Lee Henry and Miss Ebba." The rifle made another clicking sound. "I'm gonna go meet them at the door."

"What on earth are they doing here at this hour?" Sunny wondered aloud. She sounded notably relieved.

Putting a hand lightly on her shoulder, I asked, "Who's here?"

"It's all right," she assured me. "They're friends."

Tom came into the bedroom, opened the closet door, and started to put the rifle away. He hesitated a moment, muttered, "Well, on second thought—" He grabbed a shirt and threw it on, then headed out the door, still clutching the rifle. "Stay here," he ordered once more, throwing the words back over his shoulder.

"Wait a minute, Tom," Sunny protested. "Let me go with you."

Tom hesitated but finally relented. "All right. We might as well all go down. I don't imagine the Klan or whoever it was is coming back tonight. They've done what they wanted to do."

Tom headed down while Sunny, the children, and I paused to put on our robes. By the time we reached the bottom of the stairs, Tom had opened the front door and was fumbling with the lock on the screen door. The light in the hall made it impossible to see who stood on the porch, our visitors being simply two shadowy figures beyond the screen. From out of the darkness a man's voice said, "Sorry, Mr. Fulton. I know it's past midnight, but Mama come by and woke me up sayin' I had to drive her on over here—"

"It's all right, Lee Henry," Tom assured him, finally pushing open the screen door. "Come on in." He laughed briefly and added, "We were awake anyway."

A very large man entered the hall with a very tiny woman on his arm. Though the less prepossessing of the two, it was she who demanded my attention. Her dark flesh clung to angular bones, her small back was curled with age, and she shuffled rather than walked with the aid of a cane. She wore a rumpled cotton housedress—faded yellow daisies against a white background—that looked as though it had been slept in many times over. It fell to below her knees and hung loosely on her small frame. Battered leather shoes swallowed up her child-sized feet, topped by a pair of nylon knee-highs rolled down like donuts around her bony ankles. She was the picture of frailty and age, but at the same time she exuded an unmistakable strength. I could see it in the look on her face, a look of determination and resolve. She was after something, and she wasn't going to leave until she'd found it.

Without a word, she made her way past us into the living room. The rest of us followed, the children clinging wide-eyed to Sunny. In the living room the old woman flipped a switch that turned on several lamps at once. The sudden light revealed the shattered front windows and the shards of glass lying about on the carpet. Oddly, geranium blossoms mingled with the glass. One of the potted plants on the porch had been hit, its flowers hurled through the broken window. The shooting spree had also tumbled photos off the mantelpiece, upended a reading lamp, and left the far wall pockmarked with half a dozen bullet holes.

The old woman quietly surveyed the damage, then turned to us and announced, "I see dey done been 'n gone a'ready. We too late, Lee Henry."

"Couldn'ta done nothin' 'bout it anyways, Mama," the man said resignedly. "Can't stop bullets with words."

"We coulda warned dem, coulda told 'em git outta de house." She looked up into Tom's face. She had to tilt her head almost all the way back to meet his gaze. For the first time I noticed that she only had one eye. Where her left eye should have been there was only a fleshy crater. The sunken eyelids quivered, as though struggling to cling together in the middle of the empty socket. "You all right?" she asked Tom. "You 'n the chillun?"

"We're fine," Tom assured her. "No harm done except for a bit of a mess."

"Who was it, Miss Ebba?" Sunny asked. "Do you know?"

"Klan, a'course," she answered promptly. "Who else'd be? Mean 'n nasty, goin' round shootin' at in'cent peoples."

"Is it because of the school? Because we're taking a group to register on Friday?"

"Don' know." The old woman shook her head slowly. "But dat be my guess."

Tom leaned the rifle up against the living room wall and tucked his shirttail into his pants. "Do you know exactly who was in the car, Miss Ebba?" he asked.

Why, I wondered, were they barraging this little Negro woman with questions about the Klan, as though she were a routine guest at their secret meetings? I gazed at Miss Ebba in confusion.

She pursed her lips, shook her head. "Don' know dat neider, for sho," she said slowly, thoughtfully. "Don' matter none, leastways. De Klan jes' one big ugly person, is all."

I thought at once of Howard Draper, an appendage of that one big ugly person, and wondered whether he might have personally dropped off the little gift of lead before heading out into the night again. "Excuse me," I said quietly, hesitant to break in when we hadn't yet been introduced, "but how can you be so sure it was the Klan?"

The tiny woman turned to me. She gazed at me with her one eye for several long seconds before answering. "De Lawd tole me, like ever' other time. He speak to me in my dreams, tell me what comin'. Dis time, look like he shoulda give de dream a little sooner. Else Lee Henry shouldn'ta took so long gittin' his pants on."

She gave Lee Henry a glance of reprimand, and although he was at least fifty, maybe older, he seemed to wither under the look like a shamed adolescent. But only for a moment. He collected himself and said, "Now, Mama, if you lived with me and Louise like we told you to a hunnerd times, you wouldn't have so far to walk."

"Lee Henry, you ast me a hunnerd times 'n I tole you a hunnerd times, I ain't leavin' my home. Ain't dat far, leastways. You know dat."

"Mama," Lee Henry protested, "ain't nothin' close when you can't hardly walk. Take you twenty minutes just to get from your bedroom to your front door, and that ain't but fifteen feet."

"You sayin' it my fault we too late tonight?"

"I'm sayin' if you lived with me and Louise, it would save a whole lotta time when you have your dreams. Besides, it ain't safe, ole woman like you livin' alone—"

At that point Tom broke into the family squabble to suggest we all move into the kitchen for something cold to drink. I decided too that he probably wanted us away from the front of the house, just in case, though I noticed when we headed toward the kitchen he left his rifle in the living room.

It was Miss Ebba who once more led the way as we moved down the hall. It was a slow but steady procession as the rest of us followed, Miss Ebba's cane tapping out our time on the hardwood floor. A few moments later the children were curled up on a comforter in the breakfast nook, their eyes heavy again with sleep, while the rest of us sat at the kitchen table with tall glasses of lemonade.

Before anyone could speak, the old woman busied herself by staring at me, her one yellowed eye taking me in as though she'd never before seen a white woman. Her coarse gray hair was pulled back sharply from her face and tucked into several small braids at the nape of her neck. The paleness of it contrasted sharply with the mahogany sheen of her skin. She was so thin her face appeared almost skeletal, and I thought she looked like someone who had died already but was simply too stubborn to go. When she spoke she revealed an incomplete set of yellowed teeth. "We ain't been introduced," she said. "I'se Ebba Starks, and dis here's my grandson, Lee Henry Starks."

Lee Henry nodded at me and said, "How do." He was a study in contrast to his grandmother, and I wondered at the genes that had been added to the family in the two succeeding generations. He was as large as she was small, heavy without being overweight, an imposing presence in spite of his apparent timidity. He wore overalls and a short-sleeved shirt that revealed arms as thick and solid as birch trees. His hands were so big the tall glass of lemonade disappeared in their grip. I wondered at the strength in those hands and thought of Lenny Small in Steinbeck's *Of Mice and Men*—the gentle giant whose grip could easily snap a woman's neck. His fleshy face carried the scars of adolescent acne. His skin, darkened by a shadow of whiskers, was still several shades lighter than his grandmother's. He smiled at me when I said, "I'm happy to meet you," and in that brief smile I noted an unmistakable sincerity and kindness that I would later come to know as his defining characteristics.

Sunny, momentarily flustered, said, "Oh, I'm sorry, I should have introduced you earlier. This is an old friend of mine, Augie Callahan. We were children together in California."

"I'm very happy to meet you both," I said again, unsure of whether to extend my hand to them across the table. They made no move themselves to join in a handclasp, so I let my palm stay curled around the cold glass of lemonade.

"Lee Henry works down at the mill," Tom added. "One of our finest loom technicians."

The big man dropped his eyes meekly at the compliment and kept them lowered while Miss Ebba argued, "Dat just how he put food on de table. His real work be preachin' the Word o' God. He the preacher at de Baptist church, but dat don't earn him 'nuf to keep hisself alive, let 'lone a fambly."

Lee Henry looked at his grandmother. "The Fulton mill been good to me more 'n thirty years now, you know that, Mama—"

"Anyway," Tom interrupted, "you say you know it was the Klan that came around tonight, Miss Ebba?"

"Thaz right." She nodded slightly, the lids of her absent eye pulsing. "Lawd let me know in a dream. Tole me dey's plannin' on comin' by sometime tonight. Wish I coulda got here sooner." She looked down at the children asleep on the floor.

"I thought at first it might have been the two men I fired this past week—you know who I mean, Lee Henry?"

Tom looked across the table at Lee Henry, who nodded curtly. "Those two that come in drunk ever mornin' for a month. You was more 'n fair, Mr. Fulton. You give 'em more chances than any other bossman woulda."

"But if Miss Ebba says it was the Klan, then that's who it was," Tom concluded.

It surprised me that he would believe the old woman. I looked at Sunny to see whether her face held any clue as to whether Tom was simply being patronizing, but instead she returned my gaze and said, "Miss Ebba's been right too many times to discount what she says. Some time ago—how long's it been, Miss Ebba, since the dreams started?"

The old woman's jaw worked in thought before she finally said, " 'Bout a year, I guess, mebbe less, mebbe more."

"She started having dreams," Sunny continued, "in which God warns her about what the Klan is going to do."

The one-eyed seer, I thought. I tried to keep my face as expressionless as possible so no one could detect my skepticism.

"The first man Miss Ebba warned didn't believe her," Sunny went on.

"And he was probably regretting his mistake even as he died," Tom added.

I looked from one to the other. They obviously wanted me to ask, so I asked. "What happened?"

Sunny sipped her lemonade, then said, "The man's name was Amos Lowe—"

"But ever'body call him Louie," Miss Ebba interjected, " 'coz he could play de trumpet jes' like Louie Armstrong. Started playin' in roadhouses when he wuz jes' a kid. Died when he wuz jes' a kid, for dat matter. He weren't no more 'n twenty-two, were he, Lee Henry?"

Lee Henry, looking down at his glass, stuck out his lower lip to reveal the pink fleshy part inside. " 'Bout that, I'd say. Seemed older, on account he were feisty. Never heard such a smart mouth as Louie had. That's what killed him."

"He wasn't careful," Sunny said. "I guess you could say he refused to play by the rules, the white man's rules. He looked white people in the eye, wouldn't say sir or ma'am, wouldn't step off the sidewalk to let a white person pass by."

"So which offense was he killed for?" I asked.

"Pick one," Tom said. "Any one'll do. Any one is enough to get a Negro killed."

I nodded. "So what happened?"

Tom picked up the thread of the story. "One day he just went too far. He was downtown minding his own business when a couple of white boys egged him on for a fight."

Lee Henry shook his head slowly, his eyes still lowered as though he were reluctant to look at the whites seated with him at the table. "Never fight a white boy. He shoulda knowed that. No matter what they say, just walk on by. . . ."

"So they picked a fight and killed him?" I asked.

"No," Tom said. He leaned forward, crossed his arms on the table. "Louie was a skinny kid, but he was amazingly strong. He knew how strong he was because he'd been fighting other Negro boys all his life and never lost a fight. Well, he took the two young men on knowing he had a pretty good chance of leaving them in the dust. And he did too, left them both out cold in an alley."

"Shoulda knowed better," Lee Henry muttered. "Shoulda knowed a culud man can't get away with that. Gonna catch up with him sooner or later."

"Caught up wid him sooner, I'd say," Miss Ebba said.

"Did you have the dream that night?" Sunny asked.

The old woman shook her head. "Not dat night but de next one. Lawd tole me de next night Klan had plans for Louie. Told me where 'n when. I got myself over to Louie's fas' as I could to give him de warnin'. He jes' laugh. Din't belief me. Laugh in my face 'n told me I'se a crazy ole woman."

"Shoulda listened," Lee Henry whispered.

"It happened just like Miss Ebba said it would," Sunny explained. "Amos—Louie—was walking home late one night from a roadhouse where he'd been playing. To get home he had to walk along a stretch of wooded road where there weren't any houses and probably no traffic at that time of night."

"Did that all the time, Louie did," Lee Henry put in. "Walking home in the dark with his trumpet tucked up under his arm. Plenty people tried talk him outta it, told him to either sleep at the roadhouse till morning or git hisself another job. Ain't safe, a Nigra walking round 'lone at night. But he said he weren't afraid none. He was so cocky he thought he could defend hisself against most anyone. Sometimes fear's a good thing, Miz Callahan. Keep you alive." He stopped and shook his large head again.

Sunny went on, "It wasn't hard for the Klan to figure out his routine. They knew where he was working and what time he walked home. All they had to do was wait for him to show up. Of course we don't know exactly what happened that night. We only know how he ended up."

Sunny gave Tom a look that told him to finish the story. Tom sighed and glanced over at the children. Though they were sleeping, he spoke softly, as though hoping the words wouldn't enter their dreams. "They skinned him alive. Strung him up in a tree and tortured him probably for hours before finally putting him out of his misery with a bullet to the head." Tom's face was ashen, and his eyes had a faraway look, as though he could see the night that Amos Lowe died. Perhaps in a sense he did see it, because he had watched as another man died at the hands of the Klan.

We were quiet for a moment before Lee Henry added, "They even smashed his trumpet, left it danglin' on the tree with him."

Miss Ebba looked me sharply in the eye again. "It happen jes' like de Lawd tole me, word for word. I warned Louie, but he wouldn't listen."

My skepticism shivered but remained intact. There had to be an explanation of some sort.

"Word got round 'bout Louie," Miss Ebba continued, "and now peoples listen when I'se got sumpin' to say."

I nodded reluctantly. "Umm," I said, clearing my throat, "what are they going to do next—the Klan, I mean?"

The little woman leaned forward slightly, her one watery eye continuing to bore into me. "Well now, I cain't know, ken I, till de Lawd tell me in a dream." She spoke slowly and deliberately, letting me know that my deadpan expression didn't hide my doubts from her. She could see right through me.

Lee Henry pushed his empty glass aside and folded his huge hands on the table. "Whatever 'tis," he said quietly, "won't be good, you can be sho of that." He looked up at me then, as though to warn me to take it all seriously.

I did take it all seriously—the Klan, the violence, the citizenship school, the voter registration. But it was difficult to believe that God came down and told this wizened little woman what the Klan was up to, though I had to admit the story about Amos Lowe was eerie and disturbing. And come to think of it, how in fact had she and Lee Henry ended up on the Fultons' doorstep only moments after the windows were shot out of the house?

I wanted to say something, anything. "People must feel safer knowing you'll warn them about the Klan."

The old woman shrugged. "De Lawd, he pick 'n choose. Don' tell me ever'thing. Dey's some things de Klan do de Lawd don' give me no word 'bout. Ain't no one feelin' safe, chile."

"How does he decide," I asked, perhaps irreverently, "which . . . activities . . . he's going to warn you about?"

There was that eye again, that one penetrating eye, holding me in its gaze. "Who can know de ways o' de Lawd?" Miss Ebba stated firmly. "Ain't up to us to question. He do what he know be right."

For an interminable amount of time, the four of us sat quietly at that kitchen table, speaking only intermittently but mostly lost in our own thoughts, perhaps praying to whatever God we believed in.

I was thinking about T.W. and Mahlon and the students at the citizenship school who were preparing to register. I hoped that whatever the Klan had in mind for them, Miss Ebba would be given the inside scoop beforehand, in time to preach a warning. It was tempting to believe in her nocturnal pipeline to God if it meant avoiding a tragedy come Friday.

THIRTY

After the shooting I briefly considered canceling my luncheon date with Howard. It would, after all, be like breaking bread with the enemy. But in the end I decided to go. Lunching with Howard Draper, I reasoned, was for the sake of my work, a chance to gather some colorful anecdotes for my article; therefore, I was professionally obligated to meet with him.

Propelled by that convenient bit of self-deception, I entered the Magnolia Café at noon on Tuesday. Howard sat at a table near the back, just on the edge of the Negro section. When he saw me, he stood. The place was crowded, this being the lunch hour, and I suddenly felt the weight of dozens of eyes upon me as people paused and turned to see whom Howard Draper was meeting. It may have been my imagination, but a momentary hush fell over the room as I walked toward him.

He pulled out a chair for me. I acknowledged his chivalry with a polite smile and sat down. Then he sat too, hiking his chair forward and tucking his long legs under the table in one swift movement. Once we were settled, the stares receded as the chatter around us increased. I could well imagine what the chatter was about now that the diners had some new and tantalizing scuttlebutt to kick around over their burgers and fries.

He sidestepped a greeting and jumped right into an apology. "A booth might have been more private," he said, glancing around, "but they were all taken by the time I got here." He shrugged then and added, "It's not always this crowded."

"Don't worry, this table's fine," I said, picking up the menu in front of me.

He opened his own menu and scanned it. "I hope you're hungry. This may be the local grease pit, but they really do serve up some pretty good grub. Have whatever you want. It's on me."

I wasn't terribly hungry, but I pretended to read the menu with interest. Even with my eyes lowered, I could feel Howard's gaze. He seemed to be studying me. After a moment he asked, "Are you all right, Miss Callahan? You look a little tired."

How to tell him how I was, how I felt, when I could hardly unravel the mess of feelings myself? I sighed and closed the menu. "I'm afraid I didn't sleep very well last night, Mr. Draper."

He invited me to explain by lifting his eyebrows. But before I could go on, one of the waitresses arrived at our table, pulling an order pad from her apron pocket and a pencil from the cotton-candy depths of her bleached-blond beehive. Her name, Irene, was stitched onto the breast of her pink uniform. She was one of the waitresses who, according to Jerry, would give her eyeteeth for a date with Howard Draper. I was amused to notice that one of her eyeteeth actually was missing and wondered whether Mr. Draper was more active than Jerry knew. The look Irene gave me said she wasn't pleased to see me yet again sitting with Carver's most eligible bachelor. "So what'll it be?" she asked curtly. She impatiently snapped a large wad of gum while waiting for me to respond.

"I'll have a bowl of the chicken noodle soup and an iced tea," I decided.

She nodded once, took my menu, and tucked it up under her arm. She then turned her gaze toward Howard, smiled coquettishly, and to my amusement, batted her eyes. Her painted eyelids were two blue robin's eggs in a nest of clotted mascara. "What can I do for you today, Mr. Draper?" she asked, stepping so close to him that her hip almost rubbed up against his shoulder. Her voice was sultry, and she obviously wanted her question to be interpreted by the receiver as a double entendre.

But Howard was largely unaware of—or perhaps completely disinterested in—the admiration directed his way. He spoke mechanically as he closed his menu and handed it to Irene. "I'd like an egg salad sandwich and a Coke, please. And listen, hold the chips today, will you, Irene?"

"Sure, honey," she said, scribbling on the order pad. Her bright red lower lip stuck out, and I wasn't sure whether she was concentrating or pouting. When she finished writing, she tucked the second menu up under her arm, poked the pencil back into the beehive, turned on her heels, and left without another word.

Howard and I were quiet for a moment after she left. He fidgeted in his seat, then laced his slender fingers together on top of the table. Leaning forward, he frowned and said, "I hope you weren't unwell in the night, Miss Callahan."

"No, nothing like that." I sighed heavily, unrolled my napkin, and pushed the flatware into place on the paper mat. "It's just that . . . well, the house was attacked. I mean, somebody shot out a couple of windows in the middle of the night. Sent a pot of geraniums sailing right into the living room. I never did get back to sleep afterward."

He stared at me for a long minute as though I'd been speaking in a foreign language. Finally he asked, "What do you mean, somebody shot out the windows?"

I thought it an odd question, as there was nothing ambiguous about what I'd said. I repeated myself, purposely speaking slowly as though to insinuate a certain dull-wittedness on the part of the listener. "Well, you see, someone drove by the house, took aim with a rifle or a gun, and had a little target practice with the living room windows. Shattered them to bits. Right now there's cardboard covering the holes where the glass used to be."

Tired and cross, I was willing to give in to sarcasm. I thought I was irritated with Howard because he apparently wanted to play me for a fool. I don't think I was fully aware yet that I was more angry with him for not being what I wanted him to be, for not living up to what he appeared to be.

"Who," he asked with a shake of his head, "would shoot up the Fultons' house?"

I shrugged, appearing—I hoped—nonchalant. "I have no idea," I replied. I lifted my eyes, looked directly into his, and demanded evenly, "Do you?"

He tried wholeheartedly to look surprised. "No, I—no, of course not. How could I know? I have no idea at all. No . . ." He was stumbling badly. Whatever else he may be, he was not a good liar. No doubt sorry he initiated this conversation, he took a breath and dropped his eyes. "I suppose it could have been someone who's at odds with Tom. Maybe someone from the mill?"

"Hmm, yes, that's what Tom thought too. He said he had to fire a couple of men and maybe they were getting back at him for that. So that's one possibility, though we can't know for sure."

"At any rate, I trust no one was hurt."

"Only frightened. It's not something that happens every night."

"No. No, certainly not. Tom called the police, I assume."

"Well, he didn't last night, but he might have reported it today. I'm not sure what his plans were."

Howard shook his head. "I just can't imagine . . . I'm sorry that happened while you were here. I'm just glad you're all right, that everyone is."

"Well," I said lightly, "it gives me something to talk about back home, doesn't it?"

Howard gave an insincere chuckle. "Yes, I suppose so. Though it doesn't make Carver look very good, does it?"

I leaned over the table and lowered my voice. My heart pounded in my chest, but I forced myself to speak. "You want to know what I think?" I glanced around the busy café and motioned for Howard to lean closer. When he did I said, "I think it was those Ku Klux Klan people. You know, the ones who go around burning crosses and lynching Negroes."

Howard drew back abruptly and blinked, as though my face had suddenly gone out of focus. "But the Fultons are white," he protested loudly. Then, remembering to lower his voice, he went on, "Why do you think it was the Klan?"

"Everyone knows Sunny's involved in the citizenship school," I responded. "You know, to help Negroes get to vote. You did know that, didn't you, Mr. Draper?"

Howard clenched his hands together so tightly his knuckles turned white. "Yes, I know she has some part in the school, but really, I doubt it was the Klan. If they wanted to send a message about the school, there are plenty of other people they might have gone after."

"Like who?"

Howard shrugged. "Whoever the Negro leaders are. I don't know who's involved in the school myself, but it's the Negroes who are the more likely target."

"Sunny's a teacher at the school, the same as the Negro teachers."

"Yes, but she's also Tom Fulton's wife, and you have to understand that Tom Fulton is an important man around here. A big slice of Carver works for him down at the mill. Not many people would want to get on his bad side. Unless, of course, you've been fired from the mill. That seems the more reasonable explanation, don't you think? That it was someone from the mill?"

"Well," I said, sitting back in my chair and pretending to concede, "you may be right. But I suppose we'll never really know who did it."

"No," Howard shook his head again. He unlaced his fingers and began to fiddle with his napkin. "No, probably not."

"It's funny, though," I said, pausing for effect.

Howard stopped fiddling, his hands coming to rest like two beached starfish on the table. "What's that?" he asked.

"Right after the shooting someone came around to the house and told us she was certain it was the Klan."

My companion frowned and shifted in his chair. The fingers of one hand found the fingers of the other and intertwined again. "Who?"

"Someone by the name of Miss Ebba. A Negro woman. Do you know her?"

"Not personally, no, though I know who she is."

"She reminded me of you."

At this Howard appeared startled. "How so?" he asked.

"I thought she must be one of your more colorful Carver characters. She claimed the Lord told her who it was that shot out the windows. She said he told her in a dream that it was the Klan."

Howard offered me a half smile. "I see," he responded.

"Haven't you heard about her giving warnings to people who are supposedly going to be attacked by the Klan?" I pushed.

"I've heard something about it, but I wouldn't take an old woman like that too seriously." He tried to laugh, but it fell flat. "You didn't believe her, did you?"

I lifted my shoulders and my eyebrows in an odd kind of double shrug. "She may be crazy, but she just may be right. After all, she showed up right after the shooting. How did she know to come?"

Howard cleared his throat and looked around the café before answering. "Well, it was probably just a coincidence. Like I said, the attackers were most likely the fired mill hands, or maybe just a bunch of kids who got bored, had a little too much to drink and went on a wild spree. Heaven knows the young folks get bored around here, especially during the summer months. So that's another possibility." He looked quite pleased with himself for coming up with a second scenario. "Really, you have to take someone as old as Ebba Starks with a grain of salt. She's ninety-six years old. People that age"——he tapped at the side of his head——"they tend to begin to lose it up here, you know."

"Is she ninety-six?" I asked.

"Yes." He nodded. "Think of it. She was born only four years after the slaves were freed. Her own parents and grandparents were slaves on a plantation not far from here, and her great-grandfather was straight from Africa, brought over on one of the ships sometime in the eighteenth century. We think we're so far from slavery, but we're really so close to it. It's been abolished for . . . well, 1865, so that's one hundred years this year. Only a little more than Miss Ebba's lifetime."

Howard Draper seemed to know an awful lot about someone he didn't know. I nonchalantly tossed out another question to see how he would respond. "How did Miss Ebba lose her eye?"

"It was a childhood accident," he replied without hesitating. "She fell from a tree and unfortunately encountered a branch on the way down. The eye might have been saved if a white doctor had been willing to treat her. There were no Negro doctors around here back then, and no white doctor would waste his time trying to save the eye of a little colored girl."

To draw out the moment and savor it, I gave Howard a good long deadpan stare. Then I said, "I thought you said you didn't know Ebba Starks."

"I don't," he claimed, unruffled. "Like I said, I know who she is, but I've never met her."

"Yet you seem to know a lot about her."

Howard shrugged. "Small town, remember? Everybody knows everything about everybody else. The story of Miss Ebba's eye is common knowledge around here, just a part of Carver folklore."

I reached for the saltshaker, just to have something to toy with, and rocked it gently back and forth on the Formica tabletop. "What are your views on civil rights, Mr. Draper?" I asked casually.

"Civil rights?"

"Yes. Equality for Negroes and all that."

Howard stuck out his lower lip, shook his head slightly. "Well, it's long overdue, of course." He seemed about to say more when Irene brought our food and set it before us with a sniff, as though it were something offensive. Howard thanked her, but she was gone before the words had fallen from his lips. Her brief appearance, though, interrupted our conversation long enough for Howard to change the subject.

"You know," he blurted out, "I was reading the poems of Henry Vaughan last night, and I couldn't help but think of you."

"Oh?" I might have veered the conversation back toward civil rights had his mention of Henry Vaughan not seemed an odd coincidence. That was Sunny's poet, the one who wrote about God's lilies blooming in the dust.

"Yes," Howard went on, "I favor his work, really, though there are many poets I enjoy reading. T. S. Eliot, Gerald Manley Hopkins, John Milton, George Herbert, the ones that are—I don't know—spiritual."

"Aren't all poets spiritual, in one sense or another?"

"I suppose so, yes. All of them are seeking something . . . eternal, I guess you might say. Something that'll make sense out of life. But there's a difference between seeking and having found, if you understand what I mean."

I didn't understand, but I made a motion with my head that said I did. Howard shifted forward in his seat and pulled a slim volume from the back pocket of his trousers. Ignoring his sandwich, he tapped the air with the little book and asked, "May I read you just one verse of Vaughn's 'The World'?"

With my nod of assent, he opened the book and thumbed through it until he found the right page. He paused a moment, his eyes resting on the words. He seemed to be quieting himself or gathering his thoughts, as I imagined a musician must do before going onstage to perform. Conversations droned on around us, and the clattering of pots and pans in the kitchen only added to the cacophony of noise, but as he began to read, Howard drew both me and himself into a sphere of quiet, a small place isolated from the sounds and sights and even smells around us. For a moment all that existed was his voice and the words that traveled between us across the small table.

And even then I heard nothing but the first two lines. Those fifteen words captured me completely, so that though I heard Howard's voice, I could go no further with him into the verse, and didn't need to go any further.

When he finished he lifted his eyes to me without lifting his face, obviously awaiting my response.

"Would you mind," I asked, "reading the first couple of lines again?"

Down went the eyes, and in his lilting voice he read, " 'I saw Eternity the other night / Like a great Ring of pure and endless light. . . .' "

His face, as he looked at me yet again, held an expression of patience mingled with curiosity. At length I asked, "And you thought of me when you read that?"

"Yes." He nodded once, briefly.

My gaze involuntarily turned from him but, not knowing where to rest, found its way back to his face. "Funny you should think of me," I said quietly.

"Not at all," he countered, closing the book and laying it on the table. "I hope you won't be offended, Miss Callahan, but I have a deep sense that we are"—he smiled shyly—"well, for lack of a better term, kindred spirits."

I took a sharp breath and bought some time before answering by stirring salt into my soup.

Before I could respond, though, he went on, "Forgive me if I sound too forward—"

"No, no," I said, surprising even myself by jumping in and cutting him off. "It's quite all right, Mr. Draper, I—" I wanted to say I sensed it too, a kind of attraction that went beyond the physical, an awareness that this was one with whom you could share even your soul, and yet I could scarcely imagine myself joining the ladies' auxiliary of the Ku

Klux Klan, serving lemonade at KKK barbecues, sewing banners for the Klan's annual parade.

And so I said, "When I was on the plane, flying out from California, I saw a perfect circular rainbow in the clouds. I couldn't believe it. I didn't even know rainbows might appear as full circles instead of semicircles. I'd never seen an entire rainbow before. And it seemed— I don't know—I'm not big on signs, but it did seem like it was supposed to mean something. Like it was an omen of something good. And then you just now read this poem about a ring of endless light, like the rainbow, and . . ." I stopped and offered him my own sheepish smile. "Well, silly, I guess. Things like that don't mean anything."

"Well, a rainbow meant something to a man named Noah once," he offered.

I laughed nervously, feeling suddenly awkward in Howard's presence, confused by our conversation. Confused especially by my feelings. "Well, I guess I'm hardly Noah, am I, that God should choose to give me such a sign."

"You mean," Howard said, leaning forward and breaking into a roguish grin, "you're not a drunken sod?"

My forehead wrinkled into ridges as my eyebrows flew up. "Excuse me?"

Howard's eyes twinkled as though he were enjoying my confusion. "One of the first things Noah did after he got off the boat was get rip-roaring drunk and pass out naked in his tent. But of course that's the part of the story that isn't generally included in the standard Sunday school curriculum." He smiled at me gently before going on. "We're all only human, Miss Callahan. But that's the wonderful thing. Eternity is right there anyway, waiting for all of us." He made a motion with his right hand, fingers pressed together like a rosebud, as though he were pulling eternity out of the air.

I had no idea what he was talking about, but I supposed it was the church organist speaking rather than the Klansman. Or perhaps it was the poet in him; I couldn't say for sure.

He looked down at the food on the table and sighed, as though we had a tedious task before us. "I suppose we'd better eat," he suggested. "I have a music lesson in about an hour." He nodded toward the kitchen as he picked up half the egg sandwich. "Jerry's daughter—the one who plays the clarinet."

"You mean, the one who sends the dog howling for cover under the couch?" I asked.

Howard's mouth was full, but he nodded. After he swallowed, he said, "I'm afraid that really happens. I've seen it myself. Rosemary's an awful musician, but she's a sweet child."

"Tell me more about your students," I suggested, longing for simple conversation, for normalcy, for give-and-take that made some sort of sense. Howard complied, and as we ate, we talked about his students, a litany of some few budding musicians sprinkled liberally with anecdotes of arias desecrated by fumbling fingers and recitals fraught with the jarring errors of talentless youth. In spite of myself, I laughed out loud. In that hour I forgot where I was and why I was there. The people around us became mere props on a crowded stage. I gave no thought to civil rights, to *One Nation*, to my work. The excuse that had driven me into the café was all but forgotten.

For those few moments, all that mattered was Howard Draper. His voice. His face. His laughter and the laughter he drew up out of me as easily as a man drawing water out of a well after a long rain.

It felt good to laugh. It was a pleasure long forgotten, and now that I'd found it again, I wanted nothing other than to keep it, to hold it with an iron grip that neither time nor circumstance would pry open. I wanted to spend the rest of my life laughing with Howard Draper, no matter the cost.

He asked me to join him the next evening for dinner. He named a time and a place, and once again, without a lick of hesitation, I told him I'd be there.

THIRTY-ONE

"Where's the school being held tonight?" I asked Sunny.

It was early on Tuesday evening, and we were on our way to the citizenship school. A cloud of dust, like a Depression-era storm, mushroomed and whirled just beyond the car's back bumper as we headed over the dirt road toward Carver.

"At the funeral parlor," Sunny said casually.

"Pleasant," I responded. "Will everyone there be alive?"

"Should be, unless the Klan shows up in a lynching mood." She didn't so much as crack a smile. "But then," she added, "if that happens, we won't have far to carry the bodies, will we?"

"We may *be* the bodies, as far as that goes."

We rode in silence for a moment, moving forward through the heat and the dust. Thick dark clouds stretched from one horizon to the other, bringing on an early nightfall.

"Aren't you ever afraid, Sunny?" I asked.

"Sometimes," she admitted, "like last night. I'm not used to that kind of rude awakening, and I'm especially unhappy when my children are frightened. But I don't think I'm personally in any danger of being killed, if that's what you mean."

"How do you figure that? I mean, the Klan wasn't packing toy pistols when they drove by the house last night."

"No, but Tom's right about one thing—the people who did the shooting meant only to scare us, not to kill us. I can live with bullet holes in my living room. Not many Negroes get off that easily."

"But how can you be so sure you won't become a direct target? The Klan's been known to kill white people, you know. Goodman and Schwerner, remember? Last year at about this time?"

"Don't worry on that score, Augie. I'm not about to forget something that happened in my own backyard. And I'm not completely sure about anything here in Mississippi. There are so many variables, so many unknowns. But the situation for me, for us Fultons, is different than it was for the Freedom Summer workers, and I'll tell you why. The added bonus for us is that Tom employs a good percentage of Carver's work force. A lot of men in the Klan work for Tom, so ironically we have a sort of safety hatch in the mill. It's not a foolproof guarantee, but even members of the Klan are probably not too interested in killing off the source of their own livelihood—nor his wife and children, for that matter."

I nodded. Howard Draper had told me essentially the same thing during lunch.

"But I should add," Sunny went on, "that being killed and being harassed are two different things. Tom may be powerful, and we may be white, but that doesn't make us immune to the Klan's harassment. One look at my living room will tell you that."

I nodded my understanding. "And for that reason, Mrs. Fulton of Powerful White America, I still think you're brave to do what you do with the school, threat of death or no."

Sunny shook her head adamantly. "The people who are really brave are the folks planning to register to vote. Now that takes guts, to go and do something like that."

"I'm not sure I'd want to be in their shoes."

"I'm sure I *wouldn't* want to be in their shoes."

We reached the center of town, thinking of the young folks who would be going to register on Friday. Sunny knew them well, and I was just about to meet them. Already they had my admiration. What was routine for whites, going to the courthouse, involved tactical maneuvers for the Negroes. They weren't citizens entering a registrar's office. They were soldiers stepping onto a battlefield. Their small, unsharpened arrows of carefully memorized facts and figures would be pitted against the enemy's bulging arsenal of injustice. Plenty of Negroes had been wounded on that battlefield. Some had even died.

I shut my eyes against the thought of what might lie in store for these four volunteers. When I opened them again, I saw an elderly Negro woman shuffling along the sidewalk, dragging a lifetime of submission and oppression behind her. She reminded me of Miss Ebba.

"Since Miss Ebba knows the future," I mused, "maybe she can tell us whether or not the citizenship school will lead to any changes in Carver."

Sunny smiled indulgently. "Well, I'm not sure she's privy to that kind of information, even though she does seem to know what's going on with the Klan."

"Miss Ebba, the one-eyed seer."

"What was that?" Sunny leaned toward me slightly.

"I said, she's a one-eyed seer. She's got one eye completely gone and one that looks on the verge of giving out, and yet she can see into the future."

Sunny nodded. "If Miss Ebba ever tells you to run, I hope you'll run like there's no tomorrow." When I chuckled, Sunny gave me a chiding frown. "I know it sounds silly, but I can bet Amos Lowe wished he had run."

"No doubt he did," I agreed. "There does seem to be some validity to Miss Ebba's warnings. I just don't understand how she does it."

"No one does, Augie. But you don't have to understand something completely to believe it's true."

"I suppose not."

"Miss Ebba will be at the school tonight. Did I tell you she's a student?"

"No. Really?" I shook my head, amazed.

"She's been studying for a year to pass the test so she can register."

"You're kidding."

"Not at all. One of her grandkids taught her to read when she was almost sixty. She says she's a late bloomer and a slow learner to boot, but she wants to take the next step toward freedom. She has every intention of registering before the next election."

"Or before she dies."

"Actually, I think she'll make it. Before the election and before she dies both."

"If she gets registered, I'll do an entire story on her alone. Better than that, I'll write a book about her."

"There'd be a lot to say. She's a remarkable woman."

I thought about Ebba Starks for a moment and remembered what Howard had told me. "It's a shame about that white doctor who refused to help her."

"What white doctor?"

"You know, when she had that accident as a child and lost her eye. When she fell out of the tree."

"That's how she lost her eye?"

"Yes. Didn't you know?"

"No. I never asked about it, and she never told me. So how on earth do *you* know?"

"Howard Draper told me at lunch today. He said everyone knew the story."

Sunny shrugged and shook her head. "Well, I never heard it."

"He said it was part of Carver's folklore."

"Maybe I haven't been in Carver long enough to hear that one."

"Our friend Mr. Draper hasn't been here any longer than you have."

"Hmm. Well then, maybe knowing that story is required for joining the Carver Klan. Every Klansman has to know about Miss Ebba's lost eye before he can put on the hood."

Sunny laughed softly, and I wanted to join her, but I couldn't. What she said disturbed me, brought to the surface the strange juxtaposition of feelings I harbored toward Howard Draper. Distrust and curiosity. Repulsion and attraction. Disgust and desire. I, who at one time in our lives had told Sunny everything, certainly couldn't tell her this. What could I possibly say? That if he wasn't Klan, that if I didn't have to return to California, that if time and circumstances were on our side—then what? I didn't even know myself. I only knew that I didn't like the emotional knots being tied and double-tied inside of me.

"You didn't tell me," Sunny said, "how your lunch went with Howard. Did you get any good material for your article?"

"I think I did," I hedged. "The most interesting thing he said was he believes equality for Negroes is long overdue."

"Oh now, that's a good one!" Sunny exclaimed. "And I suppose he told you he's behind the colored folks one hundred percent. Maybe we should recruit him to teach music at the citizenship school. He can lead us all in singing freedom songs."

"Interesting idea."

Sunny sniffed and shook her head, muttering, "What a strange bird he is."

"Yes," I agreed. The soul of an artist. The heart of a poet. The most gentle of gentlemen and a compatriot of killers. The greatest enigma I had ever encountered.

We crossed the unmarked border into Coloredtown and soon reached the funeral parlor where the students of the citizenship school were gathering for class.

When Sunny parked the car, I got out quietly and followed her inside.

The front room of the funeral parlor was a sparsely furnished chapel, with a few scant rows of folding chairs, a podium in front, and a large wooden cross on the wall behind the podium. The larger back room was where the Robinson brothers stored and displayed coffins and, I assumed, prepared the dead for their final journey earthward. There seemed an inordinate number of coffins for a relatively small colored population. I could only surmise that in Mississippi a Negro undertaker had to be prepared for anything.

By the time Sunny and I arrived, the coffins had been pushed back against all four walls, and the center of the room was teeming with a couple dozen people. Some were young, barely past adolescence, while others were middle-aged or older. All were Negroes. A few men were arranging folding chairs into semicircles. T. W. Foss was tacking a large handwritten copy of the Fifteenth Amendment onto the inside open lid of a coffin. Wall space being limited, the coffin lid was as good a place as any to hang the document, though the irony of it didn't escape me.

Some of the younger students sat cross-legged on the floor going over notes and thumbing through books. Miss Ebba was there, seated on a folding chair in a far corner, a shawl around her shoulders in spite of the heat. She had on a pair of thick glasses but, even so, squinted her one eye at a piece of paper held close to her face. Her grandson,

Lee Henry, sat beside her, pointing toward the paper with a thick index finger to guide Miss Ebba as she read.

When we entered, Curtis and Gloria Reese stepped across the room to greet us. "Evening, Miz Fulton. So glad you could come, Miz Callahan."

We shook hands all around, and I thanked them for inviting me.

"Mahlon!" Gloria called out. "Mahlon, mind your manners, son. The ladies have arrived."

Mahlon paused in the midst of unfolding a chair, nodded, said, "Evening, Miz Fulton, Miz Callahan," and went back to work.

"We'll introduce you proper to the group before we get started tonight, Miz Callahan," Curtis said. "Won't be but a few more minutes before things get under way. Meantime, make yourselves comfortable."

"What can we do to help, Curtis?" Sunny asked.

"Not a thing at the moment, Miz Fulton."

The Reeses moved away, and Sunny turned to me. "We'll be meeting with the group that's going to register. I think Mahlon plans to go over strategy, last-minute details, that kind of thing."

"Then you don't all meet together as one large group?"

"Not generally. There are those working on literacy issues, everything from how to read to how to sign their names. Gloria and Hester"—Sunny nodded toward Gloria and another woman—"they work with that group. T.W. is working with another group studying history and law—the Civil Rights Act and the Amendments, the Mississippi constitution, things like that. Both T.W. and Mahlon know all that stuff inside out. Looks like they'll be going over the Fifteenth Amendment tonight." She nodded toward the open coffin but didn't remark on either the oddity or the irony of it. "Then our group, like I said, are those who will actually be going to register on Friday. Four young people who've been studying for months to take the test. Mahlon's been working hard with them."

"Has he showed them the scars on his back?"

"Seeing those scars is just part of the curriculum."

"And it didn't scare them out of going to register?"

"They were scared senseless before they ever saw the scars."

"Well, like you said, they're the ones with the courage, though I don't know how they do it."

Sunny nodded. "That's what courage is. Being afraid and doing it anyway."

I couldn't argue with that. "Mahlon's registered, isn't he?"

Sunny shook her head. "He's tried, but no, he hasn't been successful."

"Will he try again on Friday?"

"No. His home's in Jackson, so he can't register in Holmes County."

"Of course. I didn't remember he was from Jackson. What about T.W.?"

"You mean, can he vote in the next election?" Sunny answered the question by shaking her head in the negative.

"Okay, let me get this straight," I said. "T.W. and Mahlon are running this citizenship school, they know the Mississippi constitution forward and backward, they could pass the test blindfolded, and yet they can't get registered? Is that what you're telling me?"

Sunny nodded. "They know all the right answers, but they have the wrong color skin."

I frowned as I looked around the room. "How does any Negro in Mississippi get registered, then?"

"Good question, Augie. I'm not really sure, but I think a token few are allowed to register so that when Big Brother comes poking his nose into Mississippi's business, the state can tell the Feds that they're not discriminating. They can show them the names of the Negroes who are registered to vote, and say the numbers are small because most Negroes don't bother to register. Of course, they don't have to mention the number who fail the test or who are just turned away at the start."

I had no response for that, but none was needed. Curtis Reese glanced up at a large classroom clock high on one wall and announced it was time to begin. "We got us a special visitor tonight," he started out. "This here's Miz Augusta Callahan from Los Angeles, California. She's a reporter with the *One Nation* magazine"—here, nervous coughs, the squeaking of shifted chairs, and the shuffle of fidgeting feet became background music for Curtis Reese's speech—"and she come to do a story on us, how we's preparing to register to vote. Now, the white folks o' Carver, they don' know she's a reporter. They thinks she just a old friend o' Miz Fulton's, right?" He looked at Sunny, who nodded. "And they ain't gonna learn any different from any one o' us, right?"

A few *That's right*s echoed around the room.

Curtis nodded and smiled. "Good. Now, let's say howdy and welcome our guest."

Quiet voices rose up to greet me. "Evening, ma'am." "Welcome, Miz Callahan." "Howdy and welcome."

I smiled and nodded my greeting in return. "Thank you. I'm very glad to be here," I said.

More coughs, squeaks, and fidgeting followed.

"All right, then," Curtis said. "Let's get to work. Not much time left before our first students go to register." He lifted one large hand and pointed. "Hester and Gloria's group here, T.W.'s history group over there, and Mahlon'll be meeting over yonder with the ones going to the courthouse Friday."

The students broke up and settled into the semicircles that had been arranged for them. Sunny and I sat down in a couple of chairs that Mahlon, with a sweep of one hand, indicated were ours. I had carried a notebook in with me, which I now opened on my lap, and took a freshly sharpened pencil out of my handbag. When I looked up I found myself gazing at four fresh young faces that were, in turn, gazing at me with a mixture of curiosity and reserve.

I smiled. The two men nodded. One of the women lifted her brows suspiciously. The other woman, so petite she looked hardly older than a child, returned my smile brightly.

"Augie," Sunny said, "before Mahlon gets started, let me introduce you to our"—she paused and cast a proud glance at the group— "to our future voters."

Both of the men offered a quick response of deep-throated laughter.

"Don' know 'bout that, Miz Fulton," one said. "We still gotta convince the registrar we know how many seeds in a watermelon."

"Or how many bubbles in a bar of soap," the other added.

The two laughed heartily then, and the sound of it put me at ease. I liked people who could find humor in difficult situations. The woman who had smiled at me earlier put a hand to her mouth to suppress a giggle. The other woman, though, merely lifted her chin and narrowed her eyes at the men. "Ain't funny, you two," she said irritably. "Questions like that been keeping us from the polls for years."

"Ah, Luella," the first man said, "we're just joshin'. Gotta have a little fun 'fore we go off to war."

The smaller woman put a tentative hand on Luella's arm and squeezed it gently. "Don' worry, Luella," she said quietly. "Registrar ain't gonna ask you no stupid questions like that."

"And if he do," the first man said, "you just act like you know exactly what you talking 'bout. You just say, 'Mr. Registrar, last time I et a melon, I counted five hundred forty-two black seeds and three hundred sixty-one those li'l white seeds.' See what he say 'bout that!"

"He'd just say I be off by such-and-such a number——" Luella started.

"And if he ask you 'bout the soap," the second man interrupted, "you just ask him, you say, 'Mr. Registrar, would that be Ivory soap or a bar o' Pamolive?'"

The two men laughed so uproariously that everyone in the room turned to look at our group. "You care to share the joke?" Curtis Reese called from the literacy group.

Luella answered for the men. "They just actin' downright crazy, Mr. Reese."

"Nothing new, then," Gloria chuckled. "I swear those two always thinkin' they're Laurel 'n Hardy."

"Amos 'n Andy, more like it," Luella countered.

"Naw, child, they ain't that dumb."

Mahlon cleared his throat. "Time's wasting," he said mildly.

Sunny, obviously amused at the exchange, said, "Do you fellows think I can introduce you to Miss Callahan now?"

"Sho 'nuff."

"Please do, Miz Fulton."

"All right, then." Sunny glanced at me, then back at the young man on our far left. "This is Buford Wiley——"

"But call me Bo," he interrupted. "Don't no one call me Buford. Not even my mama, and she the one named me."

"Bo works for Tom at the mill," Sunny continued. "Well, that is to say, all four of these young people work at the mill. Tom's giving them the day off on Friday to go to Lexington to register. They know their jobs will be waiting for them when they get back."

"*If* we get back," Bo interjected.

"Bo Wiley!" Luella shrieked.

"We'll get back," the second fellow said. "Question is, in how many pieces?"

"And this," Sunny said, "is Eddie Schoby. Class clown and aspiring comedian."

"What you mean, *aspiring*?" he asked with feigned indignity. "I'm a professional. Just ask Miz Reese; she knows. I had a lead in the school play once—"

Sunny ignored him. "And the young ladies," she went on, "are Susannah Travis and Luella Owens. All of these students have been with the school since the beginning. They've been working hard, and now we feel it's time for them to graduate to the real thing—going to the courthouse to register."

Eddie asked, "You gonna be playin' that graduation song—what's it, Bo?"

" 'Pomp 'n Circumstance,' you mean?"

"Yeah, you gonna be playing that 'Pomp 'n Circumstance' song while we's marching into the courthouse, Miz Fulton?"

"Naw." Bo shook his head. "Better she be singing, 'Save Me, Jesus, I's Comin' Home.' "

I couldn't help it; I laughed out loud. I had come tonight expecting the air to be charged with apprehension, dread, maybe even hopelessness in the face of what these people were trying to do. And there was fear in the room, palpable fear. But there was also a very real sense of what I can only describe as mirth. A small flame of humor burning back a large, dark fatalism. The human heart's natural mechanism for pumping out life instead of death.

I didn't laugh alone. We all laughed, even Luella. I liked these people. I liked them very much.

After a moment Sunny responded to Eddie's question. "I'll be there, Eddie, but I don't expect to be providing any music."

Susannah asked, "You sho you ain't comin' in with us, Miz Fulton?"

Eddie jumped in and said, "No way. She'll be sittin' cross the street eatin' an ice-cream sundae while the rest of us face the fire."

"Only because that's what you wanted, Eddie," Sunny reminded him. "You said you didn't want any white ladies escorting you into the courthouse."

"That what I said?" Eddie asked in mock surprise.

"That's what you said," Sunny echoed. "And that's why we have Dave Hunsinger going in with you." She turned to me and explained, "Dave's a civil rights worker in Lexington. I don't know him, but Mahlon does. He came down last year for Freedom Summer and was supposed to go back to school in the fall—he's a student at Harvard studying law—but he decided to stay in Lexington for another year to help carry on with voter registration."

"So he and Mahlon'll be comin' in with us?" Eddie asked.

Mahlon nodded.

Luella looked at me. "You comin' to Lexington, Miz Callahan?"

"Yes, of course," I replied hurriedly, anxious to let them know of my support.

"But she'll be with me," Sunny added, "watching from across the street."

"How you gonna get a story that way?" Bo asked.

"You have an infallible memory, Bo," Sunny said, jumping in before I could respond. "You'll tell her exactly what happens in the courthouse."

"Maybe I should go in—" I started, but Mahlon interrupted by shaking his head.

"You welcome to be there, Miz Callahan," he said politely. "But too many people goin' in just gum up the works. We wanna keep it simple as possible. You talk to us after and we'll tell you everythin' that happens."

I nodded and said nothing. I wanted to go in, to be an eyewitness, but I wouldn't go against the wishes of the civil rights workers.

Bo, however, wasn't satisfied. "If we don't none of us come out alive, who's gonna tell Miz Callahan the story?"

"*Bo Wiley!*" Luella shrieked again.

"If we don't come out alive," Eddie interjected, "she'll know what the story is. No one'll have to tell her. She'll know what happened."

A seriousness, a quiet terror, fell over the group. I couldn't imagine that they would enter the courthouse and simply disappear, even in Mississippi. But neither could I imagine that they'd be allowed to register. Something was going to happen, and whatever that was, it most likely wasn't good. It was that unknown element—the question of what awaited them—that was terrifying.

After a long moment, diminutive Susannah Travis said in her tiny voice, "Miz Callahan, whatever happens to us, you tell the world, you hear? You tell the world in that magazine of yours what they done to the four coloreds from Carver, Mississippi, who tried to register." She looked at me, her eyes pleading.

"I will, Susannah," I promised. "But my hope is that you'll tell your own story, and it'll be one with a happy ending. Maybe you'll be allowed to register after all."

They didn't believe me. I could see it on all four sweaty faces. As though I needed to be reminded, Eddie said flatly, "We in Mississippi, Miz Callahan. Ain't no happy endings for niggers here, 'less you count still being alive at the end of the day."

Mahlon glanced up at the clock, his large dark eyes bouncing up to the wall and back to us with a look of authority. "All right now, enough talk. Let's go over the plan, what we gonna do on Friday."

For the next half hour, he talked about what they should wear, what time we were going to leave, what they should say to the registrar, how to react if this or that happened. Mahlon told the four young students to remember all the laws they had memorized, especially the civil rights amendments. They should fortify themselves with the knowledge that, according to the Supreme Court of the United States, they had every right to register to vote. He said they should quote their rights to the registrar if necessary. He told them to expect resistance, not only from the registrar but from whatever badge-wearing people might be hanging around the courthouse that afternoon. He talked about responding nonviolently. He reminded them about what to do, how to defend themselves, if in the process of trying to do what they had every legal right to do, they were beaten and jailed. I scribbled notes while Mahlon talked. What he said left me feeling chilled in spite of the heat.

I'd known them less than an hour, but already I felt a great affinity for Eddie and Bo, Susannah and Luella. I didn't want to see them hurt, didn't want to imagine them bloody from the batons of overzealous deputies, handcuffed, hauled off, and thrown into jail simply because on a summer afternoon in July of 1965, they tried to enter a courthouse and declare themselves worthy to be counted among the citizens of Mississippi.

At length, when Mahlon finished, he looked from one to the other of them in silence. Then he asked, "So, how you all feelin'?"

"Scared," Bo said, answering for the group. The others nodded.

"That's good." Mahlon nodded. "Give you an edge if you's a little nervous."

"Ain't a little nervous, Mahlon. We's terrified."

"You wanna back out?"

The four exchanged frightened looks. For a moment no one answered. Then Eddie said, "I's goin'."

"Me too," Susannah echoed.

"Bo and Luella?" Mahlon asked.

"Yeah."

"We'll be there."

Mahlon looked at each one again. "You goin' even if you spit at?"

"Yeah."

"Even if you arrested?"

"Yeah."

"Even if you beaten within an inch o' yor life?"

All four nodded. "That too."

"All right, then. You's ready. Friday, we go."

❦

Lee Henry Starks stood when Curtis Reese asked him to close the meeting with prayer. He shut his eyes and frowned deeply, saying nothing for a moment. He almost appeared to be in pain.

Finally he said, "Lawd Jesus, we thanks you. We thanks you that you is here with us tonight. We thanks you that you never leave us nor forsake us. Lawd Jesus, we your chillun. Your truth set us free, but in this world, Lawd, we still ain't free.

"Make us free, Lawd. Protect our four young folks gonna register on Friday. Protect 'em, Lawd, and keep 'em safe.

"And, Lawd, may they have success. Day gotta come, Lawd, when we be allowed to do what the law say we can do. Day gotta come, Lawd, when ain't no more bloodshed, no more hate. Day gotta come when we live in peace with everyone, even the white man.

"Bring us to that morning, Lawd. Bring us to that new day. Amen, Lawd, and amen."

That final word echoed around the room in the whispers of a

couple dozen voices, including Sunny's.

We rose to go. I was ready to go home. It had been a long day lived out on too little sleep. Between the heat and my own fatigue, I was beginning to feel light-headed and queasy.

I closed my notebook, put the pencil in my handbag, and shook hands with each of the four young people. "See you Friday," we told each other. Their palms were moist with perspiration. So was mine.

As Sunny and I made our way to the door, I felt a hand on my elbow. I turned to find Miss Ebba looking up at me. She was wearing the same wrinkled cotton dress she had worn the night before when she and Lee Henry came by the house after the shooting. I wondered briefly whether she had any others, or whether this was the only one she owned.

She squeezed my elbow hard and stared at me with her one disarming eye. When she spoke, her voice was raspy. "You gotta know, Miz Callahan," she said, "things ain't always what dey seem."

For a moment I couldn't answer. I waited for her to go on, but when she didn't, I prodded her by saying, "I beg your pardon?"

"Things, peoples too . . ." Letting go of my elbow, she took her glasses off and folded them up. She moved her face even closer to mine. "Peoples ain't always what dey seem."

She had to be talking about Howard Draper. Word must have reached her that I had had lunch with him at the Magnolia Café. After all, there'd been Negroes there, Negroes who might take the news back to Coloredtown as quickly as the whites might pass it around Carver. Whether through divine communication or her own intuition, Miss Ebba probably knew Howard was Klan. She was no doubt trying to warn me of his kinship with the night riders.

"Don't worry, Miss Ebba," I assured her, avoiding names, just as she was. "I understand."

"No chile," she replied, "I'm not sho you do. I wan' you to know, it's all right. You jes' go on. You don' hafta be 'fraid."

"Afraid of what, Miss Ebba?"

Before she could answer, Lee Henry came and gently placed a hand on her arm. "Let's go, Mama," he said. "I promised Louise I wouldn't be late tonight. I don't wanna be goin' back on my word."

Miss Ebba looked at me and opened her mouth to say something. I wanted her to explain, to tell me what she meant, but what she said was, "All right, Lee Henry. Les go on home, den."

Lee Henry nodded to Sunny and me and led his grandmother from the funeral parlor. After they left, I turned to Sunny. "I thought she was trying to warn me about Howard being Klan. But what do you think she meant about my not having to be afraid?"

Sunny shrugged. "I haven't the foggiest. Maybe she *is* going just a little bit senile."

We drove home then, through Coloredtown, through the white section of Carver, with the little dust storm following us like a cloud, and Miss Ebba's words trailing me like a riddle begging to be solved.

THIRTY-TWO

The veil across the sky had grown thicker in the past hour, so we traveled home under hovering storm clouds. By the time we reached the house, the rain had come, slowly at first like a timid swimmer testing the waters, then bursting into a heavy downpour. Sunny and I dashed from the unattached garage to the house, the rain beating a cold shower against our skin. We were soaked by the time we entered the kitchen through the back door.

I went to my room to dry off and thought about crawling right into bed, but it wasn't even yet nine o'clock. Besides, the rain had refreshed me enough that I decided to call my editor back in L.A. and then spend a little time going over my notes.

After changing into dry clothes I picked up the extension in the hall. As I suspected, Richard was still at his desk at *One Nation*, though it was well past six o'clock on the West Coast.

"Anything there?" he asked.

"I think I'll be able to send you a decent story."

"Go for the Pulitzer," he said and hung up. He wasn't one to waste time discussing details, not until the story had reached his desk and the scrutiny of his blue pencil.

Lightning branded jagged patterns into the night sky and thunder left the house shivering while I sat at the desk in my room, reviewing my notes. I paused over what I had written about Howard Draper after our lunch that afternoon: *Lunch with H.D. at Magnolia Café. He read to me the poetry of Vaughan. Ring of endless light. Says we are kindred spirits. I feel it too when I am with him. More lucid later—know it's a lie. How to keep sight of what he is when I'm blinded by what he appears to be?*

I read the words a second time, then scribbled in the margin, *It doesn't matter. In less than a week I'll never see him again. Stick to the task at hand.*

A series of storms, one following on the heels of the last, blew over us all night, interrupting my sleep with flashes and rumblings and the pattering of rain against roof and windows. Between the storms, my dreams were vivid and deep, images not of Lenny this time but of Howard. He was playing his violin in a clearing in the woods. Like a fiddler at a square dance, he played lively foot-stomping music that drew people out of the woods to a party there in the clearing. Only it wasn't a party, it was a lynching. Howard was providing the background music for somebody's death.

It was night, but the clearing was lighted by the fire of a dozen torches. The firelight fell across a Negro struggling on the ground, trying to escape the white men holding him down. One large white man straddled him, tying his hands behind his back. Howard played wildly but not loud enough to drown out the piercing screams of the Negro. I stood by horrified, unable to move or speak. I couldn't even lift my hands to my ears to block out the struggling man's cries: "Please, please have mersa. Oh, dear Jesus, dear holy Jesus, have mersa!"

One lone tree grew at the center of the clearing, a tall live oak. The remnants of a hundred ropes dangled from its branches, the evidence of a hundred deaths. One fresh new rope, a brand-new noose, hung there now. The other end of the rope was tied to the bumper of a pickup truck. The young colored man was dragged to the tree, the noose secured around his neck. He kicked and screamed unintelligibly now, his words no longer plea nor prayer. Howard played on. The truck was started, put in gear. The wheels began to turn. The truck moved forward, then hesitated, as though startled by the unexpected weight it was expected to pull. A little more gas, a kicking up of dirt, and the truck rolled on. The Negro's head, shoulders, back, legs rose up from the ground like a pull-tab lid yanked off a can of sardines. A tugging, a pulling, a lifting up toward the branch of the tree.

Finally airborne, the Negro kicked helplessly, frantically, as he performed the frenzied dance of a death by hanging. His wrists struggled against the ropes, his body shuddered from the shoulders down. The whites of his rolled-back eyes looked like gleaming saucers in the firelight. His mouth hung open in a silent scream as he slowly began to suffocate. Only then did I recognize who the Negro was. Bo Wiley. Strung up for trying to register to vote.

I woke up early in the morning with the sense of something both sad and ominous hanging over me, like the storm clouds that had hovered over Carver all night. The sadness and fear were for Bo. I thought of him as he had been at the citizenship school, friendly, full of humor, his sharp "A-he-he-he!" rising up out of his young chest and filling the room with infectious laughter. Now his terrified dream eyes followed me into the conscious world, and I had to tell myself that it hadn't really happened, that Bo was all right, he hadn't been lynched. In a few moments the dream images began to fade, but the sadness remained.

Footsteps on the stairs told me Sunny and Tom were headed down to breakfast. They always shared these few minutes in the morning before Tom went off to the mill. Swinging my feet out of bed, I decided to get dressed and join them.

Slipping into a sleeveless blouse and a pair of slacks, I walked barefoot past the rooms where the children were sleeping. They were attending Vacation Bible School at the Methodist church this week, but they didn't have to get up for a couple of hours yet. At the top of the stairs I hesitated a moment, then turned back to Joanie's room. I tiptoed in and knelt beside her bed. She lay on her stomach, her face turned toward me on the pillow, heavy with sleep. One strand of dark hair fell across her cheek.

I wanted to study her face a moment, to see what there was of Sunny there. I found hints, small suggestions of the girl I'd known in Boyle Heights—the plumpness of the cheeks, the flat bridge of the nose. Still, Joanie's nose wasn't the small button Sunny's had been. Her eyes weren't the winsome lidded almonds I had once so admired. Joanie's beautiful little face was a meeting of East and West, and when the blending was done, Europe had emerged over the Orient.

Sunny Yamagata's daughter was a white child with a southern accent living in the heart of Mississippi. She was the granddaughter of Chichi and Haha, the great-granddaughter of Obaasan, and yet she would probably never know—as I had known—what mochi tasted like, or how it felt to be part of a crowd yelling "Banzai!" on the emperor's birthday, or what it was to rise up out of bed at midnight on New Year's Eve to eat buckwheat noodles floating in chicken broth. Never would she sit cross-legged in the grass listening to men like Mr. Omori and Mr. Kikumura singing ballads to the sky while getting drunk on sake.

Japan was miles upon miles removed from Mississippi, and Joanie Fulton was three generations away from Obaasan, who had been born there. I viewed it as a loss, but no doubt one day Joanie Fulton would thank her lucky stars that she'd turned out the way she had. In this little girl, the land of the rising sun was setting at last, settling down into the murky dusk known as America.

In this place where the whole world converged, where every country on earth was present and accounted for, it was still those people who resembled the first white settlers who could call America home. Joanie Fulton was at home in America, though the generations of Yamagatas before her were not and had never been.

She had stopped by my room the previous day before supper, before Sunny and I left for the citizenship school. I was sitting on the seat of the bay window, propped up against two pillows, reading a novel. Whenever I traveled I took along several books to keep me occupied during the empty hours of the trip, though that particular afternoon I wasn't really reading because none of the hours of my days in Carver were empty. They were filled always with thoughts of Sunny and Chichi and Haha, and the wonder of finding them again and what it might mean for my life. And when I wasn't thinking about them, I was thinking about the folks I'd met there in Carver, like Mahlon and T.W. and the Reeses, Mayor Frohmann and Miss Ebba, and of course Howard Draper, and about the parts they all played on the stage of this little southern town.

When Joanie bounced into my room, she was wearing a sleeveless cotton dress—blue with white sailboats—and she hugged a doll to her chest. Her dark hair hung in loose waves about her neck. "Whatcha doing, Auntie?" she asked. She had started calling me "Auntie" on her own, though Ronnie still called me Miss Callahan.

"I was just . . ." I looked at the book in my hand. I hadn't even gotten past the first page. "Just thinking, I guess."

"What about?"

"Oh, lots of things."

"Can I sit on your lap?"

"Sure. Come on up."

I laid the book aside, and Joanie climbed up into the bay window and settled down in my lap, still clutching her doll. This was the first time she sat in my lap, and I didn't know—not until that moment— that my lap had been achingly empty for years.

"Auntie," she said, "I want to ask you something." A look of consternation clouded her sweet little-girl face.

"Go ahead," I invited. "Whatever it is, I'll try to answer."

She gazed at me with her serene dark eyes and asked, "Did you really know my mama when she was a little girl?"

"Oh yes," I replied, delighted that the question should be so simple, and that she would want to know about her mother and me. "I met your mother when she was just a little older than you are now."

Joanie nodded, then pursed her lips in thought. "I can't believe she ever was, though. A little girl, I mean."

I laughed lightly. "Oh, she was. I was a little girl once too, though that may be even harder to believe."

Joanie scratched an ear. She rearranged the doll so that it was nestled in the crook of her arm. "What was she like when she was little?"

"Hm, well, she was pretty and smart, and she was the nicest person I'd ever met. She was my best friend."

"Is she still? Your best friend?"

"Oh yes," I said. "She's my very best friend. I guess she always will be."

Joanie stiffened a moment, looked around the room, then lifted her face toward my ear and whispered, "She used to be Japanese, you know." Eyebrows raised, she nodded.

I nodded solemnly in return. "I know," I whispered back. "She was Japanese when I met her."

"But now she's white, like Daddy."

I let out a breath of air, not quite knowing how to respond. Her mother's sudden change of race must have been awfully confusing to a little girl. For a moment, I wondered again whether Sunny had done the right thing. "Well," I offered, "she thought it'd be best if you all looked the same when you came to Mississippi."

"I know," Joanie said, shrugging. Then she asked, "Were you Japanese too when you were little?"

I smiled then as I pondered her question. She settled her head against my shoulder, and I rested my chin on the top of her head. Lifting my eyes toward the window, I marveled at the complex layers of answers opened up by a child's simple question. "Yes," I finally answered. "But I wasn't Japanese in the same way your mother was. I was just Japanese in my heart."

"Oh," she said simply, as though my answer were perfectly understandable and not complex in the least. Maybe to a child it isn't strange at all that a person's heart can be Japanese even though her skin is white. After all, to a child, anything is possible. "Are you still?" she asked.

"Still Japanese in my heart?"

Joanie nodded. "Or are you all white now?"

I thought of Lenny and of the nameless, faceless Japanese who had killed him. I thought of Chichi and Haha and Sunny. They had names; they had faces. I knew them. After the war, when they didn't come back, I had tried to lump the good guys with the bad: "All Japanese are the enemy. All Japanese are evil." It was only now, after learning the truth from Sunny, that I could draw the Yamagatas out from the enemy camp. I could begin again to differentiate, to see the faces of individuals rather than the blur of one large group. The Yamagatas had the eyes but not the soul of the people who had destroyed my brother. And that was what made them different.

"Well, Joanie," I said, "I think a part of my heart will always be Japanese."

She looked up at me intently. "But that's okay, because you can keep it a secret," she said. "No one can see your heart."

"Why would I want to keep it a secret, honey?"

"Because if you have Japanese in your heart, people will hate you, the way they used to hate Mommy. That's why she went to that camp."

I stroked the child's hair. "Oh, Joanie, some people might have once hated your mommy because she was Japanese, but not everyone.

Only bad people hate someone because they have slanted eyes or dark skin."

Joanie sighed. She stroked her doll's hair absently in the same way I was stroking her hair. "I would never," she declared, "hate anyone for the way they look."

"That's good, sweetie," I said, "because you shouldn't."

"I hate people if they're mean, but not just because they're colored or Japanese or anything like that."

She couldn't see my smile above her head. "I bet your mommy and daddy wouldn't want you to hate anyone, even if they're mean. You don't have to be friends with the mean people, but it's best not to hate them." As I spoke, I heard the echo of Haha's voice in my words. Wasn't she the one who taught me what I was now passing on to her granddaughter?

Joanie sat up and looked at me with eyes wide. "Don't you hate anyone, Auntie?"

I didn't have to think for long. "Well, I can think of one person I'm afraid I don't like very much."

"Who is it?" she asked, settling back against my shoulder.

"An uncle of mine."

"Do you hate him?"

"Oh dear, Joanie," I sighed. "I'm afraid I probably do."

"Is he a mean person?"

"Well, in many ways, he's not a very nice person."

"Then I think it's all right to hate him. I don't even know him, but I hate him, just because you hate him."

I smiled again and sniffed out a little laugh. "Oh, sweetheart, I'm afraid your mother would be unhappy with me if she knew you hated my uncle Finn just because I do."

Joanie fidgeted in my lap and scratched at her cheek. "Well, did he ever do *anything* nice? I mean, if he did, maybe we can like him just a little bit."

My mind played back the years, looking for gestures of kindness of the part of Uncle Finn. There wasn't much to draw upon, but I was finally able to give Joanie an answer. "He was very good to my brother Lenny after he came home from the war. Uncle Finn gave Lenny a job and a place to live and treated him like his own son."

Joanie was quiet a moment. Then she said, "I guess that's enough to make me like him a little bit. What about you?"

"Well, I'll try, sweetheart."

We were both quiet then. I continued to stroke Joanie's hair, wanting to steer the conversation away from Uncle Finn. I couldn't make any promises to forgive the man.

Finally I asked, "So what does your heart look like, Joanie?"

"Umm." Her head lifted a bit beneath my chin. "Let me think. I know! Cinderella!" she said.

"Ah," I replied, "then you will marry the handsome prince."

Joanie nodded, her wispy hair brushing my neck.

I remembered her answer as I knelt beside her bed that morning and thought of how in our hearts we might be anything, and no one would know. We might even be something we don't recognize ourselves. It wasn't until Joanie had asked that I realized a part of my heart was still Japanese.

I kissed Joanie's cheek—lightly, so as not to wake her—then went downstairs to find Tom and Sunny sitting in the breakfast nook eating scrambled eggs and toast.

"Morning, Augie!" Tom called, cheerful even at this early hour.

"Oh," Sunny said, "if I'd known you were coming down, I'd have made more eggs."

I lifted a hand. "None for me, thanks. Just a cup of coffee for the moment." I poured myself a cup from the pot on the stove, then joined them at the table.

"Hope I'm not interrupting. . . ."

"Of course not," Sunny said. "We were just talking about the meeting last night."

"Sounds like everything's ready," Tom said. "And you'll be going along with the gang to Lexington, Augie?"

I nodded, blew on my coffee, sipped it. "Didn't come all this way just to miss the party."

"I hope no one in law enforcement tries to crash it," Tom shot back. "That'd put a damper on the party real fast."

"If the law enforcement officers enforced the laws that were on the books," Sunny said, "all the Negroes in Mississippi would be registered. We wouldn't have to have this little party."

Tom and I nodded. "Too bad Mississippi thinks it's exempt from federal law," I remarked.

"Federal law?" Sunny echoed. "Mississippi doesn't even follow its own state laws. Jim Crow is the police officer's handbook around here, and Jim Crow says Negroes can't vote."

Tom scooped a forkful of eggs onto half a slice of toast and popped the whole thing into his mouth. Before he had finished chewing, he said, "I still think you should have tried to get Cedric's help with this."

Sunny flashed her husband a look of disbelief. Before she could answer, I jumped in and asked, "Why do you think the mayor would help, Tom?"

Tom slurped his coffee, then reminded me of what I'd learned from T.W. at our first meeting. "Frohmann's good friends with the registrar—"

"Oh, Tom," Sunny cut in. "You know that doesn't mean anything at this point."

"Sure it would," Tom countered. "Get the mayor to escort his own would-be constituents into the courthouse. Talk his old buddy Evan Hoopes into letting them register."

"You're dreaming, Tom." Sunny stood and poured both herself and Tom some more coffee. When she sat down, she continued, "You know there's no way Cedric Frohmann would escort a group of Negroes into the registrar's office."

"How do you know? Did you ask him?"

"I don't have to! He wouldn't be stupid enough to lose the white vote by trying to gain the Negro vote. The only way we may be able to get him to influence Hoopes is if the Negroes boycott the store. Then the mayor might just be worried enough to have a little chat with his old friend."

"Maybe," Tom conceded. He was chewing again. He swallowed and sent down a gulp of coffee before going on. "I still think he may have some interest in the Negro vote with or without a boycott." He laid his fork and knife across the empty plate.

Sunny shook her head slowly. Then she looked at me and said, "Tom wants to make it four o'clock instead of five o'clock on Friday."

"What's that?" I asked.

"You know, if he doesn't hear from us by four o'clock, he'll know there's trouble. Like we've all been arrested and he'll have to come to Lexington to bail us out."

I shrugged. "How are you and I going to end up in jail if we're watching from the ice-cream parlor across the street?"

"No one's going to spend any time in jail," Tom said. He was leaning back in his chair, enjoying his coffee.

"Well, you sure are Mr. Sunny-side-up this morning, aren't you!" Sunny exclaimed. She sounded annoyed, but she followed her comment with a laugh.

"He must have gotten up on the right side of the bed," I offered.

"Why are you so sure no one's going to jail?"

"I just don't think it'll come to that," Tom said breezily.

"You think they'll be allowed to register?"

"Not likely."

"What then?"

"I think they'll just be turned away, sent home."

"Doesn't sound like much of a party," I said.

"Probably won't be." Tom lifted his shoulders in a shrug. "When Negroes go there to register from around the state, they're either turned away outright, or they're allowed to take the test but are told they failed it. That's about all that happens. Well, duty calls down at the mill." He stood, stretched, then bent to kiss his wife. To me, he said, "Augie, I know there's some danger involved in going to the courthouse, but I also know everything's going to be all right. Otherwise I wouldn't let Sunny go. Or you, either, for that matter."

"Miss Ebba hasn't been around then," I asked, "to give you any warnings?"

Tom laughed quietly as he plucked his fedora from a rack beside the kitchen door. As he settled the hat on his head, he said, "If she comes around anytime in the next couple of days, we'll know you'd better cancel the party."

After he left, Sunny and I looked at each other over our coffee cups and exchanged tentative smiles. "He seems pretty confident about Friday," I observed.

My friend sighed. "That's what he wants us to think, anyway. He knows I'm feeling a little jittery all of a sudden."

"You think something bad's going to happen?"

Sunny pursed her lips thoughtfully. "Well, I don't think anything good's going to happen. But I don't know, Augie. Maybe being with those young folks last night, seeing the fear in their eyes, kind of unnerved me. Not for the first time, of course, but now that we're actually going to the courthouse in just a few days, it all seems more real. Part of me wants to tell those kids to just stay home and stay safe."

"You know they can't do that."

"I know." She nodded. "I know they have to go. And I want them to do it. They've worked long and hard, and it's time for them to give it their best shot at the registrar's office. But at the same time I'm afraid for them. I mean, they're not just my students or some poor, downtrodden Negroes. They're my friends. I've grown fond of them. If anything happened to any one of them . . ."

Her voice trailed off, and suddenly Bo Wiley's haunted dream eyes came back to me. I had to rise from the table and pour myself another cup of coffee to get rid of the image. "Let's hope they'll be all right, Sunny." What else could I say? What assurance could I give her of their safety, when nothing was sure at all?

I sat back down, curled both palms around the cup to warm my suddenly cold hands. "Someday," I predicted, "some Negro from Carver is going to walk into that courthouse and walk out a registered voter. I don't know when it's going to happen, but it will."

Sunny sat quietly a moment, then smiled at me. "I know you're right," she said. "Maybe we'll all be pleasantly surprised on Friday."

"Anyway, no matter what, I think you and I will have to stay upbeat in front of the students. Don't let on for a second that we're nervous. They're already scared enough as it is."

Sunny conceded with a nod. She picked up a spoon and stirred the coffee in her cup, though there was neither cream nor sugar in it. "You know what I'd like to do right now, Augie?" she asked. When I shook my head, she gave me a small, embarrassed smile. "I'd like to be able to pick up the phone and talk to Mother and Papa. Funny, isn't it?"

"Not at all."

"I'm thirty-four years old, but I still run to Mom and Pop with all the news—good and bad. I still want to tell them everything."

"You're lucky you can do that."

"The problem is, I can't do it right now, since they're traveling and I don't know where they are. I wish they'd call. Though if they did, I'm not even sure I'd tell them about Friday. I wouldn't want them to worry. Comes a time when the child has to start protecting the parents, you know?"

I had no parents to protect, but I nodded in agreement. "Do you think they'll call while I'm here?"

"No telling." Sunny lifted her shoulders. "We usually talk about once a week, but it's hard to say what they'll do when they're on the road."

A weighty hush fell over the kitchen. Silently, I was willing Chichi and Haha to call. I remembered Chichi's arms around me when Sunny and I thought the Martians had landed and the world was going to end. I remembered Haha's warm hand against my cheek when Pearl Harbor was bombed and our world did end.

"I really miss them," I said, my voice a thin vapor in the air.

"I do too."

"I wonder what they would say if they called and found me here."

Sunny smiled dreamily then. "They would say 'Musume.'" Her lips stayed parted, as though she intended to say more, but her eyes drifted upward in search of the words. After a moment, she laughed quietly and said, "To tell you the truth, Augie, I don't know what they'd say."

"You know something, Sunny," I replied, "if they said only that one word, it would be enough."

THIRTY-THREE

Later that morning, after dropping the children off at Vacation Bible School, Sunny and I went to Providence Street, Carver's main thoroughfare of antique shops and secondhand bookstores. "Let's treat ourselves," Sunny had suggested after breakfast. I agreed that we could both use some time away from current events, and what better place to step out of the present than among the treasures and trinkets of the past?

We wandered among the collections of musty furniture and antiquated gadgets and knickknacks, browsed through piles of decades-old *Look* and *Life* magazines, thumbed through already well-thumbed books, and picked our way through boxes of doilies, antimacassars, and table linens. For a couple of hours I was able to forget—or at least to push to the far reaches of my mind—the look on Bo Wiley's terrified dream face, the sound of Howard Draper's voice as he read to me from his book of poetry, the scent of palpable fear in the funeral parlor as four young people prepared to register to vote.

I was lost to the lives of people who had already finished the course, who had left behind these items for me to finger through on a hot summer afternoon. I wondered, as always, who had once owned this book, that phonograph, these button-up shoes. Who were they, and what had they seen in life, and what had they known of love and fear and suffering? I liked to imagine what their stories might have been, and I gained a strange comfort from the thought that whatever they may have once faced, it was over now, and perhaps they had even come to a place of peace.

When Sunny and I got hungry, we drove to Frohmann's Department Store to eat at the lunch counter there. "You have to go to Frohmann's at least once while you're in Carver," Sunny insisted. I didn't argue. We ordered hamburgers and french fries and large chocolate shakes so thick the straws stood up by themselves in the middle of the glass.

We were served by a willowy, ruddy-faced young man who should have been in Vietnam—would have been, if he'd not been exempted by a pronounced limp. "Polio," Sunny whispered when he was out of earshot. "It probably saved his life."

At one end of the counter, a sandy-haired child in patent-leather shoes swiveled round and round on the stool while her mother, oblivious, sipped coffee. At the other end an elderly gentleman was bent over a slice of blueberry pie, scooping each small bite onto the prongs of a fork and lifting it with an unsteady hand up to his waiting lips.

The server busied himself by polishing the counter, the aluminum napkin holders, the bulbous heads of the salt and pepper shakers. He whistled quietly all the while, happy, it seemed, to be in a hot and steamy little town rather than a hot and steamy jungle in South Vietnam. On a hound-dog summer day such as this, it hardly seemed possible that our country's young men were being snuffed out by the hundreds in that little Asian nation. I thought briefly of Alan Hastings III, the fiancé of the young woman I'd met on the plane. Would this be the day he caught a sniper's bullet in the flesh? Or would he step on a land mine planted by the gooks so that his body burst open, a bloody rose in bloom? I couldn't know, would never know. But if he preferred such a death to being murdered by a Mississippi Negro, I hoped he would get what he wanted.

The blueberry man finished his pie, slipped a quarter under the plate, and eased himself off the stool.

"Take it easy, Wally," the youth called from behind the counter.

The older man saluted, gnarled hand to wrinkled brow, and shuffled out.

The coffee-drinking woman took her stool-spinning daughter by the hand and strolled into the women's department, disappearing among the cotton blouses and leather handbags. After pocketing the dime left beside the coffee cup and cleaning up the counter, the server tucked his dishrag in his back pants pocket and threw a cup of water on the grill. At once the grill glazed over with a sheet of sizzling bubbles. The young man, turning his back to us, set to work scraping the foamy field with a spatula, pushing off into a small trough a soggy goulash of leftover hamburger, steak, and onions. He was never idle, not for the entire hour we were there.

When we had almost finished eating, Sunny asked, "Well, after all that, what do you think we should have for supper tonight?"

I stirred the last bit of milkshake in my cup with the straw. I hadn't as yet told Sunny of my plans for the evening. I dreaded the conversation that would undoubtedly follow. But now that she'd brought up the subject of supper, I couldn't put it off any longer. Reluctantly, I confessed, "I'm having dinner with Howard Draper tonight."

I could well imagine the surprise on Sunny's face, though I couldn't bring myself to look at her. Instead, I concentrated on whipping the last bit of ice cream into a pool of brown milk and waited for her to say something. When she spoke, the only word that came out of her mouth was an astonished, "Why?"

It somehow didn't seem the right moment to tell Sunny about Howard's kindred spirit comment. "Because he invited me?" I made it a question, tried to laugh. But my friend was not amused.

"Do you really think you need to spend more time with him for your article, or are you just plain crazy?" Her voice was flat and tight.

I sighed, refusing still to lift my eyes. "He's an interesting character, Sunny. What can I say?"

"He's a dangerous character, Augie," Sunny countered. "You know what he is."

What could I do but nod? "Yes, I know what he is. But let me ask you something, Sunny—and I don't at all mean to sound facetious. How is it you can go to church week after week and sing those hymns with that man playing the organ?"

"Don't try to change the subject, Augie."

"I'm not changing the subject. The subject is Howard Draper, and that's what I'm talking about. My point is this, Sunny: Don't you think there's something about him that's—I don't know—unexplained? Otherwise you'd feel like a hypocrite praising God to the accompaniment of a Klansman, wouldn't you?"

She was silent so long I thought she wouldn't answer. Finally she said, "What Howard does outside the church is between him and God, or between him and the devil, one or the other. It has nothing to do with me. I don't have to justify the sins of Howard Draper."

"No," I agreed, "you don't. But I think there's something there, some sort of justification—"

"Augie." Sunny's voice was hardly more than a whisper. "Don't see him tonight."

I shut my eyes, opened them. The dismay was still on her face. "I've already agreed to see him."

"So call and tell him you're sick or that something came up."

"No." I shook my head slowly. "No, I want to go."

"Why, Augie? Why in the world would you want to spend any more time with that man?"

I pursed my lips and lifted my eyes to the lighted menu above the grill, trying to find the answer listed there among the hamburgers, cheese steaks, and hot dogs. "I don't know what to tell you," I finally admitted. "He invited me, and I said yes. Call me crazy if you want. I suppose you're right."

Sunny bunched up a napkin and dropped it on her plate. "If I were your mother," she said, "I'd forbid you to go."

"If you were my mother," I said, "you'd be long dead and embalmed with alcohol."

She frowned at me then, and her eyes were sad. "Augie," she said, "what can I say to talk you out of this?"

"Listen," I replied evenly, "all we're going to do is eat dinner somewhere and then go to some Baptist church—over in Lucasville, I think he said—where he plays the organ for the Wednesday night service. Sounds pretty benign, doesn't it? We're going to *church*, for heaven's sakes. What could possibly happen?"

"This isn't a high school date—"

"It isn't a date at all—"

"Well, whatever it is, you'll be in the company of a Klansman."

"I'm not supposed to know that, remember? As far as I know, he's just a musician who teaches tone-deaf kids how to make music, or how not to make music, as the case may be."

"So what's the point of all this, Augie? You're getting together under false pretenses. He thinks you don't know he's Klan, but you do, though you're certainly not going to let him know you know. And you think he doesn't know you're a journalist here to do a story, but maybe he does know, and maybe the whole Klan knows—and has it ever occurred to you that maybe the very reason he's paying any attention to you at all is *because* you're a journalist here to do a story on voter registration?"

It had occurred to me. The thought had more than once crossed my mind that he knew why I was here and he wanted to throw a wrench into the works to make sure there wouldn't be a story. But whenever that thought insinuated itself into my brain, I dismissed it.

"He knows I'm a novelist, but how could he possibly know I'm a journalist?" I asked.

Sunny cocked her head, two lines digging into the flesh between her brows. " 'How could she possibly know,' he asks his fellow Kluxers, 'that I'm a member of the Klan?' " She shook her head. "Word gets around, Augie. Secrets leak out. People know more than we think they know. Maybe he's even an avid reader of *One Nation*. Maybe he sees your byline every month. Ever think of that?"

I shrugged, trying to look less concerned than I felt. "So you think he's actually luring me into a triple-K trap with the intention of stringing me up?"

Sunny took a deep breath and let it out slowly. "I know it sounds dramatic, but listen, you're the one who likes to mention Schwerner and Goodman. Do you think they thought they'd end up under an earthen dam? They thought they were just going to nudge some Negroes to get out and vote, and the next thing they know they're in an unmarked grave the size of a small mountain, and their names are plastered all over the news."

She stared at me hard, then added, "Don't underestimate the ruthlessness of the Klan, Augie. You may think you're safe because you're a white woman, but I can tell you this much: any hardcore Kluxer would string up his own mother if she so much as gave a Negro the time of day."

She almost had me convinced. I felt tempted to call Howard and cancel. And yet I knew I wouldn't. I knew I'd being seeing Howard that night because I couldn't do otherwise. Part of me was afraid, but part of me knew beyond doubt that right or wrong, good or evil, Howard Draper would never hurt me. Something told me I was safe. Maybe I was a little bit clairvoyant, like Miss Ebba. Maybe some of her ability to see what can't be seen had rubbed off on me in the few moments we stood together in the funeral parlor. She had told me that I didn't have to be afraid. "You jes' go on, chile," she'd said. "You don' hafta be 'fraid." And though I didn't really understand, I would go on just as she said, and not be persuaded by fear to do otherwise.

It took me a long while to gather together my fragmented thoughts. I knew the facts about Howard. I'd laid them all out and examined and re-examined them. But there was so much I didn't know, so much no one knew about the man, and in those missing elements lay the key to Howard Draper. When I finally spoke, I surprised even myself by saying, "I'm not so sure he's Klan, Sunny." Not until that moment did I realize I'd been coming to that conclusion.

Sunny's eyes grew wide in disbelief. "Then what's he doing at the meetings? You think he's got the Klan mixed up with the Lions or the Rotary Club? You think he stumbles into the Klan meetings thinking all the while he's at a gathering of the Odd Fellows?"

I drummed my fingers over my lips and thought a moment. "That woman who talks to Tom," I suggested, "the one whose husband is Klan—maybe *she's* mixed up. Maybe she's lying."

Sunny shook her head. "Why would she lie? She has no reason to."

I pulled a napkin from the dispenser and rubbed at a splattering of chocolate shake on the counter. "I don't know how I know this, but things just don't add up, Sunny."

"What do you mean, things don't add up?" She looked at me skeptically.

I sniffed, shook my head. "I'm not sure I can explain. I mean, there's more to that man than meets the eye. There's something about him that we don't know—"

"You mean something like, instead of being a Methodist, he's actually a follower of Hare Krishna and being such a peace-loving soul he couldn't possibly hurt anyone?"

She didn't bother to hide the sarcasm in her voice. I pushed away the empty milkshake glass and looked at my hands on the counter. How to explain to Sunny what I couldn't explain to myself?

"I'm sorry, Augie, but the man is a bad seed. That's all there is to it."

"I'm not so sure, Sunny. I just have this feeling—I don't know—that there's another layer. Strip away the musician and you have a Kluxer, but strip away the Kluxer, and you're going to find something else, something that'll explain . . ."

Sunny laid a hand on my arm. "Listen, Augie, loneliness brings us to funny conclusions, makes us do funny things. Don't get me wrong but—"

"What do you know about loneliness, Sunny?" I didn't mean to come off as either angry or bitter, but the words came out sounding both.

"Enough to recognize it when I see it," Sunny returned gently. "And enough to know that it leads us down roads we wouldn't otherwise go down."

I laced my fingers together on the counter and squeezed my hands until my knuckles were white. I preferred to think I was being nudged along by a journalist's hunch, or even a woman's intuition. Not something as unprofessional as loneliness.

My old friend gave me a look of concern. "I can't tell you what to do," she said, "but I wish you wouldn't go with him tonight. If anything happened to you, I'd never forgive myself for bringing you here."

"Nothing's going to happen, Sunny. Please believe that. I'll be fine." I put on a broad smile and patted her hand. "You'll see. I will go to church with Howard Draper and live to tell about it."

"I just hope you're right, Augie." She gave my arm one last squeeze before pulling her hand away. She turned on the stool and stood up.

We left a tip on the counter, paid for our burgers, and stepped out of the air-conditioned coolness of Frohmann's Department Store into the gripping, glaring heat of the afternoon sun.

❧

I had agreed to meet Howard Draper in front of the Magnolia Café at four-thirty that afternoon. By four-fifteen I was pulling my rental car into one of the diagonal parking spaces on Main Street when he pulled up beside me in his orange Volkswagen Beetle. He waved and leaned over the gearshift to open the passenger-side door for me. I climbed out of my car and directly into his before the eyes of Carver could pick up enough news to set the tongues wagging.

"Good timing," Howard said. "We're both early."

"Great minds think alike," I quipped.

"As do kindred spirits." He smiled at me, put the car into reverse, and in a moment we were chugging forward through the heart of town. I had no idea where we were going. Howard had said he wanted to take me to his favorite place to eat, and that it was to be a surprise.

"I wish you wouldn't go with him," Sunny had pleaded, but here I was, seat belt fastened over my pale yellow dress, all strapped in and ready to go to wherever it was Howard wanted to take me.

The windows of the car were rolled down against the heat, and the hot, dusty air whipped at my face and hair. I pulled a silk floral scarf from my purse and tied it loosely around my head, knotting it beneath my chin.

Howard smiled at me again. "You look lovely today, Miss Callahan," he said. Then he added, "As always."

I thanked him, wanting to accept his words and his smile as sincere. But there remained the nagging doubt of appearances. Just as the eye falls victim to the optical illusion, so the heart falls victim to the tricks of deception. How to know what's true, what's real, when your own senses work against you?

"It's as plain as the nose on your face," Sunny argues. *"He's Klan. What else do you need to know?"*

"You gotta know, Miz Callahan," Miss Ebba breaks in, *"things ain't always what dey seem."*

"So what's the truth, then, Miss Ebba, about Howard Draper?"

"Don't get mataphysical on me, Augie. He's a bad seed. Nothing good can come from a bad seed. Take it at face value. . . ."

"You jes' go on, chile. You don' hafta be 'fraid."

"Don't underestimate the ruthlessness of the Klan, Augie. Any Kluxer would string up his own mother. . . ."

"Things, people too . . . people ain't always what dey seem. . . ."

"I know, I know, Miss Ebba. But there has to be a place where illusions end and appearances are real. If things are never as they seem, how can we make sense of anything at all?"

"He's Klan, Augie. That's all the truth you need."

"You jes' go on, chile. You jes' go on. . . ."

"Maybe," Howard said, "I should have told you to wear slacks." He glanced at my dress again, frowning this time.

"But we're going to church, aren't we?"

"Yes, but—well, you'll see."

"Yeah, you'll see," Sunny echoed.

He was dressed casually himself, a short-sleeved pale blue shirt tucked into a beltless pair of jeans. Only then did the strangeness of his garb hit me. "Do they let you play the organ at the Baptist church dressed like that?" I asked.

Howard let go one brief laugh. "Hardly," he said. "If they knew I was at the organ wearing jeans, half the congregation would report me to the church hierarchy as a heretic, and the other half would bypass that and string me up without trial."

We came to a stop sign, one of the last before the edge of town. The air around us stilled, the engine idled. I wondered momentarily whether I should open the door and flee before the car moved forward. Howard seemed to be saying that he wasn't going to play the organ at church tonight. If we weren't going to the Baptist church, then where exactly were we going?

My hand was actually raised to the door, my fingers curved around the silver chrome of the handle, when Howard explained, "I wear a robe over my clothes. So it doesn't matter what I have on underneath. No one can see. One really hot night I wore just an undershirt and a pair of cutoffs. Pretty daring, huh?"

He laughed again, and I moved my hand back to my lap. I had no idea whether I was headed for a pleasant evening with a kindred spirit or, as Sunny feared, a prearranged encounter with the Ku Klux Klan. But, surprisingly, I wasn't afraid. My hand had lifted itself to the door in a reflex of unemotional self-preservation, and that was all. I wanted nothing other than to be right there beside Howard Draper, no matter where he took me. I wanted to learn that I was right about him, that there was layer upon layer upon layer to this man, and that the very final layer was of something good.

The VW chugged forward as Howard shifted into first. We rolled out of town on the impossibly small tires of that little car, our bodies swaying with the changing of the gears, the engine rattling our insides with its noisy vibrations. After about a mile or so Howard exited the paved street and turned onto a narrow dirt road that rolled itself out through a tangle of woods. The road was a hodgepodge of light and shadow, bumps and ruts. I tasted dirt on my tongue and felt myself bathed in a layer of sweat. Sweat on my neck, my back, behind my knees. I could have reached out and grabbed leaves from the trees as we passed by.

I wanted to say something, but I didn't know what. I had so many questions, the least of which was, "Where are we going?" The most pressing was, "Who are you really, Howard Draper?"

Finally I said, "This restaurant we're going to, it's a bit off the beaten path, isn't it, Mr. Draper?"

He looked at me sideways, placidly, then smiled. "I wonder whether you would mind calling me Howard," he said.

He was avoiding the question, but I agreed to call him by his first name. "All right, Howard. So where are we—"

"And may I call you Augusta?"

"I prefer Augie. But I wonder—"

"Augie it is, then." The corners of his mouth turned up once more. "It's an unusual name. I like it."

"Thank you. Now, Howard," I tried again. "I give up. Where are we going for dinner?"

"It's a surprise, remember? But like I said, it's my favorite spot. I think you'll like it too. We're almost there."

In spite of his assurances, we didn't appear to be close to anything at all. We went on bumping over that dirt road for what seemed forever until we turned off onto an even smaller road, hardly more than a footpath cutting through the trees. We chugged up a small hill and down the other side until at length we reached a clearing. Not like the lynching grounds in the woods I had dreamed about, but a clearing in the pines that a narrow river ran through, where willows grew along the mossy banks, touching the water with the tips of their leafy fingers.

Howard cut the engine, and we sat there in the midst of the sudden silence. Slowly, the way eyes adjust to the dark, I began to hear the sounds of the woods, the bubbling of the water, the songs of the birds, the susurration of wind in the trees. The air was sweetened by the scent of pine and cooled by the shadows of the foliage reaching up toward the clear sky. Was this place of serenity where I would meet the Klan? If so, I thought, if I should die in this clearing in the woods, I hope they leave me here. It would be a good place to sleep forever.

"Well," my companion said at last, "here we are. In case you haven't figured it out, we're having a picnic."

He got out of the car, hurried around to my side and opened the door for me. He offered me his hand as I stood, and I accepted it. Then as I looked about, absently smoothing the wrinkles out of the lap of my dress, Howard folded the front seat forward, leaned inside the car, and straightened up again holding a picnic basket.

"I packed it myself. Hope you don't mind."

"It sounds wonderful."

"It's a little rustic here, I know—that's why I thought you might be more comfortable in slacks. But then you're right about wearing a dress to church." He paused once more to consider our attire. "I'm afraid I didn't plan this very well. Maybe we should have gone to a restaurant."

"Oh no! I'm glad we're here. It's a beautiful spot."

"I've got a blanket for us to sit on." He moved to the front of the Volkswagen, opened the hood over the storage space, and pulled out a lightweight blanket, the kind you might spread over your bed on a cool spring night. It was pale blue, the color of Howard's shirt and of the sky that opened clear and cloudless above us.

We found a spot not far from the water's edge. "I hope you'll be comfortable," he said as we settled ourselves on the blanket, layers of fallen pine needles a surprisingly soft cushion beneath us. "This is my favorite place in all of Mississippi. I wanted you to see it before you go back to California."

California seemed a whole other lifetime at the moment, but I decided that before I returned home I would learn the truth about Howard Draper, somehow, in whatever way I could.

THIRTY-FOUR

I slipped off my shoes and untied the knot of the scarf beneath my chin, shaking my hair free. "How did you find this place?" I asked.

Howard paused in the midst of unpacking the picnic basket. In his right hand he held a plastic bag filled with plump purple grapes. "Just luck," he said with a shrug. "Shortly after I moved to Carver I was driving around, just exploring, seeing what Mississippi had to offer. The road led me here. Now I come as often as I can. It's kind of my getaway, you know? Where I go to escape from it all." He lowered his eyes to the grapes and studied them a moment, as though wondering what to do with them. He finally laid them on the blanket as he added shyly, "This is the first time I've brought anyone along with me."

He went back to the task of pulling items from the basket. "I hope sandwiches are okay. I've got pastrami with mustard and corned beef with mustard. Not much choice, I'm afraid. But we've also got pickles, chips, cold beans, and pop."

He looked at me again and laughed briefly. I smiled in return. "It sounds like the perfect meal," I said. "I'll have pastrami."

He handed me a sandwich wrapped in waxed paper and then chose one for himself. He opened the can of baked beans with a Swiss Army Knife and poured some out onto a couple of paper plates. He tore into the bag of chips, took the lid off a jar of dill pickle spears, then held up a bottle of soda in each hand and asked, "R.C. or Grape Nehi?"

I chose the Cola. He pried off the cap with the knife and handed me the bottle. It was warm, but I didn't mind. "Oh!" he said suddenly. "Forks. And napkins. Can't forget those." His hand disappeared into the basket and came up with the forks and napkins. And with one more thing too, which he tossed onto the blanket in front of me.

"Ever read that?" he asked.

I was looking at a copy of my own book, *Soldier, Come Home*. "If you haven't," he went on, "you should. It's an excellent book."

I smiled at the compliment even as I dismissed it. "You don't have to say that, Howard, just because I wrote it."

"I'm not saying it just because you wrote it. I mean it. That book kept me up well past midnight last night. Once I got started, I couldn't have put it down if my house caught fire and burned to the ground around me. You're a gifted writer, Augie. You have a special talent."

I felt the warmth of a blush creep up my neck and into my cheeks. To divert Howard's attention from my face, I reached for the book and flipped through it. "This isn't from the Carver library," I noted lamely.

"I bought it," he said. "Actually, a friend of mine picked it up in Jackson for me yesterday. I tried to get it at the bookstore in Carver, but I'd have had to order it, and I didn't want to wait. So when Gary called and said he was coming up from Jackson to see me, I asked him to do me a favor."

I wondered briefly how Howard happened to have a friend in Jackson, but I let the question go unasked. "You know, your library in Carver has a copy. I looked it up the other day when I was browsing." I laughed self-consciously. "Well, I guess that sounds pretty egotistical, looking up your own book in the library to see whether it's there."

Howard shook his head. "Not at all. I'm sure I'd do the same."

"It wasn't checked out," I went on. "You could have saved yourself a few dollars."

"But I wanted to own a copy. After all, I know the author. Well—" Frowning, he amended his thought. "I don't know you very well, do I, since we met so recently. But reading the book gave me at least a bit of insight into who you are."

"Did it? What did it tell you?"

"That you are sensitive and intelligent. And that you've been acquainted with sadness. It's a sad book, Augie, but very real. You're not afraid to face life squarely, tell it like it is. We need people who are willing to do that, and to do it well."

I shook my head. "I don't know, Howard," I protested quietly. "Even though I make my living as a writer, I often question my ability."

"Most artists do. The ones who don't question their talent get lost in their own self-importance, and they end up doing no one any good at all."

I was quiet for a moment. Then I said, "Well, thank you for being interested in the book, Howard. That means a lot to me."

"I'm not just interested in the book, Augie." In spite of his earlier shyness, he now tried to hold my gaze. But I looked away. I was willing to talk about me, and I wanted to talk about him, but I was uncomfortable talking about us.

Perhaps Howard understood my fear, because he steered the conversation in a different direction. "Do you mind my asking you who Lenny is?" He opened the book and pointed to the dedication. *To Lenny*, it said, the only two words on the page.

"My older brother," I explained. "The book is loosely based on his life, or at least I got the idea for the story from his life. Lenny spent most of the war in a Japanese prison camp."

"Dear God," Howard whispered. He closed the book, shook his head. "What's he doing now?"

"He died—several years ago. Drank himself to death." I tried to smile but failed. "My uncle says the Japanese killed him when they captured him in Bataan, but Lenny was so tough, it took him a decade and a half to die."

Howard's eyes were full of compassion. "Your uncle may be right. It was . . ." He paused, picked up the book, and studied the cover. "Well, I can't think of a word strong enough. Unconscionable, maybe?—what they did to the prisoners in those camps. Completely inhuman."

"The Japanese?"

Howard nodded. "I don't personally know anyone who was there, but I've heard stories. I've never understood how the Japanese could be so ruthless, killing off our soldiers with no more feeling or remorse than if they were swatting flies."

"They were no worse than the Germans with the Jews, I suppose."

"Yes," Howard nodded. "What the Germans did to the Jews was just as horrible. Still, if I had been an American soldier in the war, I'd have far rather been captured by the Germans than the Japanese."

We had barely yet touched our food. I pulled a piece of pastrami out of my sandwich and nibbled on it, thinking. "I didn't know my brother, really, before the war," I said. "I was very young when he left home and joined the marines. He was going to make a career of it. I didn't get to know him until afterward, and even then, I never really knew him. He wouldn't open up to anyone. It actually was as though he came home a dead man, and we were all just waiting for his body to catch on to the fact that there wasn't any life left in him.

"So he was always something of a stranger. Still, I hated the Japanese for what they did to him. And I think that was really the hardest thing of all about the war for me. It made me hate the people that I once loved the most. See, before the war there was a Japanese family in our neighborhood who took me in, kind of adopted me. In fact, I more or less moved in with them, made myself right at home. I considered them my family."

"But what about your own family, Augie? What happened to them?"

"My father died when I was very young, and my mother, well, she kind of went around the bend, as my uncle would say. She started drinking—I don't know, maybe she'd been drinking for years and it just got worse after my father's death. So at the time I met this Japanese family, my father was dead and my mother was, well, present in body but absent in every other way. I guess that's why the Yamagatas became so important to me. I needed them, and the wonderful thing is, they seemed to want me." I paused a moment, smiling at the thought. "I even came to think of myself as Japanese. I was Japanese in everything but looks."

Howard listened intently, barely moving as I spoke. When I finished, I looked to him for a response. What he said was, "Did Helen know them too?"

For a second I was lost. "Helen?"

"Or, I guess I should say Sunny. I forgot you have a nickname for her."

"Oh!" I gave a small nervous laugh. I had to be careful about what

I was telling Howard Draper. "Yes, Sunny knew this family too."

"I suppose they were interned during the war?"

"Oh yes. They were sent to Manzanar."

"What happened afterward, after the war? Did they ever meet your brother?"

"No, they never came back to Los Angeles. I never saw them again."

Howard took a sip of his Grape Nehi and looked out over the river. "So . . ." He hesitated, frowning. "You came to resent them?"

"There was a time," I confessed, "when I would have said I hated them because they didn't come back for me after the war. And I was angry too because I saw what happened to Lenny during his little unplanned detour through Japan. After that, as far as I was concerned, all the Japanese were on my black list. But now that I'm older, I can understand things better. It took me a long time, but now I can differentiate between the Japanese who killed my brother and the Japanese who raised me. And I also realize that things happen to people, things happen in their lives, and sometimes they can't keep the promises they made to you even if they want to." Howard couldn't know how recently I'd come to realize the truth of what I was telling him, that the now of which I spoke was only days in length. Not weeks or months or years, but days.

"You've never heard from any of them since?"

"No." I was lying, and I had to turn my gaze away from Howard to do it. But I would never reveal to him that Helen Fulton was Hatsune Yamagata.

"And there's no way to find them?"

"I can't imagine how."

"But if you could find them—would you want to see them again?"

"Oh yes. More than anything."

After a moment's pause he said, "I wish I could find them for you, Augie, and bring them back into your life."

I knew he was sincere. "Thank you, Howard."

"You know, that's something else we have in common. I know what it is to love someone of another race. The person I love most in the world is a Negro woman named Trudy. She's always been like a mother to me."

I looked up at him sharply, remembering suddenly whom these

words came from. "A Negro woman?" I echoed.

Howard nodded. "Trudy played more of a part in raising me than my own parents did. Not that my parents were uninvolved. In fact, they were very good parents—loving, kind, always wanting the best for me. But Trudy and I, we had a special relationship. She took care of me from the day I was born, spoiled me like the only child I was."

"Why didn't your parents have more children?"

"My mother couldn't have children. After me, that is." He gave me a sideways glance, ate a bite of sandwich, began to talk again when he had swallowed. "Her health was never good. That's part of the reason why Trudy was hired to help around the house and to help with me when I came along. Trudy did all the things for me that my mother would have done had she been well. She fed me, cared for me when I was sick, read to me until I could read for myself, made sure I practiced the piano for an hour a day. She was gentle and fair, but at the same time she could give me a pretty good tongue-lashing whenever she thought I needed one. She said if she was going to teach me anything, it would be how to tell right from wrong."

"She sounds like the ideal mother," I commented. Meanwhile, my mind worked helplessly through a thousand tangled questions.

"She was," Howard agreed. "I consider myself fortunate, though in the past few years I've begun to think she might have missed her true calling. Trudy has a voice you wouldn't believe. She's never had any training, but she has a raw talent you don't come across very often. When I was growing up, I'd be completely mesmerized whenever she sang to me. There was this one song I'd ask her to sing again and again, 'Deep River.' An old Negro spiritual. Maybe you know it?" He looked at me. I shook my head no. "Well, whenever she came to this one part about 'the promised land where all is peace,' I'd actually get goose bumps just listening to it." Howard shook his head slowly. He seemed lost to the past, hearing again the voice that had so deeply affected him as a child.

"Sometimes," he went on, "I feel guilty that her life was devoted to me. She was a housekeeper and a nanny when she could have done something great."

"Maybe she thought raising you was a great thing."

Howard smiled shyly but said nothing.

"Did she ever say she was sorry for how she spent her life?"

"No, never."

"Then she was probably happy, don't you think?"

Howard looked at me, then away again. "I don't suppose Negroes think much in terms of happiness, Augie. Most of them are more concerned simply with survival."

I didn't know what to say. When I said nothing, Howard broke the silence by offering, "Here, let me show you her picture."

He reached around to his back pocket and pulled out his wallet. From the leather fold where he kept his dollar bills, he pulled a small black-and-white photograph. Its edges were thin and smooth, as though it had been slid in and out of the wallet many times over. Howard stared at the picture briefly before handing it to me. "On second thought," he said, "I guess you can't see much."

What I saw was a man, a woman, and a small child lounging outdoors while a distance behind them, in an open doorway of a house, a tall, thin woman stood gazing out over the trio on the grass. Her features were barely distinguishable, but her skin was so fair in the photo that if I hadn't deduced that she was the Negro, I might have mistaken her for white.

"That's you?" I asked, pointing to the child.

Howard grinned. " 'Fraid so. A few years back."

I studied the photo, trying to read from it the life Howard had lived with these people, the life he had lived while growing up. The elder Draper looked decidedly Scandinavian, with fair hair and well-proportioned features settled comfortably on a round face. He was small and compact, with broad shoulders and beefy hands, one of which he'd laid casually on his son's shoulder. His gaze was stern behind a pair of wire-framed glasses, his mouth little more than a thin line without lips. He didn't smile. Though he was seated on the grass, he had on a dark suit and tie.

"Your father looks like a businessman," I said.

"Banker, actually."

"You don't look a thing like him."

"So people tell me," Howard said, shrugging.

"Was he musical like you?"

Howard shook his head. "Not a lick of talent. My mother used to say that when he sang the hymns in church, half the dogs in Chicago started howling."

"What about your mother? Was she musical?" In the photo she didn't look musical. She mostly looked tired. I guessed her to be no more than thirty, but the illness that made her unable to produce more than one child had already claimed her. She was a small, heavyset woman, fleshy as a ripe plum, with dark circles beneath her eyes and a sag to her small shoulders. She might have been blond or she might have been gray; either way, her marcelled hair fell to just below her ears. Her face was lifted to the camera, and she smiled wanly, as though it were an effort to do so but she wanted to make that effort anyway. Not a pretty woman, she nevertheless appeared kind and gentle.

Howard laughed lightly at my question. "My mother wasn't any more musical than my father. Of course, I never said as much. If Dad started half the dogs barking, she no doubt riled up the other half. No, it was from Trudy that I got my appreciation for music."

I looked up from the photo to meet Howard's gaze. "But where did you get your talent?"

He shrugged again. "Straight from God? I mean, a lot of people have talents their parents never had. Did either of your parents write?"

I laughed and shook my head. "No. I see your point." Gazing again at the photo in my hand, I tapped my finger on the woman standing in the doorway, looking on. "And this is Trudy?"

"Yes. I thought she showed up better, but you really can't see her very well in this photo."

No doubt he had looked at this photo a hundred times, a thousand times, since leaving Chicago, and yet he didn't know how little of the Negro woman it revealed. I realized at once it was because he didn't need a photo to remember, that when he looked at what I held in my hand, it wasn't the photo he saw but the image of Trudy that was permanently fixed in his mind. Her face had been there since the time he lifted up his infant eyes to see who was holding a bottle to his lips. He had grown up with that face, lived with it day in and day out, had spent far more days and months and years with that face than I had with the faces of Chichi and Haha, and yet even I, without any photos at all, could recall every line, every curve, every feature of those faces I'd held so dear. Howard didn't need a photo either to gaze on Trudy's face.

"She still writes to me every week and begs me to come home," Howard said.

"I can well imagine she didn't want you to leave Chicago."

"No, she didn't want me to leave, and she especially didn't want me to come to Mississippi. She tried for months to talk me out of it, told me I was a fool, that I was throwing my career out the window. I told her I was just doing what I had to do. I think she finally began to understand. Even though she begs me to come home, she knows I have to be here."

"But why do you say that? If she begs you to come home, it doesn't sound like she's resigned to your being here."

Howard popped a couple of grapes into his mouth, chewed, washed them down with the warm Nehi. Finally he said, "She feels it's her duty to tell me to come home. It's just the natural extension of her years of raising and protecting me. But—and I'll never forget it—on the day I left for Mississippi, she went with me to the train station. Before I boarded the train, she took my face in her hands, looked me right in the eye, and said, 'I'm right proud to know you, Howard Draper, till I'm like to bust wide open with pride.'" Howard paused and smiled in the remembering. "I consider it the finest thing anyone's ever said to me."

"It's a beautiful story, Howard," I said, but I was thinking, *He must trust me to carry this back to California without telling anyone in Carver. Otherwise, isn't he afraid it'll somehow get back to the Klan?*

As I turned it over quickly in my mind, I decided that if the Klan found out about Howard's former nanny, so what? A lot of whites were fond of their Negro servants. Cedric Frohmann, for one. The mayor didn't make any bones about hiding it. All of white Carver had passed through his dining room at one time or another and had no doubt noticed how he regarded Celeste and the others. Why should it be any different for Howard Draper? Maybe even in Mississippi a Klansman could carry a picture of his black mammy in his wallet without too many repercussions.

No, something else was bothering me about Howard and Trudy, and I finally realized it was this: If he loved this Negro woman more than anyone else in the world, why did he come south to join the Klan?

"I guess this is a day for firsts," Howard continued. "I've never told anyone about Trudy before. At least not anyone around here."

"Is there a reason people shouldn't know?" I held my breath.

Howard stuck out his lower lip and shook his head slowly. "No. It just never occurred to me to tell anyone. I guess I'm kind of a private person at heart. But I knew you'd understand what I feel about her."

Thoroughly confused, I could only hope Howard's life made more sense to him than it did to me.

Howard looked at his watch. "I hate to say it," he sighed, "but we're going to have to head on to the church."

We gathered up the trash and the leftover food and put it all back into the picnic basket. Then Howard stood and held out his hand. "Help you up?" he offered.

I took his hand, and when I stood, he didn't let go. Not for a moment, anyway. With an unmistakable sadness to his voice, he said, "There's always so little time, isn't there?"

I nodded. "Thank you for bringing me to your special place, Howard."

He looked at me, pressing my fingers lightly before releasing his grip and letting his fingers slip from mine.

❧

For the second time in a week, for the second time in my life, I found myself in church. I sat by the aisle, in a pew about halfway between the back door and the altar. Seated next to me was a boy who managed to get the hiccoughs shortly after the opening hymn. His first explosion must have surprised even him, as it came full strength from his mouth just as the pastor stood up to read a Scripture from the pulpit. I heard the boy's mouth snap shut, saw in my peripheral vision how he turned to look at his mother, who returned his gaze with a look that said, "How dare you do that in the house of God!" The pastor slipped on a pair of reading glasses and gazed out in amusement over the top of them just in time for the second hiccough to ricochet off the walls of the sanctuary.

"Tommy, hold your breath!" his mother whispered fiercely.

The pastor pressed his lips together, seemingly snuffing out a smile, before he began to read.

Tommy drew in a deep breath and held it. His cheeks stuck out like he had a couple of Ping-Pong balls in there, and the color in his face quickly rose from pale pink to bright red. He leaned against the back of the pew, and the longer he held his breath, the further down in the pew he sank.

"Tommy, sit up straight!"

Tommy bolted upright. He let the air out with a heavy sigh. The pastor removed his glasses, closed the Bible, and started to pray. "Our heavenly Father—"

"Hic!"

"Oh, for heaven's *sake*, Tommy."

"I can't *help* it—"

"Martin, *do* something. . . ."

The man on the far side of her rose, grabbed Tommy's hand, mumbled, "Pardon us," to me, and father and son stumbled out of the pew and down the aisle. One last "Hic!" reached us before they disappeared.

Tommy's mother huffed, fanned herself with the church bulletin, touched at her neatly coiffed hair with one white-gloved hand. She glanced at me, gave me a "Boys will be boys" smile, then turned her attention back to the pastor.

My own gaze went to Howard, sitting sideways to the congregation on the organ bench. His hands were lost in the folds of his copious black gown. The pastor was making some announcements—church picnic to be held the following Sunday afternoon; the ladies' aide society would be hosting a bake sale; contributions for the food shelf could be dropped off at the church office—when Howard turned toward the congregation, settled his eyes on me, and smiled. I smiled in return. Had the first time I'd seen him really been only four days ago?

The pastor named a second hymn, and Howard lifted his hands from their hiding place and struck a chord. The congregation rose. The people around me began to sing while I continued to flip through the hymnal, looking for the page. I sensed the disapproval rolling off the woman next to me even before I saw her scowl out of the corner of my eye. Finding the page at last, I looked at her, smiled apologetically, dared her in my mind to sic Martin on me, and joined in the song.

The sermon that followed was long and tiresome. The pastor was a likeable, animated man, but the warmth of the evening was a harsh competitor. Though large ceiling fans circled quietly overhead, the church was close and stuffy. Only an occasional dusty breath of air drifted in through the open windows. The congregation became a choppy sea of waving church bulletins.

I passed the time alternately gazing at Howard's profile and at the stained-glass Christ frozen in the huge window behind the choir loft. His head had been well illuminated at first, but he grew darker as the sun sank lower and night came on. His eyes, which had gazed intently at the congregation, now seemed to begin a slow closing, as though he too had no choice but to give in to the Mississippi heat.

Finally the sermon ended, we stood for a closing hymn, sat back down for a final blessing, and then people rose to go. The woman beside me exited the pew on the far side without saying a word. Howard hadn't told me where to meet him, so I stayed where I was. A few people who passed by in the aisle smiled at me, nodded, mumbled, "Hello." They seemed reluctant to stop and greet me. Perhaps they thought a spiritual dilemma kept me glued to the seat, staring up at the stained-glass window. But I was really only waiting for their organist to find me and give me a ride home.

After a moment Howard did come to meet me, stepping down from the front of the sanctuary still in his robe. He sat in the pew ahead of me, leaned toward me with his arm on the backrest and said, "I hope you don't mind staying after for just a bit. I have something I want to give you."

I must have looked puzzled, because he explained, "I'd like to play you a few pieces on the organ while we're here. Kind of like a gift, the way your book was a gift to me."

Touched by the offer, I smiled and said, "I'd love that."

"Does it matter what time you get back tonight?"

"Not at all."

When the sanctuary had emptied out, the pastor came up the aisle from the foyer where he'd been greeting people. He wiped at his forehead with a handkerchief. "Hot as usual, eh, Howard?"

"Never seems to get any better," Howard agreed. "I'd like you to meet a friend of mine, Augusta Callahan. Augie, this is Pastor Sherman Keister. I have the privilege of serving with him while the church searches for a new organist."

The pastor held out a hand and clasped mine tightly. "A pleasure to meet you, Miss Callahan. You from around here?"

"No, from Los Angeles," I explained. "I'm just visiting friends in Carver."

"Ah." He lifted his chin, nodded, wiped at his forehead again. "I see you met the Hutchinsons. That was little Tommy there who got the hiccoughs."

"Yes," I said with a laugh. "He caused a bit of a disturbance, I'm afraid."

The pastor shrugged. "That was nothing, compared. Worst when one of the choir members passes out. Now that's even harder to ignore."

"Yeah," Howard agreed. "I hate it when that happens."

"So, Howard, you say you're staying after a bit?"

"If you don't mind. I'd like to show Miss Callahan a little bit more of what the organ can do."

"Go right ahead, Howard. Just turn out the lights when you leave. If you'll excuse me, I sent Meredith on ahead to whip up a fresh batch of iced tea. I think I hear a glass of it calling my name."

"You go on home, Sherm," Howard said amiably. "Put your feet up. Tell Meredith I'm still waiting for her to perform that solo we talked about."

"She says she will, soon as she can get over her stage fright. She says her stomach starts doing somersaults every time she thinks about it."

The pastor chuckled then and left us, unzipping his long robe as he stepped down the aisle.

When he was gone, Howard stood up and said, "You just stay right here while I go hang up this robe. Then I'll play you a few tunes."

"Should I come up to the organ?"

He shook his head. "That's too close. It'll sound better right here where you are. I won't be a minute."

I nodded and watched him disappear up the aisle and out a door near the front of the sanctuary. Then he reappeared without the robe and seated himself at the organ. He fiddled with a few stops on the large console, pressed a chord, looked at me, and at last began to play.

I recognized the songs he chose—or rather, the composers. Bach, I think, followed by Dvořák, then Pachelbel, then Schubert. There I sat, the sole member of his audience, as the notes, sweet and gentle, washed over me. Darkness came on, not fully, but falling, even as Howard played his way once more into my soul.

I wanted to stop time, to let that moment be my eternity. I

wanted to stay there forever in that cradle of song, Howard's gift to me. *So this is what it must feel like to be loved,* I thought.

But the taste of love was a short-lived sweetness, overshadowed just as quickly by the bitterness of what my life really was. As I listened to Howard play, the years rolled out before me like a scroll rolled out across a table, filled with odd scratches and marks the color of old wounds. I looked at those years, at all they contained: my father's old Plymouth colliding with a train; my mother's alcoholic breath in my face, calling me Lenny; the burning tip of Stephen's cigarette as he tells me he is off to kill the Japs. Uncle Finn's tirades, and the crucifix jumping on the wall. The empty shell of the Yamagatas' house on the morning they catch the train to an overcrowded camp. The promise, "We'll be back," and Stella and the Liddels and Jimmy Durante and "Good night, Mrs. Calabash," and my dog, Jimmy, licking the tears off my face. Waiting on the bench in front of Chichi's store. Watching and waiting. Waiting and waiting. And in place of the Yamagatas, a dead man coming home, a man as good as dead after his interim as guest of the empire of Japan. And finally the sound of a door slamming shut. The sound of a door being bolted and double bolted, and bolted yet again. Then silence.

I became an island, proving John Donne wrong. No man was an island, he said, but I was. The only friends I wanted were books; the only love I wanted was work. Books don't leave, and work doesn't make promises it fails to keep.

Howard played, night came on, and in one awful moment I realized that the place I had locked myself into for so many years was not solitude at all, but loneliness. I had imagined it a lofty place, this artist's solitude, this cozy corner where the Muse and I lingered and plotted and schemed, creating our little world of words. But it was only an empty room after all, with nothing in it. Nothing but my own cloistered and well-protected self.

So when had I turned the final bolt and stopped living? When had I chosen simply to go through the motions? Because I was as dead as Lenny when he came home from the war, and I didn't even know when I had died. I didn't know whether it had been a sudden death or a long drawn-out dying. I knew only that I was no longer alive, because what was life without love?

I had come tonight wanting to look into the heart of Howard

Draper, to find out what was real and what was not. Instead, I saw the center of my own self, stripped of illusions, scraped clear of all deceptive debris. I was Lenny, the walking dead, bumping up against the walls of my own tomb. It had been comfortable for a time, but I wasn't sure I could be satisfied there now, not after glimpsing what things might be like on the outside, where the living moved together through the rhythm of their days.

Could I go back to California and stop the game of make-believe, stop trying to be the self-sufficient island? Could I try to break out of the vault, take some risks by opening myself up to the relationships that were the normal foundation of most people's lives?

If so, then, unlike Lenny, maybe I could live again.

The music stopped, the final chord lingering a moment before drifting off into silence. Then there was only the whirling of the fans and the night songs from outside and the rush of my own blood in my ears.

I stood. Howard too rose from the organ, came down the aisle, and took my hand.

"Thank you, Howard," I whispered.

His only reply was to lift my hand to his lips and kiss it.

The ache in my heart let me know that, after all the years of dying, at least a small part of me remained alive enough to feel the pain.

THIRTY-FIVE

We drove along in a comfortable silence, the windows rolled down, the car bumping over a lengthy stretch of dirt road that would bring us to the two-lane highway leading to Carver. The only light came from the Volkswagen itself, since there weren't any streetlights, nor any sign of the moon. Even with the high beams on, our whole world was reduced to a dark, treelined tunnel, and the road ahead was revealed to us in small increments measured out by the headlights.

I still felt the warmth of Howard's hand on mine, the sensation of his lips pressed lightly against the back of my fingers. I was both happy and unhappy, and wondering still what was at the core of Howard Draper. There had to be something that made sense of all the sense-lessness, some explanation for his involvement with the Klan. In a twisted attempt at comfort, I told myself that if he really was a dedicated night rider, at least it would be easier to let him go. I couldn't imagine any other ending to our story than that of letting go.

We had driven for ten, maybe fifteen, minutes without passing another car when we rounded a curve in the road and saw a light about a quarter mile ahead. It was a single, stationary light that cast a dull glow, and only after a moment could we fully make out the truck parked alongside the road. The hood was up and a man leaned over the engine. A woman stood nearby, holding a kerosene lamp in one hand and balancing a small child on her opposite hip.

I looked at Howard, who appeared to be assessing the situation. "Looks like engine trouble," he said quietly. "I'm not much of a mechanic, but I'll see if I can do anything."

"Do you know them?" I asked.

He shook his head. "I can't quite make out who they are, but I don't think so."

Just before we reached the stranded truck, Howard pulled the Volkswagen over to the side of the road and left it idling. The beam of the headlights melted into the glow of the kerosene lamp, so that we could see the long hollow face of the woman, the balding dome of the man's head bent over the engine. "You stay here," Howard said.

He looked at me a moment, then reached for the door handle. When he did, I wanted to grab his arm and say, "Let's just go on, Howard. There's nothing we can do. . . ." But they were a family in trouble, a man and his wife and a little child, and Howard was right to stop. I didn't know why I was suddenly afraid, except that this was Mississippi, where things too often were not what they appeared, where the hate in the air was so thick it was thicker than the air itself, where nigger and nigger lover alike turned up missing, only to be found days or months or maybe years later all tangled up in the saw grass of some isolated bayou.

But then, what did that have to do with us, a white couple stopping to help a white family with engine trouble? I let Howard go without saying a word.

"Evening, friends," he called out, closing the car door behind him. "What seems to be the problem?"

The woman turned and shifted the lantern toward Howard. The child on her hip let out a wail and rubbed an eye with one fat fist. The man beneath the hood straightened up, pulled something from his back pocket, a rag that he used to wipe his hands.

Nobody spoke. Howard took a step closer. "I'm no mechanic, but I can make a call from town, send someone out if you'd like."

The only reply was the chirping of crickets and tree frogs somewhere in the woods. The man said nothing, just went on wiping his hands.

I leaned forward in the seat, watching Howard. He had stopped halfway between the Volkswagen and the truck. His elongated shadow, cast by the car's headlights, merged with the dark road ahead, as though Howard himself were melting into the darkness. For a moment no one moved, making the scene an odd tableau, a freeze-frame of a dark night on a little-traveled road in rural Mississippi. I was the invisible onlooker, lost behind the headlights, the unseen passenger in the Volkswagen. I lifted a hand to the door handle. I wanted to open the door and call Howard back, tell him these people would have to fend for themselves if they couldn't even manage to acknowledge him, return his greeting, say *something*.

Instead, I waited.

The woman turned to the man and spoke in a low voice. The man slammed shut the hood. Craning his neck toward the bed of the truck, he growled out an expletive, then demanded, "Get up!"

Howard, startled by the cry, moved one foot backward but didn't complete the step. He lifted his chin and watched as the figure of a man appeared over the roof of the truck. He was little more than a silhouette rising up out of the bed, half hidden behind the cab. He lifted a shadowy bottle to his lips, emptied it, hurled it into the woods. The glass shattered against a tree while the man wiped his mouth with his sleeve. He weaved, then steadied himself.

Howard completed the step backward, started another.

The man beside the truck cursed again before yelling, "Get on with it, Wilman!"

Howard completed the second step.

The man named Wilman placed his left hand on the roof of the cab to steady himself. "Nigger!" he yelled.

His raised his right arm, stretching it out in front of him. Lantern light glinted off the barrel of a gun aimed toward the road where Howard stood.

"Go on, Wilman!" The man on the ground went on cursing both God and the shadowy figure in the truck.

"Nigger!" Wilman held the gun in both hands now, weaved to one side, righted himself.

Howard turned to look at me over his shoulder. His body started to follow suit, a slow swinging around of arms, hips, feet, a motion abruptly interrupted when the gun exploded. I screamed, watching in horror as Howard first stiffened, then started to crumple, his face in the headlights a mask of surprise and agony. He fell with his hand over his heart.

I heard the truck's engine start, heard the grinding of gears, heard the child in the cab crying and the man in the bed laughing, but all of this reached me through a haze—the sounds tinny and faraway as though coming from an old radio turned down low—while I rushed from the car to where Howard lay sprawled in the dirt.

"Oh, God! Oh, God!" The words were automatic, bypassing my brain and rising straight up out of my heart. "Oh, God! Oh, God in heaven . . ."

The pickup sped past as I knelt on the road beside Howard. His eyes were open. I lifted his head onto my lap, slowly, carefully. His right hand lay flat across his sky-blue shirt, now dark as midnight with his blood. His eyes rolled up slowly until they met mine. They held no fear, not even sadness, only a subtle intensity, as though he were trying to memorize my face, to take it with him.

"Howard," I whispered. I cupped my palm over his forehead, placed my other hand over his own bloodied hand on his chest. "Howard, I—" I wanted to tell him that I didn't understand, that only a moment ago he was playing the organ for me in the Baptist church, and now, all of a sudden, he was lying in his own blood on a dirt road, shot by someone who had mistaken him for a Negro.

Yes, that was it. There'd been a terrible mistake. We'd obviously happened upon a setup, a trap no doubt arranged by the Klan for some unwitting Negro. And Howard had come along instead.

And yet, couldn't even one of those people see that Howard Draper was a white man, not the Negro they'd been waiting for? Maybe the gunman had been too blind drunk to tell the difference, but surely, even in the dim light, the other man and woman could see that Howard was white.

Why then, in the name of heaven, did they allow the gunman to pump a bullet into Howard Draper?

A car pulled up behind us, and a man and a woman got out. They began talking in feverish tones, but I don't know what they said. I scarcely heard anything at all. I was barely aware of anything except that Howard's eyes had closed, and that from this moment forward I would carry with me the image of Howard Draper dying on a lonesome backwoods road in a cruel and bitter place called Mississippi.

THIRTY-SIX

There's something holy about the dawn, those first moments when a crack appears in the night and the initial dim hue of daylight seeps in and slowly begins to rise. It's a resurrection of sorts, a rising up to life from out of the depths of sleep. It's the opening of the eyes, the awakening of awareness, the breathing in of heaven's breath, without which there would be no life at all.

I saw the morning come, the morning of the day after Howard was shot. It arrived as silently as a cat slinking in on airy paws across the grass. From Sunny's porch I watched the darkness recede as the sun came around again toward one more day. I hadn't slept at all. Since sometime after midnight I'd been sitting in this chair, rocking, listening, peering out at the moonless night, trying to find a way to speak to a God I'd never spoken to before.

Then, after the long dark hours, the dawn came, bringing its light, and bringing too something hushed, invisible, and yet distinctly there. A sense that if the well-designed order in the universe could assure the daily dependable rising of the sun, then the movements of my own small life as well were hinged on something other than chance. Something besides chance had brought me even to this moment, to Sunny Yamagata's porch in Mississippi on a July morning in 1965.

I watched the light rise, invading grass and trees and porch, and at length revealing even me sitting there in the same dress I'd worn the night before, the pale yellow dress now stained with Howard Draper's blood. But it was all right. There was order in my chaos, and I was at peace.

The early morning stillness was interrupted finally by the sound of an approaching car, a too loud engine needing a tune-up, four bald tires spinning over dirt. After a moment, an old brown station wagon turned into the Fultons' drive, the same car that had come to the house the night the front windows were shot out.

When the car came to a stop, Lee Henry Starks climbed out of the driver's seat. He nodded at me while barely lifting his eyes, then went around to help his passenger out of the car. Miss Ebba accepted his hand, swung her small feet down to the dusty ground, tried once, twice, and then yet again to pull herself up. Finally she stood, and Lee Henry reached past her into the car for her cane.

I rose to meet them. Lee Henry, one arm around Miss Ebba's waist, his other hand gripping her elbow, helped his grandmother shuffle from the car to the foot of the steps. She seemed to have become even smaller and more wizened in only a matter of days. She paused there at the bottom of the steps and raised her one eye to me, that imposing eye that seemed to see everything, even the unseen. It settled briefly on my bloodied dress, then lifted to my face. Miss Ebba swallowed hard while the cane trembled under her hand.

"He be dead, Miz Callahan?" she asked hoarsely.

"No, Miss Ebba," I assured her. "He's still alive."

"Bless de Lawd," the woman breathed out, a praise that was little more than a sigh. She raised a hand to her heart, and her knees must have weakened at the same time because she leaned heavily against Lee Henry for a moment. Then the two of them started the slow climb up the steps, a carefully choreographed dance of feet and cane.

When they reached the porch and stood facing me, I asked, "Miss Ebba, who is Howard Draper?"

She blinked her yellow watery eye. "Chile," she said, "dat what I come to tell ya. Where's Mister 'n Miz Fulton?"

"Sleeping. They went to bed only a few hours ago."

"Wake 'em up, chile. Dey need hear dis too."

I looked to Lee Henry for direction. He nodded. The three of us moved through the front door into the living room. Ten minutes later, Sunny and Tom were seated with us, hastily dressed. A pot of coffee was brewing in the kitchen.

Miss Ebba, dwarfed by the large easy chair in which she sat, clutched at the cane laid across her lap. She peered at each one of us in turn before she spoke, as though to make sure she had our attention. And then she began.

"No one knowed," she said, her voice still hoarse, her empty eyelid winking, "who Howard Draper wuz. Not eben Lee Henry." Lee Henry shook his head solemnly in agreement. "Had to be dat way. Uh-huh, had to be dat way."

She paused, her mouth working, as though she were chewing on her words to make them come out more easily. I leaned forward in the wing chair where I sat, waiting.

"Long time ago," she continued, "bad thing happen to my granddaughter, cousin to Lee Henry. She wuz walkin' home from her job down to the mill one ev'ning when she met up wid a group a white men. Weren't de Klan, jes' three young white boys ever'body woulda said wuz decent young men. Dey'd jes' graduated high school and were gon' start college come fall. But like so many young'uns, when dey git to drinkin', dey do foolish things, harmful things." She shook her head, gripping the cane in gnarled fists. "Raped my grandbaby, dose three boys. Done drag her in da woods and took turns wid her, and she hardly more'n a chile herself. But she end up pregnant, end up expectin' de baby a one dose white men.

"Now, her mama—dat be my daughter Hattie—she knowed dat baby gon' end up quadroon, chile of a white and a mulatto. She knowed dat coz de father white and my granddaughter half white. My daughter Hattie knowed what it wuz be taken by a white man. My granddaughter's daddy weren't Hattie's husband. Jes' a white man passin' by, passin' time, having his way wid a niggerwoman and leavin' her wid child.

"Das how Trudy born. Truf wuz, Trudy so light she almost be passin' herself. Almost, but not quite. But Hattie, she knowed Trudy baby gon' be more white den black and knowed he had a chance a passin' for sho. Hattie wuz maid to some good white folk, kind people, and dey help her 'range for dat baby be 'dopted by a white couple up north. Even 'fore she start showin', 'fore anyone knowed she got a baby growin' in her, Trudy's on a train headed to Chicagie.

" 'Go on, girl,' Hattie tole her. 'Go on, and don' neber look back.' After dat, we neber saw Trudy 'gain. But she wrote, let us know she had a baby boy, and de white couple hired her on to help raise de baby. Trudy said she wuz like de mother a Moses, raisin' her own son eben though he been 'dopted by rich folks."

She paused a moment, letting her one eye fall over each of us. "I ain't gotta tell ya, dat boy growed up to be Howard Draper." And again she was quiet, as though to let her revelation sink in. No one spoke. The coffee was forgotten; we didn't need it. We were wide awake without it.

"Howard knowed from early on he wuz 'dopted, jes' din't know de circumstance o' how it come 'bout. Not till after he wuz long growed and his parents dead did Trudy tell him de truf, dat she his mother. It wuz den Howard start thinkin' on comin' down to Carver. Wuz den what his mother said years 'fore come true—he wuz like Moses sho 'nuff, 'dopted into riches but givin' it up to set his peoples free. He coulda stayed where he wuz, coulda gon' on livin' like a white man, but he couldn't see it, he said. Said he couldn't live in de luxury o' de white north whilst his peoples still treated like slaves down south.

"And so he come. Trudy begged and pleaded wid him, but he come anyway. Come and found me and said, 'I'se yor great-grandson, Trudy's son. I need yor help.' He had hisself dis idea, gon' join de Klan, gon' go de meetin's, find out der plans and warns de Nigra folk 'forehand. He need me be de one give de warnings. Crazy ole nigger-woman havin' dreams, God tellin' her de Klan's secret doin's. I could see der wuz no talkin' Howard outta it. I said I'd help him.

"Dat what we been doin'. He hear sumpin' at de Klan meetin', he come tell me. I go on, wake up Lee Henry, have him take me where I need goin'. Somes listen, somes don't. Dem dat listen to me hab a chance, be ready for de Klan."

An unshed tear magnified her eye but didn't spill over. Her jaw worked again as she composed herself. Quietly, she said, "Der weren't no one to give me no warning 'bout Howard. I couldn't give no warning to my own great-grandbaby when de Klan had plans for him."

Miss Ebba's voice drifted off into silence. The house was still. We were all there, but in that moment, briefly, we were not together. We had each entered into ourselves to gather our individual thoughts, to come to terms with what we were hearing.

To me things finally started to make sense. Howard Draper was a Negro passing for white. That explained how such a man as he—with compassion in his voice and poetry in his heart—could be a member of the Klan. That explained the photo of a beloved Negro woman in his wallet. That explained why a drunken redneck aimed a gun at Howard while spitting out the word "nigger."

Tom suddenly stood and strode to the windows. The shattered glass had been replaced with new panes only the day before. Tom gazed through the glass toward the lawn for a long while. Finally, turning back to us, he said, "So somehow they discovered who Howard was and what he was doing."

"Somehow," Miss Ebba croaked, nodding.

Tom turned to the window again, leaned one arm against the frame and rested his chin on his sleeve. "So that's what happened, why he was shot," he said quietly. "The Klan decided they had to silence him."

" 'Course, Mr. Fulton," Miss Ebba said simply.

"Didn't he know it would probably come to this?"

"He knowed, all right. But weren't no changin' Howard's mind. Lawd knows I tried more'n once."

"I'm surprised the Klan would have trusted someone from the North in the first place," Sunny remarked. "You'd think they'd be suspicious right off the bat."

Lee Henry stuck out his lower lip in thought. Then he said, "They was probly thrilled to have themselves a nigger-hatin' northerner."

"Dey's Klan up north too, chile," Miss Ebba added. "And anyways, Howard played it like dey's recruitin' him, not other way 'round. For long time he went 'round passin' time a day wid men he figgers Klan, meetin' up wid dem at de pool hall, or mabbe in one o' da bars, says things makes 'em think he hate niggers. Oh, dey com after him, all right. Prac'ly beg him join up. He act first like he don' wan' do it, bidin' his time, lettin' 'em think dey talkin' him into it. He wuz in Carver a year 'fore he told 'em he'd join."

When Miss Ebba finished, Lee Henry said, " 'Scuse me, Mr. Fulton, but is Howard still in the hospital here in Carver? Coz if he is and the Klan find out . . ." He didn't need to finish his sentence for us to understand where his thought was going.

Tom shook his head. "After he was stabilized at the hospital here, he was taken by ambulance to Jackson for surgery. The one surgeon who might have been able to perform the operation here was unavailable."

To my surprise Lee Henry looked relieved. "He better off in Jackson."

Miss Ebba explained. " 'Bout four months ago, Howard started talkin' wid de FBI down 'n Jackson, passin' on what he knowed 'bout de Klan. De FBI dere been tryin' git info'mation on de Klan awhile now, and Howard knowed he could help. Howard said he had a man der name o' Gary Colscott. You got let him know 'bout Howard, Mr. Fulton. See if'n dey cain't do sumpin'."

Tom nodded. "Good idea, Miss Ebba. Murder—and attempted murder too, I suppose—is outside the FBI's jurisdiction, but maybe they'd be willing to offer Howard some protection while he's laid up. I'll find out the number of their office in Jackson and call them this morning. Gary Colscott, you say?"

"Dat's de one."

Gary was the name of the man who'd brought my book up from Jackson for Howard. Howard's "friend" was an FBI agent. One more piece falling into place.

"But Miss Ebba," Sunny broke in, "are you sure we can trust him? Aren't some of the FBI as bad as the Klan? I mean, they claim to be on the side of civil rights and all that, but for fifty cents they'd meet the Klan after dark and join them in a lynching. Maybe this Gary Colscott was in on the shooting."

Miss Ebba shook her head. "Don' think so, chile. It be true some FBI men hate niggers much as de Klan do. But dis Colscott fellow, Howard said we kin trust him. Said dat Gary, he a good 'n honest man. Howard, he has a way o' knowin'."

"Miss Ebba," I asked, speaking up for the first time, "how did you know to come here? I mean, how did you know we'd know anything about what happened to Howard last night?"

"I knowed you were wid him last night, Miz Callahan. He tole me the two you gon' dat Baptist church where he play de organ Wen'day nights."

"And how did you know he'd been shot?"

Lee Henry answered my question. "Nigra name o' Albert Vick works cleanup nights over to the hospital. He pass the word round Coloredtown that Howard come in wounded. 'Course most ever'one in Coloredtown thinks Howard's Klan. Don' know he's a Nigra passin'. People probly whoopin' it up right now, thinkin' the Klan shot one their own."

Tom started pacing the room. Sunny leaned forward in her chair. "They need to know who Howard Draper is, Lee Henry. We need to tell them."

Lee Henry looked at Sunny with heavy eyes. "What you suggest, Miz Fulton?"

"Lee Henry, you a preacher, ain't you?" Miss Ebba said suddenly.

"Yes'm."

"Den you gotta call a prayer meetin' at de church, call prayer meetin' for Howard and tell ever'one ever'thing 'bout him." She looked over at Sunny and Tom. "How bad off he be, do you know?"

"Well, when we called the hospital at about four o'clock this morning," Tom replied, "he'd just come out of surgery. He'd come through all right, but the doctor said he isn't quite out of the woods yet. There's always the chance of infection, though right now things look good. The doctor did say Howard was lucky. The bullet went in his upper back and straight out the front near the hollow of his shoulder. It didn't even come close to the heart or any major arteries on the way through. It was a pretty clean wound, far as that goes."

Lee Henry asked, "Those people know the man they put back together was a Nigra?"

Tom snorted quietly, suddenly amused. "Unless word traveled beyond the Klan, I imagine the hospital has him listed as white."

"Good thing," Lee Henry said. "They give him better lookin' after, thinkin' he a white man."

None of us had gone to Jackson with him, though Tom and I were at the hospital in Carver when the ambulance took Howard away. The couple who had stopped on the dirt road after the shooting had driven Howard and me to the hospital, where right away I'd called Sunny and Tom. While Sunny stayed with the children, Tom came to be with me and bring me home. Just as Howard was taken to Jackson, a police officer named Stuart Dunberry showed up to take my story and to get a statement from the couple who'd acted as ambulance drivers. While we spoke, Officer Dunberry seemed disinterested or distracted, maybe both. He fidgeted in his chair and picked at a large scab on the back of his hand. Even when I told him the first name of the man who'd pulled the trigger, he didn't bother to write it down. Instead, he'd shrugged and drawled, "Don't know no Wilmans 'round heah, Miss Callahan."

Now I understood why he wasn't interested in finding Wilman. Stuart Dunberry no doubt knew what I didn't know myself, that Howard was a Negro passing. I turned to Sunny. "Didn't you tell me the chief of police in Carver is in the Klan?"

Sunny nodded. "Bill Sturges. He's not just in the Klan, he's Exalted Cyclops of the Carver Klavern."

"Klan infiltration into law enforcement is greater than you can imagine," Tom added. "To the point almost that if you attended a Klan meeting and took away the hoods, you'd think you were down at police headquarters attending a staff meeting there."

"No wonder that Officer Dunberry wasn't interested in taking my statement last night," I noted.

I could well imagine Stuart Dunberry going back to the station and enjoying a good laugh with Chief Sturges over the downing of Howard Draper. Enraged at the thought, my one consolation was that their victory had been shortchanged. Their hit man had gotten so drunk he couldn't shoot straight. Had Wilman been sober and his aim more accurate, Howard Draper would most likely be dead.

"Wouldn't Dunberry know that Howard's been sent on to Jackson?" I asked.

Tom looked at the clock on the mantle. It was just before seven. "It's early, but I'll try to rouse the FBI right now, see if they can send someone out for security."

Tom left and I commented to no one in particular, "So I guess it's safe to assume the Carver police aren't going to try to find the man who shot Howard."

Lee Henry laughed at that, a hard and bitter laugh. "Find him? The police probly partyin' with the man right now. No sir, Miz Callahan, ain't gonna see no justice in Carver for the shootin' of a nigger, no matter how white his skin look."

"He's still in danger," Sunny interjected. "Danger from the Klan and from the gunshot wound both."

"I'll call a meetin' for tonight," Lee Henry assured her, "both to pray for Howard and to tell the folks in Coloredtown who he is. I'll get the word goin' 'round soon as we git home."

"And you, Miss Ebba," Sunny added, "maybe you shouldn't go home. You could be in danger too. Since the Klan found out about Howard, they probably know about your role in all of this too. Maybe you should stay here with us, at least for a while."

Miss Ebba smiled for the first time that morning. "I 'ppreciate yor concern, Miz Fulton," she said, "but ya'll don' need worry 'bout me none. I be jes' fine." She laughed, a throaty little laugh, before going on. "I'se ninety-six-years old. How much longer kin I have on dis earf? If'n dose men in der bed sheets wanna come round and send me on ta glory few days 'head o' my time, das all right by me."

Sunny smiled even while she shook her head. "Are you sure you'll be all right, Miss Ebba? You're welcome to stay."

"I stay heah, chile, and you be payin' for new front windows 'gain." She smiled widely, showing her yellowed teeth. Then, more quietly, she added, "I ain't 'fraid, Miz Fulton. Ain't 'fraid to live, ain't 'fraid to die. Either way, I'se in de Lawd's hands."

"Miss Ebba, how was it that Howard could be in the Klan and yet not actually be involved in—what would you call it—their activities?" I asked.

"You mean floggin' and rapin' and killin'?"

I nodded.

"Dey got a special group, call demselves Klavaliers, do most dat kinda work. Gotta get invited ta be part of de Klavaliers. Howard weren't part of dat group. He go to meetin's, rallies, picnics, dat sort of thing. Paid his dues, keep de higher-ups happy. Not ever'one in de Klan gotta go round breakin' open niggers' heads."

Tom returned then, and we looked at him expectantly. "Reached an answering service," he said. "I left a message for Gary Colscott. He should be calling soon."

"I hope it'll be soon enough," Sunny said.

Tom sat down again, looking even more fatigued than when I had awakened him. "What a mess," he muttered. "And to think when I came back to Mississippi I thought maybe I could avoid the Klan this time around."

"I wonder how they found out about Howard," I said.

"No tellin', chile." Miss Ebba shook her head. "No tellin'."

"They're all investigated by the Klan, everyone who applies for membership," Tom said. "I guess I'm just surprised no one found out about him sooner."

"And like you said, Tom," Sunny added, "Howard must have known he'd be investigated. He must have known it would only be a matter of time before he'd be found out."

"And that's part of the oath," Lee Henry pointed out. "Death to anyone tells the secrets of the Klan. Death at the hands of the brothers."

The words turned my blood cold, made me shiver in the heat. "And yet he did it anyway," I said quietly.

Miss Ebba positioned her cane on the floor between her feet and tried to lift herself up. Lee Henry jumped to help her. "We got git word 'round 'bout de prayer meetin' tonight. You folks gon' come?" She looked at the three white faces in the room.

"We'll be there, Miss Ebba," Sunny promised.

Miss Ebba nodded, satisfied. She took a step forward, stopped, looked around at each of us again. "Oh, one more thing you might wanna know. The men raped Trudy? One o' dem de mayor. Mighta been Cedric Frohmann's own seed got Trudy wid chile."

For a moment I couldn't speak. "Does he know," I finally muttered, "does Howard know the mayor may be his father?"

Miss Ebba nodded. "He knows." She lifted her thumb to her chin to indicate the dimple the two men shared. "He knows."

Tom and Sunny exchanged a look, shook their heads. Lee Henry helped Miss Ebba to the front door. I followed so I could shut the door behind them.

Before they stepped out to the porch, Miss Ebba laid a hand on my arm, an old black beautiful hand. "Chile," she said quietly, looking up at me with kindness shining in that one eye, "de Klan weren't de only thing Howard talk wid me 'bout. You pray for him, Miz Callahan. He needs yor prayers."

I nodded once, making a promise to do what I didn't know how to do. "We were lucky," I said, "to be on that road an hour later than the Klan expected. If I hadn't been with Howard, he'd have been driving home at the usual time, and Wilman might have been sober enough to shoot straight."

I smiled, but Miss Ebba didn't. She looked very serious when she said, "Weren't luck, chile. God's hand protectin' Howard."

"Then surely he'll be all right," I reasoned.

"We don' know de ways o' God," the old woman replied. "Only God decide if Howard live or die."

"But he's kept Howard safe this far——"

Miss Ebba patted my hand. "You jes' pray, chile. Pray it be de Lawd's will he live."

She squeezed my arm, then moved with Lee Henry across the porch, down the steps, into the brown station wagon. The sun was above the trees now, the dew was gone, the cool of the morning had lifted, and the air had turned warm. I watched the station wagon head for the road, watched the dust and dirt rise in its trail. *"Here in dust and dirt . . ."* I thought, remembering the poem Shidzuyo quoted to Sunny in the camp. *"Oh here, the lilies of his love appear."*

I went upstairs and lay across my bed, remembering the ride to the hospital——Howard lying unconscious on the backseat of a stranger's car, I squatting on the floor beside him. I had watched him breathe, watched every rise and fall of his chest, afraid to turn my eyes away in case, when I looked back, he might not be breathing anymore.

I shut my eyes against the memory. After a moment I told myself to get up and get out of the bloody dress and put on something clean. But I was too tired to move. I felt myself drifting, was startled and amazed momentarily as I thought again, "So Howard Draper is a Negro passing," then fell like a spiraling autumn leaf into a deep and troubled sleep.

THIRTY-SEVEN

I slept fitfully for much of the day, not waking up until midafternoon, when I finally showered and put on a clean dress. Sunny and I were in the kitchen making supper when Tom called from the mill saying he wasn't going to make it home in time to go to the prayer meeting.

"Go on without me," he said. "I'm trying to contain a few fires around here before things get out of hand."

Things had been heating up at the mill lately, Sunny explained after the call, because half the mill workers were trying to unionize while the other half were Klan or pro-Klan, which meant they were anti-union. "One more challenge for Tom Fulton in the normal course of life in 1960s Mississippi," Sunny concluded.

After supper we dropped the children off at their grandmother's and drove on to Coloredtown to attend the meeting. On the way Sunny gave me a sideways smile and said, "You were right, you know, about Howard. You said he wasn't Klan, and he wasn't. But how did you know?"

Without pause I replied, "He and I are kindred spirits." It was the only explanation I could give, and she didn't ask for more.

The "culud" Baptist church was unlike the Baptist church in Lucasville where Howard had played the organ the night before, and unlike the Methodist church in Carver that the Fultons and the mayor and anyone else who wasn't Negro or Catholic or Jewish might attend on Sunday mornings. This church where Lee Henry served as preacher was a one-room building of unpainted wood that looked as though it might cave in on itself if somebody sneezed too hard. Five loose steps of daringly balanced cinder blocks led up to the front door. Half the windowpanes were broken or missing, a series of bare bulbs dangled from exposed wires in the ceiling, and the floor sagged in the middle, right down the aisle, like the swayed back of a broken-down work-horse. The upright piano in front lacked a number of white keys and appeared to be so ancient and dilapidated that surely its days were numbered. Instead of pews, the room was crowded with benches lined up in neat rows. There were no fans to keep the air circulating, so the building was hot and close and stuffy. The only redeeming feature was a beautifully carved and polished cross on the wall behind the table that served as an altar.

When Sunny and I arrived, a beautiful young woman was singing while Gloria Reese accompanied her on the piano. The soloist's eyes were shut, her chin lifted slightly, her tongue showing pink against her white teeth as her rich soprano voice lifted up and over the room clear as the sound of wind chimes on a cold night.

"*Precious Lord, take my hand, Lead me on, help me stand . . .*"

Sunny and I stood just inside the door, listening to her from across the room of swaying backs, bobbing hats, fluttering hand-held fans. The benches were packed solid from end to end while still more people sat on the floor along the walls. I glanced at my watch. We were right on time, but all these people had arrived ahead of us, and they weren't even sure why they were there. They knew only that a special prayer meeting had been called, and so they had come.

"*Thru the storm, thru the night, Lead me on to the light . . .*"

And still they came, so that faces clustered at the windows, round dark eyes peering in from the outside to see whether there was any more room.

"*Take my hand, precious Lord, lead me home.*"

When the song was finished, the two women returned quietly to their seats while the congregation showered them with cries of "Amen, sisters," and "Bless de Lawd." Lee Henry rose from his seat in the front row, and when he turned, he saw Sunny and me hesitating in the doorway, wondering where to sit. He waved us down the center aisle, indicating with a nod that there was room on a bench for us up front. We stepped lightly down the sloping walkway, two white women cutting through a sea of black faces. Curtis Reese was there with his nephew Mahlon Jackson and a whole row of youngsters that must have been Curtis and Gloria's children. T. W. Foss was there, sitting with Bo Wiley and Eddie Schoby. I didn't spot them but later learned that Luella and Susannah were also among the crowd. I recognized the Robinson brothers who owned the funeral home and remembered one or two other faces from the citizenship school. As we moved forward, Sunny and I were greeted with smiles and nods, along with a few expressions of curiosity.

We found space on the front row beside Miss Ebba and squeezed ourselves in. Lee Henry, at the altar now, smiled, nodded, and said, "Thank you, Sister Anita, Sister Gloria, for that beautiful song." Then he opened an enormous Bible on the altar and stared at it in silence for what seemed a long while. In spite of the heat he was wearing a well-worn suit and tie, and sweat rolled down the sides of his face, down his neck, onto the stiff starched collar of his clean white shirt.

"Brothers and sisters," he began quietly. He finally looked up then and walked around to the front of the altar, his eyes scanning the congregation like two searchlights trying to cut through heavy fog. "Brothers and sisters," he began again, "we's here tonight because a man needs our prayers, a man we mighta once sworn stood against us, but a man who was for us all the while. A man who left his home up north, who left behind a good life to come down to Miss'ssippi to help his people, same way Moses left Pharoah's palace to help the Jews find the Promised Land."

His gaze moved from one side of the church to the other and back again. The hush that had settled over the place was unnerving. Little snakes of sweat began to slither down my own back. Lee Henry went on.

"The man I'm talkin' 'bout tonight is Howard Draper."

Behind me a few gasps rose, followed by whispers that rippled over the room and brought the word "Klan" to my ears.

"Some of you all know by now, some don't," Lee Henry said, "who Howard Draper is and what he done. If you don't know, I'm here to tell ya. Listen up, friends."

I could sense the congregation leaning forward on the benches just as I had leaned forward in the wing chair early that morning while listening to Miss Ebba. The faces in the window to my right drew closer as the listeners there strained to catch every word.

Lee Henry started to pace as he spoke. "Two years ago, Howard Draper left Chicago, left his home, and come on down to Carver. He left that big city, he left his work, and he come all the way down here to Carver, Miss'ssippi. Now, you might ask, why? Why would any white man do that? Why would any white man come here, to a no-place town like Carver, Miss'ssippi?"

He paused, seemingly waiting for an answer, though no one ventured a guess as to why a white man would leave the North to come to Carver, Mississippi. "I'll tell you why," Lee Henry said at last. "Howard Draper come down here because he not a white man. Howard Draper a Nigra, jes' like you 'n me."

More gasps, and someone cried, "Lawdamercy, cain't be true!"

"Is true!" Lee Henry called back. "Howard Draper a Nigra! He my own cousin! He Miss Ebba's great-grandson, son o' her granddaughter, a woman some you mighta knowed once, Trudy Loomis. His skin may look white as any white man in Carver, but in his veins runs culud blood. And you all know, any man got culud blood be a Nigra, no matter if his skin be like Snow White. He still a culud man."

"What dis all about, Lee Henry?"

I turned to see a white-haired, neatly dressed man spring up from a bench near the center of the church. He held a weathered fedora in both hands over his chest, kneading the rim as he waited for an answer.

"I'm gittin' to it, Solomon," Lee Henry said. "Sit yourself back down and give me time. I'll tell ya everything you's needin' to know."

But the man didn't sit. "I'se heard tell Howard Draper ridin' wid de Klan. What you sayin' he a Nigra? He yor kin?"

"Howard Draper *was* Klan." One large gasp escaped the congregation, but Lee Henry ignored it. "Sit yourself, Solomon. Give a man a chance."

"Sit yourself down, Solomon, so's we can heah Lee Henry out," a woman chided. It must have been his wife, because Solomon sat.

But even as he sat, another wave of murmurs rolled over the room, cresting in one person's cry of, "Lee Henry telling de truf, Miss Ebba? Howard Draper yor kin?"

Miss Ebba pulled herself up with her cane and did a slow shuffle to the front of the room. She straightened herself up to her full height, drew in a deep breath. "Dis man yor pastor," she chided quietly, nodding toward Lee Henry. "Been yor pastor goin' on twenny year now. You knowed better den to ask me dis man be lyin' to you."

"Mama?" A woman in the front row raised a tentative hand. She was seated beside me, just beyond the gap left by Miss Ebba. I hadn't noticed her until she spoke. "Let me tell 'em, Mama."

Miss Ebba looked startled. "You sho, Hattie?"

In response Hattie rose and moved forward. When she stood beside Miss Ebba, it was easy to see that she was the older woman's daughter. She was taller and heavyset, but still the resemblance was unmistakable. "Lee Henry ain't lying," she stated quietly but firmly. "Somes you too young to 'member, but somes you was here when I sent my baby girl off to Chicagie. When she lef, Trudy was carryin' a white man's chile." Her eyes clouded over, but her voice remained strong. "Din't never want no one to know, but now you know. And now that chile done come home. I'se only jes' now learnt mysef that Howard Draper my grandson. Only learnt jes' today. I'se proud o' him, o' what he done."

She fell silent and looked around the room. After a moment a woman's voice reached her. "We's wid ya, Hattie, honey. We's wid ya."

There was a mumble of general agreement. Miss Ebba and Hattie exchanged a glance; then the older woman let her eye roam over the crowd, as if daring anyone to doubt the integrity of her family again. When she was satisfied her message had been received, she said, "Now you go on, Lee Henry. Tell 'em what happen, what Howard done."

Lee Henry stood quietly while Miss Ebba and Hattie made their way back to the bench and eased themselves down. While he waited, he folded his hands together, made a steeple out of his index fingers, and lifted his hands to his lips. His eyes were downcast, and he appeared deep in thought. Finally, when the air was so thick with expectation it was hard to breathe, he took off his jacket, laid it across the table, and began to speak.

"Here's the story, friends, brothers, and sisters. Here's the story." And he told them, without mentioning the name of Cedric Frohmann, of how Trudy Loomis had been taken by a group of white men, and of how she went north and gave her son over for adoption to a white couple. He told of how she stayed as maid and nanny and how she raised that little boy. And how, when he was grown and he learned who he was, he decided to come back to his roots to help the people who needed him. Lee Henry told of how Howard Draper joined the Klan and turned their secrets over to Miss Ebba so Miss Ebba could go around to the colored folks in danger and give out warnings. He told of how Howard Draper had put his life on the line for the very people sitting in this church tonight, put his life on the line to try to save them from harm and even death. And he told them of how Howard Draper had been shot down on a dark road the night before, shot down no doubt by a member of the Klan, and of how he needed their prayers now to recover from the bullet wound that might have taken his life.

And then Lee Henry Starks began to preach. "I wanna tell ya, Howard Draper's the Moses of our day. He our Moses! He didn't hafta come down here. No suh, coulda stayed where it was safe, where he had a home and a job and money in the bank. Coulda stayed there and lived like a rich white man! But no, he like Moses. Howard Draper regarded disgrace for the sake o' Christ as of a greater value than all the treasure o' Egypt." Lee Henry stretched out the word "all" so that it lasted several seconds, while his hand took in the room in a sweeping motion that ended with his index finger pointing upward over his head.

From a back row a single voice reached forward. "Tell it out, Brother Starks."

Lee Henry loosened his tie, slipped a finger in his collar, and stretched his neck. He pulled a handkerchief out of a back pocket and wiped at the sweat on his face. Outside the windows hands began to swat at mosquitoes. A host of insects buzzed and fluttered around the light bulbs overhead. The church was busy with the sound of paper rustling as people fanned themselves against the heat.

"Brothers and sisters," Lee Henry went on, "Howard Draper was like Moses. But, friends, he was like someone else too. I say, he was like someone else, and that man was *Jesus*! I say, Howard Draper was like *Jesus*—"

"Tell us how, brother."

"Because *Jesus* come down . . ." Lee Henry's finger flew up toward the ceiling, then down toward the floor. "I say, *Jesus* come down. . . ." The finger went up and down once again. "I say, *Jesus* come down to earth when he coulda stayed in heaven enjoyin' all the riches of the Lawd's kingdom."

"Dat's right."

"Amen 'n glory now."

Lee Henry pulled out the handkerchief again and wiped the sweat from his forehead, his lips, his neck. The crowd waited expectantly for him to go on.

More quietly, he said, "Now, you maybe say to me, 'Brother Starks, Howard Draper ain't Jesus. Howard Draper ain't the Son of God.' And my answer to you gonna be, I know that. I know he ain't Jesus. What I'se sayin' is, Howard Draper be *like* Jesus because he have the love of Jesus in him. He have the love of Jesus in him, and that's why he could leave everything up north and come down here to live and maybe even to *die* for his dark-skinned brothers and sisters."

He paused, looked around, paced in front of the altar. "Now lemme tell you something 'bout this man Jesus."

"Preach it, Brother Starks."

"You go on, Lee Henry. We's listenin'."

"Lemme tell you something 'bout the Son of God."

"Tell it out, preacher."

Lee Henry stopped, stood still, shouted, "Now, Jesus weren't no white man—"

"No, he weren't!"

"Amen to dat!"

"Bless de Lawd, brother."

"And Jesus weren't no Nigra man—"

"No, weren't no Nigra neider. . . ."

"What Jesus was, was a Jew. When the Lawd come down and put on skin, it was Jewish skin. Not white skin, not culud skin, but somethin' somewheres in between. Now, Jesus, he lived over there in a place called Israel, and at that time, Israel be jes' 'bout the center of the world. Jesus lived smack dab in the middle of the world, surrounded by Africa 'n Europe 'n India 'n China. And because of that, you know what I think?" His voice rose. "I say, do you know what I think?"

"Tell us what you think, brother."

"Speak on, Lee Henry, we's listenin'."

"I think maybe Jesus had a little bit o' the blood o' ever' race on earth runnin' in his veins! I'm sayin' here tonight, brothers and sisters, that Jesus weren't no white man—"

"Amen and alleluia!"

"And Jesus weren't no culud man—"

"Bless de Lawd anyway—"

"And even though he had hisself Jewish skin, he weren't jes' a Jew neither. I'm sayin', seems to me the Son of God be *all-l-l-l* colors, jes' the same way light be all colors. Light be all the colors all mixed up together, 'n you know what the Scripture say 'bout light!"

"Tell us 'gin, preacher."

"Go on now, Lee Henry."

"Scripture say, 'The Lawd is my *light*—' "

"Bless de Lawd!"

"Scripture say, 'God the light of *life*—' "

"Praise de Lawd!"

"Amen and amen, Lawd Jesus."

"Scripture say, 'God is light, 'n in him be no darkness at all!' "

"Dat's right, Lawd Jesus."

"Praise de Lawd Jesus."

The handkerchief appeared again, and Lee Henry paced before the altar, wiping futilely at the fountain of sweat his face had become.

And in that momentary pause I saw again the circular rainbow that I had seen from the plane window, the colored light that seemed to be a message written across the sky. And I heard Howard's voice as he read the words of Henry Vaughan, "I saw Eternity the other night / Like a great Ring of pure and endless light. . . ." And now Lee Henry, bearer of the final image, the one who made all the pieces come together into a recognizable whole, Lee Henry calling out that Jesus, the Son of God, is the light of life.

I had only that one brief instant, but I saw it fully, and capturing it, I held it to my heart. Jesus, Son of God, ring of endless light, circle of eternal life.

When the handkerchief disappeared into the back pocket, Lee Henry abruptly stopped pacing and looked straight down the center aisle. "Funny thing 'bout blood," he said quietly. "White folk say you got one drop culud blood, you culud. Don't matter your skin white as Howard Draper's, don't matter you look whiter 'n any man put on the Klan hood. Don't matter if your mother white, your father white. Don't matter at *all* what you look like. You got one drop culud blood, then you culud.

"But, friends, you know what the Bible say 'bout blood?"

Lee Henry went around the altar and flipped through the pages of the Bible until he found what he wanted. This time Miss Ebba piped up, "Speak it out, Lee Henry. We's waitin'."

"Says here," he went on, "says here in the book of Acts that God 'hath made of one blood all nations of men for to dwell on all the face of the earth'! You hear that, brothers and sisters?"

"Amen!"

"I say, did you hear that, brothers and sisters?"

A voluminous "Amen!"

"Acts seventeen, verse twenty-six, God 'hath made of *one* blood all nations of men for to dwell on all the face of the earth'! You know what that means?"

"Preach it, Brother Starks!"

"Means there's only *one* kind of blood in the world! Means there ain't white blood and culud blood and Jew blood. Means there's only one kind of blood and that blood in *all-l-l-l* us!"

"Amen to that, brother!"

"Blood all the same!"

"Praise Gawd!"

"I say, blood all the same!"

"Alleluia!"

"Yes, oh yes, friend, blood all the same."

Lee Henry walked around to the front of the altar once more and sighed heavily. "But even back when Jesus was walkin' the earth, there was all manner of hate. All manner of hate because people was diff'rent. And you know who was the nigger back then?"

"Who, Lee Henry?"

"Tell us, preacher."

"The nigger in Jesus' time was the Jew. The Jew was the one hated, oppressed by the white man. And that's what Jesus was. Jesus Christ was a Jew. When God come down, he put on the skin of the nigger of the Roman Empire. Come down and put on the skin of the slave. Come down and put on the skin of the peoples that was hated and pers'cuted and oppressed.

"I'm tellin' you tonight, brothers and sisters, Jesus knowed what it was to be hated."

"Yes, he did."

"Jesus knowed what it was to be looked down upon, spat upon, beaten."

"Bless de Lawd."

Loudly, with every word emphasized, Lee Henry declared, *"Jesus knowed what it was to be killed by the people that hated him!"*

"Amen."

"Alleluia."

"Praise de name of de Lawd."

The room fell suddenly quiet then. So quiet I could hear myself breathe. I didn't dare move as I waited for Lee Henry to go on.

"Well, lemme tell you something, friends," he finally said.

"Say it, Brother Starks."

"Lemme tell you this. It was wrong then, 'n it wrong now. I say, all the hate that killed the Lawd Jesus was wrong then, and it wrong now."

Amens rolled down the aisle like bowling balls, crashing up against Lee Henry where he stood before the altar.

When the noise died down, Lee Henry asked quietly, "We gonna let hate win?"

"Uh-uh, no suh."

"Hep us, Lawd."

"I say, we gonna let hate win?"

"Never, Lawd!"

"Cain't let it, Jesus!"

"What we gonna do, brothers and sisters?"

"Gon' pray!"

"What else we gonna do, brothers and sisters?"

"Gon' believe!"

"That's right!" Lee Henry smiled like a schoolteacher looking out over a well-versed class. "That's right. We gonna pray, and we gonna believe. We gonna pray God's love come over the world! We gonna believe that love gonna win!"

"Amen!"

"Praise de Lawd!"

"And lemme tell you something else, friends."

"Tell us, Brother Starks."

"Lemme tell you this 'bout the Klan. They's a group of men who plan evil 'gainst everyone not just like them. Lemme tell you what gonna happen to them. The Klan, they got themselves a motto. Got themselves a motto they took right outta the Good Book, right outta Hebrews. Motto says the Klan was there yesterday, Klan be here today, and the Klan gonna be here forever. Lemme tell you what that is, friends. That's *blas*phemy! Plain, cold blasphemy, same as spittin' right in the face of God. Because that verse, it speakin' 'bout *Je*sus. That verse 'bout *Je*sus, and the Klan got no business takin' out the name of Jesus and puttin' in the Klan instead." Lee Henry narrowed his eyes and peered over the heads of his listeners. "Woe to him puts hisself in the place o' God."

"Amen, brother."

"I say, *woe* to him puts hisself in the place o' God!"

"Amen, brother!"

Quietly, in almost a whisper, he said, "The punishment for blasphemy be death."

He folded his hands over his heart for a moment, then let them drop to his sides.

"Only God be forever," he said simply, looking out over the crowd. "Only God be forever." He sighed deeply, as though a struggle had ended.

After a long moment he straightened his shoulders and went on speaking quietly. "My friends, I wanna tell you that the evil gonna end. Day's gonna come when evil gonna end. And when that happen, when the evil end"—his voice rose in volume as he lifted one hand upward, index finger pointing somewhere over our heads—"my friends, when the evil end, the good gonna keep right on goin'!"

Lee Henry Starks became a statue then, eyes forward and finger outstretched, as though he were both pointing toward and looking right into forever. I almost turned to see whether a light had been turned on at the back of the church, because whatever it was back there that Lee Henry saw, the reflection of it glowed in his eyes the way fire dances in the eyes of onlookers. Or maybe those two dark orbs were simply shining with a certain ineffable hope.

Finally he lowered his hand and shook his head slightly as though awakening from sleep. He looked around the room at the faces peering up at him, mine included. "Till that day, friends, we gotta be faithful. There's a man needs our prayers tonight, a man lying in a hospital bed, shot in the line of duty, the duty of protectin' his people. Howard Draper was willin' to put hisself in danger for your sakes 'n mine. Who be willin' now to take his need for healin' to the throne of God, to ask for mercy?"

In the next moment someone stood and prayed, and then in turn, someone else, and someone else. Men, women, even children stood to offer up a few words, to ask for healing, to plead for mercy. Time dissolved in this vast, many-voiced chorus of prayer, and I found myself lost to the beauty of it, captured by its simplicity, comforted by the faith of these people who spoke to a God they believed not only existed but loved them. And I realized maybe that's what prayer was after all, the simple cry of the heart, a crying out to the one who was faithful enough to bring on the morning at the end of every night.

"Please protect Howard," I thought, and as though she had heard my inward prayer, Miss Ebba beside me whispered, "Amen."

THIRTY-EIGHT

We were little more than halfway to Lexington when Luella asked us to pull over. Three minutes later we were back on the road, leaving Luella's breakfast behind on the shoulder of Highway 17.

"Sorry, Miz Fulton, Miz Callahan," she mumbled. She was slumped down in the backseat, her eyes shut, her head resting against the upholstered leather. Her forehead and upper lip sparkled with tiny beads of sweat.

"No need to apologize," Sunny assured her, glancing up at Luella's reflection in the rearview mirror. "I can understand your nervousness."

"Would you like some soda?" I offered. "It might help you feel better." At my feet was a small ice chest of cold drinks Tom had suggested we bring along.

Before she could answer, I opened a bottle of R.C. Cola and handed it back to Susannah, who in turn held the cold bottle up to Luella's forehead. A small smile trembled on Luella's lips. "Feels good," she said weakly.

"Think you can drink some?" Susannah asked.

Luella nodded and took the bottle from her friend. But instead of drinking, she gazed out the window at the passing stretch of longleaf pine. "Been scared all my life," she said quietly, "but ain't never been as scared as I am this minute."

It was Friday, July 30, the day that had been chosen for the four young residents of Coloredtown to go to the Holmes County Courthouse to register. Mahlon was in the car behind us, his uncle's 1954 Pontiac station wagon. With him were Eddie and Bo. They'd been like mannequins, stiff and silent, when we met outside Reese's General Store that morning. When I greeted them, they mumbled a reply, but otherwise appeared as wide-eyed and frozen as a couple of deer caught in the headlights of an oncoming car. I didn't have to wonder where their laughter had gone.

"You don't have to go through with this, you know, Luella," Sunny said. "We could let the other three try to register today, and you could go back another time."

The young Negro woman shook her head sadly. "Naw, Miz Fulton. Don't matter whether I go today, next week, next year. I'll still be jes' as scared. Might as well go today."

We drove in silence for a few miles. My sympathy was with Luella and the others, but my thoughts were with Howard Draper. The word from the hospital that morning was that Howard had been moved from the intensive care unit to a private room. That meant he was improving. Several FBI agents had volunteered to stand guard during their off hours, so someone was posted at the door of Howard's room around the clock. If the Klan didn't figure out some way to get at him, and if no unexpected postoperative complications set in, chances were good for his full recovery. But those seemed like two big *ifs* to me, and I continued to worry.

To get my mind off Howard, I turned toward the two young women in the backseat and smiled. "I don't think I mentioned how nice you look," I said. They were all dressed up as if they were going to a wedding or some other festive occasion. They both wore short-sleeved cotton dresses, clean and neatly pressed. Luella's was navy blue with large white buttons reaching from the rounded collar to the pleated skirt. Susannah's was a pale green with imitation lace for trim around the neck and sleeves. Too, they both wore white beaded gloves, slightly tattered hats, and low-heeled shoes that had recently been given a coat of white polish.

Susannah smiled at me, giving me her eager wide-toothed grin, but Luella shook her head and mumbled, "Thank you, Miz Callahan, but I reckon I don't look nothin' but sick."

"You look wonderful, Luella," Sunny offered. "I want you to know I'm proud of you both. It takes a lot of courage to do what you're doing."

Susannah said meekly, "Thank you, Miz Fulton."

Luella moaned and said, "We ain't there yet, Miz Fulton. Bo and Eddie, they may be carryin' me into that courthouse. How good am I gonna look then, nigger woman come to register can't even stand on her own two feet?"

"You'll feel better once we get there," Susannah kindly predicted.

Luella moaned again and said nothing.

"You know," Sunny chirped, trying to sound reassuring, "I really think the worst that'll happen is they'll turn you away without even giving you a chance to take the test. They'll come up with some excuse or other to keep you from trying. So then we'll go on home and try again later. You have every right to do what you're doing, you know. Just remember that. The law's on your side."

"We in Miss'ssippi, Miz Fulton," Luella said flatly. "Federal law don't stand no chance against old Jim Crow."

Sunny had made the same comment only a couple of mornings before, but now she said, "If you really believe that, Luella, we might as well turn right around and go back to Carver and just do away with the citizenship school altogether." I knew she was trying to conceal her own doubts for the sake of the two women in the backseat. Someone had to try to paint a smile on old Jim Crow's face, or the prospect of confronting him would simply be too bleak.

Luella's response was to shut her eyes and shake her head.

"How many times you think we gonna have to try to register, Miz Fulton?" Susannah asked.

"I have no idea. But we'll keep going back to the courthouse until you're registered, no matter how many times it takes."

"Lawdamercy," Luella mumbled as she sank back down in the seat. "Jes' kill me dead now, Lawd, and get it over with."

Susannah looked sideways at her friend and clicked her tongue. When she spoke, there was an unmistakable sense of awe in her voice. "Day's gonna come," she said quietly, "when some Negro's gonna be the first culud person in the history o' Carver to register to vote.

Might jes' be me, Lawd willin'. 'Magine that. Might jes' be me."

On that note, we caught our first glimpse of the Holmes County Courthouse situated on a hill in the center of town, this Holy of Holies that was open to all but the Negro, who entered at his own risk.

Mahlon parked about a block away on Mulberry Street. Sunny and I dropped the women off there, then drove on to the square surrounding the courthouse. We found a parking space in front of the ice-cream parlor that would serve as our lookout post. We both ordered a cherry Coke from the pimply faced kid behind the counter, then settled ourselves at one of the tables on the sidewalk out front.

By the time we sat down, our five young people, including Mahlon, were already halfway up the walk leading to the courthouse. The men were dressed as nattily as the women, with white shirts and dark ties, carefully creased slacks, and shoes that, according to Eddie, had been polished just that morning with a rag and plenty of spit. They were a fine-looking group, ready and wanting to take on the responsibility of voting. I could only hope that somehow—by a twist of fate, an outright miracle, or a momentary act of conscience on the part of the registrar—they would be allowed to do what they'd come to do.

The courthouse itself was a stately two-story brick building topped by a tall clock tower painted white. The upper story had arched windows. The bottom-story windows were embellished with ornate keystones. The building had four entrances, one on each side of the square, reached by climbing two or three steps up to an open four-columned porch.

A young white man standing on the porch lifted an outstretched hand to our group as they approached. "That must be Dave Hunsinger," Sunny explained. "The local civil rights worker who'll go with our group into the registrar's office."

When the party reached him, Dave Hunsinger shook hands with each of them, then led the way in through the heavy double doors. When the last one disappeared inside and the door closed behind them, I said, "Well, Luella made it in on her own two feet."

Sunny smiled. "I knew she would."

We fiddled nervously with the straws in our Cokes, but we didn't drink. Neither Sunny nor I could take our eyes off the entrance to the courthouse. A few cars passed by on the one-way street. Shoppers moved in and out of the stores around the square. Not far from where we sat, an elderly Negro swept the sidewalk with a push broom. I heard the whisk of the broom before I turned my gaze away from the courthouse to look at the old man. His lips moved as he worked, and every so often, if he was turned toward us just right, I could catch a note or two of whatever it was he was singing. Doubtless some freedom song or a gospel song, one of those choruses that looks to a time far beyond the present.

I wondered whether he'd ever tried to register to vote and decided he probably hadn't. I watched while the white folks on the sidewalk passed by him without a glance, certainly without the nods and smiles with which they greeted each other. At best, he was an extension of his broom; at worst, he wasn't there at all. He was just a nigger, a man without a life, without a mind, without a soul.

I wondered what he had seen as a Negro in Mississippi. I wondered what he had experienced in his life, a span of time stretching back some sixty years or more, to the very beginning of the century. What stories could he tell me, not of how he lived but of how he simply survived in such a place as this? That one sidewalk sweeper was a gold mine of stories—tales of prejudice, perseverance, tragedy, maybe even hope—if anyone dared to dig beneath the skin and find out what those stories were.

I was studying him, lost in thought, when he glanced up from his broom and noticed I was watching him. For an instant his own tired eyes—the whites darkened to the color of weak tea, the bottom lids as droopy as a hound dog's—widened in surprise or fear or both, and just as quickly dropped again. He turned his back to me and wandered off sweeping in the opposite direction.

Negro men were lynched for meeting the eyes of a white woman. Negro men were lynched for less than that. This old man had managed to survive some sixty years in this white man's world, and he wasn't about to take any chances now.

As I watched him move away, Sunny announced quietly, "Here they come."

I looked back in time to see our group exit the courthouse one by one, then gather on the porch, where they lingered, talking among themselves.

"Well," I remarked, "that was too quick for them to have been allowed to register."

"I wonder what Hoopes's excuse was," Sunny said, sighing. "Maybe he was leaving for an early lunch, or he doesn't register on Fridays anymore, or he ran out of registration forms. It'll be interesting to hear what he came up with."

"At least they all came out in one piece."

"Yes. But what do you suppose they're talking about?"

"No telling. I'm sure they'll fill us in when they get here."

Several minutes passed and they didn't leave the porch. From the waving of hands and the shuffling of feet, they appeared to be in a heated discussion. At one point Mahlon lifted a hand in our direction, and we saw Dave Hunsinger gaze over at us briefly. A few moments later all heads nodded, and Dave Hunsinger stepped out from the group and took long strides down the sidewalk. No one followed him.

"I wonder what's going on," Sunny murmured.

Saying nothing, I shook my head. I kept my eyes on our little group clustered there outside the courthouse, looking small and overshadowed by the imposing brick building. In another moment, the five of them moved off the porch. But instead of walking toward Mulberry Street where the car was parked, they stopped and kneeled down on the walkway leading up to the courthouse steps.

"They're holding a kneel-in?" The inflection in Sunny's voice made it not so much a question as a statement of disbelief.

By then Dave Hunsinger had reached us. He was a tall, compactly built young man with fair hair and ruddy cheeks. He sported a flattop, and his deep blue eyes peered out from behind a pair of dark horn-rimmed glasses. Unlike the others, he was casually dressed in a striped T-shirt, beltless jeans, and tennis shoes. He looked like the All-American college kid, which, had it not been for Freedom Summer, was in fact what he would have been.

"You're Helen Fulton?" he asked, and when Sunny nodded, he held out a hand for Sunny to shake. "Dave Hunsinger," he said.

"Hello, Dave. Happy to meet you." She tilted her head toward me. "This is my friend, Augusta Callahan."

The young man shook my hand and said, "Pleasure." Without wasting any more time, he went on, "They were turned away flat out."

"What excuse did Evan Hoopes give?" Sunny asked.

Shaking his head, Dave explained, "We never even got to see Hoopes. We ran into a deputy who stopped us in the hall, asked us our business, and said the registrar was on vacation. He wouldn't even let us get as far as the office to see for ourselves. We asked him when Mr. Hoopes would be back, and he said he didn't know." The young man shook his head again in obvious disgust. "Ten to one Hoopes is in there right now, registering a white couple that came in by the north entrance as we were leaving."

"Well, I don't know. That couple could be in the courthouse for any number of reasons," Sunny suggested.

"Doesn't matter," Dave interjected. "That deputy was lying. I don't know his name, but I've seen him before. He's textbook Klan, fits the bill to a T. You don't even have to wonder what his take is on civil rights."

"So you've decided to hold a kneel-in? We hadn't been planning on that."

"These young people have been trained in nonviolent demonstrations—"

"But do you think it's the wisest thing to do at this point?"

Dave nodded. "Absolutely."

"They all agreed?"

A nod toward the courthouse lawn was Dave's answer. "Listen," he said, "I gotta make a phone call. Time to rustle up the troops."

"But—"

Before Sunny could say more, Dave Hunsinger turned and headed down the sidewalk, disappearing into a drugstore.

Sunny looked at me, her eyebrows raised. For a moment neither of us spoke. Then she said, "We've talked about kneel-ins and the like at the school, but I wasn't expecting to get involved in all that today."

"I guess they decided there's no time like the present."

Sunny studied the young people kneeling on the courthouse lawn. She pulled at her lower lip, then let her hand drop as she said, "Heaven knows, this isn't going to end without trouble."

Down the street Dave Hunsinger exited the drugstore and, his long strides carrying him back across the square, rejoined the group at the courthouse by kneeling beside them. Sunny and I watched in silence as, a few minutes later, about a half dozen more young people—white and Negro both—hiked across the courthouse lawn and added their bodies to the protest. Over the next fifteen minutes, they continued to come, two from one direction, three from another, a handful from yet another street, until the number of young people kneeling there in the grass had swelled to several dozen.

"From the looks of it," I said, "he really has called in the troops."

"They must all be young people involved in the civil rights movement here in Lexington."

"I'd say that's a pretty good guess."

"It's almost as though they were on standby, just waiting to come."

"Maybe they were, or maybe they're on perpetual standby, ready for anything."

"I'm not sure I like this, Augie."

"Well, it does look like the party's getting a little more wild than we anticipated. Complete with music and everything." The gathering crowd had started singing freedom songs, the songs that served as background accompaniment to the turbulent times we lived in. How many newsreels had I seen of people singing their hearts out while they marched, kneeled, protested, picketed, and got their brains bashed in by the local police?

"Maybe I should call Tom now," Sunny said, more to herself than to me, "let him know what's going on. I don't think we're going to get through this without any arrests."

The old Negro stood on the edge of the sidewalk, clutching the handle of the broom with both hands, gazing intently at the crowd on the courthouse lawn. His expression gave no clue as to his thoughts, whether he looked upon the protesters as a bunch of foolish young scalawags, or whether he admired their courage in this act of civil disobedience. He lifted his cap, wiped his brow with his forearm, settled the cap back on his head, and went on watching. He'd seen plenty in his day, and this was one more show in the long struggle for equality for his people.

And there I sat, with my hand on a cold glass of cherry Coke, watching as well. But all at once I knew I was tired of watching. I'd seen the Yamagatas lose everything because of the slant of their eyes and the poetry of their name, and I could do nothing. I'd seen intolerance for years as I wrote my stories on race relations for *One Nation*, but beyond putting words on paper, I'd done nothing. I'd watched as Howard Draper was gunned down because some of the roots of his family tree were planted in Africa, and I hadn't been able to do one thing to keep it from happening.

But now I was witness to a group of young Negroes turned away from doing what they had every legal right to do, and this—this one act of injustice—I could do something about. I could take a stand against it, say by my actions that it was wrong, let that deputy and the registrar and everyone else in Lexington know that something wasn't right here, and it needed to be changed.

"Where are you going, Augie?"

I scarcely realized that I had stood, that I'd pushed my chair away from the table and I'd already taken a step toward the street. Where was I going? "I'm going to join the kneel-in, Sunny."

"Are you nuts?" She caught my gaze and held it. "I invited you out here to write a story, not to protest. It's dangerous, Augie."

"That didn't stop Howard Draper, did it?"

"Augie—"

"You don't have to come, Sunny. But I can't just sit here and watch from a safe distance."

She stared at me for a long moment. I could see a conflict going on behind her eyes. She was thinking of Tom, no doubt, and the children. Maybe she was thinking of the scars on Mahlon's back. But maybe too she was thinking of a family wearing numbered tags, carrying what was left of their belongings, leaving home to catch a train to only God knew where. Because just as she turned her gaze back to the courthouse, a passing car raised the dust on the road, and maybe the dust Sunny saw wasn't the red dust of Mississippi but the dry dust of an internment camp in a California desert. And maybe the music she heard wasn't just the voices of a bunch of idealistic young people, but maybe it was the music of a Salvation Army band in Hollenbeck Park that called out to Sunny in a way I couldn't hear. Because when she turned back to me, the conflict was gone, and in the next moment we were crossing the street.

THIRTY-NINE

We were kneeling on the courthouse lawn, squeezed in between Bo and Susannah, singing freedom songs, sweating, swaying under the blazing afternoon sun, our knees and the balls of our feet pressed against the hard earth, aching, when the fear began to creep in. "Keep your mind on the songs," I told myself. But my mind wandered anyway.

It traveled aimlessly, pausing on the open casket of the young Negro Emmet Till, his face beaten beyond all recognition. Could have been an old man, not a fourteen-year-old boy who'd innocently uttered a few foolish words to a white woman.

It recalled the photos of the broken, bullet-riddled bodies of the three civil rights workers pulled from the earthen dam right here in Mississippi only last year.

It entered the Mississippi jail where, two years earlier, Fannie Lou Hamer was clubbed almost to death with billy sticks because she had sat her black body down at a lunch counter in a bus terminal. Imagine ordering a hamburger and ending up ground meat yourself. Didn't matter that she was a woman. No, here in the bitter arena of civil rights, women found themselves equals at last, treated every bit as cruelly as their male counterparts.

Not even white women were safe. Viola Gregg Liuzzo was killed by the Klan for assisting Negroes during the march from Selma to Montgomery. She was a white housewife from Michigan, a mother of five, who'd been watching reports of the march on television when she decided to go down and help. It was the last thing she ever did. Her selfless gesture earned her two bullets in the head.

I fought the urge to stand up and run, to save my own white, womanly skin. "You don't have to do this," I argued with myself. But then, neither did Howard Draper have to do what he did. He did it anyway, knowing the danger and the probable outcome, because the good in him wouldn't let him do otherwise.

I kneeled on, until I felt the knees of my slacks becoming one with the grass and the dirt. I kneeled until I thought the sun would melt me into a puddle of flesh and blood on the grounds of the Holmes County Courthouse. We were ignored so long I began to wonder whether anyone in the courthouse would bother to notice us, or whether our only adversaries would be the heat, the thirst, and our own aching limbs.

No one showed up to question or reprimand us. No one left or entered the courthouse, at least not on the south side where we were. It almost seemed that the people whose attention we wanted were determined not to give it. It seemed they wanted us to wear ourselves out, to decide on our own to get up and go home. Even the shoppers around the square appeared more interested in pursuing the sales than in becoming spectators to yet another protest. Our only silent cheerleader was the old sidewalk sweeper who occasionally, in between sweeps, paused to look our way.

We went on singing. When one song finished, someone started another and everyone joined in. When I didn't know the words, I faked it. I pushed away thoughts of battered bodies, tried to draw strength up out of the words of the songs. Keep your eyes on the prize. This little light of mine, I'm gonna let it shine. Ain't gonna let nobody turn me around. . . .

At long last a very young, sunken-chested deputy sauntered out of the double doors and walked to the edge of the porch. He stopped there and leaned up against one of the columns. I was almost relieved to see him. Still, initially, he gave no indication that he saw us. Reaching into the breast pocket of his uniform, he pulled out a pack of cigarettes, retrieved one, tapped it against the column and stuck it into the lipless slit that was his mouth. Then he rummaged around in the pocket of his tan, neatly creased slacks, found the book of matches he was looking for, struck one and lighted the cigarette. He put out the match with a flick of his wrist and tossed it to the ground. Then he proceeded to smoke as nonchalantly as if he were on his own front porch, looking up at the sky rather than at the mass of protesters on the grass, even—unbelievably—amusing himself by blowing smoke rings, watching the circles enlarge and expand until they drifted away.

No words would have spoken more loudly his contempt for us. We went on singing, by now the same songs over and over. He went on pretending we weren't there. A full five minutes went by as he worked on reducing his cigarette to ash.

"Bo," I asked, "is he the deputy who kept you from seeing the registrar?"

Bo squinted in the direction of the man and nodded. "He the one, Miz Callahan."

Finally, after what seemed an interminable amount of time, the deputy flicked the butt to the ground just as he had the match. Only then did he push himself away from the column with his shoulder and move down the few steps to the sidewalk, his thumbs looped in his belt.

He paused then and let his gaze wander over the crowd. He was finally willing to see us, and his expression said he had come upon something as disgusting as fresh, steamy horse droppings left in the middle of a public square. He shook his head as he began to saunter down the walk. As he strolled, the singing petered out until only two or three voices limped along to the end of the chorus, and then there was silence, a nerve-wracking hush.

I dropped my head, suddenly intent upon the grass at my knees, and waited. All my muscles went taut, stiffened against what was about to happen. I tried to keep my breath even, a quiet calculated in and out, so as not to give in to panic. But for the first time in my life, I knew what it was to be weak with fear.

"You know ya'll breaking the law heah, don't you?" The deputy's words startled me, though they were neither harsh nor loud. It might have been their very evenness that made them all the more dreadful.

From out of the crowd someone answered, "No, sir." I recognized the voice, and in a moment I spotted Dave Hunsinger. "You're the one breaking the law, sir."

Smoke Ring swung around until he was facing Dave. "That right?" he asked in the same even way. "How's that, boy?"

Dave Hunsinger didn't hesitate. "The four Negroes who came to register this morning have every legal right to vote. Your not allowing them to register leaves you standing in the way of justice."

Smoke Ring's eyes were squinted against the sun, but still it wasn't hard to see the flash of annoyance in them. "You know, boy," he drawled, "I've had just about enough of you coming 'round to the courthouse with your nigger friends. You're not even from around heah. Why don't you go on back where you came from and get your nose outta Mississippi's business?"

"Civil rights is everybody's business, sir."

Smoke Ring took a few swaggering steps closer to where Dave knelt in the grass. "That right, nigger lover?" The words slid out on an oily wave of contempt.

But Dave Hunsinger wasn't about to slip and fall. "Yes, sir, it is," he said firmly.

"You think we heah in Mississippi need outsiders tellin' us how to handle our niggers?"

"Apparently so, sir, since you're not doing a very good job of it yourselves."

"Don't get smart with me, son."

"No, sir. Just stating a fact."

Smoke Ring turned then and walked a few feet back up the sidewalk. "Heah that, men?" he hollered. A half dozen or more deputies had gathered on the courthouse porch in the last few minutes. "This nigger lover from the North thinks we don't know how to handle our own culud folk."

Laughter rumbled from the deputies while one voice called back, "We could show him just how well we handle our niggers."

"And nigger lovers," a second voice added.

Smoke Ring turned and sniffed out a laugh as he looked back over the crowd. "Naw," he sneered, "we don't want no trouble, do we?"

Somehow, I sensed that trouble was exactly what was coming.

Smoke Ring took his nightstick out of its holster and swung it nonchalantly at his side. "Why don't ya'll just break it up, go on home like good little girls and boys?"

"We're not going anywhere till you let us see the registrar." It was Dave Hunsinger again. I wondered how his voice could be so steady. I was trembling all over and beginning to feel light-headed.

The nightstick suddenly landed on Smoke Ring's palm, slapping against the flesh. "Told you, boy. He ain't heah today."

"We'd like to see for ourselves."

The deputy was suddenly angry. Up to now he'd been having a little sport, enjoying the feeling of power, but finally there'd been enough said to kindle his fury. I could see it in the way his shoulders stiffened, his jaw clenched. He moved toward Dave Hunsinger until he stood directly over him. Slapping the nightstick repeatedly against his open palm, he hollered, "You callin' me a liar?"

Dave looked up, peering fearlessly from behind his horn-rimmed glasses. "No, sir. I'm just saying we have a right to see for ourselves."

"You ain't no resident of Mississippi, boy. You got no such right."

"The four Negroes who came to register today are residents of Mississippi, and they have every right to see for themselves whether or not the registrar is in his office."

I was certain that at any moment the nightstick would come crashing down on the young civil rights worker's head, and I felt my own body stiffen against the blow. But it didn't come. Instead, Smoke Ring turned and moved slowly across the grass until he stood in front of Bo Riley. Because I was next to Bo, the deputy also stood in front of me. I quickly dropped my eyes again, narrowing in on the tips of the shiny black shoes that had come to rest just inches away from us. There wasn't anything extraordinary about those shoes, and yet in all my life I had never seen anything quite so foreboding.

"You're one of the niggers that come to register, ain't you?" Smoke Ring accused. His voice was steady and quiet again.

In my peripheral vision, I could see that Bo too had his eyes focused on Smoke Ring's shoes. "Yessuh," he whispered hoarsely.

"What's that? I can't hear you, boy! Speak up!"

"Yessuh," he said more loudly this time.

The nightstick slapped against the open palm at regular intervals now. "You think you got a right to see the registrar?"

I heard Bo suck in his breath, then clear his throat. "Yessuh." His

Adam's apple rose and fell. "Yessuh, I do."

Slap, slap, slap. "How long you lived in Mississippi, boy?"

"All my life, suh."

"How long's that?"

"Twen'-one years, suh."

Slap, slap, slap. Smoke Ring was enjoying himself again. "You ain't learned much in twenty-one years, have you, boy?"

Bo fidgeted on his knees, and I understood his dilemma. How to answer such a question?

"I said," Smoke Ring repeated, more loudly, "you ain't learned much in twenty-one years, have you, boy?"

Bo sounded resigned. "No, suh. Guess I ain't."

"You tellin' me a dumb nigger like you thinks he can vote?"

Again Bo was silent. By now the other deputies had stepped off the porch and spread out among the crowd. A pair of steel-tipped cowboy boots came and joined Smoke Ring's shiny black shoes. At eye level was a belly that had seen too many beers. The buttons of this deputy's shirt were severely strained at the waist so that bits of pink and hairy flesh showed where the shirt didn't quite come together. I didn't raise my eyes high enough to see his face, but I could imagine the double chin, the sagging jowls. He must have had a wad of chewing tobacco in his jaw, because before he spoke he snorted, cleared his throat, and in the next moment a glob of brown sputum—a moist little comet—landed on the grass at Bo's knees.

"Nigger givin' you a hard time, Floyd?" he asked Smoke Ring.

"Nigger ever give a person anything but a hard time, Hank?" Smoke Ring/Floyd responded.

The hands that hung at Hank's sides had fingers like thick sausages. He lifted one of those hands now, pointing one sausage finger at me in a gesture that took my breath away. "Who's this, boy?" He directed the question at Bo and spoke as though my presence, out of all the people there, was a personal affront to him.

Bo fidgeted again, shook his head. "Don't know, suh."

"You don't know? This lady's kneeling heah in the grass right alongside of you, singing right along with all your freedom songs so you's can come on in heah and register to vote, and you're telling me you don't know who she is?"

Sweat trickled down my back from something other than the heat.

The ache in my knees became almost unbearable. I thought in another moment I might fall forward right onto the steel tips of Hank's cowboy boots, but I willed myself to stay upright.

"Yessuh," Bo said.

"Yes, sir, what, boy?" Hank growled.

"Don't know who she is, suh."

Like Floyd, Hank removed his nightstick from the holster. "And I'm saying you do."

"It's true," I blurted out then, looking up at the man. The double chin was there, the sagging jowls, just as I'd expected. But I could never have imagined the intensity of hatred in his dark eyes as he looked from me to Bo and back again. "He doesn't know me."

Floyd took over then by spitting out an expletive and noting, "You ain't from heah, neither, judging from the way you talk."

"No, sir." I shook my head.

"You another one of those do-gooder civil rights peoples?"

"Not exactly, sir."

Slap, slap, slap. Floyd said, "Now whatta you mean by that? Either you are or you ain't."

I thought a moment. "Then I guess I am," I said.

"Girl," Hank complained, "you're a pretty little lady, but you're just as dumb as this nigger."

He pointed at Bo with his nightstick. I said nothing.

I had lost all sense of time, all sense of what was going on around me. I was scarcely aware that Sunny was on the other side of me, her shoulder only inches from mine. I didn't know what the other demonstrators and the other deputies were doing. The whole world had been reduced to Bo and me kneeling on the courthouse lawn, and Floyd and Hank standing over us with their inane questions and their fidgety nightsticks.

" 'Course she's dumb," Floyd was saying. "She's one of them nigger lovers from the North. Ain't nobody dumber'n them."

Sunny's hand was on my back. "Don't say anything," she whispered. She needn't have said it, not to me, anyway. The conversation was making me sick and angry, but I wasn't about to respond to it. The two deputies were obviously chiding the crowd on to a riot. That way they'd have a solid excuse to make arrests.

Hank slipped the tip of his nightstick under Bo's chin and tilted up his head. Bo complied, but he kept his eyes lowered. Sweat rolled down the side of his face. The muscles in his jaw twitched.

Hank's words broke the unbearable silence. "You havin' your way with this white woman, boy?"

Bo shuddered. His Adam's apple bobbed several times, as though it were a sentence stuck in his throat. "Nawsuh," he whispered at last.

"I say you are."

The nightstick lifted Bo's chin up a little higher. Bo resisted slightly, pursed his lips. "Nawsuh, I swear. Don't know her, suh."

"This is getting way out of hand, deputy." Sunny's voice, calm and even, startled me. "Four Mississippi residents came here to register to vote, and if you would just let them see the registrar—or else see for themselves that he isn't here—we could all go home peacefully."

"And just who are you, little lady?" Hank spat out the words slowly, along with another brown pellet of tobacco juice that he aimed off to his left.

"It doesn't matter who I am," Sunny replied. "What matters is the law, and like the gentleman said, you're breaking it."

Floyd and Hank laughed gleefully at that, Hank's belly rumbling like gelatin. "*We're* breaking the law?" Hank echoed. "Lady, we could haul all of you away right now on charges of unlawful assembly and disturbing the peace."

Sunny appeared unperturbed. "If you will just let us attend to our business, sir, we'll go away quietly."

Hank had let his nightstick drop from Bo's chin. He clenched it at both ends now, like a batter warming up behind home plate. "Lady, you deaf or something?" he said. "Floyd told ya'll already, Mr. Hoopes ain't heah today. You don't need to be snoopin' 'round his office to see whether it's true or not."

Floyd muttered, "Another dumb nigger lover."

I had begun to wonder what was going to break the standoff. What would allow us at long last to rise from our knees, uprooting ourselves from the courthouse lawn? Something had to happen to bring an end to this protest. One side would have to give in or give up, and neither side was willing.

But the next moment put an end to my wondering. Bo Wiley decided he'd heard all he was going to hear. Floyd's comment about Sunny had barely left his lips when Bo leapt up and tackled the skinny deputy to the ground. I remember crying out and starting to rise, one hand stretched out toward Bo, but from that moment on, everything was chaos.

I didn't even rise up fully before I felt a sharp pain across my back. It was Hank's or maybe some other deputy's nightstick crashing down against my shoulder blades. At first I was only stunned, but quickly the numbness escalated into intense pain. It traveled the length of my back, detoured into my arms, and dropped all the way down my legs to my feet. I fell to the ground, only vaguely aware of the tangle of bodies, the screams, the shouts, the jostling of the crowd above me, and Sunny's voice calling out my name. I didn't struggle against the hands that pulled my arms behind my back, nor against the metal bracelets suddenly slipped around my wrists, clicking into place. Something—a tight grip on my upper arm—lifted me from the ground and led me to a waiting paddy wagon in the street. Inside, pressed against sweaty bodies, amid the stench of perspiration, surrounded by curses and moans, I found myself bumping along the streets of Lexington on the two-block trip from the county courthouse to the county jail.

FORTY

We were separated, men from the women, and thrown into cells that cut us off by sight, if not by sound. Traditionally, inmates were separated by color as well, but in our case white and Negro women landed in the same tank there in the Holmes County jail. I suppose law enforcement thought integrating us would add insult to injury, but in reality it was a comfort to have our little group of women from Carver together.

In all, twelve of us squeezed into a cell meant for four. Women crowded the cots of the two bunk beds and spilled over onto the floor. One rested her back against the toilet. Another lay beneath the dripping sink, using her arms as a pillow. The place was close and hot and dim, the one overhead window so high as to be almost useless for letting in air and light.

We didn't talk much among ourselves at first. Though united in a common cause, we Carver folks and Dave Hunsinger's girls had nevertheless been total strangers until a couple hours earlier. Now our circumstances made for awkward introductions. We were tired, thirsty, scared, and locked up, making the usual *How do you do?*s irrelevant.

Not all of the protesters had been arrested, obviously. Only a chosen few from the dozens of men and women kneeling on the grass. Still, the deputies had managed to round up the entire Carver group, men as well as women, and I considered that a good thing. Sunny and I felt responsible for Luella and Susannah, and at least this way we knew where they were.

The two of them sat together on one of the lower bunks, leaning up against the cinder-block wall. Susannah had lost gloves and shoes in the scuffle, and her stockings had been ripped beyond all possible mending. Her feet, small and pink soled, stuck out from the side of the cot and hung over the concrete floor like a couple of lost puppies. Half of her imitation lace collar had disappeared somewhere in the fray, the other half clung to her dress by a few tangled threads. Her hat sat askew so that it dipped down over her eyebrows, but she didn't bother to rearrange it. Her eyes were wide but unseeing, staring straight ahead. She made me think of British children crawling dazed through the rubble of London after another night of the Blitz.

Luella had fared a bit better, coming through the scuffle and arrest with shoes and hat still in place. She even yet wore her beaded gloves, though they were streaked with dirt. She sat beside Susannah with her legs drawn up, her arms clasped around them as though she were trying to curl herself up into a ball. She had a twig in her hair, and a few blades of grass were pressed into crisscrosses on her knees, but her eyes spoke of her amazement that she'd come this far without being done in by either her own fear or a deputy's baton.

They were the only two women in the cell wearing dresses. Dave Hunsinger's girls were a rather scruffy lot, uniform in their clothing and hairstyles, as though conforming to a certain image of civil rights workers. Six white women and two Negroes, they all wore blue jeans or cutoffs, tie-dyed T-shirts or sleeveless blouses, and tennis shoes or sandals. The white women wore their hair long and parted in the middle, except for one, whose hair was curly like mine and had to be held in place with two large barrettes on either side of her head. One of the Negro women sported the newly popular Afro. The other had her hair pulled back into several tight braids.

In addition to being hot, tired, dirty, and thirsty, most of us were aching somewhere, rubbing wrists that had been handcuffed, holding ribs that had been jabbed, nursing a bump on the back of the head. I asked Sunny if she was hurt, and she said no, but that exchange seemed to rouse her out of her own personal stupor, and she began asking around to see if everyone else was all right.

Stretched out on the bare mattress of the second bottom bunk was a lanky blonde, her face hidden by her hair and her right hand. I had thought she was crying silently or even trying to sleep, but when Sunny spoke to her, the girl lifted her hand to reveal a bloody mass of hair and flesh.

"Natalie!" cried another young woman. She joined Sunny at the bunk and bent over her friend. "I didn't know you were bleeding like this! Why didn't you say something?"

Without waiting for an answer, she jumped up, removed one of her sandals—a leather thing with a sole that looked like a tire tread—and started banging on the bars of the cell. "Hey!" she called out. "Hey, we need medical attention here!" She was, it was easy to tell, one of those "do-gooder, nigger lovers from the North," maybe from the Boston area, if I knew my accents. Definitely not a native southerner, this one. She looked about twenty, and she had that air of confidence and determination common to most young civil rights workers. Her long brown hair was tucked behind her ears, and she had on a T-shirt that sported a peace symbol and the words, "Make love, not war."

When she got no response, she yelled again, beating the bars with the dull-thudding sandal and throwing out a few curses for good measure. At last we heard a door open, then footsteps on the concrete floor. A young man whose badge was brighter than his perceived intellect paused outside the cell and stared at us in silence.

"Well?" Boston cried, pointing her sandal toward the cot where the wounded girl lay. "Aren't you going to do something?"

The deputy's gaze followed the sandal and landed on the wounded blonde. "Wha' the matter with her?" he asked. He chomped on a toothpick, rolling it from one side of his mouth to the other with his tongue.

"She has a rather bad cut on her forehead," Sunny answered. "If nothing else, we could at least use some ice until she can get out of here and see a doctor."

The deputy stood there another moment as though he couldn't quite comprehend what was happening within his field of vision.

Boston let go another string of curses, questioned the gene pool from whence the deputy sprang, and ended her tirade with, "What's the matter with you? Get the ice! Now!"

He shrugged. "Don't got no ice heah," he replied, unruffled. The toothpick rolled sluggishly across his chapped lips.

"Then how about a towel?" Sunny asked. "Do you at least have a towel or something?"

He shrugged again. "I'll see."

He disappeared, then reappeared a moment later with a towel so dirty it might have been hanging in the men's room for the past several months. Before handing it over, he took the toothpick out of his mouth—the end of it was frayed so that it looked like a tiny whisk broom—and waved it toward the bunk where Natalie lay. "Best not get blood on that there mattress," he warned. He gave the towel to an infuriated Boston, who threw her sandal at him as he made his way back down the hall. She must have missed, because we heard the door shut behind him without incident.

Boston carried the towel to the sink and, calling down curses upon the uncivilized and unregenerate South, moistened the cloth with cold water and carried it to her friend. "I can handle it," she told Sunny brusquely, dismissing her. Sunny hesitated a moment but finally turned away and joined me again on the hard but surprisingly cool floor.

"Well, Stanley," she said, looking around the cell and feigning a smirk, "this is another fine mess you've gotten us into."

"Sorry, Ollie," I deadpanned. "Hey, stick with me. We'll go places."

Sunny sniffed out a chuckle while looking at her watch. "Well, anyway, it won't be long before Tom figures out something happened, and he'll come bail us out."

"I wouldn't be surprised if Dave Hunsinger had someone standing by too. Maybe we'll be out of here soon enough to save Tom the trip."

Sunny nodded. "Maybe." Then she added, "How's your back?"

"Throbbing," I replied.

"Let me see."

I obediently turned and let her lift the back of my blouse up over my shoulder blades.

"You have a nice red line there that'll turn into a beautiful bruise. But you still won't be able to compete with Mahlon when all's said and done."

"Thank God for that." She let my blouse drop, and I turned back toward her. "I have to say, I admire the way you stood up to those two deputies. I was trembling so hard I was barely able to stay upright, and here you weren't even afraid."

Sunny shook her head. "You've got that wrong, Augie. I can think of only one other time when I was more afraid, and that was when I thought the Martians were going to disintegrate us with their heat-ray guns."

I smiled at the memory of the two of us huddled in Sunny's closet, waiting for death on the night before Halloween. "I remember," I said. "It seemed so real. Remember that neighbor kid who came flying in the front door? The one who told us New Jersey had been blown to bits and we needed to evacuate while there was still time?"

Sunny and I laughed quietly. "Yeah," she said, "and when I saw him later, he said he'd known all along it was just a hoax, and that he was really just trying to scare us."

"Liar," I replied, shaking my head. "I don't think anyone thought it was a hoax at first, not even Chichi and Haha."

"They had a few doubtful moments too, I think. But at least the whole thing made Obaasan laugh, so it was worth it. That's the only memory I have of Obaasan laughing."

We fell silent a moment, and while neither of us spoke, I listened to the pain in my back. Only one stroke of the baton and my whole body ached. What must it have been like for Mahlon when he was given the beating that left him so terribly scarred? What must it have been like for Fannie Lou Hamer, or for any number of others, black and white, who'd been beaten to within an inch of their lives? What must it be like for those who are beaten time and again, fresh wounds on old scars, layer upon layer until finally their backs become an archaeologist's study in injustice?

Pushing against the thought, I said, "I wish Chichi were here right now to tell us this is all just pretend."

Sunny shut her eyes and nodded. "I wish he were here too, and Mother as well, even though they can't tell us it's all just pretend."

"Even if they couldn't say anything at all, it would make all the difference in the world just to have them here."

"I know."

"I miss them."

"So do I."

"Where do you suppose they are right at this moment?"

Sunny offered a brief shrug. "No telling. They could be anywhere."

"Then I wish we could be anywhere with them."

A smile crept across my friend's lips. "Here we are again, a couple of thirty-four-year-old kids, wanting Mom and Dad."

"You bet I do. They always made everything all right, no matter how awful things were. And anyway, I only had a mother and father for three years. That wasn't enough. I was cheated."

"You'll see them again."

"Do you think so?"

"Yes. Once they know I've found you, nothing will keep them from seeing you."

"I hope so." Silence. Then, "Did you ever think, when we were kids . . ." My voice trailed off. Of course we never thought of jail cells, of civil rights, of racial injustice. We were of two different races, but before Pearl Harbor I thought of that only as a wonderful thing, a clear distinction between the family of my birth and the family of my heart. The distinction wasn't yet a division, and I was full of hope for how life might unfold for us. "Whoever would have thought," I rephrased it, "that the two of us would end up in jail together?"

"Well," Sunny said, resting her head against the cinder-block wall, "it's not the first time I've been locked up, is it?"

"I thought you'd never been arrested for your civil rights work before."

Sunny shook her head. "I'm talking about Manzanar."

A glance around the cell told me that some of our fellow detainees hadn't even been alive during the Second World War. Others had been merely infants. Undoubtedly, not one of them knew about Manzanar. The Japanese internment camps weren't talked about much after the war. The whole affair had become hush-hush in the way a demented great-aunt or an embarrassing family episode is considered taboo for dinner conversation. Twenty years later, most Americans didn't know the camps had ever existed.

"But at least the Japanese in the camps," Sunny continued, "didn't have it half as bad as the Negroes in the South."

"Maybe not," I conceded, "but you can't belittle your own suffering when your family lost everything."

Sunny shut her eyes. She was remembering something, and I waited, giving her time to remember. Finally, she said, "When we were in the camp, Shidzuyo said to me once, 'It's hate that's the prison, Hatsune.'" She opened her eyes then and looked at me. "She always called me Hatsune, never Sunny. Anyway, one day we were walking around the camp, just walking to pass the time and to look at the gardens that were beginning to bloom that spring, and as always there was the barbed wire and the guard towers and those men up there looking down at us with their guns. I told her the day would be perfect, if not for those men in the guard towers. I told her I hated them, because they kept us there in that prison. And, typical of Shidzuyo, she turned the whole thing around. She told me that the only people who were in prison were the ones who hated other people, because it was hate that got people all bound up in chains, so bound up that they couldn't even live. The best those people could do was just exist. But she said that if you don't have hate inside you, then no matter where you are, you're free."

She turned her gaze from me then. After a long moment, I asked, "Who's free then? Anyone?"

Sunny moved her head from side to side, a slow movement against the cinder-block wall. "I thought about it a long time that afternoon, and I finally decided I couldn't help it. And that's what I told Shidzuyo. 'I can't help it, Auntie,' I said. 'I hate the white people who put us here and took everything away from my mother and father.'"

She paused. I waited. After several drawn-out seconds she went on. "Shidzuyo said, 'Well, then, that's your choice. You'll have to live with it.' Well, I told her I couldn't help but hate them for what they'd done, and she just said, 'You *can* help it, Hatsune.' 'How can I help what I feel?' I asked. And she said, 'You can listen to your mind instead of your emotions.' I told her that no matter what, I could never love them, even if in my mind I thought I wanted to. And she said maybe not, but that I could decide to forgive them, and that would be even better."

I considered my friend's words, and I considered my friend—who she was, who she had become. "You have forgiven, haven't you, Sunny?" I asked.

"I have to forgive again and again, because I still find myself pulled to just give in to what I feel. The truth is, I can't completely get beyond the anger—not just about Manzanar, but for what I've seen in all the years since. What I've seen here in Mississippi. There's so much, Augie. This race against that race, these people against those people. And it's not just races, you know, but this class against that class, and men against women, and one family against another, until it all just seems endless."

I drew in a long breath as I thought about Sunny's words. "It does seem endless. And hopeless."

At that, Sunny smiled, an unexpected and reassuring smile. "Still, in the end, I do believe things won't always be the way they are now, Augie," she replied.

I wanted to ask her what she meant, but before I had the chance we heard a commotion from somewhere beyond the cell: a door opening and banging closed, muffled angry voices, the sound of a scuffle or of someone being dragged along the floor.

"What's going on?" Sunny asked.

"I don't know." I slid across the floor the few feet to the bars to get a better view, but there was nothing to see except the empty hall.

"Think we're being bailed out?" one of the women asked.

No one answered.

In the next moment we heard a man's voice. The words were mostly indistinguishable, but the tone was one of fury. Then another voice, murmuring. Then the angry voice again, shouting threats, tossing out curses. Then a frightened, "Nawsuh. I swear, suh." Several voices now, taunting, angry, followed by "Please, please don't. . . ." And then a thud and a piercing scream.

Luella jumped off the bunk and hurried to the bars of the cell. "It's Bo," she said quietly, her hands gripping the bars. "Deputies beatin' Bo."

From the other side of the jail we heard the shouts of the men, the voices of Mahlon and Eddie and Dave Hunsinger and a dozen others.

"You have no right—"

"We'll contact Washington—"

"You can't do this—"

"We'll see to it there's an investigation—"

"Hold on, Bo—"

"We're with you, brother—"

And from that other awful place there in the Holmes County jail came the repeated thud of something dull and heavy pounding against flesh and the cries of the young man whose courage I admired and whose humor had made me laugh. I shut my eyes against the anguish ripping through me with every one of Bo Wiley's screams. Cradling my forehead in the space between two bars, I found myself alternately thinking, *Dear God, please make them stop,* and, *Hold on, Lenny. I'm coming! I won't let them hurt you, Lenny!* as the cries of Bo Wiley became the cries of Lenny Schuler that had so often interrupted the nights of my youth.

Sunny came and put an arm around me. The jail was a tangled riot of men's and women's voices, calling out, cursing, crying. One of the women in our cell hollered over and over, "You can't do this! You can't do this!" But they could do it, and they did. And they knew they would get away with it, without consequence, no questions asked.

Finally, suddenly, the jail fell silent. Then we heard what must have been the heels of Bo's spit-polished shoes being dragged along the floor as the deputies hauled him back to the men's cell.

No one moved. We were waiting for something; I don't know what. Finally Luella turned slowly and went back to the bunk where she buried her face in her hands and wept.

Sunny and I knelt on the hard cold floor, immobile, still clinging to the bars. Without looking at her, I said, "I hate the men who did that to Bo. How can I not hate them?"

For a moment she said nothing. And then she offered me again her cryptic prediction, "It isn't always going to be like this, Augie."

Somehow, it didn't seem a satisfactory answer to my question.

❦

Hours passed. No one came to bail us out. Sunny kept looking at her watch and muttering, "I wonder where Tom is." We exchanged small talk with Dave Hunsinger's girls, enough to learn some of their names and where they were from and how many times they'd been arrested. One of their co-workers, a guy named Aaron Wexler, was supposed to have bailed them out, but he hadn't shown up either.

"Something fishy's going on here," announced Boston. Her name was Ellen Parsons, and she was a student at the University of

Massachusetts—or had been, before Freedom Summer. Now she considered it frivolous to devote time to learning when a person could actually be out doing something. She said when she'd done her bit for Negroes, she was going to start in on equal rights for women.

Our other cellmates were from out of state too, except for the two Negroes who had been born and raised in Lexington and recruited to the work by Dave Hunsinger. The one with the braids said it was her dream to ride the rails north and settle down somewhere just this side of the Canadian border. She wanted to get as far away from Mississippi as possible, because she was coming to the conclusion that the South would never change.

Small talk did little to speed up the passing of time. No food was brought, and we were hungry. We took turns drinking water from the tap, but that hardly filled our stomachs. No one showed up to tell us what was going on—not the sheriff, not even his deputies.

We wondered how Bo was. We were afraid to call out to the men in case our jailers should retaliate by beating Bo again or by choosing someone else to rough up. Sunny worried about Tom and the children. I thought about Howard and wondered whether I would ever see him again. I wanted to let him know I was proud of what he'd done.

Dusk fell, followed by darkness. A single dull bulb blinked on overhead to light our cell.

"We have rights, you know," Boston muttered to no one in particular, and no one answered. She sounded worn out, and as though she were pondering the futility of her own words.

All we could do was wait. Think and wonder and wait.

Finally, at about nine o'clock, something happened. It wasn't what we'd been hoping for, but it was something we needed without even knowing we needed it. The men on the other side of the jail started singing. They started in once again on the freedom songs we'd all been singing together on the courthouse lawn. When their voices reached us, the women perked up and exchanged glances. Some even smiled.

"That's all right," they sang. "That's all right. You go brute me, you go scorn me, / You go scandalize my name. / Since my soul got a seat up in the Kingdom, / That's all right."

In a mean Mississippi jail, on a hot summer night, it was all right. I pictured the young men huddled in their small cell, mentally picking up anger, humiliation, and fear and setting it aside to go on singing about hope in the face of hopelessness.

Who knows, maybe something is hopeless only when we're not willing to sing anymore.

FORTY-ONE

Tom Fulton and Aaron Wexler spent hours demanding to be allowed to put up bail, but they were repeatedly turned away. Five times they were told that the amount of bail hadn't yet been determined and they would have to return in an hour. After five hours, Tom called Cedric Frohmann, who was known to be friendly with the sheriff of Holmes County, a man with the dubious name of Elwood Posse. A brief but reportedly heated conversation between Cedric and Elwood led to our eventual release. We left our cells to find Tom still in the process of upbraiding the deputies with a whip of furious rebukes. But when he saw Bo half stumbling, half carried out of the jail by Mahlon and Eddie, his anger escalated far beyond words. He was speechless. And in the silence of that white-hot anger, I think he finally heard the voices of Hollis's animals calling him out of the South.

Dave Hunsinger and his co-workers scattered into the night while our own small group headed back to Carver. We returned in the cars we had come in, except for Bo. We carefully settled him into the backseat of Tom's car with a blanket under his head for a pillow.

On the way home we drank the sodas still in the cooler, and it took the edge off our hunger. We rode in silence, and halfway home the two young women fell asleep, Susannah's head on Luella's shoulder.

It was past midnight when our little caravan of cars broke the darkness of Coloredtown's unpaved and unlighted streets, soldiers returning from battle, a defeated battalion.

Mahlon veered away with a quiet farewell toot of his horn, dropping off Eddie before returning to the Reeses' home over the store. Tom went directly to Dr. Dawson's office to deliver our one serious casualty into the hands of the only Negro doctor in Carver. Fortunately he was at home when the makeshift ambulance arrived. He answered Tom's knock right away and, still wearing nothing but the shorts he slept in, set about stitching Bo's bleeding scalp and binding his broken ribs.

Meanwhile, Sunny and I took the women home, Susannah sleepily padding across the hard-packed earthen walkway in her bare feet, but straight up and dignified, at long last settling her hat back into place before opening the front door. Luella, when she said good night, hesitated a moment, turned back to us, and said, "You ever gonna take another group to register, Miz Fulton?"

"Yes, Luella," Sunny replied. "I'm sure we'll go back."

"Don't go without me."

Sunny smiled. "We won't. Good night, Luella."

"Good night, Miz Fulton, Miz Callahan."

We went home then, Sunny and I, and in his separate car, Tom. We wished each other good-night with the unspoken agreement that we would talk about what had happened in the morning. For now we needed rest.

I crawled wearily between the cool sheets, thankful to shut my eyes. At once I fell into a dreamless sleep and slept late. It was the sound of Lee Henry's car coming up the drive that woke me close to noon. He and Miss Ebba came by every day to get an update on Howard. Without a phone they weren't able to call for themselves, but Tom was checking in with the hospital every morning.

I sat up to a wave of nausea—too little food, too much heat, the continuing ache in my back. But it passed and I dressed, washed my face, and tried to tidy up a bit, then went downstairs to meet the Starks. They were sitting with Sunny in the living room drinking iced tea. Tom, I knew, was at the mill, as he often was on Saturdays. When I appeared, Lee Henry's eyes said I looked as bad as I felt, but he collected himself and gave me a smile.

Miss Ebba set her glass on the small table beside the overstuffed chair. She had on a different dress today, a sleeveless brown linen with yellow buttons the size of quarters up the front. But she wore the same battered shoes, and her ankles were circled by the same nylon donuts. "We hear," she said mildly, "de two you spent time in de Holmes County jail yestiday, Miz Callahan."

I offered a brief laugh and sat down in the wing chair. "Yes, we did, Miss Ebba. The accommodations were lacking, but it was an interesting experience nevertheless."

Lee Henry leaned forward and said, "We're right sorry that happen to you, Miz Callahan."

"Don't be, Lee Henry. I'm glad I was behind bars with the good guys instead of outside with the bad ones."

Lee Henry nodded and sat back. The straps of his overalls stretched snugly over his huge shoulders, the buttons straining against the metal loops holding up the bib.

"I've been telling them about what happened yesterday," Sunny said, "but they'd already heard some of it on the grapevine. Everyone knows that Bo's laid up at Dr. Dawson's. A whole handful of young people from the school have volunteered to go to the courthouse next week to try again."

"In spite of what happened to Bo?"

"More likely because of it."

The room fell quiet. The laughter of the children playing outside drifted in through the open windows.

Miss Ebba turned her one eye to Sunny and said, "When dey go, I'm gon' wid dem."

"Now, Mama——"

"Hush, Lee Henry. I done made up mah mind. I ain't been studyin' all dis time for nothin', you know. I'se been preparin' to regista, and regista I will, eben if it kill me."

"Or you get killed in the tryin'."

"Might be so, Lee Henry, but I won' sit by no more. I done learnt what I need to 'bout registrin', and it's time I go do it."

Sunny sighed. She looked at Lee Henry. "She's determined, Lee Henry. I don't think we can change her mind."

"You cain't," Miss Ebba said firmly.

"But we'll have to have another meeting of the school to decide exactly when we're going, and"—Sunny shifted her gaze to Miss Ebba—"who's going."

"I'm gon'," Miss Ebba said, making the decision final.

Lee Henry sighed heavily. He looked from his grandmother to Sunny and changed the subject. "Well, we didn't come to talk about registrin', we come to learn about Howard. Tom call the hospital this mornin'?"

I looked eagerly at Sunny, who nodded. "Yes. Howard's doing fine, as well as can be expected. They're still concerned about infection, but so far there doesn't seem to be any sign of one. He's eating a little bit, even asked for butter pecan ice cream yesterday—said he had a craving."

"Mus' be a good sign," offered Lee Henry. "Dying man don't ask for ice cream, does he?"

"Can he hab vis'tors yet?" Miss Ebba asked, ignoring Lee Henry's speculation on last requests.

"He can have one visitor for a few minutes at a time."

Miss Ebba nodded, took a deep breath, let it out. "Will one o' you go, den, take a message to him? Tell Howard sumpin' face-ta-face for me?"

"What is it, Miss Ebba?" I asked.

"Tell him, go on home, go on back to Chicagie. Dat boy's work done here. No more he can do. Tell him go on home 'fore anythin' worse happen."

Surely Howard already knew his work was done here, that the only thing left for him to do was go home. But I decided Miss Ebba wanted to send him home with her blessing, to let him know he had done what he could, and it was time now to leave.

Sunny looked at me. "You want to go?" she asked.

She knew I did. Miss Ebba too.

"Yes," I said simply.

"In a little bit I'll call the hospital and get directions for you," Sunny volunteered.

"You lemme know what he say," Miss Ebba instructed.

"I will," I promised.

"Tell dat boy I love him, but I don' neber wanna see his face in Miss'ssippi 'gain."

I smiled. "I will, Miss Ebba."

She nodded her satisfaction, then she and Lee Henry rose to go. The phone rang and Sunny excused herself to answer it, but I walked the Starks to the front door and stepped with them out onto the porch. At the top of the steps, Miss Ebba said, "I hear dat courthouse don' have too many steps."

"No, just a few," I assured her.

"Good thing too. I'se gittin' too old be climbin' up 'n down too many steps."

"Mama," Lee Henry complained mildly, "you gettin' too old for most ever'thing anymore."

"Hush, Lee Henry," Miss Ebba scolded. "I can still keep up wid you, cain't I?"

"Yes'm," Lee Henry muttered. "But maybe that ain't sayin' much, seein' as I'm just this side a old myself."

"Well, quit complainin', old man, and hep me down the car."

Their friendly sparring continued until both car doors had slammed shut, but even then, as they pulled away, I could see Miss Ebba's hands waving, her jaw flapping. I laughed. My laughter sailed across the open, sun-filled air. I was happy, giddy as a schoolgirl on her first date. I was just a couple hours away from seeing Howard Draper.

❦

When I reached the hospital in Jackson, a nurse directed me to Howard's room with the words, "It's the one with the man standing outside the door."

He was an FBI agent in street clothes, and his eyes latched on to me and didn't waver as I made my way down the hall.

"You Augusta Callahan?" he asked without preamble when I'd reached him.

I said yes and nodded. Sunny had told the hospital I was coming.

"Can I see your driver's license?"

I fumbled about in my purse, pulled out my wallet, and gave him the license. He inspected it, looked at me, looked back at the license, then returned it to me. "You the one who wrote that book?" he asked.

"Yes," I replied. "Are you Gary Colscott?" He nodded. He still hadn't smiled, though I offered him one now. "You bought the book for Howard when he couldn't find it in Carver?"

Gary Colscott shrugged. "Least I could do. He's helped me out a great deal."

"I hear he was feeding you information."

The agent nodded toward the open doorway. "That's why he's here."

"Ruthless, aren't they?" I asked, speaking of the Klan.

"Someday we're going to hang those rodents from the end of their own rope." His words were tinged with anger, but he finally smiled. He nodded again toward Howard. "I think he's asleep, but why don't you go on in?"

I did and saw that Howard's eyes were closed. I walked to the side of the bed, wanting just to be near him. I could wait, I thought, until he wakes up. I was in no hurry. I wouldn't leave without giving him Miss Ebba's message.

He was hooked up to an IV that dripped a clear liquid methodically into his left arm. His face was pallid, drained of all color, whiter than white. Even his lips were pale, so that the dark whiskers on his cheeks and jaw looked like penciled dots across the bleached canvas of his skin. His hair was a startlingly dark crown, and for the first time I noticed faint hints of gray. One too long strand fell forward over his forehead, touching the lid of one eye, and instinctively I lifted a hand to brush it back from his face.

When I did, his eyelids flickered and opened. He gazed up at me a moment, not as though he were trying to recognize who I was, but as though he were trying to decide whether I was really there. Finally he whispered, "Augie?"

"Hello, Howard." I finished brushing the hair from his forehead and gave him a smile.

When he spoke, his voice was raspy, "Augie, I'm sorry . . ."

He paused to moisten his lips, and I took the chance to ask gently, "What could you possibly have to be sorry about?"

"Putting you in danger. I never should have . . ."

"I never went anywhere I didn't want to go. It was all my own choice. . . ."

He shook his head slowly. "I had no right."

"But, Howard, I—"

"That first night, at the mayor's house . . ." He paused, cleared his throat, ran his tongue over his dry lips once more. "I told myself,

418

Draper, old man, don't be a fool. Leave her alone. But then I saw you again at the café . . ."

"I know. I know, Howard, and it's all right."

He gazed at me, searching my face, my eyes. For several moments neither of us spoke. Finally I said, "I have a message for you from Miss Ebba and Lee Henry."

A small smile played across his lips. "I think I know what it is. Tell me anyway."

"Go home. Go back to Chicago."

The smile grew wider. "I guess I've worn out my welcome here in Mississippi."

"More like, your cover's been blown."

Howard nodded, an almost imperceptible nod. "Miss Ebba told you about me?"

"Spilled the whole story."

He looked pensive a moment, then lifted his free arm and crooked a finger to draw me closer. When I leaned in toward him, he said quietly, "My cover hasn't been blown completely, you know. They've got me in the white section of this hospital." He winked then and put his finger to his lips.

I laughed quietly. "Your secret's safe with me," I assured him. "But listen, Howard, you'll leave, won't you? Go back to Chicago?"

Howard shrugged. "Maybe I could join the Klan here in Jackson or in some other small town."

"I hope you're kidding. It won't be long before the whole state of Mississippi knows one of the members of the Carver Klavern was a Negro passing. That's sure to make Carver the laughingstock of the White Knights."

Howard smiled again, but it was a wan smile and unconvincing. "I didn't want Cedric Frohmann ever to know I'm his son."

"But there were three men involved. How can you be sure Cedric Frohmann's your father?"

Howard raised a finger to the dimple in his chin. "Where do you think I got this?" Without waiting for an answer, he added, "Of course, I can't be completely sure, but I look more like the mayor than I do the other two men."

"Well, okay, but why do you think the mayor will find out he's your father?"

"The Klan must have found out about Trudy, about her going north when she was carrying me. Else they wouldn't know about me, that my mother's a Negro woman. The mayor's not Klan, but he knows what time it is. He'll find out one way or another why I was shot."

"You mean someone in the Klan will tell the mayor he's your father?"

Howard shook his head. "I doubt the Klan knows who my father is. All that matters is they know who my mother is, and that she's colored. For all they know, my father's a Negro too. Maybe high yellow, but still a Negro."

"But I still don't understand. So the mayor will find out you were shot for being a Negro, but why is that going to tell him he's your father?"

"Well, Cedric was drunk when he and the others raped my mother, but not so drunk he doesn't remember. He knows who raped and when he raped her. Put two and two together and he'll figure it out." He looked up at me, his eyes large. "See, I think the rape is why he backed out of Ole Miss and went to school up north instead. I think Cedric wanted to get away from the memory of what happened and from the place it happened."

"At least that means he's got some sense of right and wrong."

"Actually, I've come to believe he's a good man at heart, a good man living in a bad place at a bad time." Howard drew in a deep breath and let it out slowly. "When I came to Carver, I had nothing but contempt for Cedric Frohmann. But then I got to know him. Funny thing is, now that I know him, I genuinely like him. He did something awful where Trudy was concerned, but I think, when the alcohol wore off, he was sickened by the whole thing. It was like, well, it was the one aberration in an otherwise good life, the one reckless moment. That's how I've come to think of it, anyway. And to some extent I've even forgiven him."

"So that's why you went to the mayor's house every Sunday? To be with Cedric Frohmann?"

"Yes."

"You know, don't you, that everyone thought it was because you were interested in his daughter."

"Yes, I'm well aware of what Carver thinks," Howard confessed lightly. "And I never meant her any harm, but it wasn't Betsey I was interested in. That weekly invitation to their home was more than I'd ever hoped for when I came to Carver. I thought I'd see Cedric only from a distance, learn about him through hearsay. Ironically, because my father was interested in me as a son-in-law, I was able to spend a lot of time with him."

Out in the hall a medicine cart rattled by on squeaky wheels. A doctor was paged. Gary Colscott coughed, reminding us that he was there.

"You know, Howard," I said, "if Cedric Frohmann hadn't done what he did, you wouldn't be here."

"Yes, there's that," he agreed quietly. "Edit the rape out of the story, and I'm gone right along with it."

"So something good came out of something awful."

"I'd like to think so," Howard admitted. "At least if I can make my life count for something. I thought I was in a unique position to help the Negroes of Carver." He shifted slightly in the bed, wincing as he moved, his eyes becoming lines. Then he gazed up at me again. "Well, now you know why I left Chicago to come to a nothing town like Carver, Mississippi."

I nodded. "Yes, now I understand."

"But in spite of my good intentions, I didn't really accomplish much, did I?"

"Oh, Howard," I countered, "more than you can know."

He shook his head. "I would have liked to have done so much more. I was just getting started, just beginning to pass on information to the FBI and . . ."

"Now, you listen to me, Howard," I interrupted, trying to sound firm. "You did more than most people would do. Far more. You think very many people would put their life on the line to come down here and try to outwit the Klan?"

It was a rhetorical question, and Howard didn't answer.

"Anyway," I said, "I'm glad your cover's been blown. It was killing me, trying to figure out how someone like you could be involved with the Klan."

Howard's gaze widened. "You knew I was Klan before Miss Ebba told you?" When I nodded, he asked, "How'd you know?"

"There's a leak down at the mill. One of the wives of a Klan member tells Tom, and Tom tells Sunny. When I arrived in Carver she greeted me with the news that Howard Draper was a church organist by day and a Klan member by night. I was fascinated."

Howard laughed and shook his head. "So you were trying to figure me out."

"Yes. I knew there had to be some sort of explanation, something no one in Carver knew about. Something just told me you weren't Klan, but I would never have guessed you were a Negro passing."

With those words his face became a blank slate from which I could read nothing. Then he appeared troubled or sad, or maybe he was simply weary from the exertion of talking. He closed his eyes, and when he opened them I could see a hint of fear reflected there.

"What is it, Howard?" I asked.

"I'm wondering . . ." He paused. He glanced toward the window, then looked back at me. "I'm wondering what you must think of me now, now that you know I'm not really a Klansman, but I *am* a Negro."

I don't know whether it was the fear in his eyes or the pain in his voice or the implication behind his question that touched me so deeply, but suddenly his image was blurred by the tears I couldn't hold back. I wasn't sure I could speak aloud for the lump in my throat, so I leaned forward, closer to his face, and whispered, "You ask me what I think of you?" I shook my head and one tear slipped down my cheek so that I was crying even while I laughed. "I'm right proud to know you, Howard Draper, till I'm like to bust wide open with pride."

And then my cheek was pressed against his lips, and he was kissing away my tears, kissing away all the years that reached back from that day to the day I decided not to love, and farther back still, back to a time before Lenny, before Chichi and Haha and Sunny, before Mother and Uncle Finn and Aunt Lucy, all the way back to the day I came to be named Augusta through someone's carelessness. A newborn baby, red, wrinkled, squawking, but willing to love and wanting to be loved because that is how we are made. Bolts unlocked and years swept away and suddenly, a new beginning. Like Snow White, I was brought back to life by a simple kiss. Sometimes that's all it takes to come back from the dead. A simple kiss, and there you are.

FORTY-TWO

I'd never come up against writer's block until the day I sat at the desk in Sunny's guest room staring for more than an hour at a clean piece of paper in my portable typewriter. My editor had sent me to Mississippi on good faith, expecting me to come back with a worthwhile story on voter registration in a town where not one Negro was registered. More than a week later, as I sat down to begin the story, the number of Negroes in Carver registered to vote was still zero. What mattered was that they had tried—that was the story. They had tried and they would try again, and that was the core of what needed to be said.

My notes lay scattered in piles on the desk like subpoenaed witnesses waiting to testify. But I wouldn't let them speak. I was too engrossed in listening to something else. Another story was taking shape in my mind, and if I didn't listen right now, this minute, I might not have the chance again.

Part of the story was taking place beyond the open window even now. For the hundredth time that afternoon Joanie peddled her little pink bicycle to the end of the driveway and back toward the house, training wheels kicking up dust. She'd been at it for the last half hour, up and back, up and back, crying out at intervals, "Look at me,

Mommy! Look how fast I'm going!" And Sunny calling from the porch, "Good job, Joanie. Soon we'll be taking those training wheels off!" In the side yard, Ronnie and two of his Little League friends took turns at bat while Tom played pitcher with a softball. I couldn't see the boys from where I sat, but I could see Tom, and I could see too the occasional ball that went flying past him almost all the way to the road. Little boy voices filled the air with cheers, laughter, and good-natured ribbing.

I liked the sound of it, of this family and their young friends enjoying a lazy Sunday afternoon. And I thought, *This is life*. This is the best it has to offer. Because who in the world doesn't want simply to be at peace, enjoying their loved ones on a sunny Sunday afternoon?

It was what I wanted, certainly, though I'd denied it for more years than I could count. But it wasn't too late. There was still time. And the fact that I had years ahead of me to live—to *really* live—was a gift. An undeserved gift, pure and simple.

I turned my gaze back to the typewriter, to the empty page, to the handwritten notes on either side of me. I'd have to work up those many disconnected notes into a reasonable whole, turn it all into readable copy. I would do it. But probably not today. Today was for something else, for listening to the stirring of a different story.

My mind skipped back to that morning in church where two odd things had happened. The first was the way in which the pastor glossed over Howard Draper's absence. "Our usual organist is ill," he explained perfunctorily. "Miss Lucinda Craft has graciously agreed to fill in for him until his return."

At first I thought he must be joking, but it didn't take me long to decide that he and everyone else was simply willing to play along with this strange half-truth. Surely most everyone knew by now that Howard had been shot and wouldn't be coming back. Not that there had been any reports in the *Carver Clarion*, or should that be *Karver Klarion*, the editor himself being Klan? No KKK newspaperman would allow the news of a Klan shooting to make headlines. But there were quicker ways for news to get around than through the daily paper, and I had no doubt the news about Howard had made the rounds more quickly than usual.

This was Mississippi, after all. Everyone knew, but no one was going to talk about the unthinkable. That a Negro would have the nerve to pass for white! That a Negro would worm his way into the Klan! An embarrassment never to be lived down. Best, at least in public, to pretend that Howard Draper had simply fallen ill, and if he never showed up at the organ again, well, Lucinda Craft did a fair enough job on "He the Pearly Gates Will Open." Who's to complain about that?

The second odd thing was the arrival of Betsey Frohmann on the arm of a strikingly handsome—and extremely fair-haired—young man. I nudged Sunny as the couple made their way toward the front of the church to sit with the mayor and his wife. Not that Sunny wouldn't have noticed them anyway. The service was already under way when the couple sauntered down the aisle like a couple of honored guests at a wedding. It was obvious they had come late to the service expressly for the purpose of being seen.

"Who's that she's with?" I whispered to Sunny.

"Never seen him before."

"How could she have come up with him so fast?"

Sunny shrugged. "You got me on that one. He must have been waiting in the wings somewhere."

"Do you think she's devastated to know she was in love with her own half brother?"

She shook her head. "She'll never know Howard was her half brother. Only a very few people will ever know that."

I considered that for a moment, then nodded my understanding. Only Miss Ebba, Lee Henry, Sunny, Tom and I, and the mayor himself—if, as Howard said, he put two and two together—would know the paternal identity of Howard Draper. Certainly it was not a confession the mayor would want to make to his wife and daughter.

"But she's most likely learned by now that Howard's mother was a Negro from Carver?" I said.

"Oh yes, I'm sure."

"Then at least she knows she was in love with a Negro."

"Yes. And that would devastate her more than knowing she was in love with her own brother."

No doubt Betsey Frohmann hoped Carver's memory of her link to Howard Draper would fade more quickly if she was seen in the company of a blue-eyed blond. No colored blood in this one, no sir, not a drop.

It's just as well, I thought, smiling to myself. Howard Draper didn't love her anyway.

I was so lost in thought I didn't hear Sunny enter the room. When she spoke, I actually jumped in my seat.

"Sorry to scare you," she apologized, laughing. "Hope I'm not interrupting."

"Look for yourself." I waved a hand toward the typewriter and the empty page.

Sunny nodded sympathetically. "Having trouble coming up with a lead?"

I shook my head. "It's not the lead so much as the whole story," I confessed.

"You don't think there's anything to write about?"

"Oh no. No, there's definitely a story here amid all these notes. It's just that . . ."

When I didn't go on, Sunny prodded, "Just what, Augie?"

"I don't know. I mean, I came here expecting to do another civil rights story, and I will. It's just that, well, there's another story too, one that starts in Hollenbeck Park on a summer day when a Salvation Army band is playing." I took a deep breath, let it out. "It's about a little girl in Buster Brown shoes and another little girl who needs a family and finds one." I looked up at Sunny. She was smiling. So was I. "It's a story about losing and finding. It's about a Japanese woman who becomes white, and a white man who's really colored, and a white woman with a Japanese heart who falls in love with a white man who's really a Negro passing. It's a love story." I laughed lightly, shook my head. "I never thought I'd write a love story, but that's what I want to write."

Sunny put a hand on my shoulder, giving it a squeeze. "Then that's what you should write, Augie."

"I will," I responded. "I think I'll do just that."

I cleared the desk of my notes. I'd get back to them, but not today. Another time and place were calling me back to themselves, and I answered their call, sailing back across years to one auspicious day in my childhood. My fingers began to move over the typewriter keyboard, the clicking of keys filling the room. If I worked for an hour I could come up with at least a few pages, at least a beginning.

Outside the window life went on, but I wasn't in Mississippi anymore. I was a little girl named Augie Schuler wandering the streets of Boyle Heights. . . .

FORTY-THREE

That night around the Fultons' dining room table, we played Monopoly until long past the children's bedtime. By ten o'clock Joanie was asleep with her head on the table, her small fist clutching a plastic hotel and twenty-one dollars in Monopoly money. Tom carried her up to bed, and Ronnie followed close behind. Sunny and I moved to the kitchen to have a cup of tea and to spend a few moments together before going to bed.

"When will you be going back to L.A.?" she asked.

"I'm not sure. A couple of days, most likely."

"I hate to see you go."

"I hate to go."

We sipped our tea. We listened to the chorus of crickets and tree frogs beyond the open windows.

"It doesn't seem right, somehow," she said. "Now that we've found each other again, it seems we should go on being together."

I nodded. "How much longer do you think you'll stay in Carver?"

"I really can't say. Probably not long. Even this past week I've seen a change in Tom. He's never been happy here, but at least he was willing to stay for the mill. Now it seems as though he's lost that willingness."

"It'd kill Corinne if he moved back north."

"It'd kill Tom if he stayed down here."

She poured herself some more tea, stirred a bit of sugar into it. "We have to stay in touch."

"Of course we will," I said, surprised she felt that was something needing to be said. I added, chuckling, "Sean McDougall is no longer my mailman, remember? If you write, chances are I'll get your letters."

She smiled wanly. "We'll fly out to L.A. sometime to visit you. Certainly Mother and Papa will want to go. Has the old neighborhood changed much?"

"A little. Not too much. Even a lot of the same people—older now, of course."

"I haven't been there since the war. It would be strange to go back."

I shrugged. "It's the same old place. I don't think you'd have any trouble recognizing Boyle Heights."

She dropped her eyes to the teacup, lifted them again. "But I don't think Boyle Heights would recognize me."

She had a point. "No matter, really. As Thomas Wolfe said, you can't go home again. None of us can."

"And yet Boyle Heights still feels like my home in so many ways."

"Maybe because Carver doesn't. I suppose we always want to have someplace that feels like home."

"What feels like home to you, Augie?"

I thought a moment. And I knew she was right. "My home is a little white house on Fickett Street where I live with you and Chichi and Haha."

Sunny nodded, her eyebrows raised. "Do you think we could ever all be together again, living in the same place? The same city, at least?"

A night owl hooted somewhere. I paused to listen. "I don't see how. But I for one feel pretty lucky to at least know where you are. We're lucky to have found each other after so many years."

"Yes," she agreed. "Yes, we are." She looked at me, her head tilted slightly, her face soft with concern. "What about you and Howard? Do you have any plans?"

Sighing, I pushed my teacup away from me. "I don't know. Nothing's been said for sure. I do know he'll be going back to Chicago, and I'll be going back to L.A."

"But you do love him, don't you?"

"Yes, I think I do." I paused, smiled. "As much as you can love a person you've known for only a week."

"And he loves you?"

I had to think about that. "I don't know how to answer, Sunny. He hasn't said anything—about a future."

Sunny looked at me a long moment before saying, "Are you content to go back to California and go on the way you were?"

I shook my head no. "I don't think I'll be going on the way I was. I mean, you're a part of my life again—you and Chichi and Haha. That changes everything."

"But is that enough?"

"It has to be."

Sunny looked skeptical. "I'd like to see you happy, Augie."

Another sigh, and I felt the lines forming between my eyes as I wondered how to answer. "I think I am happy, Sunny. Happier than I've been in a long time."

She smiled, then rose and carried our teacups to the sink. When she turned toward me, the smile had disappeared. "But you shouldn't have to be alone."

"I'm not anymore. As long as I know where you and Chichi and Haha are, I'll be all right."

"Well, you'll always know exactly where we are."

"Then I'll always be perfectly all right."

Sunny turned off the kitchen light, and then we climbed the stairs and said good night.

Instead of going to bed, I returned to my desk. Talking with Sunny had churned up feelings and memories that I didn't want getting lost in the caverns of sleep. I jotted down pages of notes by hand so as to avoid the clacking of the typewriter. A couple hours later, at about one in the morning, I gathered up the pages and, feeling satisfied, finally decided it was time to sleep. But before I could rise from the desk, I glanced one last time out the window and was surprised to see a hazy light in the distance, rising ghostlike over the tops of the trees. What was out that way, I wondered, to the east of the Fultons' house? It took me a moment to reorient myself, but then I remembered. The Big Black River. And Coloredtown.

I rose slowly, my eyes on the glow above the trees. I pushed the chair away from the desk with the backs of my knees. The light was coming from Coloredtown, rising up and spreading out against the dark night sky, and that could only mean one thing.

Quickly I ran to the bedroom next to mine. "Sunny, Tom," I cried, "I think there's fire in Coloredtown."

They were awake at once. "What's going on?" Tom asked.

"I see light above the trees, over in the direction of Coloredtown."

Tom jumped out of bed, threw on a robe, and headed for the hall. Sunny and I joined him at the window, looking out over his shoulders. The light was brighter now, a rosy glow like an ill-timed sunrise pushing its way into the night sky.

"You're right," Tom said. "The whole place must be up in flames."

He turned then and pushed past us, disappearing into the bedroom. When he came out, he was dressed and buckling the belt of his jeans.

"Tom?" Sunny asked.

"They'll need all the help they can get," Tom muttered, "and I hardly think the Carver fire department is going to respond." He was angry again. And I understood. Would it never end?

"I'm going with you, Tom," I called out as he headed down the stairs. I was still wearing the casual slacks and blouse I'd changed into after church, but I ran to my room to get my shoes. When I returned to the hall, I was surprised to see Tom waiting for me on the stairs. "Let's go," he urged.

Sunny took a step forward. "I should go too, Tom," she offered, but her husband shook his head and replied, "No, stay with the kids. And anyway, the train."

I didn't know what he meant by the last, and at the moment I didn't care. Sunny gave us a worried look. I responded by saying, "We'll be back as soon as we can." She walked to the head of the stairs, watching us as we hurried down. I felt her eyes on our backs, though I didn't turn around. My mind was already in Coloredtown, taking inventory of the folks I'd met there. The men and women of the citizenship school. The young folks I'd gone with to Lexington and been jailed with. The families that had filled the Baptist church the night of the prayer service. And of course Miss Ebba and Lee Henry and Hattie Loomis—members of Howard's own family. Coloredtown was full of Howard's family.

Who was hurt? I wondered. And had anyone been killed?

Tom and I arrived to find the whole of the business district up in flames, the entire row of stores, offices, and homes that made up the center of Coloredtown. The general store and the Reeses' apartment, the funeral parlor, the barbershop, the clothing boutique, the Chat and Chew, Dr. Dawson's office, and the living space above it. They were all connected and all burning.

When Tom slowed to a stop by the side of the road, he muttered only one word: "Klan." He needn't have said it. I already knew.

The place was a Dantean nightmare, the inner circle of hell set down in the middle of Carver's Coloredtown. People were running, hollering, screaming, crying, dark silhouettes against the huge inferno devouring the heart of their town. The heat from the blaze was intense, searing my skin even from a distance. The air was hot and smoky, making it an effort simply to breathe.

Tom and I stood immobile by the car for a moment, arrested by the sight in front of us, not sure how to begin to help. He must have forgotten I was there, because in the next instant he found his legs and sprinted toward the fire. In its light I saw him grab somebody's arm. That unidentifiable someone waved his other arm toward the flames, and Tom disappeared with him around the back of the burning buildings.

Before I could will myself to move and follow Tom, I noticed someone lying beneath a tree not far from where we'd parked. As I stepped closer, the face of the young man took on shape in the firelight. It was Bo Wiley.

Moving to his side, I knelt on the hard-packed earth, just at the edge of the blanket where he lay. His eyes were open. A white bandage circled his forehead. A second one, larger, hugged his otherwise naked chest. He held one hand against his ribcage, as though to still the ache.

"Bo," I said gently.

He turned his eyes to mine; the reflection of the fire danced in the dark spheres. "Miz Callahan," he whispered, sounding surprised.

"Are you all right?" I asked.

He shut his eyes and nodded slightly. "Doc helped me out here soon as the fire started. Leastways the night riders didn't stay, so's we could get out. Jes' threw their firebombs in the windows and left."

"Has anyone been hurt?"

Bo licked his lips before answering. They were dry and cracked. I wished I had some water to give him. "Don't know, Miz Callahan," he replied.

I looked toward the burning buildings, then back at Bo. "How long ago did they come?"

" 'Bout half hour, give or take."

It didn't matter, really, when they'd come. What mattered was that they'd come at all, and what they'd done. "I'd better go help, Bo. Will you be all right?"

Bo nodded. "They's haulin' up water from the river. But"—he winced, shook his head—"it no use . . . all lost. Whole street's gone."

"Maybe something can be salvaged," I offered lamely, knowing full well that Bo was probably right.

"You go on, Miz Callahan," Bo nodded once toward the fire. "I'se all right. I'd help too if I could."

"You just rest, Bo." I touched his shoulder lightly, and he pulled away. Not because of pain, I knew, but simply because I had touched him. It was a reflexive action, nothing more. But I was surprised and hurt, because I hadn't expected it from Bo. We had protested together on the lawn of the courthouse, and he had tried to defend and protect me. We'd been hauled to jail together in the same paddy wagon. We had shared something that was about race but beyond race.

And yet, he was still a Negro, and I was still a white woman, and even after all that we believed in, and all that we had done, we were still different, because the world said it was so. The fear of whites had been bred into Bo Wiley since the day he was born, and it was a fear he would never outlive. A time might come when a Negro man—Bo Wiley's son, or his son's son—might look into the eyes of a white woman without fear, but what had taken years to make would take years to unmake as well.

I pulled my hand back. He dropped his eyes.

"You rest," I repeated. And then I rose and made my way through the heat toward the fire.

The next several hours were spent in a losing battle against the flames. Two long bucket brigades stretched from the back side of the buildings to the Big Black River, and I joined one of them, stepping in between Curtis Reese and a young woman I didn't know.

"Is anyone still inside, Curtis?" I hollered over the roar of the fire.

His dark skin glistened with sweat that flew from his face when he shook his head. "Don' know for sho, Miz Callahan," he said, "but I think ever'one's out."

"Anyone hurt?"

"Some burns. Don' know how bad."

I saw Tom up close to the buildings, throwing water on the fire. I didn't know how he could bear the heat, but then I saw that the lines rotated so that no one person was close to the flames for long. The one who threw the water onto the fire carried the bucket back down to the river while numerous other buckets made their way, passed hand to hand, up the line. Even children helped, boys and girls no older than eight, nine, ten. Most of them barefoot—most everyone barefoot, in fact, having been called up out of bed when the fire broke out.

We must have known it was hopeless. How could we not? We needed fire trucks, hoses, gallons of water. All we had were a few dozen buckets, and the water we tossed on the flames was swallowed up as quickly as a sprinkling of rain over miles of sand dunes.

But we did it anyway. Bucket after bucket after bucket. Hand to hand to hand. Reaching, passing, reaching, passing. Running, stumbling through the woods to the river. Feet making trails in the sandbar at the river's edge. Oh, the cool sand, the cool water! Scoop the water into the bucket, haul it up, pass it on one more time. Never mind the dizziness from heat and smoke. Never mind the hands aching with blisters. Don't think about the aching muscles, the sheer exhaustion; just keep moving. Take the bucket, pass the bucket. I never knew water was so heavy. Bumping up against other bodies, who was that? I would say I'm sorry, but no time to talk now. No breath to talk. Everywhere, people gasping, coughing. Sweat dripping down faces. Tears running down cheeks, tears from the smoke, tears from the heart. Twigs snapping underfoot, water sloshing onto stomach, arms, legs. No stars overhead, only a thin slice of moon somewhere beyond that cloud of smoke. The flames are the lantern we work by, an eerie, shifting light. Will morning never come? And all around me, splintered prayers drifting upward with the smoke: "Lawd, help us, God,"

"Gimme strength, Jesus," and sometimes just, "Lawd, Lawd," because beyond that, as the hours dragged by, there was really nothing else to be said.

I prayed myself, wordless prayers, asking for the strength to keep going. I fought against the temptation to lie down on the floor of the woods and give in to the sleep of exhaustion.

Is this how you felt, Lenny? I wondered. *Is this how you felt, day after day, year after year, when you were sick and tired and hungry and you had no strength left, but you had to go on living anyway? Oh, how did you do it! How did you ever make it back to Boyle Heights alive?*

Maybe, like Uncle Finn said, it was the O'Shaughnessy blood in him that kept him going during the war. Or maybe it was just the will to put up a fight, even though he knew he was defeated. Maybe he figured if he was only going to die once, it wasn't going to be because his skin was white and his eyes were round and that wasn't the right way to look in Bataan in 1942.

If I told them, would the people here in Coloredtown believe that my own brother had suffered because he was white? That he'd been starved and beaten and faced with the unspeakable horrors of a labor camp because he was an American in Bataan when the Japanese invaded? Would they understand that as long as hate existed, no one was safe, not even a white man from America, land of prosperity, home of the free?

The roof of the Reeses' store and home caved in, burning log crashing down upon burning log, black smoke billowing out of the open store windows like the tongues of schoolchildren wagging at us. Then the roof of the barbershop next door went down, and then the café, then the clothing boutique, and so on all the way down the line, dominolike, until the entire stretch of buildings folded in upon itself with a huge resigned sigh.

We went on fighting the fire, though there was little left to save. After an indeterminate amount of time—maybe an hour, maybe more—the flames finally lost their momentum. They settled into a smoldering rumble, like sated gluttons content to lick their fingers before lying down to sleep.

At last the buckets stopped. The woods grew silent. People appeared frozen in place, trying to take in the loss, the destruction. Morning had come with our hardly being aware of it, creeping in over the Big Black River while we stood dumbfounded, gaping at what was left, which was nothing at all. Just a pile of black ashes, dotted with a red glow of embers, and white smoke rising up into the still morning air.

Only after what seemed a very long time did people begin moving about, hugging each other, comforting each other. Some sat alone on the ground, looking numb, defeated. Some wept, their faces buried in their arms. Others moved away individually or in small groups. The Reese family stood by the ruins of their home and livelihood, their arms around one another. The Robinson brothers gazed across the ashes of the funeral parlor. I could see all the way across the dirt road to where Tom had parked the car a few centuries earlier, and to where Bo Wiley still lay on the ground. A small crowd had gathered there. The wounded? Dr. Dawson was wrapping what looked like a cloth bandage around the arm of a young man. Where he got the bandage I couldn't imagine. His office and all his medical supplies were gone. Maybe it was just a piece of clothing or a shredded pillowcase brought from someone's home. A woman walked among the crowd, ladling out drinking water from a bucket.

I stood where I was for a long while, made immobile not by the exhaustion but by the enormous sadness in my chest. Sorrow for the people of Coloredtown, sorrow for Lenny, sorrow for everyone who had to live in a world where fear outweighed certainty, and the only certainty was that we all of us had to live in fear.

Lee Henry stood amid the smoke of the dying fire holding a bucket still filled with water. It dangled uselessly at his side, clutched in his huge paw of a hand. He stared at the charred remains of Main Street, and I wondered what he saw, what he was thinking. Could he still see into forever, where the good keeps right on going? Or had the window been shut and locked, the curtains drawn?

I went to him, asked quietly, "What'll happen now, Lee Henry?"

He didn't look at me but kept his eyes straight ahead. "We start buildin', Miz Callahan."

"Can all these people start over?"

Lee Henry's chin fell and rose once. "We can, Miz Callahan."

I looked around at the exhausted, shell-shocked people still milling about. "How soon do you think you can start to rebuild?"

"Today," he said, "Lawd willin'." He looked at me then, and his eyes had that same look they had had at the prayer meeting. I recognized what I saw there. It was hope. I wanted to latch on to it, to take it in and make it my own. I wanted to see into forever, the way Lee Henry did. How do you keep holding on to the good? I wanted to ask. But someone called for him, and Lee Henry excused himself and walked away.

Tom was nowhere around. I decided to look for him. Maybe we could get a few hours' sleep and then come back to help with the cleanup.

A car entered Coloredtown then, rolling slowly across the baked earth that had only recently been Main Street. I turned, zombielike, to gaze at it. It took me a moment to realize it was Sunny's car, and that people were with her. She must have come to help, I thought, and had stopped to pick up a couple of recruits along the way.

She parked the car right in the middle of the street, opened the driver-side door and stood up, her one arm on the top of the door, the other on the roof of the car. She stared at the charred ruins of Coloredtown, and even from a distance, through the drifting smoke, I could see the dismay on her face. After several moments, she bent down and said something to the people in the car. The front and back doors on the passenger side opened simultaneously and a man and a woman stepped out. They obviously weren't prepared to help put out a fire. He was wearing a suit and a fedora; she, a skirt, blouse, and a small, stylish hat.

At least, I thought, if I couldn't find Tom, Sunny could take me home. I could leave a note on Tom's car saying Sunny had come by and I'd returned with her. Sighing, I willed my exhausted legs to move, to take me to the road and Sunny's car. Never had I been so drained, so weak. And maybe that's why I had almost reached the car before I realized who was there.

I stopped short, bumping up against a wall of disbelief. My breath caught in my lungs. My heart stopped, then jump-started on a quick surge of adrenaline. I shut my eyes against the smoke, shook my head, looked again.

They were so small, so much smaller than I remembered, and old now, and gray. And yet it was unmistakably they, the mother and father I had not seen since 1942. They studied me, as though trying in turn to find in my face the little girl they had once known, whom they had once called Daughter.

With great effort I moved forward. Sunny came around to their side of the car. She was smiling.

"I don't . . . I don't understand," I stammered. It was all I could think to say.

"They called from Vermont on Saturday when you were at the hospital with Howard," Sunny explained. "When I told them you were here, they said they'd catch the next flight to Jackson. They've only just arrived here on the train. We went home first, but they were so anxious to see you, they insisted we come find you."

My mouth was open, but there were no words inside. Sunny continued, "I didn't tell you because I wanted to surprise you."

She had succeeded. I looked at the man, who had removed his hat and placed it over his heart. I shook my head. "You came all this way?" To Mississippi, a place you had never been, where you swore you would never come?

"Musume," Chichi said quietly, gently, in the voice I remembered so well. "How could we not come when we learned that you were here?"

The eyes behind his glasses were moist, and I felt tears running down my own cheeks, no doubt cutting little rivers into the dirt and soot that covered my face. Haha stepped forward then and lifted her hand to my cheek and held it there. She simply looked at me, like a mother seeing her baby for the first time, with unmistakable surprise and joy. I cupped my hand around hers and felt the warmth of her palm against my skin, and it felt just as it had on the day that Pearl Harbor was bombed and our little world was blown apart.

But that didn't matter now, because suddenly Chichi and Haha and Sunny and I had fallen into one another's arms, crying and laughing and talking all at once. And with that, right there in dust and dirt, ashes and soot, God's love appeared, because in spite of everything that had worked to keep us apart, we had found each other at last. Or perhaps it was that we had been brought together. Either way, something good had broken in, a shaft of light had broken through, creating a little window, a little looking-out place from which I could see the vast expanse of goodness that kept right on going, all the way into forever.

FORTY-FOUR

After promising Richard he would indeed see an article before summer's end, I took a brief leave of absence from the magazine to spend some time in Carver with Chichi and Haha. We had so much to talk about, so much catching up to do, and so much to remember. I told them of how Uncle Finn had intercepted their letters so that I didn't know where they were, and of how I had spent the war years with my cousin Stella, and of how, every time Jimmy Durante signed off with, "Good night, Mrs. Calabash, wherever you are," I thought of them and cried. I told them of how Jimmy and I sat on the bench outside the old store watching for their return, and when I told them that, they cried. It seems we cried a lot together, but we laughed more than we cried, and every night we stayed up late, sitting at the kitchen table drinking green tea. Haha and I held hands across the tabletop, her hand so tiny now in mine.

Of course, their being in Carver meant the cat was out of the bag as far as Sunny was concerned. Not long after Carver was struck dumb with the news that one of its leading citizens was a Negro, it was hit on the other jaw with the revelation that Tom Fulton's wife was Japanese. It was a one-two punch that left the little town reeling. To think that these two well-liked, well-respected people weren't really Caucasian!

Afterward, it was almost as though people began to eye each other suspiciously, wondering who else might be living under a false cover of whiteness.

Howard found it all pretty amusing when I told him about Sunny. "And here I thought I was the only masked marvel in Carver," he said. "I never would have guessed Helen Fulton had a more interesting act going than I did."

I laughed with him but added, "She had a little help from a surgeon, remember. Your act was completely natural."

Howard sat in a chair by the window in his hospital room. He was growing a little stronger each day. "Is that why she was so involved with the Negroes, helping out with the citizenship school—because she knows what it is not to be white?"

I had to think a moment. When Sunny and I were shopping just the day before, we'd overheard—were meant to overhear—what one woman said to another: "It's no wonder she was always spending so much time with the niggers. She's as good as one herself."

To Howard, I said, "I think her experiences as a Japanese had something to do with her wanting to have a hand in civil rights for Negroes. But you know, I think if she'd been born white, she would have done exactly the same thing. She's just a good person. She's someone who wants to see justice done."

Howard nodded his understanding. "So what will the Fultons do now?" he asked.

"They're going back north," I said. "Back to Cincinnati where they met, and where Sunny's parents still live."

"Are they leaving because they think they have to leave, now that Carver knows about Sunny?"

"Actually, no. You know, Howard, a lot of people are really sick at the thought that Sunny's Japanese. There've been anonymous, sometimes threatening, phone calls in the middle of the night, that type of thing. And some people ignore Sunny now, or purposely turn a cold shoulder when they see her. And of course there's the Klan, who like Japanese about as much as they like Negroes, but"—I laughed a little "then again, the Klan doesn't like anybody very much, not even each other, I think."

Howard nodded, offered a shrug.

I went on, "And then there's Tom's mother, who's furious that Carver now knows her daughter-in-law is Oriental and her grandchildren are half-breeds. She won't even speak to the Yamagatas, and she's threatening never to forgive Tom for bringing this shame on her."

"But she's known all along Sunny was Japanese?" Howard interrupted.

"Yes, but she came to accept Sunny after the surgery that left her looking white."

Howard shook his head. "Amazing," he retorted quietly.

"Yes, so it's been a shock to Carver where lots of people are like Corinne Fulton, with that same attitude. But at the same time, there are some who are completely different. All week Sunny's friends have been calling and coming around to the house, saying they're surprised, but that it makes no difference to them at all that her family's Japanese. Many people have made the Yamagatas feel welcome. And you know what else? Some of these same people, you probably know them"—— Howard nodded when I told him some names—"have been helping out in Coloredtown, helping clear away the debris, donating food and clothes, even making commitments to help rebuild. It's pretty unbelievable."

Howard smiled. "That's wonderful news, Augie."

"I guess tragedies tend to generate their own goodness, in an odd sort of way. At least they give people an opportunity to rise up and help, and happily there are those in Carver willing to do just that."

"I never doubted that Carver had its share of good people."

"Yes," I agreed. "Sunny warned me not to stereotype when I came here. But, anyway, about Sunny and Tom, they really don't feel they have to go back to Cincinnati, but they want to. They think now is the right time."

"And the mill?" Howard asked. "Will Tom sell?"

I shook my head. "Not right away. For now, he's going to leave it in the hands of someone he trusts, someone who can oversee its operation until Tom can decide when and if to sell."

Howard looked out the window, then back at me. "I guess you had your own act going for a while there, huh? Undercover reporter for *One Nation*?"

"Sunny and I thought it'd work out best if I didn't let on."

"How's the story coming?"

"Well, I've got a lead."

"I'm anxious to read it whenever you get it finished."

"Yeah," I sniffed, "so is my editor."

We fell silent then. A small breeze drifted in through the window, bringing with it the scent of pine needles. Howard shut his eyes a moment, opened them, looked at me. "It's been quite a trip for you, Miss Augie Callahan," he said quietly. "You found your family at the end of the rainbow."

I shook my head in wonder. "I can hardly believe all that's happened, Howard."

He smiled, a small, wistful smile. "And what about now? What are your plans after you leave Carver?"

"Actually, the Yamagatas and I have been talking about my moving out to Ohio. Chichi and Haha tell me they have a big house. They've invited me to live with them for a time—for as long as I want, they said."

"What about your work with the magazine?"

I drew in a deep breath, let it out slowly. "I want to write another book," I said. "Chichi said their home would be a quiet place for me to write. I think I'm ready to leave the magazine and concentrate on books—novels. With the help of the Yamagatas, I think I can do it."

Howard nodded, raised his eyebrows. "It sounds ideal."

"It does, doesn't it? I'm still trying to take it all in, to believe it's all real."

"I'm glad for you, Augie." Howard reached over and took one of my hands in his. "I'm really glad for the way things have worked out for you."

With our fingers intertwined, I took a moment to study our hands. I was a fair-skinned redhead, but his skin was only a few shades darker than mine. I couldn't help but smile. What did it matter, after all? It made no difference to me how dark or how fair his skin was. I loved those hands, loved the music they made, loved the person they were attached to. I raised my eyes to Howard's. He was gazing intently at me.

"Chicago isn't terribly far from Cincinnati."

I shook my head. "No, not very far."

"I don't want to let you go, Augie."

"You don't have to, you know."

Howard smiled faintly as he stroked the back of my hand with his thumb. "Believe it or not, I've never been to Cincinnati."

"I hope you'll get to know the city a little bit."

He raised my hand to his lips and kissed my fingers. "I plan to get to know the city very well indeed."

He returned to Chicago by plane a few days later. When he called me that night, he told me that Trudy was in a state of near euphoria because her baby was safely home. "She's looking forward to meeting you," Howard said, and I told him to tell her I hoped it would be soon.

The sixth of August marked the twentieth anniversary of the bombing of Hiroshima, the beginning of the end of the war that had separated me from the Yamagatas. On the sixth of August of that year, 1965, President Johnson signed into law the Voting Rights Bill. The ninth of August marked the twentieth anniversary of the bombing of Nagasaki, which led to the eventual surrender of the Japanese and the coming of peace. On the ninth of August of that year, 1965, Mayor Cedric Frohmann escorted Miss Ebba Starks into the county courthouse in Lexington, Mississippi, where she became the first Negro citizen of Carver to register to vote.

On that same day Sunny and I celebrated our mutual thirty-fifth birthday. "Did you know," Chichi asked me, "that people born on August 9, 1930, are very special?"

"Yes, Chichi," I said. "Someone told me that when I was a little girl. I've never forgotten."

"There is something else, Musume, a saying we have in Japanese. Did I ever tell you?" Chichi paused briefly and smiled. "It goes like this, *Umi-no-oya-yori mo sodate no oya.*"

I thought a moment, shook my head. "I really don't remember whether I ever heard that or not. What does it mean?"

"It means, Musume, 'Your adoptive parents are your real parents.'"

I smiled at my father in return. "Well, Chichi, as you know, I've never been very good at Japanese, but I could have told you that in English a long, long time ago."

EPILOGUE

The old bench is still here, where, on an early autumn day in 1938, two little girls became friends. Funny how a chance encounter can completely change the course of a life. I shouldn't use the word chance, though. I've decided that I don't believe in chance anymore. As a writer, I know a plot when I see one, and I know too that a story can't be the result of purely random happenings. Someone has to plan it out and put it all together and make the events add up to something in the end. And on this day, August 29, 1965, as I sit here in Hollenbeck Park, I know that my life is good, and that it is unfolding according to some plan that I can't always understand but that I can put my hope in. Any story that brings me back to Sunny and Chichi and Haha is more than I could ever have imagined myself and had to be written with love in mind.

I am on my way to see Uncle Finn. It's Sunday morning, and I know he and Aunt Lucy will be home. I haven't seen them in, well, I can't remember how many years exactly, but I know it's been quite a few. Aunt Lucy calls me once in a blue moon, but that's as far as we go in the family relations department.

Uncle Finn suffered a heart attack some years back. He never fully recovered, maybe because he went on eating just as much, drinking just as much, and being just as mean as ever. He did sell the hardware store after that, though, and retired to a sedentary life in his easy chair. He bought a television set in 1959 that, as Stella puts it, keeps him occupied while he's waiting to die. "God knows he should be dead already," she told me once with a grunt of distaste, "but he's just too stubborn to go." An old family trait, if Uncle Finn was right about Lenny. But I figure I'd better get around to seeing him before his stubbornness gives out. His O'Shaughnessy blood isn't going to keep him alive forever.

Whether or not Uncle Finn will want to see me, I have no idea. Still, I'm on my way, and he can slam the door in my face if that's what he prefers. But I think of how he could have slammed the door on us when Mother showed up on his doorstep with four of her children all those years ago, and he took us in. He let us live there long after my father's insurance money ran out, so I guess there's something to be said for that.

I had planned to take the bus all the way from my apartment to Fresno Street, but I decided to get off near the park instead. Walking the rest of the way buys me some extra time to think and to build up my courage.

The park is quiet, filled with birdsong and shade and a few people strolling aimlessly arm in arm by the lake. I'd like to think the whole world is so peaceful, but of course I know it's not. When I returned to Los Angeles on August 14, the Watts neighborhood was in its fourth day of rioting. The Negroes had risen up to protest years of impoverishment and segregation. Citizens clashed with police, buildings went up in flames, stores were looted, and it seemed the whole place would be completely wiped out before the rioters were finally subdued. More than thirty Negroes died. More than a thousand were injured. And on and on it goes. I didn't have to stay in Mississippi to witness the devastating effects of injustice.

The sun is rising up toward noon. It glitters on the lake and shines on the spot where a Salvation Army band once played. I rise from the bench and head toward Louis Street, deciding suddenly to swing past the Yamagatas' old house. Like Uncle Finn, it's something I haven't seen in years.

The house on Fickett Street looks a little older now, a little weatherworn, but what to expect after a quarter century? Some time ago it was painted a pale green, but now that paint is peeling, coming off in small flakes like dead skin. It should be painted again. This house deserves to be kept up. It's the keeper of a lot of memories, my memories, and they are happy ones.

Three children play on the front lawn, all girls. The strikingly blond hair that they share tells me they are sisters. They are playing with their dolls, having a tea party there on the grass, much as Sunny and I used to do when we were children. I hope that the happiness we knew in this house lingers here still so that these children feel it at night as they lay in their beds, waiting for sleep.

I turn away from what was once the Yamagatas' home, and my home, and head toward Fresno Street. What will I say to Uncle Finn when I see him? I know what I'd like to say. I'd like to tell him that there is no such thing as "they" or "them." That there are only individuals with layer upon layer of experience, ideas, hopes, dreams, beliefs. That there are some Japanese who are really Americans, some whites who are really Negroes, some Irish-German-Americans who are really Japanese at heart. And that in spite of what a person appears to be or not to be, it's the heart and not the face that matters.

This is what I would like to say to Uncle Finn, but I know I won't. I'm not going to him after all these years to tell him about the human heart. Even if I did, I'm not sure he would understand. I'm on my way to Uncle Finn's house for the sake of my own heart, that place that had become cold and bolted shut, beginning all those years ago when I lived in the attic of his house.

I won't even tell him I forgive him, because he would neither know nor comprehend what I'm forgiving him for. But I'll forgive him anyway. Silently, inside myself. And that should be enough.

I stand on the doorstep of his house, my heart pounding. He'll answer the door when I knock. He always answers the door. Finn O'Shaughnessy, king of the house, keeper of the gate. He answered the door when my mother and her children showed up on his doorstep that day in 1938, and he took us in. He answered the door when Chichi came looking for me in 1945, and he turned him away.

I knock. And in a moment the door opens, and there stands Uncle Finn. He is older and heavier, and his red hair is now gray and very thin on top. He is wearing an undershirt, gray trousers, white socks. His tired eyes look startled for a moment, as though he recognizes me but can't remember my name.

But then he smiles, that little twist of the mouth that passes for a smile with Finn O'Shaughnessy.

"Hello, Uncle Finn," I say.

"Well, I'll be . . ." He scratches the bald spot on the top of his head, turns and yells over his shoulder, "Hey Lucy, get out here. We got company."

He turns to me then, opens the door a little wider, takes a step back. "Come in, Augie. Take a load off. How in the world ya been?"

He calls to Aunt Lucy again, his words peppered with oaths.

Amused, I can't help but smile. He hasn't changed. But I have. I step into Uncle Finn's house and quietly shut the door behind me.